Allison Brennan worked as a consultant in the California State Legislature before leaving to devote herself fully to her family and writing. She is a member of the Mystery Writers of America and International Thriller Writers. She lives in Northern California with her husband Dan, and their five children.

Visit Allison Brennan's website at
www.allisonbrennan.com

FATAL SECRETS

A NOVEL OF SUSPENSE

ALLISON BRENNAN

PIATKUS

PIATKUS

First published in the US in 2009 by Ballantine Books,
an imprint of The Random House Publishing Group,
a division of Random House, Inc.
First published in Great Britain as a paperback original in 2009 by Piatkus

A CIP catalogue record for this book
is available from the British Library

ISBN 978-0-7499-0956-7

Printed in the UK by
CPI Mackays, Chatham ME5 8TD

Papers used by Piatkus are natural, renewable and
recyclable products sourced from well-managed forests and certified in
accordance with the rules of the Forest Stewardship Council.

Mixed Sources

Product group from well-managed
forests and other controlled sources
www.fsc.org Cert no. SGS-COC-004081
© 1996 Forest Stewardship Council

FSC

Piatkus
An imprint of
Little, Brown Book Group
100 Victoria Embankment
London EC4Y 0DY

An Hachette UK Company
www.hachette.co.uk

www.piatkus.co.uk

Six years ago, a woman I'd never met before came up to me at my first RWA meeting and said, "You're going to sell your book." I thought she was insane. Instead, she was psychic.

This one's for you, Anna Stewart.

ACKNOWLEDGMENTS

I'd like to thank several people who were generous with their time and knowledge in helping me keep my facts straight. If I got it wrong, it's my fault alone.

My gratitude and appreciation go out to Jim Battin, Igor Birman, Kalen Hughes, Karin Tabke (who is always willing to listen to me complain), and special agent Steve Dupre. If there wasn't an FBI file on me before, I'm sure there's one now!

Those who know me know that I can be forgetful, especially when on deadline. I'll likely be writing future "corrections." I neglected to acknowledge Sgt. Lorenzo Duarte of the Santa Barbara Police Department for answering many questions for my last book, *Sudden Death*—on his day off. Thank you!

Most of today's heroes we'll never see. My extra-special appreciation goes to someone I can't mention by name. I am humbled by the dedication and commitment of so many of the agents in Immigration and Customs Enforcement, who are battling the evil of human trafficking against overwhelming odds.

On June 4, 2008, former Secretary of State Condoleezza Rice said, "Globally, human trafficking is a multidimensional threat: It deprives people of their human rights and dignity. It increases global health risks. It bankrolls the growth of organized crime, and it undermines the rule of law."

According to a State Department report, approximately 800,000 people are trafficked across international borders each year. Eighty percent are women; half are minors. It is estimated that *millions* of people are trafficked for forced labor and sexual exploitation within national borders.

For more information about this worldwide tragedy, visit the "Major Publications" section of www.state .gov.

PROLOGUE

Twenty-one Years Ago

Sonia was thirteen the first time she killed a man.

She and Izzy were prisoners in a filthy basement, the sound of men stomping above making Sonia jump when dust rained on her. Izzy cowered in the far corner on a foul-smelling, stained mattress atop the hard-packed dirt floor. The older girl spoke with an odd Spanish dialect that Sonia barely understood—that is, when Izzy spoke at all. During the hours they'd been imprisoned together, Sonia had learned her name, but not much else.

Sonia's father had taught her a variety of languages and dialects over the years. The importance of establishing a rapport with the villagers required being a quick study of both verbal and physical language. She'd eagerly participated in the lessons because she'd wanted to earn her father's rare praise. If only she'd known the truth.

If you'd known the truth, you'd be dead.

For ten days, through fear and anger and guilt so foul-tasting she could barely eat even when allowed a stale meal, she mourned all she'd lost. Her innocence, her father—her very identity.

Sonia drew in a sharp breath, swallowing the tears

she could no longer afford to shed. If she wanted to survive, the suffocating self-pity had to end. She would find a way out.

When they left Belize ten nights ago, there'd been more than thirty girls crammed into the back of the truck. Sonia could hardly breathe through the stench of fear, vomit, and urine. Some cried. Some screamed. Some fought back.

Those who fought were beaten or raped. One girl had been shot and left to die by the side of the blistering-hot dirt road. Sonia wanted to believe that it was all a nightmare and she'd soon awaken in a hut, one of hundreds she'd slept in over the years, alone and lonely, but safe.

You were never safe. It was an illusion.

What happened to the other girls from the village? Where had they been taken? Why had Sonia been separated from them and locked in this filthy underground room with Izzy?

From what she'd learned eavesdropping, Sonia had been sold to a powerful man who wanted a virgin bride. Her captors snickered when they said "bride," and Sonia didn't know what would happen after the man claimed her. Would he rape her? Kill her? Would he keep her prisoner? Would he share her with other disgusting perverts?

Sonia had to get out—before she was turned over to the man who wanted to buy her as if she were property. She hoped Izzy would go with her, but every time she illustrated her escape plan using hand signals and some words Izzy understood, Izzy shook her head and pointed to her threadbare mattress, as if this were something she was resigned to.

"*Esclav,*" she'd repeat, which made no sense to Sonia.

The closest word it might mean was "slave." The unspoken fear of slavery was as real as anything in her life; perhaps that was why she couldn't accept it, couldn't acknowledge that she'd been sold into slavery by her own father.

The door at the top of the basement stairs rattled as a key turned in the lock. Izzy jumped at the sound, and Sonia's heart pounded. She crammed her skinny body tightly into the corner, glancing right and left like trapped prey, knowing there was no weapon, nothing to save her. She had searched the barren room many times in the last twelve hours.

A hulking man lumbered down the rickety wood stairs, clutching the solitary railing that seemed too thin and too old to hold his ample weight. His name was Carlton and he'd been there when Sonia had first been taken away. He'd watched with a half-grin as her father had shot the village elder when he tried to stop the caravan from taking their daughters.

It's your fault, Sonia. Curiosity killed the cat, sweetheart, and you've been too damn feline for too long.

She forced her father's last words to her deep into the back of her mind. If she thought too much about him she wouldn't be able to find the strength to fight back. And she wasn't going to die, not like this, not as a slave.

Carlton swaggered across the dirt floor, his head brushing against the naked lightbulb hanging from the ceiling of the twelve-foot-square room. The dingy yellow glow against the windowless walls cast darker shadows in the corners, where spiders ate their silk-covered meals. There was no way out except for the door at the top of the stairs.

He turned to where Sonia cowered. She tried to hold her chin up but her body trembled and her eyes darted away from the man dressed in black. He was younger than her father, overweight, and balding. He reeked of cigarettes and beer, and the butt of a handgun protruded from the waistband of his pants.

Carlton spoke in unbroken English. "You're the one I want."

Sonia's burning gaze turned to his, startled. Was this an order? A demand to meet her fate? His dark eyes stared at her chest, his scowl revealing crooked yellow teeth. She glanced away, embarrassed and angry and more terrified than when she saw her father kill.

He reached over and pinched her nipple. She shrieked, then bit her tongue, her fear swallowing her bravery. She shrank against the cold cinder-block wall and silently prayed, not believing it would do any good. Not after what she'd seen. He grinned at her, jerked down the arm of her loose-fitting blouse, and slapped her shoulder. Pain flared from where his fingers had burned her skin, marking her as his property. She refused to cry out, instead biting her tongue again, this time so hard she tasted blood.

"This makes you chattel." He pressed his thumb into her healing flesh until her tears spilled over and she barked out an agonized sob.

He laughed cruelly. "You think you're something special, Sonia Martin. You're just a woman. Don't forget it. You're pretty now, you'll bring in good money, but your beauty is short-lived, and if you're trouble, you'll be dead."

She spat blood-tinged saliva in his face and immediately knew she'd made a mistake. His lips curled and he backhanded her so hard her head hit the wall and her vision blurred. His fat diamond ring cut her cheek. He kicked her in the stomach and would have beaten her to death if a voice from the top of the stairs hadn't stopped him.

"She's not yours." He sounded American. Had they traveled far enough to reach America? Possibly, but she didn't think it would help. She was a stranger here, a foreigner. Illegal.

"She fuck—"

"I don't care if she bit your dick off, you are not to touch her again or I will kill you. You'd better hope she heals quick, or the boss will take it out of your share of the profits. Take the whore and be quick, the others want a turn before the trucks arrive with the rest of the merchandise."

The door slammed shut and Sonia scrambled to the far side, away from this horrible stranger who glared at her as if he would enjoy squeezing the life from her body.

"*Puta*," he whispered. "You're trouble, no one listens. Don't even think about disrespecting me again, or I'll beat the shit out of—" he stopped himself and turned his anger on Izzy. Sonia suddenly understood. The man upstairs wouldn't let him touch Sonia, but the other girl was fair game.

He barked out a crude order in Spanish. Sonia didn't believe she'd heard right until Izzy, tears streaming down her pretty brown face, began to unbutton her simple cotton dress.

"Watch, bitch. You'll be doing the same thing as soon as your owner gets tired of your attitude. You're only a virgin once. Once that's gone, you're just a whore."

He slapped Izzy, and Sonia jerked as if she'd been hit. Izzy sobbed and took her dress off faster. She was naked underneath, her thin body scarred. Sonia's fists clenched. Her head ached; her cheek dripped blood onto her torn, dirty dress. She hated feeling so helpless, but she didn't know what to do.

Izzy laid down on the mattress. Carlton unzipped his pants and took out his penis; Sonia turned her face into the wall, eyes tightly shut. Izzy wasn't fighting him, but she was crying. How many times had men forced her?

Sonia wasn't naïve—she knew enough about what happened when young girls were lured by promises of jobs and money. They were forced into labor or prostitution. Izzy had been part of this life for a long time, ashamed and broken. Sonia wanted to help her, but she couldn't even save herself from the fate that awaited her.

Sonia hadn't been lured. She'd been sold because she'd discovered her father's true mission. Mission!

You have been blind for a long time. Blind until it was too late to save anyone, even yourself.

"Look!" Carlton demanded.

Sonia trembled, her arms wrapped around her head. Izzy cried out and Sonia screamed.

"I told you to watch," Carlton sneered as he raped Izzy. "Watch or I'll hurt her. Or maybe you like that."

Sonia reluctantly dropped her arms. Carlton had Izzy on her face and was raping her from behind. He was a giant compared to the teen. Tears of rage and fear escaped and Sonia wiped them away. She would not let him see her cry again. Could not let him know that he'd gotten to her. She choked on a sob.

His hands were on Izzy's neck and he pushed her into the mattress as he worked himself up into a frenetic release. Izzy's face . . . something was wrong. She was in distress, a different pain than before.

"Stop!" Sonia cried. "You're hurting her!" She jumped up, stumbled toward the rapist, and pushed him with all the strength she found. He didn't budge. She hit him on the head, her hand burning with pain. He groaned.

"I'll get you, bitch."

"You're killing her!"

He didn't understand, or didn't care. Sonia screamed for help, then kicked him as hard as she could in the testicles.

Carlton's voice reached a high note and he collapsed next to Izzy. His face was contorted and red as he cupped his balls.

His expression told her he would kill her.

"Izzy," Sonia squatted, turned her over. "Izzy—"

She was dead. Sonia had seen dead people before; she knew Izzy was gone. Blood oozed from her mouth. Her chest wasn't moving.

Carlton groaned, pulling himself up into a crawling position. "You're dead," he rasped.

She started toward the stairs for help, but then she saw the gun. It had slipped out of his loosened pants and fallen silently to the mattress next to Izzy's broken body.

Sonia dove across the floor and grabbed the gun before Carlton realized he'd lost it. She didn't know much about handguns, she was only familiar with rifles used for hunting. But rifles had safeties, and she glanced down. Saw a similar switch and pressed it down with a shaky thumb.

He came at her and she pulled the trigger hard. The recoil surprised her and the bullet went high—

—right into the rapist's face.

She heard shouts from upstairs, the sound of boots running across the basement ceiling.

They're going to kill you. Oh God, Sonia, what have you done?

She dropped the gun, then picked it up again. She might have a few seconds. That was all she needed to run.

Sonia ran to the top of the stairs and pounded on the door. "Help! Please! He killed her! Help!"

The shouts on the other side of the door took on a frantic urgency, and she heard voices all around, inside and outside the house.

Breaking glass made Sonia cry out, and she ran back down the stairs, tripping over her own feet and falling face-first onto the dirt floor. The air rushed from her lungs and she couldn't move. What was happening? With no windows, she'd lost all sense of day and night. She was lost, alone with two dead bodies, and a few bullets were not going to save her. There was gunfire above her head and she jumped, her chest hot and struggling for a breath.

She crawled over to the far wall, where she could see the shadows at the top of the stairs. Hands shaking, she pointed the gun at the door.

Stop shaking. Stop it or you'll miss. You can't miss. You have to kill them or you'll die.

Sonia didn't want to die. She didn't know where her steel will to survive came from, but it fully emerged there in the basement, gun in hand, and her hands steadied. She braced her fists on her knees; she tried to swallow but her mouth was so dry there was nothing but the taste of copper and dirt.

More breaking glass, and smoke came from under the

door. Oh, God, no! They were burning her alive, a prisoner. She screamed.

Amid the shouts she heard a word she thought was only in her head.

"Police!" More shouts. Thumping and crashing and a scream. How long did it last? A minute? Ten? An hour? Sonia didn't know. But there was no sound of fire, no smell of burning wood. She watched the top of the stairs and waited. She didn't dare go up there, not now. What would they do to her?

The door opened and a bright light blasted into the room. She shielded her eyes and bit her lip.

"This is the police! *Policia!* Put down your weapon! Now!"

Could she believe them? There were so many people, so much noise her ears rang. She dropped the gun and expected to feel the pain of bullets hitting her chest. She closed her eyes and made herself as small as possible.

Several men descended cautiously and inspected the small room. One man approached her.

"Honey, you're safe now."

She didn't believe him. She'd never be safe.

He repeated his words in Spanish, though she'd understood his English.

Sonia peered at him. He wasn't young or old; his face was hard but his blue eyes were kind. He asked her name.

"Sonia." She looked over at where four men were covering the bodies. "He killed her," she whispered. "He raped and killed her. I-I got his gun. I had to."

"Shh, Sonia. Honey, it's okay. You're safe. You're alive. I'll make sure you get home."

She started shaking again, and then the tears came. "I can't go home."

"No one blames you—"

"He'll kill me."

"Who?"

"My father. He sold me to those men. Me and— What happened to the others? They separated us. What happened to them?"

Grief crossed his face and Sonia knew the answer wasn't good.

The cop slung his rifle over his shoulder and picked her up. "I'm getting you out of here. My name is Wendell Knight. I'm a Texas Ranger, and you're safe with me."

CHAPTER
ONE

"They'll fire you."

ICE Agent Sonia Knight gave her partner a sideways glance and rolled her eyes. "Not if we succeed."

Trace shook his head. "I want this bastard as much as you, but we're walking a very fine line here."

"We're so close."

"We could both end up dead."

"Our witness has risked everything to give us this information. If Jones gets even a whiff that Vega is turning state's evidence, he *and* his pregnant wife are dead."

"Don't think it."

"You know it. He hasn't checked in for three days, which isn't like him."

"Kendra Vega is fine. We checked on her yesterday afternoon."

"For now. But Vega could be getting spooked. It's one thing to talk about getting out of the business, but doing it is another story. These people are ruthless. Vega knows it."

"And you pulled every string and called in every favor to get them into witness protection *when* he delivers the goods. You can't do squat for him unless he comes back with the promised intel."

True, but Sonia feared that Xavier Jones was untouchable. He'd been getting away with trafficking in humans for years because his instincts were sharp and he trusted no one. That one of his top security men came to her three weeks ago to make a deal was a miracle. She wasn't going to blow it—she wanted Jones in prison and the Vegas safe. That's why not hearing from Greg Vega for the last three days disturbed her. Where was he? Why hadn't he checked in?

"I wish we had better information," Trace said, not for the first time.

They were hiding among the pine trees near Devils Lake, appropriately named considering that the son of the devil, Xavier Jones, owned hundreds of acres in the Sierra Nevada foothills abutting the lake. She could see his house with field binoculars, and tonight, like the last two nights, it was dark.

"It will happen this week."

"This is our third night watching Jones's place. He's out of the state, like Vega reported last time he checked in. The kid could be wrong."

"He's not." They'd contacted the Transportation Security Administration. Xavier Jones hadn't used his passport. He usually traveled by private plane, both retaining a pilot and having a license himself. Tracking small craft was much more difficult, making the last few days even more frustrating. He could be back in northern California now for all they knew.

Sonia had spent long days talking with ten-year-old Andres Zamora just to get him to trust her. He told her everything he remembered about his family's abduction and his brother's murder. It all held together, and he had the scars to prove it.

"I should never have run."

"You did the right thing. Your brother told you to go."

"I should have stayed to find Maya. She is all I have."

"Don't give up on your sister."

"How could she survive what they do to her? I don't even know where they took her."

Sonia didn't have an answer, because she didn't know if she could find his sister. Eight days was a long time in the vile underworld, and thirteen-year-old Maya had most likely been sold before she ever set foot in the United States. If she even ended up here. They'd been separated during the journey, and Andres had no idea where they'd been when she'd been taken away. He'd ended up being smuggled in by truck, then boat.

Sonia frowned at Trace. "If you're worried about a reprimand, I'll tell them I lied to you like I lied to the rest of the team." She hadn't wanted to be dishonest, but she felt as if she had no choice. Her boss wouldn't have authorized this stakeout on the word of a pint-sized illegal immigrant.

Trace slammed his fist on the ground. "I can't believe you said that."

"I'm sorry." She stared through the binoculars at the dark house. She didn't want to hurt Trace, but he hadn't been in the trenches long enough to know how brutal this business was. That the buying and selling of humans was even thought of as *a business* angered Sonia and kept her focused on the prize: slapping cuffs on Jones and getting him into an interrogation room.

"No you're not. You think you're protecting the team, but you're only hurting yourself. Don't be the martyr, Sonia. You're too damn good. I'm a big boy, and I could have told you to fuck off, or told Warner that

Vega didn't give you this intel. I backed you up because I trust your instincts. I just don't want you to be blinded because—"

Their earpieces came to life.

"Beta Two reporting three vehicles approaching from the west at approximately forty miles per hour, headed toward the residence."

Beta Two was stationed at the fork, and there were only two private homes off this road, one being a vacation home belonging to a Silicon Valley executive who came up here quarterly.

Adrenaline flushed her system and she was ready to rock and roll. *This* was what she lived for. It was 0100 with a near-full moon.

"ETA?"

"Ninety seconds to our post."

"Stand down. Do not engage—Beta Four, circle—"

She was cut off mid-sentence. "They're Fibbies," Beta Two said.

"*What?*"

"Grille lights just went on. Red, white, and blue."

Sonia slammed her fist against the nearest tree trunk. She watched the road and seconds later red and blue lights flashed intermittently through the trees lining the private road off Lake Amador Drive. She heard someone—it sounded like veteran Joe Nicholson—say, "She's gonna fuckin' blow like Mount Vesuvius."

"Wish I could see it," his partner replied.

"Wish I were on vacation."

They were talking about her, and they were right. She had had more problems with the fucking FBI than any other law-enforcement agency. And now they'd blown her operation. How did they get wind of the stakeout?

Why didn't they call and find out if anyone was investigating Jones? They acted as if they were the only federal law enforcement in the country. Jones was ICE territory, and Sonia was going to make damn sure the FBI knew it. Innocent children were going to die if they screwed this up.

She watched as three black Suburbans drove onto the wide, circular drive in front of Jones's towering home, lights flashing, screeching to a halt as if they were in some B movie.

Federal heads were going to roll. Sonia would see to it. Personally.

She issued orders to her team, then turned to Trace. She was about to tell him to stay put, but shut her mouth. He was no longer a rookie, having been with her team for two years. "Ready?"

He nodded. "Don't be rash."

"This isn't the first time the Fibbies have screwed up one of our ops."

"You don't have to tell me that, but don't forget: more flies with honey, right?"

"I don't want to catch them, I want to swat them."

She and Trace ran low to the ground toward the residence. They were a good hundred yards or more off, but made it to the rock-strewn edge of the drive through sparse foliage without being seen by the feds. They halted behind a boulder where they could watch the action. Doors opened and at least eight Fibbies oozed from the interior, black bulletproof vests with bold white letters proclaiming their authority: FBI.

Homeland Security trumped the FBI every time, and she'd make sure the idiots who had driven into her stakeout damn well knew it.

They were dressed in black tactical gear, and she pulled her hat from her pocket that identified her as ICE, peeled down the flap on Trace's back revealing the same acronym, and clipped her badge to her belt. Trace did the same. She motioned to her partner and mouthed "*On three.*" They emerged from the large, decorative rocks only feet from the nearest agent. If she had been one of the bad guys, she'd have an ideal head shot. Hell, with her weak hand she could have taken out three of them without breaking a sweat. Incompetent jerks. Did they know who they were up against in Xavier Jones?

She strode toward three agents surveying the layout. One black-vested agent tried to stop her, flashing his badge and saying, "Ma'am, we'll have to ask you to speak with—"

She pointed to her badge, glanced at the name sewn onto his vest. "Who's in charge, Ivers? Elliott? Richardson?"

"I—"

A black-haired agent approached. Sonia recognized Sam Callahan, Sacramento FBI's SSA for white-collar crimes. Political bribery and money laundering. What was he doing here when Jones's crime was far more international—and deadly—in scope? "Callahan. Surprised to see you here."

"Right back at you, Sonia." He nodded at Trace. "Anderson."

She couldn't hold back her frustration. "You just destroyed nearly two years' work! Is covert not in your vocabulary? We're in the middle of a major investigation. Did you just not feel like contacting us?"

Callahan straightened and reddened. "We have a subpoena."

Subpoena? "For what? No one cleared it with me. This is my operation—we're dealing with immigration and human trafficking here, out of your jurisdiction." She was just getting started. "Dammit, Jones probably has people watching this place. And I know he has security—" she gestured toward the security cameras her team had identified three days before. "You blew it, Callahan."

She started to kick the door of one of the SUVs, then pivoted before her boot made contact. She was pissed off, but she'd take out her frustration on the racquetball court later.

What was she going to tell Andres? She pictured his troubled face, his warm brown eyes, begging her to find his sister. Andres had been here, at the Jones house. He'd seen the gate, had known about the mermaid fountain— completely out of place in the foothills. This was where Sonia had to start looking for Maya.

She needed to talk to her informant, Greg Vega, but she couldn't jeopardize him, not when they were this close. He'd missed two scheduled contacts, and she desperately wanted to pull him now, but her boss made it clear: no hard evidence, no witness protection. Toni Warner was playing hardball with Jones's key man because Vega was certainly no saint. Complete immunity and witness protection would only be worth it for ICE if they got something, or someone, big in return.

The passenger door on which Sonia had nearly taken out her anger opened. A man stepped out, clearly in command as evidenced from the quiet that descended among the other FBI agents. Unlike the rest of the feds in black SWAT gear with FBI-logo jackets, this man was dressed like a wealthy corporate attorney in a sharp charcoal-gray suit, crisp white shirt, and dark blue tie. He filled the suit beautifully, but looked like he'd be more at home wearing a black flak jacket and carrying an M16.

The suit shut the door and stared down at her with eyes so dark brown she couldn't see the pupils. Sonia unconsciously straightened. He wasn't as tall or big as she'd first thought—just over six feet and 180 pounds was her guess—but his commanding presence made him appear larger. She noted that he wore a double shoulder holster; on one side, the standard-issue Glock; on the other a definite nonissue HK Mark 23, a .45-caliber pistol that was used by U.S. Special Operations Forces.

Who *was* this guy?

"Callahan," he ordered, "walk the radius, make sure the perimeter is secure before we serve the subpoena."

"There's no one inside," Sonia snapped. "And no one's coming with you and your clowns parked like we're having a damn party."

"Now," he said.

Sonia glanced at Trace and jerked her head toward Callahan. He joined the FBI team dispersing to search the immediate perimeter.

"You blow my investigation and start issuing orders?"

"I have a subpoena," he said.

"Give it to me."

His expression changed almost imperceptibly with a mere hint of a smile. "It doesn't have your name on it, and I didn't hear you say *please*."

Sonia hated to be ridiculed. "There are lives at stake! Do you think this is a damn joke?"

His face hardened. "Follow me."

He turned and walked toward the edge of the driveway, beyond earshot of the remaining agents, expecting her to follow. She did, if only to explain that she was at the top of the chain of command. And though she knew she'd been "rash" (as Trace would say), she wasn't about to apologize.

When they were out of sight of his team, he turned and glared at her. His body was so rigid and still, she suspected he was made of stone. For the first time, Sonia saw true impassioned anger in someone other than herself. She resisted the urge to take a step back.

"There was obviously a serious lack of communication between our agencies. If I had known ICE had a covert operation, I would have pulled back. But I am *this close*"—he put his thumb and forefinger a half inch apart close to her face—"to nailing Jones on money laundering and racketeering, and frankly, I don't give a damn how that bastard goes to prison, as long as he's locked up for the rest of his pathetic life."

Sonia swallowed and took a deep breath. Money laundering? "I understand your enthusiasm," she said, failing to hold back her anger, "and I don't give a rat's ass how we nail Jones, but there are huge concerns here of which you aren't even aware! Jones is suspected of orchestrating a full twenty percent of our human trafficking problem in the U.S. I have a lead on a missing girl who is supposed to be here tonight!" That wasn't completely true. It was only the men who had taken her in the first place. But Sonia desperately wanted Maya to be here as well. Chances were slim, but it was not an impossibility.

She was just getting started. "You send Jones away for laundering, that does nothing but cause a minor ripple in his organization. Another pervert will step in and take over. It'll never stop until we nail every leader of every port in every country. It'll never stop until we have all the names. Jones is the key to that information. He's the middleman who knows *everyone*!"

No matter what she did, how many of these bastards like Xavier Jones she threw in prison or deported or interrogated, there were a dozen more ready to take their place. The cycle was endless. As Renault said in *Casablanca,* human life is cheap. Children bought and sold like grain, stripped from their families and sent all over the world to be the toys and property of the rich, the depraved, the desperate.

She turned her back on the man in charge. She didn't even know his name, but she didn't care. She had to find some way to reach Vega, to make sure he was safe, to push for the hard evidence so she could protect him and his wife. What was the FBI's raid going to do to her inside man? Was Jones going to think one of his people turned? Would he look at Vega? Would he increase his surveillance on his own people?

"Sonia—"

She whirled around and glared at him. The stony look was gone. It was replaced by something that bordered on compassion.

"How do you know my name? You're new here. I don't know you."

"Your reputation precedes you. Which is, frankly, the only reason I'm not writing you up."

Writing *her* up? For calling him to the carpet because he walked into the middle of *her* stakeout?

"You don't have the authority, or the grounds."

He looked amused. That irritated her. She remembered Trace's comment. *More flies with honey.*

"Look, Agent . . ." she waited for him to fill in the blank.

"Hooper," he said.

"Hooper. I have a witness to protect. Your operation here is jeopardizing him. You need to leave."

He didn't say anything. She almost lambasted him for being rude, then noticed that he was listening to his earpiece, his expression unreadable. Into his sleeve he said, "I'll be right there."

"Not without me."

He didn't say anything for a moment. He was looking at her with . . . what? Pity?

Her stomach flipped with the all-too-familiar sensation of being watched, analyzed, and dissected. She didn't know him, but he knew her. How much did he know? Her past wasn't a deep, dark secret, but it certainly wasn't something discussed around the watercooler.

He nodded. "Of course. I wouldn't want to work with anyone else."

His temper had deflated a fraction and some of her steam dissipated. Still, she felt like a bug, the antennae twitching on her head, picking up a danger signal.

She just wasn't sure if it was from arrogant Agent Hooper or something else. Something far more dangerous than the FBI.

CHAPTER
TWO

Xavier Jones was a businessman in all aspects of his life, from personal to professional. Every decision was weighed carefully, but quickly: did it benefit him and add to his power base? Minimizing risk was his strength, and in his businesses, both legal and illegal, risk was part of the game.

He would not allow anyone to jeopardize what he had built, especially a *child*.

Xavier caught Greg Vega's eye and tapped his watch, then pointed to the cockpit of his Learjet. They'd been delayed leaving Mexico; now all he wanted was to land and take care of the schedule changes that had come up after the Zamora kid disappeared. Vega left the cabin to talk to the pilot.

Xavier leaned back into the leather seat and sipped his cabernet. It had been a productive trip. He'd finalized an agreement that would continue the flow of merchandise through his network instead of diverting a portion to a competitor. He persuaded the seller by highlighting Sacramento's many benefits—ease of access by plane, boat, and truck; not as heavily monitored by authorities as major ports like San Francisco and Long Beach; and since most of the merchandise left the area within forty-eight hours, the centrally located city provided another layer of protection to those involved. Once his plans were clearly presented, almost everyone Xavier spoke with agreed that his location was ideal. And no one had more experience.

Vega returned and sat across from Xavier. "We're east of Fresno. Twenty minutes and we'll be descending."

"Good. Any word on the kid?"

"No. I have feelers out everywhere. He seems to have disappeared."

"No one disappears. He's hiding. Find him."

As far as Xavier was concerned, the kid knew nothing, but when Marchand found out he had escaped, the man became livid. Xavier feared little in a business that bred violence, but he was more than a little wary of Noel Marchand. Xavier was cold; he had no qualms about killing those who interfered, but it was never personal, and he took no pleasure in murder. Marchand, however, enjoyed it. It wasn't just business with that man.

"You contacted Child Protective Services?"

"Yes, sir. I looked at all possible kids before we left town," Vega said. "He wasn't there. I swear, Mr. Jones, he's nowhere. He probably got lost and died in the woods."

"If you say that one more time, I will shoot you myself. Until we find his body, he's alive. Understand?"

"Yes, sir."

More likely the brat had made it into the city and was living off the streets. There was an extensive runaway population in Sacramento, a big city that pretended it was a small town. The kid spoke no English, had never been to America, and was distrustful of people in uniform. All that played in Xavier's favor. *If* the police picked up the kid, he wouldn't talk. And if he did talk, he didn't know anything of true value. It had been more than a week, and everything he *might* have learned had all been changed. Xavier had never set eyes on the kid, and even if he fingered one or more of Xavier's men, Xavier wasn't worried. He picked men who had families for a reason. They would remain silent.

It was Marchand who was turning this minor annoyance into a major headache.

"Finding the Zamora kid is our number-one priority. When you find him, you know what to do." Xavier sipped his wine, then asked, "How's Kendra?"

Vega paused. "Doing well."

"The baby is due soon. A boy, you said."

"Next month."

"Wonderful. I hope this is resolved by then so you can spend time with your family. If the situation is taken care of to my satisfaction, I'll give you time off to spend with Kendra after she gives birth."

Again, silence. Xavier smiled at Vega, satisfied that his message had gotten through. The slight panic in the eyes, the resolve settling across his hard face: Vega was solid and would do the job he needed to do.

"Thank you, Mr. Jones. I appreciate it. It will be handled."

"Is my driver waiting?"

"I'll check. Excuse me."

Vega went to the rear of the plane and Xavier took out his planner, making a meticulous and coded annotation regarding the Saturday-night exchange. The merchandise should have arrived tonight, which was earlier than Xavier preferred, but the storage facility was secure.

He closed his planner and returned it to his breast pocket, then leaned back in his seat. He had just closed his eyes when his business line beeped. He answered.

It was Paul Haas, his accountant. "Are you in town?"

"We're about to land."

"The feds are all over your house."

Xavier sat straight up, his blood pressure rising. "Why?"

"They got a subpoena. Your financial records."

"Financials? What the hell does that mean?"

"I don't know, I haven't seen the subpoena. It's probably taxes."

"My taxes are clean."

"I know, I know, but—"

Xavier interrupted. "Do they have an arrest warrant?" He would not go to jail, even for the night. It was a disgusting place filled with pathetic and sick petty criminals. He would have his pilot turn the plane around and go back to the border. They had plenty of fuel, and he had more than enough money to keep the U.S. government at bay while he fought back.

"No, just a subpoena for your records. But—"

"There's nothing at the house."

"Then why are they there?"

"They're not at your office?"

"No, but I don't keep anything important here."

"What about my downtown offices?"

"As far as I know, they're only at your house, but that doesn't mean they won't go downtown next."

He glanced at his watch. "It's after one in the morning. Why so late?"

"The judge just approved the subpoena. You need to talk to Leland. He can probably fight it in court. But this means they've had a grand jury convened for God knows how long—they couldn't get a subpoena like this without one."

His attorney might be helpful in these circumstances, but Xavier wanted more information before he acted. Information was the difference between a bad businessman and a good businessman. Xavier might be able to diffuse the situation without causing a ruckus.

"Get me the details first. I want to know how the investigation started, when it started, and why. I want to know what they know. I want everything about the FBI agents in charge. Then we can decide how to proceed."

"It was Dean Hooper who went before the judge."

Xavier felt an inner twinge, of what exactly he was uncertain. Not a man prone to fear, this painful knot in his stomach made him tense and unsteady.

The FBI's top cop for white-collar crimes, Dean Hooper's reputation was legendary in Xavier's circles. He'd been the man who took down Ricardo Tattori, a crime boss in Chicago, reputedly a distant relative of the fallen Bonanno family of New York. Hooper had also led the takedown of someone closer to home, Thomas "Smitty" Daniels, who had been Xavier's competitor in the importation of human beings. While Xavier was pleased that Smitty was out of the picture—he was a vile businessman, sampling his imports too regularly and trolling locally—he was displeased that Smitty had been fingered by the government. Though Smitty was now dead after a shoot-out with the feds, Xavier had feared the man had left evidence implicating Xavier or his people. The subpoena tonight proved that his fears about Smitty's troubles were well founded.

But that was four years ago, and Xavier had cleaned

enough of his books in a sufficient manner. His confidence was high that Hooper would find nothing in his records, and had someone talked, they wouldn't have been able to tell the whole story. Spreading pieces of information among several people had saved his businesses more than once. None of Xavier's associates had enough pieces of the puzzle to take him down.

Still, Hooper could be a big problem. He had the reputation of being a tenacious bastard.

"Xavier?" Paul whined. "Are you there?"

"I think I'll go home."

"Didn't you just hear me—"

"The best way to confront pompous prick cops like Dean Hooper is head-on. Show him that I have nothing to hide, that I am not scared of what he might find. That he sought to deliver the subpoena while I was out of town—rude, to say the least. I should be there while they paw through my things."

"But—"

"Trust me. Who was the judge?"

"Barnhardt."

"Hmm." Barnhardt wasn't one of his, but he also wasn't one of theirs—the jurist distrusted cops as well as criminals. A wild card. Xavier didn't like the unknown. Like the missing Zamora kid. He wondered why Hooper had gone to a judge like Barnhardt. He'd have thought Tucci was the more logical choice, considering that he liked fishing expeditions. Perhaps Tucci wasn't available.

Vega said from the rear of the jet, "Your driver is at the runway."

"Good. Did he say anything?"

"Excuse me?"

"Are there any problems down below?"

"No. Nothing. He's been there since eleven-thirty, like you asked."

His driver doubled as a bodyguard. Xavier liked Chuck. He was quiet, punctual, and lethal, all appreciable qualities. He was beginning to think maybe Chuck could replace Vega—if a replacement was necessary. He hoped not. It would be messy, since Vega had been with him for many years and the other men took orders from him as well. Xavier didn't want dissension, but sometimes it became unavoidable.

He could always make it look like an accident.

If it was necessary.

The Learjet descended and touched down at the private airstrip outside Jackson. As they taxied to the waiting Escalade, Xavier called his favorite information broker.

"Darla, it's me. I need you to find everything you can on Dean Hooper, an FBI agent currently in Sacramento."

"Do you have anything else on him?"

"He arrested Smitty."

"Good place to start. I'll call you tomorrow."

"Sooner, Darla. I'll make it worth your time."

The rumors were wrong: Sonia Knight wasn't just pretty, she was a knockout. Long, long legs packaged seductively in jeans that hugged round hips; a masculine black T-shirt that couldn't hide her feminine attributes; and functional black boots that only added to her allure. Hell, Sonia would look good in a burlap sack.

To avoid looking at the sexy ICE agent, Dean Hooper pulled out his notepad and scrawled notes he didn't need to write. He still saw her hazel cat eyes watching with the quiet intensity of a feline predator deciding when to pounce on a mouse. Any other woman with looks like Sonia Knight and Dean would suspect—rightfully from his experience—that she'd obtained her position on her back. But Sonia was not a woman to compromise, either a case or her principles. In that, her reputation was dead-on. Fiery, dedicated, smart, and a marksman. He'd seen the first three in short order; he looked forward to seeing her in action as well.

No warm-blooded male could ignore the passionate and notorious ICE agent, but Dean put his physical reaction on the back burner. He had a more immediate concern: Jones wasn't home. He should have been here an hour ago. Dean had planned the raid to coincide with his return. Had someone talked? Alerted Jones while he was still in the air that the FBI was coming? Dean didn't see how—he'd gone to the judge at the same time Jones was scheduled to land.

There could have been delays, Dean knew, but he didn't have anyone inside the organization to give him up-to-the-minute status reports, and he feared Jones would flee if he knew the FBI was on his ass. He had enough money to make it extremely difficult for anyone to find him. Especially since Dean didn't have an arrest warrant and not enough evidence for the U.S. attorney to take over the case.

He'd already taken a huge risk going to Barnhardt and pushing for a full-on search-and-arrest warrant without actually wanting it. He'd played a delicate game, but in the end got exactly what he wanted: a limited and specific subpoena for Xavier Jones's personal and professional tax records at his home. He didn't expect to find anything, but he couldn't tell that to Barnhardt. A man like Jones wouldn't leave incriminating documentation lying around where it could be easily seized. What Dean needed to complete his analysis were the unconnected details, but those innocuous items wouldn't give him enough cause for a warrant. He had to use Jones's link to a known criminal to make the case to Barnhardt.

All Dean wanted to do was rattle Jones's cage. Make him nervous. Force him to make bad decisions. But men like Xavier Jones didn't rattle easily. The subpoena was just the first step. He *did* keep a record of his illegal finances somewhere; Dean would find it. It's what he did best.

Having ICE and Homeland Security involved was a problem, but not such a hindrance that Dean couldn't turn it to his advantage. He needed to make a few calls to neutralize Sonia Knight. She was a hothead who could jeopardize his investigation. Corruption of this magnitude demanded patience and finesse.

Sam Callahan returned with Sonia's partner and reported that no one was on the property.

"No one?" Dean asked.

"I could have told you that," Sonia Knight snapped. "We've been sitting on this house for two days."

Dean wanted to ask why, but that would have to wait. "Did you reach his attorney?" he asked Sam.

"Left a message at eleven-thirty when we left Barnhardt's house."

"Has his plane landed?"

"What?" Sonia asked.

He raised an eyebrow and said rather mockingly, "You didn't know he was out of town? I'm surprised."

She tensed and Dean was almost sorry that he'd rubbed it in, but she'd pissed him off with her not-so-veiled comments about his motivations. He cared more about the people Jones hurt than he wanted to talk about.

"He didn't take a commercial flight," she snapped.

"He has a private plane. Learjet."

"I know that." But it was clear from her expression that she thought it was still at the airfield. Which made him think she had some bad intel. Or was ICE running with too much work and too few resources, like the FBI?

"We're on the same team," Dean said, extending the olive branch. "I want to compare notes. But right now we need to prepare for his arrival." He glanced at his watch. "It's after oh one hundred hours. When did he land?" He'd been told Jones was going to be back between eleven-thirty and midnight, which was why he had delayed arriving by an hour.

"Twenty minutes ago."

Sonia put her finger to her ear, listening. Dean waited, hoping she would share the information without being asked. Any branch of Homeland Security could be dicey to work with, but ICE used to be independent, and while the FBI didn't have the best relations with their sister agency, Dean had never encountered any problems himself.

Sonia said, "Jones's car turned off the highway. ETA four minutes."

"You really do have a—" he stopped. An idea occurred to him. "Jones knows who you are." He said it matter-of-factly.

"Of course he does, I've been in his face enough."

"Right now I'm serving a limited warrant for specific financial documentation."

"Why would—"

"I don't have time to explain, but I'm asking you to trust me. Take your partner and go back to your surveillance post. You're entrenched right now; we didn't make your team anywhere on the property."

A hint of a cocky smile emerged on her lips. "Of course you didn't."

He gave her an appreciative nod. "You train your people well. I'm asking you to let me serve the subpoena and shake Jones's confidence. Then we'll leave, and you monitor comings and goings, see who Jones taps when he's on the hot seat. Do you have a wiretap?"

"Do you?"

"Dean," Sam Callahan interrupted. "Three minutes."

"We'll meet at the FBI office at noon," Dean said. "Okay?"

"We'll meet at my office at one," Sonia said. "Full disclosure."

He extended his hand to seal the agreement and smiled. "My office. One is fine with me. I have too much paper and equipment to transport downtown, and believe me, you're going to want to take a look at it."

Her hand was soft and cold, but her grip strong. "Don't disappoint me." She reached into her pocket and dropped an extra-strong magnet into his hand, then gestured toward the security cameras around the house. "The security office is in a room off the kitchen. The door is unmarked. If you don't have a warrant for the tapes, you might want to erase them—though I don't really care one bit if Jones knows I'm on his ass."

Sonia didn't want to walk away, but Hooper's identity

threw her off her game. She hoped she hadn't given away her surprise when the Fibbie gave his full name. *Dean Hooper.*

She had already started down the porch steps when she remembered the reason she was here in the first place. She ran back up the stairs and leaned close to Hooper's ear. He smelled of expensive cologne and leather. Voice low, she said, "I'm looking for an Hispanic teenager, a thirteen-year-old female. She was kidnapped from Argentina two weeks ago, and I have good reason to believe that Jones knows where she is. If you see or hear anything—"

Sam said, "Sixty seconds."

Sonia caught Dean's eye. He'd understood. Motioning for Trace to follow, she ran down the stairs and stayed low to the ground, in the shadows, until she was out of sight.

Dean Hooper. She hadn't made the connection when he had first introduced himself as Hooper. Agent? An understatement if she'd ever heard one.

Everyone in the business for more than a couple years knew Assistant FBI Director Dean Hooper. The FBI's own Eliot Ness. He'd said her reputation preceded her? She had nothing on Hooper, and under any other circumstances she may have had a fan-girl moment and asked about some of his more interesting cases.

She didn't like that a fed with such a high rank was on Jones's ass, because while she wanted to nail him, she needed more than his tenure in prison. She needed information, and her man inside was still working. If Hooper acted too soon, she'd lose names and files and more people—women and children—would disappear or die. What was he doing in the field, anyway? She assumed he worked out of Washington; if he was in Sacramento or San Francisco, she would have known.

Sonia didn't partner well. She thrived in her authority and command of her office, but trusting a partner only resulted in disaster. She called Trace her partner, but she was technically his supervisor, so she didn't have to worry about him making decisions without consulting her, or going behind her back to plan an operation that could get agents hurt or worse.

But Dean Hooper had looked her in the eye with a confidence that spoke of unwavering honesty, and she wanted to trust him. She had no choice, really. He'd blindsided her with not only his arrival but his identity. And if Xavier Jones thought that the FBI and ICE had made a major connection in his activities, he'd cut his losses and run.

She'd give Hooper tonight.

Sonia heard her team report that Jones's black Escalade had pulled to a stop in the driveway. She and Trace sprinted to their original position and she grabbed her field binoculars to observe the scene at the house.

"What's going on?" Trace asked her.

"A minute." She watched Dean Hooper on the porch, standing next to Sam Callahan. Dean was an inch shorter, but with a far greater presence, for lack of a better word. She watched as nothing happened for a full minute. Then the driver got out.

Sonia's mouth went dry. The coffee she'd been drinking all night churned painfully in her gut, and she froze, staring. She had to be wrong. It had been years since she'd seen Charlie Cammarata; how could she instantly recognize him?

As the driver closed his door, she saw part of Charlie's

familiar arm-length tattoo. But her mind filled in the rest of the intricate black cross with vivid, blood-red letters dripping down the center:

La vendetta è mia.

Vengeance is mine.

What was the disgraced, renegade ex-ICE agent doing working for a known criminal?

What are you up to, Charlie?

Charlie opened the back door of the Escalade and Xavier Jones, the devil himself, stepped out. Sonia had half a mind to put him in her sights and kill him. That she also wanted to put a bullet in Charlie scared her. She thought she'd gotten over his betrayal. She thought she'd forgiven him.

The urge was short-lived—going to prison wouldn't help them find Maya or any of the buyers Jones supplied with a steady stream of young foreign women. She needed the bastard alive in order to identify and arrest every damn one of his business associates. She would go through their files one by one and track down every woman they'd sold into sex slavery or forced labor and give them a future. The ones who were still alive.

She watched Jones walk to his front porch, and his confident stride and arrogant half-smile told her Hooper's arrival wasn't a surprise. Sonia noted that Charlie acted like a bodyguard, imposing and fearsome. Greg Vega was there, too, and she sighed in relief. She'd been worried about her spy, knowing the huge risk he had taken in contacting her. But he was safe, at least for now. She hoped he had something solid for her so she could get him and his pregnant wife into a safe house.

Charlie glared at the feds while Callahan handed Jones the warrant. Did Callahan or Hooper or any of the other longtime agents recognize him? Probably not. Charlie's punishment had been swift, and while it hadn't involved prison time, he'd lost everything. As well he should have. Before his fall from grace, he'd been primarily undercover, and few agents outside of the then-INS knew his name, let alone his face.

Charlie was here because he had his own vendetta against Jones or someone close to Jones, Sonia was certain. Charlie did nothing without revenge as the motive. It didn't matter if it was his revenge or that of others—at least, that's how it had been in the past. But now? Sonia didn't know. She hadn't seen him in ten years. Was he the feds' contact? It made sense. How Hooper knew about the travel, when they left the airport. But Sonia didn't see a man like Charlie Cammarata giving anything to the FBI. He'd never had an ounce of respect for that agency; he'd barely tolerated his own employer.

Dammit, she wished she could hear what they were saying! Sitting on the sidelines was excruciating, almost as painful as giving up control—and to the FBI, no less. She hoped she wasn't making a huge mistake giving Hooper the lead.

"Dammit, Charlie, what are you doing with Jones?" she muttered.

"Who?" Trace asked, looking through his own field goggles. "Who's Charlie?"

Trace had been in high school when Charlie was fired. He wouldn't have known him. "Charlie Cammarata," she said reluctantly. "My partner when I was working out of El Paso."

She breathed easier when Trace didn't comment, thinking he didn't know about what happened. Her relief was short-lived.

"Why is a former INS agent working for Jones?"

Trace sounded like Charlie had gone to the dark side, become one of the bad guys. And while Charlie was no saint, he wasn't trafficking in humans. "If I had to guess, he's working a job."

"For us?"

"No." For himself.

"We have to report it."

"I know."

"I can do it," he said quietly. "Considering your history with—"

"I'll do it," she snapped. Trace didn't know half the history she had with Charlie Cammarata. Most of the closed-door disciplinary hearing ten years ago with the Office of Professional Responsibility was still classified or sealed, and Sonia would make sure it remained so as long as she breathed.

But Charlie's involvement with Jones was one big-ass fucking wrench in the works.

CHAPTER
THREE

Towering was the only word Dean Hooper could think of to describe the Jones residence. With three-story ceilings, a sweeping staircase, and an excessively large great room with floor-to-ceiling windows, during the day it would have a view of Devils Lake and the San Joaquin Valley beyond. The decor was dark, rustic, and minimal, with a cloying scent of Pine Sol and wood polish. Not a speck of dust or a cobweb in sight.

Jones had his fingers in many, many pies outside of his consulting firm. He owned enough property to make Donald Trump jealous, and enough toys to send up red flags to the IRS. Had Dean not already been looking at Jones after taking down Thomas Daniels and finding Jones's name in Daniels's records, the IRS would have launched their own investigation. But Jones had been audited twice in the last eight years, and the IRS could not find anything illegal.

His longtime friend, a U.S. Treasury Department analyst, had told him, "My gut tells me the guy is dirty, but every path I follow somehow ends up legitimate. I've been working on this for months and I'm no further along. You're the whiz kid. Maybe you can find what I'm missing."

Dean didn't always like his reputation; it put him in a

place with few friends and lots of people waiting for him to screw up. But he did see patterns of illegal behavior in the numbers that others missed, including computers. It was the human element. Putting the information together in different ways and factoring in human psychology, coupled with the personality of his target. That experience, and intuition, couldn't be replicated by a computer.

This was the first time Dean had met Xavier Jones in person, and he wasn't wasting a moment. Already he had better insight into his character and personality. Clean to a fault. Sanitary. Uptight that strangers were in his house touching his things. Extremely confident that the FBI would find nothing incriminating, irritated and arrogant at the same time. There was nothing personal— no photos, diplomas, or awards of recognition. If he had any of these things, they were hidden from guests.

"I'm happy to assist in your investigation, Agent Hooper," Jones said, "but I'm afraid you aren't going to find what you're looking for."

"What am I looking for?"

Jones shrugged, his smirk arrogant. "Who knows? A businessman does well, and the government thinks I don't pay my fair share. I can assure you, Agent Hooper, my tax returns are squeaky clean."

And that, Dean knew, was his biggest obstacle. As far as he could figure, Jones *was* paying his taxes. Jones's main business enterprise was his consulting firm—he lobbied both state and federal governments on behalf of a huge number of clients, mostly the big-money players like city government, Indian gaming, and labor.

Jones glanced at the armed goon standing at his side and Dean said in a preemptive move, in case Callahan didn't see the weapon strapped to the goon's belt, "You do have a permit for that gun."

The hulking man stepped forward. His tattoo bulging *ndetta mia* on his arm. Vendetta? Interesting.

Jones stopped his bodyguard with a glance. "He doesn't need one. He lives here."

"And did he bring the gun into Mexico?"

"You're beginning to irritate me, Agent Hooper."

I'm sure I am.

"Just want to make sure your gorilla doesn't make any sudden moves."

The gorilla comment made the goon scowl.

"You may leave now, Agent Hooper."

"I'd love to, it's certainly past my bedtime, but the subpoena states that you are required to turn over all financial documents immediately to my office. Agent Callahan will go with you and provide a receipt for everything we confiscate. We'll also require your hard drive and any other computers, flash drives, or disks you have."

Anger and annoyance crossed Jones's face. He didn't like being told what to do. So Dean pushed, refraining from showing too much satisfaction. He loved his job.

"We can wait for your attorney if you like, but I'm not leaving until we have everything we came for."

"You're fishing, Agent Hooper. I'm not giving you anything. My attorney will be fighting this subpoena in court first thing tomorrow morning."

Dean showed a concerned, understanding expression. "I understand your frustration, Mr. Jones, but you can't refuse to comply with this subpoena. The judge agreed that to leave the documents in your possession could potentially cause said documents to disappear or be altered. We have the authority to seize everything in this warrant now, and I only offered to wait for your attorney as a courtesy."

A fire lit Jones's eyes and Dean caught a glimpse of the criminal underneath the facade of a respected businessman. Cold, calculating, and criminally brilliant. Dean saw his own head on a platter held by Jones, and that pleased him. He was getting to this guy, which was the whole purpose of this exercise.

I will put you in prison, Xavier Jones. That's a promise.

Dean kept a level head and let Jones quietly fume. Patience was, fortunately, Dean's strong suit. Jones quickly got himself under control, showing Dean that while he was a narcissistic racketeer and suspected human trafficker, self-preservation was at the top of his list. He wouldn't slip up because he lost his temper. He was too sharp for that.

Yet Jones's methodical approach to business might also be his downfall. Criminals like Jones need to keep all of their accounts balanced, all the dollars counted and recounted. Dean could use that. Already, after ten minutes in Jones's presence, he had new ideas to pursue using Jones's financial history as the foundation for his case. Watching his reaction had proven hugely beneficial, as Dean had suspected.

Finding ICE Agent Sonia Knight involved with this character could prove to be a real break. She might see something he didn't because she knew far more about the money trail in human trafficking than he did.

Sonia Knight had testified in no less than five major human trafficking cases in the last two years. Dean had watched one hearing on closed-circuit television after

Knight's squad had taken over an FBI case and arrested a husband-and-wife team who lured women from China to be domestic servants. Only "servant" meant "slave" to those who held the contracts. The women, here illegally, were stripped of all their papers and identity, and then subjected to forced sex, long hours of labor, and no pay—all "earnings" were used to repay the "fee" to bring them to America in the first place. They were kept in line with threats and their illegal status. Sonia's team had uncovered the operation and took all the players out. It was a major coup for ICE. Sonia's written report on how the investigation played out was now used as part of ICE and FBI undercover training.

Dean had long admired Sonia Knight, but he wasn't sure he'd be able to control her. A case like Xavier Jones required delicacy.

Jones said to his gorilla, "Watch them closely. They take nothing that isn't explicitly on this warrant. Understood?"

"Yes, Mr. Jones."

"I'll be in my bedroom."

"I'll join you," Dean said. No way was he letting Jones out of his sight until Callahan had everything in their possession. "Call in the rest of the team, Sam. It's going to be a long night."

Dawn broke over the Sierra Nevadas, tracing the mountains in bright orange. Any other person would have paused to stare at the awesome vista, but Xavier Jones had no use for pretty scenery. He'd been quietly fuming at the way his possessions had been handled by the FBI. Pawing through his personal belongings, touching his clothing—everything would have to be laundered.

He wasn't surprised when his phone rang before six a.m., not thirty minutes after the FBI left. Nor was he surprised that it was Marchand.

"I heard about your trouble."

"It's not a problem."

"It had better not be."

His anger at what the FBI had put him through simmered. They would find nothing in his records; did they think he was an idiot? They were fishing, nothing more, but the knowledge that they had a grand jury giving his finances a rectal exam infuriated him. He was quite good with his money and he knew no one had talked. Everyone had as much to lose as he did, but more than that, no one had all the information necessary to do him serious damage.

"You have no need to worry about your shipment," he said.

"We're not going to talk about this here."

"I have protection." No way was the FBI wiretapping his phone. He had state-of-the-art security to prevent it.

"We'll meet. Tonight."

Xavier didn't like Noel Marchand, but he was one of his best customers, on both ends—importing and exporting. In this business, one didn't have to like one's business associates. As long as they paid and did their job with discretion, Xavier was happy to do business with them. Besides, he wasn't in it to make friends. He'd buy whatever friends he needed through his philanthropic donations.

"Here?" Xavier asked, loath to bring the man into his sanctuary, but it was a gesture of goodwill, and right now Xavier needed to keep Marchand happy.

"Of course not. Midnight. Your restaurant."

Xavier had purchased a riverfront restaurant last year and was renovating it. The place was convenient and private, off the west River Road. It was Xavier's turf, so Marchand wasn't overly upset.

"I'll be there."

He hung up and stood on the balcony of his bedroom. Marchand was a minor annoyance compared to what had just happened with the FBI. They had gone through his *things*. Pawed everything with greasy fingers. Pictures were crooked, drawers misaligned, dirty footprints on his polished wood floor.

He dialed his secretary on her cell phone. She worked out of his consulting office, but handled both personal and professional appointments. And while he had no desire to screw her, Denise provided him with a weekly blow job that was satisfying. He refused to stick his dick into any man or woman; what other men had been there before him? Disgusting.

"Call in the cleaning service," he demanded. "I need them to come early—I want the house cleaned top to bottom, before noon."

He next called Craig Gleason, the attorney and head lobbyist who ran the day-to-day management at XCJ Consulting. "I'll be coming by late this morning for a briefing. Have you had any strange calls or visitors?"

"Define strange."

"This isn't a joke, Craig. There's been some excitement here at the house. I want to make sure that reporters and other vultures aren't circling."

"It's a Wednesday during the middle of a budget crisis in the California capitol—business as usual."

"Good. Just put everything I need to know together and the status of the key bills we're pushing. I'll give you one hour; use it wisely."

"Yes, sir."

More often than not, for the last twenty-some years he had called himself Noel Marchand. He stood on the balcony of his penthouse suite at the Hyatt Hotel across from the California State Capitol. He rarely came to America, and when he did he took a great many precautions. Of course, he was registered under a false identity: Pierre Devereaux, a French Canadian from Montreal. It amused him to remember that he had, in fact, been born in Montreal and was part French Canadian. But his life as Franz Corbert had ended when he was nine, when his father killed his mother and fled to South America with Franz and his younger brother Tobias. He'd never returned to Canada even after his father died; he had no attachment to the country.

Nor did he care for the United States. He could not be king here, no matter what he did or who he controlled. He preferred places where he could wield power so great that when he killed, no one questioned his action. Where, when his car drove past, people cowered. Where, when he walked into a room, the women did what he said, and if he had to punish them, no one asked why.

Americans had money, and rich Americans liked their toys. He provided the toys; Xavier Jones provided the buyers.

His business certainly wasn't limited to the States, but Americans usually overpaid for everything, and considering the risks of importing under the federal radar,

Noel felt justified in charging his North American buyers far more than he needed to cover his expenses.

He paced his hotel room, antsy, yet well aware that keeping to himself until the Saturday-night exchange would protect him. The less time he spent in the States, the less opportunity that a savvy cop might recognize him. He wasn't worried about just any cop—there were only a handful who could identify him as Noel Marchand—but one of those called Sacramento home. He wouldn't have come here this early at all, except for the situation with the Zamora kid.

Noel Marchand deplored incompetence, and until this last week, Xavier Jones had been the pinnacle of professionalism and discretion. And while Jones had made good on providing another boy, letting the first one escape was a disaster. Perhaps not for Jones, but to Noel the boy was a threat: the brat had seen him.

The Zamora kid needed to die or disappear—Noel didn't much care which, as long as he didn't talk to anyone. Though even if he did tell what he knew, putting all the damning information together would be virtually impossible. Only the fact that Noel was in the same city as the kid made the risk a sliver more than nonexistent. But what really irked Noel was that *he* had made two mistakes. First, he had underestimated the boy, never suspecting that Andres Zamora would run when he had the chance. Most of his captives were too scared to flee, knowing they would be hunted down and severely punished. Noel's second error was in not leaving at least one family member alive as leverage over the two Zamora kids. Threats against family back home were the single best tool to keep the slaves in line.

Noel didn't make mistakes like these. He'd been furious that the mother had challenged him, that the brother had attacked him, that the girl had wanted to renege on her agreement. Allowing his anger to dictate decisions inevitably led to problems. Problems like a missing kid in California who could identify him.

Noel was successful because he was discreet. He employed enough people, and paid them well, to ensure that he could fill the high demand for males and females of all ages and types. While he specialized in teenage and young adult females for prostitution throughout the Western Hemisphere, he also provided a few bonded workers when the money was good enough. When he was putting together his next shipment of females, he'd received an order for two boys. One of the girls he'd spoken with had two brothers. She was eager to bring them along, with his promise that they, too, would have jobs in America.

He lied smoothly. But almost immediately there were problems with the older Zamora. And when the younger boy saw him dispose of the mother—who had become a major liability, he had had no choice but to kill her—Noel should have also shot the two boys and put the girl on the truck alone. But he was on a tight schedule and timing was critical. His trip to California was far more important than the troublesome Zamora family.

Noel was upset by the series of events that resulted in the younger boy ending up under Jones's watch, of course, but he could let it go because, ultimately, the situation wasn't completely Jones's fault. What truly frustrated him was the FBI looking at Jones. He didn't care one iota that the warrant was for financial records, Jones was a threat to Noel if he was arrested. Noel knew exactly how the government worked. They did what he did—leveraged. You give me this, we'll give you that. The only difference was that Noel's punishment was far more permanent than prison if the person didn't agree with the terms.

Jones was a potential threat. And while Noel didn't want to kill one of the best people he'd ever worked with in this business, he wouldn't lose sleep over it.

Noel was training someone to take over for Jones should it become necessary. They might have to make the change sooner than planned, since business demanded continuous adjustments in personnel.

And if he had to let Sacramento go altogether, so be it. He dealt with other brokers like Jones. While there were few with Jones's breadth of clients—and the added service of providing squeaky-clean money was a major allure—Noel could withstand some losses in order to protect his larger empire. Obviously, the "squeaky-clean" money Jones guaranteed was being looked at by American law enforcement. It was no longer safe to do business with him.

Noel made his decision. He'd gather the rest of the information about Saturday's exchange, ensure that the girls had arrived safely and were secured, and then kill Jones.

His assistant came in through one of the suite's doors and cleared his throat.

Noel motioned for Mr. Ling to join him by the balcony window. Ling was Chinese, bald, and in his early forties. He could kill a man with little effort, and had a sharp intellect. He'd been with Noel for more than a decade.

"Yes, Mr. Ling?"

"Tobias neglected to properly dispose of the girl."

Noel's fists clenched, the only outward sign of his anger. His brother was yet another liability. Had he been able to leave him behind in Mexico, he would have. But the last time he left Tobias for more than a day, his brother had disappeared for three weeks and left behind too many dead bodies for Noel to cover up. Noel resented having to care for the twisted, weak retard. Before their father had died, Noel didn't have to see or talk to Tobias. But now he was truly his brother's keeper—a job Noel resented.

"I should have killed him when Father died."

Mr. Ling bowed in agreement, though both men knew that Noel wouldn't have done it at the time. His father had asked him to spare Tobias. And Noel had genuine affection for the brilliant man. After traveling throughout South America for years, Johan Marchand settled farther north, in Mexico, and turned a small brothel into a thriving international organization of prostitution. Because Noel had the charm, good looks, and ability to lie as smoothly as he killed, he went on the road most of his early adulthood, recruiting or kidnapping young women to feed the business. It was lucrative and satisfied the wanderlust of his youth.

Women were good for not much outside of sex, and most of them couldn't even do that right. So when Tobias killed for the first time, when he was fifteen and screwing one of the whores their father had given him as a birthday present, Johan finally admitted what Noel had known from the beginning: Tobias was not right in the head. Not just dumb as an ox, Tobias had been killing animals from when he was young not for sport or pleasure, but just because, as he once told Noel, he liked to hear their bones break.

Johan had allowed Tobias an occasional whore. Four out of five ended up dead, and Noel had had to clean up after him, until Noel convinced his father he was a better recruiter. Johan agreed and taught Tobias to clean up after himself when Noel traveled.

Obviously, the lessons hadn't stuck. Noel could no longer afford to spare his brother's life. His father would understand. Hadn't Noel risked enough by letting Tobias play? It was over.

"Where is he?"

"In his room."

"Watch him. I don't trust anyone else. I'll come up with a plan, but he won't be returning to Mexico with us."

"Of course, sir."

"Send a team to retrieve the body."

"They're already on their way. She was left in a potentially exposed place."

"What the *fuck* did he do?"

"He dumped her in the river, but her arm got caught on a bush and he didn't want to get wet."

Tobias couldn't swim. Noel should drown him. Would serve him right.

Have mercy on him, son. Tobias doesn't have full mental faculties.

Noel would live up to the promise he made his father for mercy. He'd put a bullet in his brother's head before he weighted him down and tossed him into the river. By the time his body surfaced, Noel would be long gone, and he had no plans to return to the States. Ever.

"Four days," Noel said. "Four days was all I needed and he screws up in less than six hours."

"And Jones?"

"We'll see to him tonight. In the meantime, I want full backgrounds on all his employees—"

"You have that, and—"

"Go deeper. I want to know who they've talked to and where they've been in the last two months. I want to know who tipped off the FBI about Jones, and how much they know about me. I don't give a fuck what happens to Jones, but I'm not going to let them take me down with him."

And at this point Noel would prefer to just kill everyone involved in Jones's operation. Unfortunately, in the States, the murder or disappearance of a couple dozen people would cause more than a small ripple in the landscape.

"Give me everyone who has any hand in our business, and everyone who's just window dressing. We'll pick and choose, decide who stays and goes. Start building a list of people I can trust to do their job right."

Noel would find out who tipped off the FBI and make a clear statement. No one would dare turn against him.

Not that it would matter. In four days he'd be back home, safe, far away from the long arm of American law enforcement. They'd need an army to get him.

CHAPTER
FOUR

Sonia could have taken half a day personal time after working through the night, but she had too much on her plate to even think about sleeping. And if she did stop home for a couple hours of downtime, she feared that seeing Charlie again would trigger the nightmares she'd buried long ago.

She had to get this part over with.

She dialed the assistant special agent in charge of the San Francisco Regional ICE office—based in Oakland.

Toni Warner supervised all field offices in the large, multistate territory. Sonia had met her nearly ten years ago when she was transferred from Texas to the San Francisco office, and though they butted heads as often as not, there was no one in the business Sonia had more respect and admiration for. Toni was smart, savvy, chic, and ruthless.

"Warner."

"It's Sonia. I have news."

"You have Jones in custody and a solid case to turn over to the DOJ."

"Not yet."

"Please don't tell me to turn on the television."

Sonia cringed. Last year, she'd been caught on film in an unfortunate situation taken completely out of context. She'd led the raid of a sweatshop that "employed" illegal aliens. Only these illegals were indentured servants—not only smuggled into the country but held against their will making a dollar an hour, half of which went toward their room and board. When she'd burst in, one of the supervisors had cracked a whip across the back of a minor, a twelve-year-old boy Sonia later learned had been working there since he was seven. Sonia had seized the whip and snapped it toward the asshole who abused children. It cut across his face—she had never intended to actually hit him, only scare him. When she escorted him out in cuffs, she still had the whip and the press filmed them—highlighting the bastard's split face.

Sonia wouldn't have changed anything—she'd wanted to do so much more when she saw the squalid conditions in which these people lived and worked—except in hindsight, she should have put a bag over his head and handed the whip to Trace.

"I saw Charlie Cammarata this morning."

Toni was silent. Sonia squirmed uneasily, speaking quickly. "He's driving for Xavier Jones. I saw him get out of the Escalade with Jones early this morning while surveilling the house. He's up to something." She dreaded asking, but had to. "Has he been reinstated? Without telling me? I understand, but I should have—"

Toni interrupted. "Charlie hasn't been reinstated, at least to my knowledge, but I'll find out. I can't imagine ICE bringing him back, but stranger things have happened."

"Is he working undercover for another agency? The FBI maybe?"

"The FBI?"

"They served a warrant on Jones this morning. Tax evasion or money laundering, I didn't see the papers, but I'm meeting with the head agent this afternoon."

"Did Cammarata see you?"

"No. The last time I heard from him was four years ago, when he called me from Mexico about the container ship going through Panama with captives from eastern South America. You know that." And Sonia had had nightmares for months after just hearing his voice. She'd felt weak and stupid for letting the past hurt her. Why couldn't she just forget? But seeing Charlie today was already stirring up the awful memories. Ten years was a long time; it should be enough time to get over nearly dying.

It's not as simple as death.

"I didn't know the FBI had an open investigation on Jones." Toni sounded as ticked off about it as Sonia had been when she first saw the Fibbies roll on scene.

"Neither did I, but I think this goes way high up the ladder. The agent in charge is Dean Hooper."

"Assistant Director Dean Hooper?"

"The one and only, and Sam Callahan—he's the SSA in charge of white-collar crimes—he's answering to Hooper. Not only is it highly unusual, I don't remember ever hearing about an A.D. in the field serving warrants."

"Hooper's an anomaly," Toni said. "We have jurisdiction here. Do you want me to knock heads together and find out what's going on?"

"I'd love it, but that's not going to help nail Jones. I'm going to find out what Hooper has. If Jones has been playing with his books and we can prove it, maybe that'll give me the leverage to make a deal. Names, routes, places. We can do heavy damage to the human trafficking business in the western U.S. if I can entice Jones to cooperate." Sonia didn't want to cut any deals with that bastard, but she had to look at the bigger picture. Either way, Jones would go to prison.

"I like it. You have my support."

"What I'm really worried about," Sonia continued, "are the Fibbies coming in wanting to make a big splash. The economy sucks, and politicians are always looking for scapegoats. Taking down a rich tax evader like Jones gives them headlines and crowing rights. And you know damn well the FBI wants those headlines to justify their existence and their budget." Homeland Security, and ICE as a major investigative agency, took care of potentially deadly situations quietly and out of the prying eyes of the media. The public knew little of what ICE and other agencies had thwarted not only now, after 9/11, but before.

"I'll make some calls—about Hooper's investigation and about Cammarata. Quietly. No need to get feathers ruffled unless we are prepared to pluck them."

"I'll let you know what Hooper has and we'll go from there."

"I'll back you up, Sonia, but let me be the bad guy. You know I love you and you're my favorite agent, but you're impulsive, and your temper is going to get you in trouble." *Again.*

"Understood. Thanks, Toni. And let me know what you learn about Charlie as soon as possible. If he's in this on his own, I have to get him out. He could screw up our investigation big-time."

"You certainly don't have to tell me Cammarata is dangerous. Are you prepared to arrest him?"

The pastry she'd scarfed down on her way to the office swam uncomfortably in the pool of coffee sloshing in her stomach. "Absolutely. I'll do anything to protect the integrity of this case. I'm not about to let Jones walk free on a technicality."

CHAPTER
FIVE

At FBI headquarters Dean Hooper coordinated the organization of evidence they'd seized from Xavier Jones's house that morning. He had nearly the entire white-collar crimes team working on analyzing every piece of paper and computer file, but he took the one thing he really wanted back to his desk. With everyone else on his team in the conference room or out in the field, he was alone.

Dean turned the day planner over in his hands. It was a half-size seven-ring executive planner, one day per page, covered in black leather. Pages could be removed or inserted as needed. It was in the seemingly innocuous details of Jones's daily activities that Dean would find the path leading to hard evidence and, ultimately, a conviction. Everything he had now was circumstantial. Dean needed solid proof.

Jones was meticulous, and judging from how he reacted to agents going through his things, he was likely obsessive-compulsive. He practically had a coronary when Dean moved a vase an inch off-center. Jones strode over to the table and put the vase back dead center, perfectly symmetrical.

Oh, yeah, the guy was anal to the nth degree.

Technically, Dean didn't have a warrant for the day

planner, but when he looked through it at the house he noted that Jones listed all his bank account numbers and meetings he had with his accountant. That put the planner under "financial" in Dean's book, so he seized it.

Jones wouldn't be so dumb as to write down anything blatantly illegal, but he would have a schedule of his meetings and within the meetings, and the empty spaces, there would be a pattern. Next, he would check the planner against Jones's known whereabouts and determine if there were any codes in the seemingly innocuous content. In addition, if specific meetings coincided with seemingly *legitimate* bank deposits or withdrawals, Dean could look at those entities to see if he had cause to get a warrant for *their* records.

Criminals had become extremely sophisticated over the last decade, and money laundering increasingly complex. While many bad guys use the tried-and-true methods—such as putting their cash into small, legitimate businesses to clean it—with the sheer amount of illegal money changing hands, criminals had to develop new and innovative ways to wash large amounts of money and get it circulating.

Dean could have delegated this rather mundane task of inputting Jones's schedule into a database, but he had better luck identifying patterns and anomalies when he was the one typing the information. His mind processed it differently, he supposed, or maybe it was simply that how he wanted the information logged maximized his ability to recognize patterns. His database was easily sorted by date, dollar amount, entity, account number, or any other field, but Dean preferred analyzing the raw data by date. He'd found that while criminals tried to randomize their activities to avoid detection, they usually set meetings or bank deposits on a regular day or time. Dean had taken down Thomas "Smitty" Daniels because he cleaned his money on the first Monday of every month.

Daniels's scam was good. Dean wouldn't have figured it out so quickly without the specific time frame. Daniels was a landlord purported to own dozens of rentals. He deposited rent—in cash—on the first Monday of every month. That was a big red flag. How many landlords had all their tenants pay on time? Dean scoured the property records and found that Daniels was claiming to own property that he, in fact, didn't own, and collecting "rent" from people who didn't exist. He wouldn't have been caught if he hadn't had to increase the deposits, which alerted the FBI to a change in deposit history. By law, all banking transactions over $10,000 were reported to the FBI. Most were legitimate and, in real estate, substantial deposits and withdrawals were common. But Daniels had gone from deposits of between forty and fifty thousand a month to deposits of ninety thousand.

When Dean looked at the records, all deposited at the same time of the month, all cash, he launched the grand jury investigation. He didn't know how Daniels was making his illegal money—he had wrongly assumed drugs, which accounted for an estimated ninety percent of laundered money in the United States. It didn't take long to learn that Daniels was involved in sex crimes, specifically kidnapping minor female runaways for Internet pornography.

Xavier Jones's name had come up in the course of investigating Daniels, but there was nothing substantial in Daniels's records implicating Jones in criminal activity. The major impetus was an old photograph of Jones and Daniels with a group of known or suspected criminals. It was primarily Dean's gut intuition after seeing that photo that had him looking closely at Jones for the last two years.

Dean suspected that Jones was involved with the illegal sex trade, but there was no evidence pointing directly at him, and until he learned that ICE was involved, he had assumed it was prostitution—Jones had contact with known prostitution rings. Dean knew less about the international scope of Jones's activities than ICE agent Sonia Knight—human trafficking was primarily under the domain of Homeland Security. And while he *should* have known about the ICE investigation, even in this new era of sharing information, not all information trickled down—or up—to the right people.

He wanted Sonia to look at all his information immediately. He had a feeling she'd see things he didn't because her experience tracking the buying and selling of people was legendary.

That Sonia Knight had been sold into slavery as a child, then escaped, was in itself an incredible story; that she'd become a decorated special agent in immigration was even more extraordinary. He hadn't been blowing smoke up Sonia's very attractive backside when he told her there was no one else he'd rather work with. She had a reputation for being not only a hothead, but intelligent, extremely knowledgeable, and compassionate. She took risks, probably too many, but in Dean's experience it was only those agents willing to put their reputation and life on the line for justice who made the difference. He'd admired her from afar for years, but in all honesty he never thought he'd have a chance to work with her. DHS and the FBI were completely separate agencies; he hadn't even known she worked from the Sacramento field office.

If she had records of shipments in and out of the area that Jones was suspected of orchestrating, maybe adding that information to his database would make existing information pop, and he could follow that thread to the proof he needed for the U.S. Attorney to indict.

Tracking money wasn't the sexiest job in the FBI. Most agents wanted to work counterterrorism or violent crimes; those who were technology savvy, like Dean, usually found themselves in cybercrimes. But white-collar crimes pulled Dean in like nothing else. It came down to trust: if you couldn't trust your government, your small businesses, your corporations, society fell apart. Criminals reigned, and law-abiding citizens suffered financially, emotionally, and physically. Anarchy was the end result of doing nothing.

And, frankly, crunching numbers and pattern recognition were his strengths. His father never understood. Clint Hooper had been a beat cop, working the streets of Chicago until the ravages of too many cigarettes and too much fat put him in an early grave. He'd been a good cop, had taught Dean and his younger brother, Will, right from wrong, but a cop was all he was. When Clint Hooper was home, he wanted to be out on the streets. When he went to their ball games, he was always with the other cop dads. As a result, Dean lived with cops, socialized with cops, didn't know anything else but the life of a cop. He'd wanted something else.

So he joined the military through the ROTC program and planned to be a career Marine. It wasn't his first choice—he'd always excelled in math and had considered teaching or being a CPA—but the pressures of a blue-collar father thinking accounting was for wimps had him looking to prove his manhood when he really should have had nothing to prove to anyone except himself.

He'd learned his lesson, but not before his dad died. He left the Marines, got his degree, and, because of an aptitude test, was recruited into the FBI. He ended up doing what he was good at coupled with the only thing he truly knew and understood: being a cop. Maybe it was in the blood. And that was okay with Dean. This was where he was supposed to be; there was nothing else he wanted to do.

Sooner than he had expected, he was done inputting the information from Jones's day planner. Nothing jumped out right away, so he looked again, for notes and odd marks. There were none. The planner was as neat and efficient as Xavier Jones's house and physical appearance. His perfect, crisp, all-caps printing was neither too small nor too big, with little deviation—Dean had to look closely to see any differences between the same letters. Virtually every "E" looked identical. Almost impossible to do by hand, but the writing was definitely ink. All black, fine felt-tip.

The handwriting analysts would have a field day with this, if they could get anything useful, other than what Dean had already figured out about his personality.

Dean looked at today: Wednesday, June 3.

11:00 a.m.	*BRIEFING @ XCJ*
12:00 p.m.	*LUNCH @ CHOPS: CLIENTS*
5:00 p.m.	*DRINKS @ FRANK FATS: CLIENTS*

Odd. He looked back at all the previous meetings. Jones never identified who he was meeting with, but he always had a location. Was the location a code? Or did he not want a physical record of the people at the meeting?

XCJ was Jones's lobbying firm. Again, Dean flipped through the book. He had no business listed except weekly "briefings"—almost always on Mondays, except today.

Was that because he'd been out of town this past Monday?

There were no appointments scheduled for this week Monday or Tuesday, the days he had been gone. Dean looked at the book closely. Several things had been whited out. Again, meticulously. And because it was felt-tip, Dean couldn't see the impression of the individual letters through the white-out, so he couldn't re-create the meetings that had been canceled. He turned the page to see if he could read the bleed-through and decipher the backward text. The flip side had been whited out as well.

Maybe the evidence response team could come up with something, but Dean wasn't holding his breath.

Another thing that stuck out to Dean was that for a multimillionaire philanthropist who owned several businesses and millions of dollars in property, there was surprisingly little written in the day planner. The e-teams unit had already informed Dean that Jones didn't use the calendar on his computer. They were looking at possible online calendars by going through his browser history, but they had to re-create the history since Jones used sophisticated software to permanently erase his files and Internet travels.

Who else might keep a calendar for Jones? He couldn't keep all his plans and meetings in his head, could he? Maybe his cell phone, but Dean didn't have a warrant for phone records. And Jones wouldn't put anything incriminating on it. With one of his employees—that was more likely. Separating himself from any record of illegal activities by having a third party involved.

Employees . . . how did he pay his employees? Cash? That wasn't enough to prosecute, especially if there was a record of it. Dean noted large withdrawals from Jones's bank account once a month. Payroll? Maybe. He had employees through two businesses: XCJ Consulting and XCJ Security. Dean had taken a look at the tax forms and nothing jumped out at him as odd about the businesses, other than that they were very profitable— and Jones was paying his required taxes on the profits.

Sam Callahan walked over to Dean's cubicle and said, "We missed breakfast. I'm starved. I'm going to the deli down the street. Want something?"

Dean glanced at his watch: 11:00.

He knew where Jones was going to be at noon. Dean would be interested in finding out which "client" he dined with after his trip down south.

"How about a working lunch?"

"What's up?"

"Let's head downtown. Chops."

"You've been here three weeks and I've never seen you eat anywhere other than this desk or the conference room. How do you know about Chops?"

He tapped Jones's day planner. "Jones seems to think it's pretty good. Has lunch there every week. In fact, he'll be there today."

"What about our meeting with Sonia Knight?"

"We'll be finished by one. I just want to see who Jones likes to eat with."

Sonia left her office early so she could swing by her adopted parents' house before driving across town to the FBI's headquarters. They lived in the established neighborhood of South Land Park, where stately homes and classic Tudors and Craftsmans had been built over more than one hundred years to create a warm, inviting, and pricy feeling to the tree-lined, curving streets. She lived in a small bungalow only two blocks from her parents, and her brothers, Riley and Max, shared a house a few blocks in the other direction. A Marine, Max returned home only a few weeks a year and was currently deployed in Afghanistan, where he'd recently re-upped for another three-year tour, so Riley pretty much had the place to himself. But they congregated in the family house. Few days went by without visiting her parents.

Sonia found Andres after getting an "anonymous" tip that a ten-year-old boy who'd been held against his will at Jones's house would be walking along Ione Road. She'd assumed that the untraceable email came from Greg Vega, who had every reason to be paranoid; now she wasn't so sure. She'd gone easy on the kid after learning what he'd been through and his declaration that he'd never seen Xavier Jones, didn't know who he was, and just wanted to find his sister and go home.

Sonia couldn't send him home, and she hadn't yet

been able to locate Maya. The safest place for him was with her parents while Sonia worked discreetly through the system to find his family in Guatemala. Sonia had been fortunate to find a home after she'd been rescued; but she'd seen what happened to the kids who went through the system. There was little anyone could do except send them home. Those they rescued weren't only illegal immigrants kidnapped or smuggled into the country under false pretenses, many were runaways taken off the streets by predators with the promise of food and shelter. After they were separated from any friends they may have made, they were forced into prostitution. Some of the kids were kidnapped young and trained to be whatever the buyer wanted—a sex slave, a servant, a soldier—or as Sonia had heard child soldiers called, cannon fodder.

The truth was, they saved very few once the victims disappeared into the human trafficking network. With over eight hundred thousand women and children manipulated or kidnapped each year, the situation was out of control. The United States, with other countries, made small inroads into the illegal system, but the evil continued to grow until sometimes Sonia felt it was all but hopeless.

Except that she personally had saved numerous victims and helped them get their lives back. That alone made it worthwhile. As long as she focused on those she helped, she could do the job. And she had the most incredible support system in her adoptive family. She knew her life would have been far different, and much worse, if they hadn't been there for her. If they hadn't given her unconditional love and a real home.

She knocked on the door, then entered with her key. "Mom? Dad? It's me."

"In the kitchen," Marianne Knight called out.

Sonia walked through the cluttered but immaculate living room and formal dining room to the bright kitchen in the back. Her mom was at the stove grilling sandwiches and brother Riley was drinking coffee and lounging in sweats and an old Led Zeppelin T-shirt. He worked swing shift in the Sacramento Police Department—four to midnight—and lunchtime was his breakfast. He was a year younger than Sonia, though they'd gone through high school in the same grade because Sonia had had to play catch-up when she came to live with the Knights.

She affectionately punched Riley on the arm with a "Hey" and hugged her mom.

"Nice surprise," Marianne said. "I'll grill another sandwich."

"I don't have time," she said as she poured herself a cup of coffee. "I need to talk to Andres."

"You can take it with you." Marianne's tone said no arguments.

Riley smirked when Sonia glanced at him. "Don't fight it, sis. Besides, you can't live on coffee alone."

"I had breakfast."

"Ha. Let me guess: drive-through Starbucks, blueberry scone."

"They were out of blueberry by the time I got there," Sonia retorted. "I had to get vanilla."

"You slept in so long you missed out on blueberry scones?" Riley teased.

"I was on a stakeout. Didn't leave until nine a.m."

Marianne frowned as she took a perfectly toasted ham and cheese off the pan. "And you haven't slept?"

"Trace drove back," Sonia lied, only so her mom wouldn't worry. "I had nearly an hour of sleep."

Riley gave her the look that said *bullshit,* and whether Marianne believed her or not, she didn't let on. "An hour's sleep isn't good for your reflexes," she said. "Be careful today."

"Where's Andres?"

"At the park with your dad. Owen is teaching him baseball. Andres is a natural, has taken to the sport better than Riley and Max."

"Not for lack of trying," Riley said.

"They'll be back any minute," Marianne said.

"How's he doing?" Sonia asked, sitting across from Riley. He gave her a look, obviously curious about her stakeout. *Later,* she mouthed. Riley knew she was going after Jones, but she didn't want to go into details in front of their mom. It was a clandestine investigation, and she technically shouldn't have talked to Riley about it, but she had needed his help to find Andres last week after the anonymous email. And she liked to talk to her brother. He was easygoing and smart. He both listened and offered sound advice.

"As good as can be expected," Marianne replied. "He's worried about his sister, of course, but he's eating well and seems to enjoy going to the park. And before you say it, yes, we're keeping a close eye on him."

"I know," Sonia said.

The back door opened and Owen and Andres walked in, all smiles, with balls and bat and a large German shepherd who bounded over to Sonia when he saw her, and sat at attention, his tail barely restrained. She scratched the former police dog between the ears. "Hey, Sarge, I missed you, too."

Andres's smile faltered when he saw Sonia, and she felt awful that he expected bad news from her. "Hi, Andres," she said in Spanish with a smile. "I hear you're the next Jose Canseco."

He beamed nervously, glancing up at Owen. After family, Owen's next love was baseball.

"I have tickets to the Giants game tomorrow," Owen said, "and I'd like to take Andres if it's okay."

"Sure," Sonia said. "It sounds like fun."

"You can come?" Andres asked hopefully.

She shook her head. "Sorry, I have to work."

"I have the day off," Riley said. "I'll go."

Andres smiled.

Sonia glanced at Riley, but said nothing. She knew he didn't have the day off—he worked Monday through Friday—but their parents didn't seem to catch on and Riley subtly shook his head at her.

"Andres, I have a couple questions for you."

"Wash up," Marianne interrupted, pointing them to the sink. "Lunch is ready."

Sonia glanced at her watch. Marianne handed her a paper bag. "You can eat in the car, dear."

She kissed her mother's cheek and took the bag. "Thanks, Mom."

When Andres sat down, Sonia said, "Andres, when you left the garage where you had been held, you said that a man left the door unbolted and told you to run when he walked away."

Andres nodded, his brown eyes troubled.

Sonia took a picture out of the folder she'd brought with her. "Is this the man?"

Andres looked at the photograph of Charlie Cammarata. Riley tensed beside her. Sonia hadn't told her parents about her history with Charlie, but she kept few secrets from her brother.

"*Si,*" he said. "He said run."

Sonia's chest tightened. Charlie was in the middle of a dangerous game. "Thank you." Her voice was clipped as she forced a half-smile. She had to find Charlie and talk to him. Something big was going on, otherwise he wouldn't have sidled up to a known trafficker like Xavier Jones. Charlie would have been more likely to assassinate Jones than go undercover and work for him simply to gather information.

And, Sonia reminded herself, Charlie was no longer in law enforcement. But that didn't mean that an agency wouldn't hire him freelance, even though he was a volatile maverick.

"I need to go," she said, standing.

"I'll walk you out," Riley said.

She wished she could avoid her brother, at least until she had more information, but he'd hound her until she talked.

She grabbed her lunch and kissed Andres on the head. "I'll see you later, okay? Have fun at the ball game."

Before the front door shut, Riley asked, "What's that bastard Cammarata doing here?"

"I don't know," she admitted.

"Dammit, I don't like this. He almost got you killed, Sonia, because he was a selfish, conniving rogue agent. And he was the one who freed Andres? What about his sister? Did he sell her? So he could track down her buyer?"

Sonia had always been quick to temper, and her

brother set her off worse than anyone. "That's not fair," she said. "Don't you dare bring that up—"

"It's true. He used you, Sonia. And you nearly died. Cammarata should have been put in *prison*, not just lost his badge."

"Charlie snapped, but he was a damn good agent for a long time."

"Don't you defend him!"

"I'm not. I'm the one who turned him in!"

"And you've felt guilty about it ever since."

"If the situation was reversed, wouldn't you? The blue code is just as real to federal cops as it is to you. So don't tell me you wouldn't feel exactly like I did when I testified against Charlie, and don't talk about him like he was a criminal. He made a mistake—"

"He made *a lot* of mistakes." Riley ran both hands through his disheveled hair. "Sonia, I'm sorry, but I love you and I hate what he put you through."

"I'm okay."

Riley put his hands on her shoulders and looked hard at her. "Are you?"

"*Yes*. I'm fine. I can handle Charlie. But I'll admit this situation has me confused. My boss is trying to find out if Charlie is working undercover—freelance, maybe— for another agency. The FBI is after Jones for money laundering. There's no trail on where Maya was taken. I'm at the end of my rope and am going to be late for a meeting with the FBI white-collar crimes unit to share notes on Jones. And to be honest, I don't know what else to do but go along with them."

"You can use what they have as leverage, get the information you need."

"Absolutely. The thing is, I don't think they have any-

thing solid, either. I think they have what I have: circumstantial evidence that is pointing to Jones, but with no
hard facts to haul his ass into an interrogation room.
But with Charlie inside—"

"Who would bring him on? No one trusts him."

Sonia straightened. "That's it."

"You've lost me."

"No one trusts him, but when you're desperate you
will do anything."

"Still lost over here."

"I know who hired him. Or rather, not who but why."

"This dumb cop is still in the dark," Riley said, irritated.

Sonia rolled her eyes at him. "Think about it. Charlie
is a renegade, but he's shared key information with ICE
when he has it. He's still involved, but in the private sec-
tor."

"Who would hire him?"

"Someone desperate."

"Who's desperate enough to hire a volatile, disgraced
cop who *might* share information when he feels like it?"

Sonia cringed. Riley was dead-on. Charlie only tossed
them intel when he couldn't do anything with it. But
sometimes, law enforcement's hands were tied and
Sonia didn't blame private citizens from doing everything in their power to find missing loved ones who all
too often disappeared outside U.S. borders.

She said, "The last time he contacted me was four
years ago. He gave me information about three college
girls who'd gone missing during spring break. He'd been
hired by one of the girls' parents. If you're desperate
enough, you'll do anything to find out what happened
to your child."

Riley's voice softened. "I remember. They were found dead."

She nodded. "But he had information about the trafficking ring that abducted them, and we were able to put together an international task force and take down several of the key players. I've heard through the grapevine he's been taking cases like that for years."

"And you think this is one of those?"

"It makes sense. And I know exactly who to call."

"Don't tell me."

"Kane Rogan." She pulled out her cell phone.

"I thought Rogan hated him as much as I do."

"Maybe, but they were Marines together and Rogan has been known to take similar assignments. Maybe he's familiar with whatever Charlie is working on. If not, he has enough contacts to find out."

CHAPTER
SIX

Promptly at noon, Xavier Jones walked through the entrance of Chops, a downtown Sacramento restaurant popular with the legislative and lobbyist crowd. Dean and Sam had used their badges to get a good table in the corner with a view of the entrance and most of the restaurant.

Jones entered alone, but he walked over to a booth in the back room where two men had been seated only a few minutes before. Once he sat down, Dean could no longer see him.

"Did you get a picture of those men?" Dean asked Sam, who'd been taking digital photos of everyone who entered the restaurant since they'd arrived.

"Yeah," Sam said, flipping through the images on his camera. He turned the small screen toward Dean.

"Clear. Great." The waitress came by with their order. "Can you box this up for us?" Dean asked. "We're going to talk to someone in the back and we'll pick it up on our way out." He handed her his credit card.

They walked into the back room and approached the booth. Though Jones obviously recognized them, Dean still took out his badge and held it up—more to piss Jones off than because he needed to identify himself to the men sitting across from him. "Assistant Director

Dean Hooper, Federal Bureau of Investigation," he said formally. "I just need to follow up with Mr. Jones, if you don't mind."

The only sign that Jones was more than a little irritated was a vein throbbing on the side of his neck, and a jaw clenched so tightly that Dean expected to hear his teeth grind.

"This can wait," Jones told Dean. "You have no right following me."

"I didn't follow you. Agent Callahan and I were having lunch and saw you walk in. It saves me another trip to your residence. But I'll come out this afternoon if that's better for you."

One of the two men said as he stood, "We'll give you a minute, Xavier—"

"No," Jones commanded. "Sit down."

It was an order, and the man sat. Interesting, Dean thought. What businessman would talk to his clients like that?

"Agent Hooper, I know exactly what you're trying to do, and it's not working. You have nothing and you'll find nothing because there is nothing. This is a complete waste of taxpayer money, and your boss will realize that sooner rather than later. I don't have to talk to you. Leave, or I'll call the police, have you removed, and sue you for harassment."

"That sounds like fun," Dean said. "I haven't had a chance to meet any local police." He slid into the seat next to Jones. "And you are?" he asked the men across from Jones.

"Don't answer," Jones said.

"I'm just making conversation, Xavier," Dean said.

Jones leaned over and said in a voice so low that Dean

was certain no one but him heard the threat. "You do not want to make me angry."

Dean whispered, "Yes, I do. I'm closer than you think."

Certain he got his message through to Jones, Dean stood and smiled humorlessly at the men. "Enjoy your lunch."

As he and Sam were walking away, a fourth man approached the table. "What's going on?" Dean heard the stranger say.

"Shut up and sit down," Jones growled.

Dean whispered to Sam, "Get his picture."

"Already done, boss."

"Don't call me that."

"That was impressive," Sam said quietly. "I'm learning more from you than I did at Quantico."

"Sometimes, you learn more by playing up to the stereotype."

At the reception desk Dean signed his credit slip and grabbed their lunch. Sam said, "Well, that was a ballsy move. If Jones is half as dangerous as Sonia Knight thinks he is, you'd better watch your back."

"I hope he goes for me. It'll be easier to put him in prison."

They stepped out of the restaurant into the dry Sacramento heat. "Not if you're dead," said Sam.

Sonia was halfway to FBI headquarters when her cell phone rang. She grabbed it, hoping it was Kane Rogan. But it was Grace Young, her administrative assistant.

"Hey Grace, I'm on my way to FBI headquarters. Are they already calling? I'm only a few minutes late."

"The FBI hasn't called, but Simone Charles from the

Sacramento Police Department is on the phone and says it's urgent."

Sonia frowned as she maneuvered her car through lunch-hour traffic. "I don't know her. What's it about?"

"She didn't say, but asked for you specifically. I tried to put her off, but she's stubborn, said she was at the hospital. I didn't know if it was about your brother, the cop—"

Sonia's stomach flipped, but she'd just left Riley at her parent's house and he was fine. "No, I just saw him. I'll talk to her. Patch her through."

When Sonia heard the *click-click* of the transfer, she said, "This is Sonia Knight."

"Agent Knight, I'm Simone Charles, supervisor with the forensic investigation division of SPD. I have a rape victim here at Sutter who I think you're going to want to see."

"How'd you get my name and number?"

"A memo you issued a couple years ago on criminal tattoos."

Sonia remembered the memo. She'd sent it out three years ago, when she was first promoted to SSA of the Sacramento field office after raiding a brothel near the Oregon border. It had been full of illegal Russian women who'd been branded with an ownership tattoo. She compiled a list of all known tattoos and sent an extensive memo to local and federal law enforcement about what to look for on both victims and suspects. She'd received only a few calls over the years, but this was the first in her jurisdiction. And the first about a victim.

"You said a rape victim?"

"Yes. I heard you work exclusively on human trafficking cases, but the tattoo is a close match to one of the descriptions on the memo. My Jane Doe is Caucasian, blond, blue eyes. I don't know where she's from. I'd think she was a runaway or something, except for the tats."

"Russian?"

"Doesn't have the bone structure, but maybe she's part Russian or European. Frankly, she looks like the girl-next-door type. At least, that's how I'd imagine she'd look if not for the blood and bruises and broken nose and cracked ribs."

"Where'd you find her?"

"On the bank of the Sacramento River near Discovery Park. A fisherman found her early this morning, naked and half submerged. He thought she was dead, didn't approach, and called nine-one-one. When the emergency crew arrived, they discovered she was breathing and rushed her to Sutter Hospital. I just finished taking the rape kit and collecting trace evidence. She's in bad shape, and the doctor isn't optimistic about her chances."

"Is she conscious?"

"No, hasn't been since she was found."

"What does her tat look like?"

"Four stars on her upper left bicep, then a number: D1045. Does that mean anything?"

"I haven't seen those numbers before, but the stars? Yeah. They mean something." Sonia unconsciously flinched, as if she'd been poked with a sharp needle. "I'll be right there."

Noel Marchand concluded a particularly lucrative deal in Brazil over his secure cell phone, and rewarded himself with an after-lunch shot of fifteen-year-old Scotch whisky he'd brought with him. Laphroaig. He'd imported it from Glasgow, one of the finest, richest-flavored Scotches he'd tasted.

He brought the glass to his lips, sipped, reveling in the warmth that brought his taste buds to life. At home, he'd enjoy having one of his in-house women take his cock in her mouth while he listened to classical music from the early Baroque era, especially Monteverdi and Buxtehude. But he'd have to make do with a sip or two—and no blow job—because there was much work to be done.

His phone rang and he answered without identifying himself. "What?"

"We have a problem."

It was one of his local men. "I don't like problems."

"We went to retrieve the used merchandise. It's not there."

"Did you check the morgue?" A problem, but not fatal.

"She's at the hospital."

Noel slammed down the phone. He crossed his suite and threw open the door to Tobias's bedroom. Mr. Ling sat at the desk with his laptop computer. There was no one else who could control Noel's brother, and Ling was an expensive babysitter. "She's not dead," Noel said through clenched teeth.

He unsheathed his knife, staring at his brother. Tobias smiled sweetly at Noel, then turned back to the ridiculous cartoons he watched most of the day. He didn't notice Noel's rage or the knife, or how close Noel was to slitting his throat right then. Since the day he was born, Tobias had been Noel's fucking albatross. Noel had finally broken out on his own when he was twenty, only to be once again shackled to the lunatic after their father died.

"Mr. Marchand," Ling said quietly. "There's a better way."

Ling was right. "We still have a major problem," Noel said.

"I'll get our best people on it."

"I want the bitch dead before she opens her fucking mouth."

CHAPTER
SEVEN

Sonia arrived at Sutter Hospital on F Street and found the criminalist packing up her equipment. "Simone Charles?"

The young woman turned, looked Sonia up and down. "Agent Knight."

"Sonia."

Simone said, "I'm done. There's nothing more I can do for her except run the rapist's DNA through the system."

"He left sperm?"

"Plenty. Normally I don't assume we have anything from the rapist, but I'm pretty confident that our perp left enough evidence in and on her body."

"Didn't you say she was found in the river? Wouldn't that contaminate DNA?"

"Yeah, but she wasn't completely submerged nor was she in the water for long. I recovered enough uncontaminated sperm, as well as skin and hair under her nails, that I think I'm going to get a solid report. It's like the guy is either stupid or wants to be caught."

"Or both," Sonia said, frowning.

"What's wrong?"

"If this is a typical rape, I don't see how the tattoos play in. My perps are usually better about disposing of their victims. They also don't kill them until they become too much trouble. They make their money with living, breathing women."

"Maybe the tats have nothing to do with trafficking. I called because the memo stuck with me over the years, and when I saw the stars, I just knew."

"I appreciate it," Sonia said. "Is she conscious?"

"After I spoke with you on the phone, she came to briefly. She panicked, which isn't surprising, then had a seizure. The doctors got her stabilized and gave her something to calm her down, but she's unconcious again."

"Did she say anything?"

"No. She can't talk. The doctor says she has a crushed larynx, she'll be lucky to ever speak again. They're going to take X-rays and tests."

Sonia's skin crawled. "Her larynx was *crushed?*"

"My best guess is that the bastard strangled her while he was getting off. The doctor is being very protective, jumped down my throat when he found out I called you. He understands we need to talk to her as soon as possible for a description of her attacker, but it's obvious she underwent a major trauma. She might not remember any useful details. He doesn't want her under any unnecessary stress."

"Who's the detective in charge?"

"Homicide detective John Black. We were initially told the victim was deceased, so until we got here we didn't know she was still fighting for her life. John's good. He's keeping the case."

"Great." Sonia glanced at the closed door and said, "You need a guard on her."

"Don't know if I can do that," Simone said. "You can talk to John. He's still at the scene."

"She's in danger. If they find out she survived, they'll come after her."

"Maybe you'd better clue me in on the situation."

The truth was, Sonia didn't know what she was dealing with.

"How old is she?"

"Minor. Fifteen or sixteen."

The right age. "Can I take a look at her?"

"And then you'll tell me what's going on?"

"Yes. You need to know what to look for, and I'll want to talk to Detective Black as well."

"The memo is about human trafficking. Is that what the tattoos mean?" Simone asked.

"Branding the victim with a tattoo or burn mark is becoming more commonplace. Some of the more high-tech organizations use GPS chips to track their victims, but the permanent markings are for ownership, and GPS is used to ensure their total compliance. Even if the victims are unsupervised for a time, GPS keeps them from escaping. They implant the chips usually in the shoulder or back of the neck." Sonia hit her forehead with the palm of her hand. "We need to X-ray the victim immediately. I might be able to find it on an external exam, but if it's been a while it might be harder to locate."

Simone's jaw clenched with indignant anger. "I'll get the doctor."

A male voice interrupted, "No one can talk to my patient right now."

Sonia turned and faced the man in a white coat who came out of the victim's room. His full head of close-cropped silver hair suggested senior citizen, but his face was smooth and youthful. He was closer to forty than sixty, and wore silver-rimmed glasses over blue eyes that defied Sonia to take a step toward his patient.

"Dr."—she looked at the name embroidered on his white coat—"Miller, I'm Agent Sonia Knight with Immigration and Customs Enforcement. I don't need to talk to her now, but I do need to see her injuries and the tattoo on her arm. And—"

He interrupted. "Ms. Charles has already photographed what you need. You can get it from her."

Sonia appreciated a doctor who protected his patients, but she was not the threat. "Doctor, your patient is in grave danger. We need a guard on this door."

"I'll notify security."

"No. I mean a real cop, twenty-four/seven, at no time can she be left unwatched. If she's who I think she is, some very bad people will do anything to make sure she can't talk."

"She may never talk again. Her larynx is crushed. She's lucky to be alive."

Lucky. The girl would be lucky if she could forget for five minutes what had happened to her this morning, and the days, weeks, and months leading up to this brutal attack.

"I'm not leaving here until an armed guard is standing outside her door. It can be ICE, it can be Sac P.D., it can even be the FBI, I don't give a damn, all I want is that girl to be safe." Sonia pushed aside her windbreaker revealing her gun and badge, and crossed her arms, putting her back to the door. "And I need to inspect her body immediately. She may have a GPS tracking device embedded under her skin, which means the person who did this to her already knows where she is."

Dr. Miller partly relented. "I'll put hospital security on alert and have someone at her door until the police arrive."

"We may need to move her. If she has a—"

He shook his head. "She's in no condition to be moved. If you are certain she's in danger, fine. Bring in an officer and we'll make it work."

Not good enough, but Sonia needed to confirm the microchip before she pushed to move a critically injured victim to another facility. "I also need the names of the nurses and orderlies who are assigned to this room. They need to be cleared, and then only those who are cleared will be allowed into the room, with an officer present."

"Isn't this overkill?"

Sonia had lost too many witnesses to the cutthroat brutality of traffickers. "Hell no. I don't know if it'll be enough. Under no circumstances is she to be identified as Jane Doe."

"We already—"

"Change it—now. Call her, um, Simone, what's your middle name?"

"Ann. Why?"

"Call her Ann Charles. Change every record in the system. They'll find a way to get in and search for Jane Does. They will be looking for her, they've already started." Of that, Sonia was certain. She hoped it wasn't too late to thwart them, or at least stall them.

It was obvious that Dr. Miller was finally taking her seriously. "I'll get right on it."

"Doctor," Sonia asked, "what are her chances?"

"That she regained consciousness, even momentarily, is a good sign, but . . . there's extensive damage. She needs surgery, but right now surgery is too dangerous. If it wasn't summer, she would have died of hypothermia. Even in this heat, her body temperature was far too low. I don't know the extent of all her injuries. She's going for a CAT scan in thirty minutes."

"Do you have a portable X-ray available?" Sonia asked. "We need to know what we're up against."

"I'll have it brought down. Give me a few minutes." He walked briskly down the hall, pulling a nurse along with him.

Sonia turned to Simone. "Can you get someone from Sac P.D. down here before that?"

"I'll do my best." Simone picked up her phone.

Sonia said, "Turn around and man the door. Be alert."

Sonia slipped into "Ann Charles's" room before Simone could stop her.

She let the door close.

"You can't be in here."

Sonia faced a seasoned nurse who was monitoring several humming, beeping machines while writing on a chart. The victim was the only patient in the 4-bed ICU room. "I'm Agent Sonia Knight with Immigration. Dr. Miller said I could see the patient." She showed the nurse her badge.

The nurse shook her head. "I doubt that. He allowed the police department to collect evidence, but the patient is in—"

None of the staff's efforts to protect Ann would matter if her attacker tracked her to Sutter Hospital. These people were ruthless; they would kill anyone who got in their way. While most of the brutal violence associated with trafficking occurred outside U.S. borders, there had been a marked increase over the last few years of "unsolved" murders that ICE believed were a by-product of the more-than-$23-billion-and-growing human trafficking business.

"Five minutes," she told the nurse as she approached the victim.

The nurse called security and stood sentry at the foot of the bed. "Don't touch her," the nurse growled, but made no move to throw Sonia out.

The victim had clearly not been meant to survive. Her skin was bruised, a bandage covered half her head, and numerous cuts had been cleaned, interspersed with bandages over the deeper injuries. Amazingly, her beautiful face was unmarked except for a couple of minor scratches. But her throat was dark purple with a bruise pattern that clearly outlined fingers.

Previous victims flashed through Sonia's mind. She'd seen similar marks before. In southern Mexico she was part of an international task force that uncovered an unmarked grave of more than a dozen women, all killed at different times. The most recent victim in the grave had been dead for less than forty-eight hours and bore similar violent bruising that covered her entire neck.

Though the task force had thoroughly investigated the murders, they'd never had a suspect. DNA was collected, but it didn't match any known individual in CODIS. Mexico and other countries had their own CODIS systems, but their data was less complete than in the United States and Europe. Still, it was worth sending the DNA samples Simone collected to all countries in the western hemisphere that had the capability to run them against their files. The chances Ann's rapist and the Southern Mexico killer were one and the same were slim, but because human trafficking was involved the odds increased slightly.

Sonia's rage bubbled as she pictured the brute who had caused such pain and trauma to an innocent girl. She had to find the bastard and stop him. But even then, Ann's safety was at risk. If she had been a captive, they wouldn't let her live to tell her story or finger any of them. Sonia had to know what she was dealing with.

"Ann" was in a deep, drug-induced sleep, on breathing equipment and an IV. Her neck was bruised, in a partial brace, and Sonia didn't dare feel around for the chip and risk further injury. She'd have to wait for the X-ray.

Traffickers inserted GPS chips when they planned to keep the victims alive and working, either in hard labor or prostitution. The implants, even when they didn't function properly, kept them in line, because everyone believed they would be found even if they escaped. Some victims had cut out the microchips, but it wasn't easy or safe. The back of the neck was a quick and easy incision with the least chance of infection, but the device was almost impossible to remove without assistance.

Sonia felt the nurse watching her closely, but she had no choice. She reached out quickly and pushed up the sleeve of Ann's gown to see the tattoo.

The four stars were so familiar Sonia almost felt that she knew the girl. Of course she didn't, not personally, only girls like her. She could have ended up like Ann. She also could have ended up dead. That she'd been one of the few to escape before suffering such physical and emotional trauma brought on mixed emotions. Relief and joy, guilt and sorrow. Knowing there were others not as lucky as she'd been. Others like Ann. Like Izzy . . .

The nurse grabbed her arm. "Detective, you need to leave right now. You think you can come in here and manhandle my patient?" she said in a loud whisper. "Do you know what this girl has been through?"

"I know a hell of a lot more about what she's been through than you."

Sonia jerked her arm away from the nurse and gently dropped the gown back in place. She didn't know what the numbers meant—she had never seen anything similar. They didn't look right, as if a different ink had been used. But there was no way the nurse would give her the time she needed to concentrate on the oddity.

The door opened and a security guard stepped in.

"Escort this woman from the hospital," the nurse demanded.

"I'm leaving," Sonia said.

"I'll take you out, ma'am," the guard said.

"I'll wait for the doctor." She stepped through the door. Dr. Miller came running and frowned.

"Agent Knight, I told you not to speak to the patient."

"I didn't talk to her. I needed to see something."

"If you want my help, I suggest you follow my rules." He dismissed the security guard. "The portable X-ray is on its way. Wait here. Or I *will* have you removed from the hospital." He stepped into the room to calm the fuming nurse.

Simone grinned. "You have balls."

"So they tell me. Can you rush the DNA tests? Or send some evidence to the DHS lab? It's a long shot, but because we're dealing with likely human trafficking, our suspect could be a foreigner. DHS works closely with the FBI and law enforcement abroad."

"Consider it done."

"Maybe we'll get lucky with an I.D." As she spoke, she emailed her boss the information she had.

"I just hope he's from a country with an extradition treaty," Simone said. "What about the tattoo?"

"The stars are related to her destination. These girls don't mean anything to them—they're property. The marks tell them how to sort their 'property' to make it easier to inventory and distribute."

"How can you talk about human slavery so matter-of-factly?" Simone asked, incredulous.

Sonia bristled, then bit back her temper. The criminalist was asking a valid question. Still, she responded with a question. "How can you collect evidence off a rape victim?"

Simone shook her head. "It's not the same thing."

"We all deal with our jobs the best we can. I have to be objective or I can't do my job."

"I'm sorry. That was rude of me."

Sonia pressed her palm to her forehead and said, "I overreacted."

Sonia had been accused of being both overly passionate and overly clinical, which used to amuse her until she realized most people didn't want to see either extreme. They didn't want to discuss serious crime clearly and rationally to solve the problem, nor did they want to hear about their own culpability in ignoring the problems in the first place. If it didn't touch their lives, they feigned ignorance. They didn't want to know if the clothes on their back had been sewn by a slave or if the shoes on their feet had been glued by an eight-year-old.

"I'm going to check on the X-ray," Simone said and went to find a nurse.

Sonia's phone vibrated. She glanced at the number. It showed a 916 area code and nothing else. Federal. "Hello?" Oh, shit. She was way late to her meeting with the FBI.

"Sonia Knight, please."

"Hooper, right? I'm sorry."

"You did remember our meeting then."

"Yes, I'm really sorry. It couldn't be avoided."

"I spoke with Toni Warner. She said the FBI is welcome to work with you and your partner, Agent Anderson. I don't know if that's in our best interest."

She paused a beat, her nerves prickling with restrained anger. "Excuse me?"

"I don't have time to play territorial games or wonder if you're going to hold back crucial information." Dean's high-and-mighty arrogance—his superior tone— irritated Sonia and she bristled.

"I don't play games," she snapped. "I resent the accusation."

"How can I be sure? I thought we agreed to share information. Yet you don't even have the courtesy to tell me you're running late. My time is as valuable as yours."

"Look, Hooper, I'm happy to work with you on this, okay? But right now I have a delicate situation and I can't stroke your ego." Sonia winced. Sometimes her mouth worked faster than her brain. She softened her voice and added, "If you can give me an hour, I'll be there. I promise."

There was a long pause. "I think I owe you an apology," Hooper said, startling Sonia into silence. "I didn't mean to jump down your throat. I don't have an ego, Sonia."

She must have touched a sore point with Hooper. "Okay, no ego. Neither do I." She suddenly laughed, and it felt surprisingly good.

"Did you just laugh?" He sounded surprised.

"I might have." She took a deep breath and said with a smile, "I think we should both admit that we have small, manageable, unobtrusive egos."

Dean couldn't stifle his own chuckle. "I think I can agree with that."

Diplomacy was never something Sonia cared much about, but right now, working with the FBI on the Jones case was critical. There was too much at stake. And Sonia would do anything—perhaps even make a deal with the devil himself—to find Maya Zamora alive and reunite her with Andres.

"Let's regroup this afternoon." She glanced at her watch. "It's two, as soon as I get a guard on my victim, I'll leave—"

"Victim? What happened?"

"This isn't connected to Jones." At least she didn't think it was. Jones was a middleman; he wasn't suspected of killing any of the people he traded in. Still, the FBI could help. "However, I was hoping to get some assistance." She quickly explained to Dean what happened to "Ann" and her likelihood of being forced into prostitution. "The tattoos are a dead giveaway that she's a victim of human trafficking. We have DNA from her rapist, and it's clear that he intended to kill her when he threw her in the river. How she survived the ordeal is a miracle. Simone Charles from forensics is sending DNA samples to the DHS lab for processing and comparisons with foreign CODIS databases. I was hoping you could clear the way of bureaucratic obstacles and help process the evidence on your end."

"I can help. Sometimes being an assistant director has huge advantages. I'll email Ms. Charles my secretary's contact information and put in a few calls."

"Thank you, Dean. I really appreciate your help." Sonia gave him the details, then hung up.

Simone approached when she saw that Sonia was off the phone. "I spoke to Detective Black. He's getting a twenty-four-hour guard approved right now. We'll have someone within an hour."

"The FBI is pulling out the stops on DNA. Dean Hooper is going to email you with instructions." She wrote down Dean's contact information for Simone.

Dr. Miller returned with a nurse and a table of equipment, including an X-ray machine. Sonia was relieved that the doctor was taking Ann's condition seriously. "I'll personally see to it that if there is a damn computer chip in my patient's neck no one can track her down."

"Thank you, Doctor. Do you know when you'll take her into surgery?"

"She's stable right now and she'll be taken down for a CAT scan shortly. I'll know more after that."

"Please wait until the guard shows," Sonia said. "Or I can go with her." Sonia needed to get back to the Jones investigation, but she couldn't leave Ann vulnerable. She was torn between the two cases.

"It'll be at least thirty minutes."

"When you remove the GPS chip, I want it. We might be able to trace it." A long shot, but Sonia was willing to go down any path to find everyone responsible for Ann's condition. It wasn't only the rapist who was culpable. Who tattooed her? Who put the numbers on her? Who brought her to this country in the first place—or kidnapped her? How long had she been forced to prostitute herself? Where? Were there more like her in Sacramento? Sonia knew the answer was *yes,* but she didn't know where to start other than getting Xavier Jones to talk.

Sonia stared at Ann's door, willing the girl to recover. She was another key; like Andres a victim, but she'd also been part of the organization. She could testify, she could lead Sonia to where she'd been imprisoned. Describe her attacker. Ann was a key witness, another reason they needed to protect her.

Most victims of human trafficking were dead when Sonia found them. Or they'd been rescued before they learned anything about the illegal underground. Ann was rare and her survival paramount.

Riley, Sonia's brother, stepped out of the nearby elevator. He was dressed in uniform and Sonia asked, "What are you doing here?"

"I heard through the grapevine that you were involved and needed police protection for a rape victim." He tilted his head toward the criminalist. "Hi, Simone."

"Riley."

"Thanks, Riley." Sonia filled him in on the case as quickly as possible. "I'm glad you're here. I feel much better leaving Ann in your hands."

"Ann? You know who she is?"

"No, but I don't want her identified as a Jane Doe. Be careful, Riley. These people are ruthless."

"Right back at you, sis."

Sonia left the hospital, relieved that Ann was in good hands and that the doctor was serious about protecting both her identity and her life. She called Toni Warner as soon as she got into her car. "Anything about Charlie?" She asked without preamble.

"I've talked to everyone who would know about an undercover operation concerning Jones," she said, "and no one is claiming involvement."

"That doesn't mean there *isn't* something going on," Sonia said. While the various branches of federal law enforcement had been working together better since 9/11 unified their key mission statements and goals, there were still clandestine operations throughout the country and the world. Sonia knew; she'd been part of several post-2001. But because of her position and reputation Toni had the right contacts. She'd get a hint of an operation if one existed. It would just take time, and every passing day made it harder to find Maya.

"Tread carefully, Sonia. Cammarata is a loose cannon and dangerous."

"He's not going to hurt me." *Again.*

"Not intentionally, but he's always felt his causes were just, his actions necessary. He's always believed the ends justify the means, Sonia. And frankly, I don't care how noble his goal is, Cammarata cannot break law after law. It's why he was fired, it's why he's been blacklisted, and it's why you, and others, were nearly killed. Don't trust him because you think he feels remorse over what he did ten years ago. Trust me: I know Charlie Cammarata, and any guilt he feels is far outweighed by his personal mission to save the underdog at the expense of those he thinks should take care of themselves."

"I'll confront him and get him to talk, haul him into custody if I have to," Sonia told her boss.

"Bring backup, Sonia. You can't trust him."

CHAPTER
EIGHT

Dean had been so busy working on coordinating DNA testing of Sonia's rape victim that he didn't notice it was well after three in the afternoon. He'd talked to Quantico and they would expedite the tests, with results sometime next week. With their current workload, that was the best Dean could hope for. He also contacted local authorities and arranged for some of the evidence to be shipped overnight to Virginia. And when put on hold during numerous calls, he had time to update his charts on Xavier Jones's businesses.

He was concentrating on an updated printout of his spreadsheet when Sam Callahan escorted Sonia into the small conference room Dean had taken over when he arrived three weeks ago.

"How's the victim?" Dean asked Sonia after Sam excused himself to finish up paperwork from the warrant last night.

Sonia shook her head. "She's in bad shape, but alive. She has a chance. Maybe not a *good* chance, but so far she's holding her own. I may have to run if the hospital calls. I want to be there when they take the GPS chip out of her neck."

"Excuse me? GPS chip?"

"Human trafficking has heralded in the twenty-first

century with even more innovative ways to keep their victims captive." She glanced around the conference room, her hazel eyes taking in Dean's charts, diagrams, and extensive printouts. "This is all Jones?"

"Taxes, corporate filings, Fair Political Practices reports, SEC filings, any public information."

She flipped through one of Jones's tax returns, her brow furrowed. "Math isn't my strength."

"We all have our talents. Sit down." He pulled out a chair and she sat heavily. Dean doubted she'd slept since the stakeout. "Where do you want to start?"

"I want to know how you started looking at Jones and why you didn't notify anyone."

Dean bristled, but then realized Sonia hadn't intended to be insulting. "Fair enough. Do you remember a criminal named Thomas Daniels, aka Smitty?"

She arched her narrow brows. "Of course I remember him. The FBI went after him on money laundering and racketeering. He was killed trying to avoid arrest."

"I'm the one who shot him," Dean said. His cool tone belied his mixed emotions in being forced to fire on a suspect.

Her expression softened in understanding. "I'm sorry."

Dean had looked at Sonia's record, knew she'd used lethal force in the past as well. It wasn't something to take lightly, and unfortunately the movies often portrayed law enforcement as trigger-happy, gun-wielding vigilantes, when in reality it came down to reluctant but necessary use of force.

"When we went through his records, we put together his money-laundering scheme. Quite brilliant in its simplicity. Understanding the process helped us close other investigations where we didn't have the evidence because we hadn't yet caught up to the new systems criminals employed. We've been ahead of the curve for a while now—taking down nearly everyone we've targeted these past four years. Except Jones. He's been eluding me for too long."

"Did Smitty give Jones up?"

"No, he never talked to us. Everything we learned came from his records, which were disorganized. It took over a year of painstakingly analyzing his cryptic notes to discover that Smitty had a business association with Jones. I never figured out it was human trafficking—" He shrugged in frustration. "But we were close. I'd thought prostitution."

She nodded. "Smitty was a competitor. He specialized in runaways. Jones works with coyotes—human smugglers—south of the border, all the way to South America. But while Jones can bring in more merchandise, his expenses are higher than Smitty's. He makes his money on volume, while Smitty lured young runaways off the street and then relocated them all over the continent where they couldn't easily get out if they wanted to. Many of the girls he manipulated had been sexually and physically abused as children and felt they deserved whatever happened to them. Smitty was really good at spotting the damaged teens."

"You worked on his case, too?" Dean asked, surprised she knew so many details but he hadn't worked with her on the case.

She shook her head. "He was dead before I transferred to Sacramento, but I knew him as one of the players. Unfortunately, he was out of my squad's charter. My job has always been international trafficking, and after nine-eleven it's included a focus on potential terrorist trafficking, specifically disbanding hidden cells throughout the country."

"But your heart isn't in it."

"My heart is with the victims. I've done my fair share to prevent terrorism, but it's hard to focus on that when hundreds of thousands of innocent young people are lured or kidnapped into prostitution or labor camps."

Dean watched Sonia closely. She was impassioned, but also a realist. There was little they could do to stop these horrendous crimes, but she was determined to do everything possible to thwart their opponents. He admired her drive, her dedication, her passion for her job and the people she helped, as well as the people she put in prison. Sonia wasn't a woman who would ever stay on the sidelines. Like him, Dean doubted she had much of a life outside the job.

Sonia asked, "What did you find that put Jones on your radar?"

"A thin file. Nothing I could use in court. We originally went after Daniels for racketeering because he was working with major drug smugglers out of Stockton. He was responsible for laundering their money, and had a scam of claiming income from property rentals that didn't exist. It took time to catch on, but the banks involved alerted us after he changed his deposit habits, and we launched a grand jury investigation to figure out exactly where his money was coming from. It took a few months and physically viewing the properties to realize what his scam was.

"We didn't go after him right away because we wanted to build a case against the entire organization. Our profilers said he wouldn't rat anyone out—he was former military and extremely disciplined. So we began surveillance and Jones turned up in one of our photos. Because Jones was a well-known philanthropist, we didn't make him a priority, but after Daniels was killed, I found a memo that mentioned Jones and a bill of sale for property in Amador County. Nothing on the surface seemed illegal, and after looking into the property we couldn't find anything wrong with the sale. Callahan went out and interviewed Jones and his answers raised no flags. It went on the back burner until we closed out the Daniels case. But while logging in evidence months later we found another photograph of Daniels, Jones, and some others taken years ago in Mexico—analysts identified the area as Laguna Tres Palos, outside Acapulco. It made Jones's statement to Callahan that he was only an acquaintance of Thomas Daniels suspect. I started looking closer at Jones's business—maybe he was now laundering money for drug smugglers since Daniels was gone. I pulled his tax returns and saw that he had ample wealth with no major red flags, but after talking to specialists with the IRS, it seemed that Jones made a lot of money very quickly. He was paying his taxes, but his earnings far exceeded the normal range for companies like his. We looked at his businesses. Everything looked in order . . . but the association with Daniels bugged me, so I pulled together everything I could get my hands on. When I had the minimum information I needed, I launched the grand jury investigation."

Dean saw that Sonia was absorbing all the information. "Wow," she said, eyes wide and sparkling. "And you got a warrant on that? Vague gut instinct?"

"No, that was just the beginning."

"So you don't have an informant?"

"No. I wish I did. We discreetly approached some of

Jones's people and determined they aren't willing to talk or they don't know enough to help."

"And how did you get the warrant you executed last night? They're not easy to come by."

"On a wing and a prayer," Dean mumbled.

"Excuse me?"

"Full disclosure: I don't have a case. But I have a terrific assistant U.S. attorney who put together a solid argument with legal precedent. I have strong hints of a case, I know in my gut that Jones is corrupt—his lobbying firm charges his clients more than any other state or federal registered lobbyist. But I can't get anyone to talk, and because Jones is meticulous about his filings, there's nothing, not even an error, I can nail him on. If his clients are willing to pay, what can we do? Is it extortion? Bribery? We're looking into possible political corruption—that's Sam's primary focus, at least until I arrived—but we can't find anything there, either."

"It's hard for that many people to keep a secret that long. Politicians may be scumbags, but they're not usually murderers or involved in human trafficking."

Dean cracked a wry grin. "True, but there have been exceptions. Did you know that back in the 1920s a legislator shot his chief of staff in a lover's triangle involving the secretary?"

"You're a font of murderous trivia," Sonia said with a smile. "I haven't really looked at Jones's lobbying other than a cursory examination—do you think something's there? Or that he's using the business to pass through his trafficking profit?"

"I've looked, but I don't see how he's doing it. Every dollar he gets from clients is reported, we've verified with the clients' own reporting, and everything matches up. So if Client A pays twenty thousand dollars for consulting services, Jones is reporting twenty thousand dollars—not thirty or forty thousand as I'd expect if he were washing illegal dollars."

Dean continued. "When you look at his two primary businesses—the lobbying and the security business—they're very lucrative. More lucrative than similar businesses. I want to take another pass through the companies, the staff, the clients. That was what I was in the middle of when we decided to shake Jones up."

"That's all this exercise was about? Shaking Jones up?"

"I just wanted to see what he would do. So far, he's holding to schedule. I checked his calendar and he showed at his meetings today. I'll track him tomorrow as well, see if he's changing any of his plans. He didn't like me stopping by his lunch date this afternoon."

"Date?" She raised an eyebrow.

Dean waved his hand. "Just an expression. It was a meeting—him and two clients, men—businessmen, possibly his Indian gaming clients. Sam is running their photographs through the database. We know the fourth man, who arrived late, is his chief of staff at the lobbying firm, Craig Gleason. We took a surface look at him at the beginning, nothing popped, but we're digging deeper into his background. I have a pair of agents staking out his plane, and if he attempts to leave we'll take him into custody."

"On what grounds?"

"Attempted flight to flee prosecution."

"But you don't have that."

"No, but it'll stop him from leaving for forty-eight hours and I'll get it."

"And here people think Homeland Security has loose rules."

"I follow the rules," Dean said firmly, "I just make the most of them. There are more rules protecting criminals than defending our right to pursue them. I'm not trampling on any of his rights, but I'm going to make damn sure he doesn't leave the country. I have his passport flagged as well. If he tries to use it, the FBI will be notified and he won't be allowed to board the plane."

"Do you really think Jones is running his human trafficking profits through his businesses?" Sonia asked, somewhat skeptical. Dean understood her confusion— white-collar crimes were a far cry from anything she'd worked on.

"Yes, but how? See, small-time drug dealers make their illegal money selling drugs; then they invest that money in a legitimate business, and over time, that business is in the clear. The statute of limitations is five years. If they stay clean for five years, and we don't catch wind of their activities, they've won."

"That's if they aren't still committing crimes," Sonia said.

"Exactly. And there's Jones's property." Dean crossed the room and flipped over a whiteboard. On the back was a map of the greater Sacramento area with two dozen color-coded dots. "Each dot represents land or a business Jones owns. The red dots are vacant or unimproved land. The blue dots are occupied—he owns several properties where some of his employees live, plus his residence, and an apartment building. The green dots represent businesses. So far, everything is legit—unlike Smitty, these people actually exist. We've looked into *their* finances, thinking maybe he's paying his employees cash, but so far everyone seems to be living within their means."

Sonia stared at his map.

"Do any of these dots mean anything to you?" he asked her. "I haven't found a pattern yet."

"I don't know," Sonia admitted. "Have you been to all these properties?"

"Between Callahan's team and myself, we've visually inspected every one."

"Have you run them against local crimes?"

"Excuse me?"

"Murder, for example."

"There wasn't a need to."

"Maybe you should."

"What would that prove?"

"I don't know. But here"—she pointed to the foothills where Jones had extensive holdings—"is a good place to hide bodies. Or people."

"Have you looked at his property as part of your investigation?"

"My investigation is new."

"But you said this morning that you've been after Jones for years."

She turned to him, looking sheepish. Dean bristled. He didn't like being lied to, especially when he'd been up front since the beginning. "I *have* been after Jones for years," she said, "but I didn't launch my investigation officially until one of his top people came to me wanting witness protection in exchange for testifying against him."

Dean's voice was low. "And you didn't tell me?"

"I didn't have time last night," she snapped and rubbed her eyes.

"This is important, Sonia. You should have told me right off."

"I *did* tell you I had an informant," she replied. "I wasn't going to risk him by going into the details in front of everyone and their brother."

"Everyone? You think that one of my *people* is leaking information?"

"I didn't say that."

"You implied it."

"Even my office doesn't know who the informant is. Only my partner, Trace, and my boss. And the U.S. marshals who are putting together their witness-protection package."

"Their?"

"My informant is married. His wife is pregnant. He came to me when it became clear to him that he couldn't walk away with his life. He was worried about his wife, and I believed him. I don't have to like him, or what he's done."

"And you still don't have enough to get Jones?"

"This man has killed on Jones's orders, has transported sex slaves, and has named some of the players—but there is no proof. It's his word against Jones's, and the lawyers felt that we didn't have even a fifty percent chance of making it to trial against a well-known philanthropist who gives more than a million dollars annually to local charities. My guy can't be wired because Jones has an elaborate security system. Jones randomly searches people who work for him. He sweeps his house, phones, and offices regularly for bugs. But my informant confirmed everything I suspected. I just need hard evidence!" She slammed her fist on the table.

"Together we're going to nail him," he vowed.

"I'm counting on it." When she looked at him, Dean was surprised at the vulnerability behind her determined expression.

"It's Greg Vega, Jones's head security chief. He's been with Jones for years."

Dean appreciated Sonia's revelation. The admission had been hard, and Dean respected the trust she'd placed in him. "I'd like to talk to your informant."

Sonia balked. "You can't."

"Don't you trust me?"

"It's not you, it's the system. The fewer people who know about Vega, the better chance he stays alive."

"He might have information you don't know to ask about."

She stiffened as if he'd offended her. "I know my job."

"And I know about racketeering. I need to know how Jones is laundering his money. I can't imagine he's smuggling people in and out of America for fun. He's getting paid well for it."

"True, but—"

"We took down Al Capone for tax evasion. We have better laws now to stop criminals like Xavier Jones. I just need the money trail, and then I can nail him. Protect your informant. I don't want anything to happen to Vega or his family. Trust me, Sonia."

Sonia saw that Dean meant every word he said. She had no doubt he would do everything in his considerable power to protect the Vegas. She wanted to trust Dean. Why was it so hard to give him that one olive branch? Trust was the most important thing between partners—and that was the crux of the problem. Charlie had not only betrayed their partnership, but he had also destroyed the trust inside of her. It had taken her years to rebuild her confidence in others.

Silence hung between them, and Dean's entreaty turned to anger. "I see."

He didn't see; he couldn't know what had happened. Not everything. And she couldn't tell him like this, she didn't talk about it. Ever. But she didn't want this riff, she liked Dean, she needed him to take down Jones. Time was critical. She had to share something, so he understood why she was hesitant. She released a long, frustrated sigh. Dean turned from her, but she grabbed his arm to pull him back, her fingers gripping rock-hard muscle beneath his expensive tailored shirt.

"I lost an informant nearly four years ago," Sonia said. "Before I was transferred here. A nineteen-year-old prostitute from Argentina. I was born in Argentina and I used everything in my arsenal to bring her on board. I pleaded with her, I threatened her, I guilted her into it. She was scared to death, but she knew what happened to the younger girls, girls who had become her sisters and friends. She wanted it to stop."

Sonia dropped her hand and turned away from Dean, looking at the neat stacks of paperwork but not seeing anything but a blur of black and white. Why was this so hard to say out loud? Not a day went by that she didn't remember . . .

"Her name was Maria. She had tattoos like Ann, who's fighting for her life at Sutter Hospital. Not four stars, but a square with an overlapping cross. She finally agreed to help me after one of the younger girls was murdered by a john. Maria realized that none of them were safe. It took me *months* to work on her, primarily because I was undercover and only there one day a week. I was the "nurse" giving them their Depo-Provera shots, checking them for pregnancy and STDs, and treating their cuts and bruises."

"How long were you undercover?"

"Fifteen weeks. We could have gotten them for illegal prostitution, but I needed to prove they were smuggling in not only illegal immigrants but also minors against their will. I wanted the whole chain, not just that one link." Every night she'd left reluctantly, wanting to take all twenty-four girls with her. Help them. Protect them. That she couldn't tore apart her heart.

"Did you get them?" he asked quietly.

"Oh, yeah. Twenty-seven people went down in that sting, from low level thugs to the coyotes who transported the girls to leaders controlling multiple such places. We prosecuted nine, the remainder fled. Five were extradited last year and are awaiting trial, and the rest we can't touch. They're not Americans, and they've gone to ground. But, all in all, the operation was a huge success. For everyone except me, that is."

Dean was right behind her, she could feel his breath on the back of her neck. "What happened to Maria?"

She blinked back tears. "Two days before we took them down, Maria gave me vital information. I had everything we needed, but she was giddy—there was a new shipment of girls coming in that night. I staked it out, but it was a bust. The next morning, Maria was dead. She'd been set up, and—" She stopped. He didn't need to know everything.

"Did they know it was you?"

"Yeah. I fucked up, okay?"

"But you got them."

"Maria not only died, she was tortured. They shipped

off half the girls before I could get them out. I found some of them, but . . . it's not just about putting the traffickers behind bars, it's about saving innocent people. Maria should never have died. I should have sensed it was a setup, but I was so high on the power of the hunt, of nailing these guys every which way I could, I was blind."

"And you don't want to risk it again."

"I can't!"

"I'm not a risk, Sonia. You agreed we'd work together. I can't work with you if you don't trust me. It's your call."

Sonia wanted to. God, she wanted to, but she suddenly felt the vise tightening and everything was moving too quickly. She needed time to think.

Her phone rang and she excused herself, relieved that she could buy a couple of minutes. Dean walked out, mumbling something about water. He was angry, and Sonia wished she could patch things up. Dean wasn't Charlie, she had to trust him, somehow.

"Hello," she snapped into the phone.

"Sonia."

The deep voice was none other than Kane Rogan. She breathed easier. Kane had never let her down. She wanted to trust Dean like she did Kane, but she didn't *know* the fed. Yet, she didn't really know Kane, either. Other than the fact he'd saved her life.

"Thank you for returning my call."

"You don't call often."

"Charlie Cammarata."

The silence was so complete Sonia could picture Kane as a statue, calmly assessing a threat before he acted. "What about him?"

"I saw him today. Working for a trafficker. You've hired him in the past—do you know what he's working on now?"

"I haven't hired him in ten years." Kane spoke clearly in a low, deliberate tone.

She swallowed uneasily. She'd angered him without intending to. "I know, but you've been in contact."

"I've sent jobs his way. When no one else was willing to take them."

"Recently?"

"I referred him to a woman whose daughter went missing last year while on a cruise. Security determined that she fell overboard after drinking too much. The mother was not convinced. However, the police were, and they closed the case."

"That's all?"

"In these last few years. Cammarata has become un-dependable."

"Would you still have her contact information?"

"Of course."

"What about Charlie's?"

"Yes."

"I need to talk to him."

"Very well. I assume you know what you're doing, but remain aware that Charlie is not the same man he was ten years ago. And he wasn't trustworthy then."

"I understand," she said softly, clearing her throat. "I appreciate your help."

"You can call anytime, Sonia."

"I know."

"Let my brother know if you need anything. Duke will drop everything to assist."

"He doesn't even know me."

"I know you. Watch your back, sweetheart." Kane hung up.

Ten seconds later the contact information she wanted came through on her text messaging. He included his brother, Duke Rogan's, private cell phone number.

She trusted Kane Rogan with her life. If it weren't for him, she would have died ten years ago when Charlie went off on his own mission and left her, only a year out of training, in a situation that forced her to kill for the second time in her life.

But Kane was God-knew-where fighting battles only true heroes had a chance of winning. Once she had called him a cat with nine lives, and he'd actually *smiled*—a rarity.

If she could trust a man she saw once in a blue moon, why couldn't she trust FBI agent Dean Hooper, a man she was working side by side with? She already knew more about Hooper after knowing him less than twenty-four hours than she did about Kane, a man she'd known for ten years.

Dean returned with two bottles of cold water and handed her one. Nothing had looked so good; she was parched. "Thank you," she said.

He didn't ask, he simply looked at her with piercing brown eyes that demanded answers.

"All right," she said. "I'll set up a meeting with my informant. But first, there's something else you need to know."

Riley Knight stood sentry outside Jane Doe's hospital room. *Ann*, he reminded himself. That was so like his sister to give an unknown victim a personal name. One of the psychological games traffickers and other abusers used to demoralize their victims was to dehumanize them, make them forget they were individuals and program them to believe that their only value was in what they did and not who they were. Naming people "Jane" or "John Doe" grated on Sonia like fingernails on a chalkboard, though she'd never said anything.

There were many things Sonia never said, but after twenty years of being virtual twins, Riley knew her better than she knew herself. This was no exaggeration; Riley didn't think Sonia cared to be introspective. Like any good cop, she could handle her complex and emotionally demanding job because she could compartmentalize. That trait enabled her to put her past in a box she rarely, if ever, opened. But that didn't mean her past didn't shape her present and future. Maybe that was why Riley still worried about her even though she was one of the most self-reliant people he knew.

He hoped Charlie Cammarata—that bastard who nearly got his sister killed—didn't mess her up with whatever insane mission he was on. She had never spoken about it again, after telling Riley what had happened on that undercover assignment ten years ago. But Riley couldn't forget that Cammarata had set up his sister so he could get the glory. Cammarata had never apologized for what he had put Sonia through, only said he was sorry that "it had gone too far" and he "never meant for her to get hurt."

Cammarata was like an extremist Muslim on a jihad; he didn't care who he hurt as long as his goal was achieved. Riley didn't give a rat's ass how noble the goal was; the bodies Cammarata laid in his wake made him the enemy. Riley didn't want one of those bodies to be his sister.

Dr. Peter Miller left Ann's room, acknowledged Riley, and walked down the hall, passing Detective John Black, who approached with a cup of coffee. "Thought you could use some," he said.

"Thanks." Riley sipped. It was nowhere near as good as his mom's.

"I have Ericson relieving you at twenty-one hundred. You good till then?"

"I'm good."

"Then I'll see you in the morning. Let me know if there's any change. We have no witnesses, except that girl."

Black walked off and Riley sipped the coffee, then put it on the low table next to him. He wasn't sleepy, his shift had technically just started a couple of hours ago, and he had plenty of energy. His mom didn't understand the allure of the swing shift, but for Riley it was great. He'd always been a night person, and now he had an excuse to sleep until noon.

An orderly approached and ignored Riley, making a move to open the door.

Riley blocked him. "You're not authorized to enter this room."

"Sure I am," he said, showing his name badge. *Jose Martinez.*

"You're not on the list."

"I'm just changing bedpans."

Riley didn't budge.

Martinez swore. "Look, my boss is gonna get on my ass if I don't get this done. I don't know why I'm not on your friggin' list. Let's go talk to him, fix this."

Riley didn't like the way Martinez's eyes darted back and forth. He squinted at Riley with dark mousy eyes.

Riley glanced at the photo on the name badge again and realized this man wasn't Jose Martinez. Same general look and race, but two different people.

"Let's call him," Riley said, motioning to the house phone. "What's his name?" He needed the fake orderly to believe he was playing along, to get him away from Ann's door. As casually as he could, he tapped a code into his radio with his badge number and "officer needs assistance" signal. He hoped Black was still in the building with his radio on.

The imposter nodded, moved toward the phone, then started running down the hall.

"Shit!" Riley started down the hall, then stopped. He couldn't leave Ann, and the fake orderly was acting overtly suspicious. A decoy, Riley realized, to get him away from the door.

He whirled around and saw a tall, lean, blond Caucasian male with his hand on Ann's door. Where had he come from so quickly?

Riley commanded, "Don't move."

The man didn't stop and in three long strides Riley was in a position to restrain him. The man pivoted and backed into Ann's room. He had a scalpel in his right hand, and something Riley couldn't see in his left.

"Security!" Riley yelled at the top of his lungs and saw a nurse scurry toward a phone.

Riley couldn't let him near Ann. He grabbed his Taser, but the suspect kicked his wrist. Riley held on to the Taser, but his arm went straight up, and his attacker lunged with the scalpel aimed at Riley's neck as if it were an ice pick.

Riley faked right, then pivoted left toward Ann. The

suspect was fooled by the move, but recovered quickly and tackled Riley, plunging the scalpel high in his thigh. Riley bit back a scream as the sharp blade was pulled several inches up his leg. He Tasered the bastard in the chest, but the darts bounced off. He had a fucking vest on!

Already the perp was scrambling up and moving fast toward the unconscious girl. Riley grabbed his legs and pulled him down. Then saw what the attacker had in his left hand: a syringe. If that syringe had pricked him or Ann, Riley was certain they'd be dead.

Sweating, his vision blurry and fading, blood flowing from his leg, Riley grabbed the killer's left wrist and slammed it hard against the floor. Again. Again. The perp said nothing, but he grunted in pain and frustration. Riley didn't see the scalpel coming toward his head.

There was commotion behind him, then a sharp pain in his cheek, and John Black shouted, "Knight!" Riley sensed more than saw John grab the suspect's right hand and slam it against the floor.

"The syringe!" he tried to shout, his words slurred.

Black's hands reached over and clasped the perp's wrist, squeezing, and Riley heard bones crack and the bastard beneath him scream in pain.

"I got him," Black said.

Riley rolled away and lay there, barely registering two cops cuffing the blond man and pulling him out of Ann's room.

"Riley," Black said. "Help's on the way."

"Should be," Riley said, seeing nothing but gray. "I'm in a damn hospital."

Black ripped Riley's pants away, grabbed a blanket

from the foot of Ann's bed, and applied pressure. "I got your radio signal," he said.

"It happened so fast." Riley was quickly fading. "I'm okay."

"You damn well better be. Your sister scares the hell out of me."

"Call her."

A doctor and three nurses came in. Black said, "I'm staying with the girl. Get him stable. I need to talk to him ASAP."

CHAPTER
NINE

Dean could tell Sonia's decision to bring him fully on board had been difficult, but it was the right choice. If they were going to take down Xavier Jones, she had to trust him without reservation. There was no middle ground.

She said, "I set up layers of security measures to protect Vega. It's not even easy for me to talk to him quickly without jeopardizing him."

"What's he doing? Trying to find files or photographs—"

She shook her head. "I need to catch Jones red-handed. I need a location—to observe an exchange of illegal immigrants for money. Hell, I'd get him on smuggling aliens into the country if I could, but he doesn't get his hands dirty. What he *does* do, though, is meet with the principals. It might not be at the same time as the exchange, but it's being discussed, and if I can get in, if I know where the meeting is, I can plant hidden cameras and microphones. Vega said there's something going down soon, but I don't have an exact date or a location. All I know is it's local. And it's connected to three dozen kidnapped teenage women from China. As soon as I know the details, we'll set up the stakeout. We're only going to get one shot. Either we get Jones, or I have to pull Vega and put him in protective custody because Jones will know who ratted him out."

"Is that why you were at Jones's house last night?"

"Not exactly."

"Exactly what then?"

Sonia sat down again and rubbed the back of her neck. Dean resisted the urge to massage her shoulders. She was uncomfortable and Dean wanted to make her feel better. He knew how it felt to have a case grab you and tighten its grip until every muscle in your body was pulled taut. Sonia looked like the weight of the world rested on her pretty shoulders.

"Last week I had an untraceable email about a boy who had been held captive at Jones's house and escaped. I was given the general area where he'd be, and after searching for a couple hours with my brother, a Sac P.D. cop, we found him. Andres Zamora. I thought Vega had given me the tip. Andres speaks little English, but I'm fluent in Spanish. The kid is ten. He was abducted from Argentina two weeks ago, along with his thirteen-year-old sister, Maya. Their mother and older brother were murdered when they tried to stop the abduction."

"Jones?"

"No. I showed Andres his picture and Andres had never seen him before."

"Then how did he end up at Jones's house? How did he know it was Jones's house?"

"He didn't. My anonymous informant did. I asked Vega about it when I could set up a call the day after, but he claimed he didn't know what I was talking about—he knew the kid had escaped, but said he hadn't sent the message. I didn't believe him. No one else on Jones's staff would have turned and known to call *me*. Anyway, Maya had been separated from her brother after two or three days, probably before they hit the American border. She was taken on another truck, and Andres was taken by boat. He remembers being crammed into a hold with dozens of other boys from eight to sixteen years of age, but doesn't remember how long. Days. They gave him fresh water and one small meal daily. He thinks there were four meals. They were not allowed on deck. At one point, the boat was boarded—probably by the Coast Guard, based on what he heard—and their captors threatened that if any of the boys made a sound they would all be killed.

"After that, Andres found a hatch off the hold and hid inside—mostly because it gave him a little more room to move around. When the boat docked and no one came for him, he realized he couldn't get out. A day later he was discovered and brought to Jones's house. I've shown Andres pictures of Vega and everyone else on Jones's staff, but he didn't recognize anyone.

"Until this morning."

Sonia opened a file and took out a photograph of a forty-something man with short-cropped dark hair graying on the sides. He looked younger than Dean remembered, but just as hard.

"Jones's driver," Dean said.

"His name is Charlie Cammarata. He's a former Immigration agent."

"Former?"

Sonia's eyes glistened, but when she blinked the pain was gone. She was all business. "Yes. He was my training agent. He went rogue. I turned him in, testified against him, and he was fired and stripped of all commendations and his pension. He disappeared—though I've heard from him a few times. He likes to feed me information, and frankly, it's been damn good information. But . . ."

"But what?"

"Nothing."

"Sonia."

Dean waited until she looked at him, then continued. "But what?"

"I wish he would leave me alone. I don't want his help and I don't want to talk to him. Yet the one time I could use good intel, he decides to play undercover spy and go deep into Jones's operation without giving me a heads-up. I was hoping he was working for you."

"He's not."

"I didn't think so. You and he wouldn't get along."

"You're right, I don't think we would." Dean didn't like what Sonia *wasn't* saying. He had a feeling there was far more to this story than she'd told him. But instead of pushing her, he asked, "He called you about Andres?"

"Yes. And when I talked to Andres today, I found out that Charlie Cammarata intentionally let Andres go. It was no accident. He probably knew what was going to happen to the boy, and Charlie wouldn't be able to let him die. Not a child."

Not a child? Did that mean he'd let an adult die to protect his cover? Dean wanted to ask, but didn't.

Sonia continued. "I need to get to Charlie. I have to talk to him and find out what he's doing, but I have no way to approach him without setting off warning bells with Jones. I don't want Charlie dead, I just want to cut him out. If I go in and arrest him, Jones may think we're getting too close and cancel whatever is going down in the next couple of days. I'm hoping you can help me."

"You want me to slip him a note or something?"

She shrugged. "Or something." Her intention was clear.

Dean nodded. "I can do that."

Sonia continued. "We have to be extremely careful how we handle this. If we push Jones, he could cancel or divert the suspected shipment and we lose the victims. They'll be sent underground so fast that even if Jones told us everything he knew, we'd never be able to find them. I have to have solid confirmation as to their location before we arrest Jones."

"I understand," Dean said.

Sonia glanced at her phone and frowned. "Hello?"

As Dean watched, Sonia's face paled, and her bottom lip quivered, then her jaw tightened and she stood up, moving toward the door. "I'm on my way."

She snapped her phone shut. "Someone tried to kill Ann tonight and stabbed my brother. I have to go."

"I'll drive you."

"No—"

"You're shaking."

"I am not." She stared at her hands as if she couldn't believe they had betrayed her fear.

Dean took both her hands and squeezed. They were icy cold and he rubbed them between his palms. "If it were my brother, I'd let you drive."

"Thank you."

Sonia could scarcely breathe until she saw Riley.

It took pulling her badge and pitching a fit before a

nurse let her look through the window of the surgery where Riley's leg was being stitched. A bag of blood dripped into his arm. "Why the blood?" she demanded.

"I'll explain in the lobby," the nurse said.

Dean took hold of Sonia's arm and led her back to the waiting room. She was grateful for the support. She didn't know if she was going to lose her temper or collapse. Every nerve ending burned. Riley was not just her brother, he was her best friend. If he died . . . she didn't realize she was shivering until Dean put his arm around her shoulders. She took a deep breath and asked, "The blood? And why does he have a bandage on his cheek? When—"

The nurse, Tina according to her name badge, interrupted. "He lost a lot of blood. He was fortunate that no major artery was severed, but the cut was four inches long, and deep enough to cause extensive blood loss. We got to him quickly. A couple days' bed rest and he should be up and around."

"And Ann?"

"Ann?"

"Ann Charles—the Jane Doe he was protecting—where is she?"

"Detective Black supervised her move to another wing. I can take you."

"Please do."

"Thank you," Dean added.

Sonia glanced at him. He was a rock, which calmed her tremendously. "Thank you for coming with me," she whispered.

"No thanks are necessary," he said.

They passed at least a dozen cops and detectives between surgery and Ann's new room. Whether they were there because of the attack on Ann or to check on Riley, Sonia didn't know, but she appreciated the strong police presence.

Outside Ann's room were four uniformed officers and the towering Detective Black. He approached when he saw her. "Let's go in here," he said, opening the door to an empty room. "I had them clear this wing. We're going to have a rotation of six officers—two on the victim, two on the grounds, and two roaming."

"I should have done that from the beginning," Sonia said, critical of herself.

"You?" Black said, dark eyes showing some of the pain that Sonia felt inside. "This isn't on you."

"What happened isn't on anyone," Dean said. "Someone wants that girl dead, which makes me believe that she knows who tried to kill her. She can I.D. him."

"Exactly," Sonia said. "What happened, John?"

"Someone tried to get into the room dressed as an orderly. He acted suspicious, distracting Riley, then another man slipped through the door. Riley tried to Taser him, but he had a vest on. He stabbed Riley with a scalpel, then made a move toward the victim with a syringe—we now know it was liquid arsenic, which would have killed anyone with a fraction of the dose in the tube— Riley tackled him, I came in, and we subdued the perp with no further incident."

"Who is this guy? Her rapist?"

"We don't know, but we have his DNA and we'll find out damn quick. He tried to kill a cop, he's not getting off."

"I want to talk to him."

"He's going through booking right now."

"I don't care, I need to talk to him. Ann has a unique tattoo on her shoulder, and—"

"I know what it means, Sonia. But right now no one's talking to him. He's said only four words. 'I want my lawyer.'"

Sonia kicked the empty bed. "Shit!"

"He's not getting bail," John pointed out.

"That's not the point. I need to know what he knows."

"He's a cold bastard. He had no identification on him. He refuses to tell us his name. He even refuses to tell us who his lawyer is. I suspect that when he doesn't report in to whoever he's working for, we'll have a lawyer show up at the jailhouse claiming to represent him."

Sonia's fists clenched and she closed her eyes. "You printed him?"

"Of course. Sooner or later, we'll find out who he is."

"I need his picture."

"Within the hour."

Dean said, "If you have his DNA, prints, and photo sent to Quantico, I'll pull some strings as well."

"I don't think he's an American," Black said.

"Does he speak English?" Sonia asked.

"Yes, with an accent."

"Hispanic?"

"No. Blond, blue-eyed, Caucasian. Eastern European of some kind."

"He could still be a citizen," Sonia said. "There's a large Russian population here. How old?"

"Thirties."

Sonia rubbed her eyes. She didn't have any evidence

or information that Xavier Jones was working with any of the Russians. They liked to keep their smuggling in-house, so to speak. Jones worked with a variety of nationalities, and with Smitty Daniels out of the way, Jones had something of a monopoly. But that didn't mean someone wasn't freelancing. Or this had nothing to do with Jones, was simply one more tragedy in this business of human trafficking. It just wasn't going to stop.

Dean asked, "How's Ann?"

"The same. The doctor said that's good, her body's fighting back. They're planning surgery for tomorrow. There's damage to her kidney, and possible internal bleeding. Dr. Miller says as long as she doesn't get worse, he's putting her on the table at oh six hundred hours."

"You'll be here?" Sonia said.

"Along with half the Sacramento P.D. Nothing is going to happen to that girl, Sonia. I give you my word."

When Sonia's parents arrived at the hospital, Dean left and called Sam Callahan.

"Where's Jones right now?"

"At his house."

"What about his driver?"

"He dropped Jones off at five this evening and left. I don't know where he went."

"I need to talk to him. I thought he lived somewhere on Jones's property."

"What I got out of him last night was that he lived in a cabin on Jones's property, not in the house itself."

"Can you email me directions?"

"Sure." Callahan sounded like he wanted more, but when Dean didn't elaborate, Callahan said, "Do you need backup?"

"Not now."

Dean followed the directions to Jones's property, passed Jones's driveway, then turned onto a narrow, gravel-lined road a mile farther up the main road. It was after eight in the evening, and the summer sun was just descending on the horizon though the temperature still hovered in the high eighties. Dean was ready to crash; it had been a long day, starting late the night before when he'd pleaded his case for a warrant to Judge Barnhardt. Had less than twenty-four hours passed? It seemed like days.

This was his last task, then he would return to his borrowed apartment and crash. Tomorrow promised to be another long day.

A sporty sedan was parked in the carport of the small cabin. Dean drove up and parked behind the car. Lights glowed dully behind drawn shades. All he knew about Charlie Cammarata was that he and Sonia used to work together, and Cammarata got himself fired, with Sonia's help. Cops rarely turned in other cops unless the situation was so egregious that there was no avoiding it. Problems were usually dealt with internally.

The situation involving Sonia and Cammarata must have been huge. Dean wondered why he didn't know about it—except, it *was* Immigration. People thought the FBI kept things close to the vest; they'd never worked with ICE before. They gave tight-lipped a whole new meaning.

The cabin was small, one room by all appearances. A small porch up three steps. Nothing homespun, in all appearances vacant except for the car and lights.

Dean had to assume that Jones had the cabin bugged, so he needed to make this look good.

He rapped on the door, searching his memory for the goon's name, the one Jones used. He didn't know—Jones had never used it in front of him. He glanced at the message from Sam Callahan. In the subject line:

CHUCK ANGELO

"Angelo! This is Agent Hooper with the FBI. I have some questions."

"Get the fuck off my property."

"I'd be happy to put you under arrest."

"Bullshit, you fucking federal prick. You have nothing to arrest me for."

"Aiding and abetting."

On the other side of the door Cammarata laughed. "I know the law better than you think."

"I'm sure you do. Five minutes."

"Fuck off."

"I'm not going anywhere. I'll call my partner to get the arrest warrant—"

The door opened. Cammarata had a gun in his hand. He was shorter than Dean by an inch, broad-shouldered with a barrel chest. Solid muscle, this guy worked out regularly. He was in his late forties but had the physical body of a man ten years younger. The lines around his eyes betrayed his age: they had seen the world.

On the table behind Cammarata was a virtual arsenal of weapons, one of which was disassembled. Cleaning supplies were visible, and the pungent scent of solvent hung in the stifling heat.

"You should open your windows," Dean said, "unless you're getting high off the fumes. Which is a crime."

Cammarata glared at him.

"Can I come in?"

"No."

Dean shrugged casually. "We didn't get a chance to talk this morning. But I wanted to make sure you understood that we're investigating Mr. Jones on money laundering and racketeering. Very serious charges. You'll be charged as an accessory when I prove my case. And I *will* prove my case. I'm giving you the chance to help. I'm sure—"

Cammarata rolled his eyes and started to close the door. Dean stuck his foot between the door and jamb. Cammarata glanced down and said, "You want that foot shot off, don't you?"

"You are treading in dangerous waters, Mr. Angelo."

"So are you. I have nothing to say."

"Are you certain—"

"Back off."

"I tried." He extended his hand. Cammarata made no move to shake it. Dean pushed the small piece of paper between his fingers so it couldn't be missed.

Cammarata glared at it.

"Just drop the good-cop act, you're all a bunch of fascist pricks."

Dean dropped his hand, letting the note fall to the floor. Cammarata made an aggressive move toward him, his foot falling squarely on the paper. "Get off my property or I'll file charges for harassment."

"You'd better watch that temper of yours, Chuck, or I'll be hauling you in just because I don't like you."

Cammarata dragged his foot—and the paper—inside and slammed the door shut.

Dean got back into his car and hoped Sonia got what she needed, but after meeting the man, Dean doubted Charlie Cammarata cared about anything but his personal cause, whatever that was.

CHAPTER
TEN

Noel Marchand did not react well to bad news.

Mr. Ling drove. They were headed to the river, to his meeting with Jones. Noel glanced at Tobias in the rear seat watching the lights pass by as if he were a child. Noel harbored no guilt for what he planned.

That Johan had failed to terminate the whore made this miserable day worse. What was so complicated about walking into a hospital room and injecting arsenic into the veins of an unconscious girl?

Mr. Ling said, "Perhaps we should abandon this project and go home."

Ling meant home to Mexico, not the hotel. If any other employee suggested such a thing, Noel would have killed him. But he valued and respected Ling, whose advice and loyalty were exemplary.

"Perhaps," he said without seriously considering the option. "There is a lot riding on this exchange. A new venue, a new client, new opportunities. I like their innovative ideas. Interactive online sex. Brilliant. We provide the girls, and we get residuals for years. Like royalties on movies. One girl will pay off long after she's used up. And they want a minimum of two hundred annually? No more dealing with middlemen like Jones."

True, Xavier Jones had originated this deal and expected a cut from every sale, but a dead man couldn't get paid, could he?

"We can approach them later. When things settle."

"I appreciate your concern, Mr. Ling, but it won't be much longer. If we abandon this deal now, they'll go to someone else—like the damn Russians. I'll be cautious. On our other matter of the girl, find an attorney and educate him. As long as Johan doesn't talk before Monday, the attorney will be paid handsomely."

"Very well, Mr. Marchand."

Noel wasn't personally worried about Johan. He was a hired assassin and didn't know anything about Noel or Tobias. His contact was Mr. Ling.

Mr. Ling continued. "I've narrowed the possibilities of Jones's betrayer."

"Who are the lucky dead men?"

"Craig Gleason, his chief of staff."

"Gleason?"

"Thinking as Machiavelli would, he may figure that with Mr. Jones out of the picture, he would rise quicker in the hierarchy."

Noel considered the arrogant lobbyist. "He doesn't have the balls to risk it."

"You may be right."

"Anyone else?"

"Gregory Vega."

"Far more likely—he certainly has the spine for it. He's straightforward and has been with Jones for many years." Noel had intended to put Vega in charge once Jones was out of the way. If he was a traitor . . . "Why him?"

"His wife has been getting her affairs in order."

"Elaborate."

"She allowed her magazine subscriptions to lapse. She's searched the Internet for houses and school districts in other states."

"School districts?"

"She's pregnant."

"And Jones didn't insist on terminating the pregnancy?"

"It's not his child."

"Does not matter. Kids are nothing but problems. They force Americans to make stupid business decisions. But that's no reason to think Vega is talking to the feds."

Mr. Ling pushed a button on the dashboard of the car. He said, "After our conversation this morning, I took the liberty of planting a bug in the Vega residence. He sweeps the place regularly, but I thought it wouldn't hurt to try one. He doesn't sweep daily, after all."

Another reason Noel appreciated Mr. Ling: his foresight.

"This conversation took place shortly before we left the hotel."

Through the car speakers, an indistinct verbal banter could be heard over the clattering of dishes. A chair scraped the floor. The pouring of liquid, ring of utensils.

"It's great, Kendra," a male voice said. Greg Vega.

"Thanks."

"You shouldn't be on your feet. I don't mind eating takeout."

"I like to cook. The baby likes it. If it's a girl, what do you think about the name Emily? I know, it's trendy, but 'Emily Vega' has a nice sound. Or Elizabeth."

"You like the 'E' names? For a boy you wanted Ethan."

"You nixed that idea."

Noel snapped, "This is ridiculous."

"It gets better."

If Noel was willingly going to have a kid, he would choose the name. He didn't give a damn what the whore wanted. She'd be dead as soon as she delivered. There would be no emotional maternal influence over any child of his.

"—in Pennsylvania."

"Shh," Vega said.

"Do you think they'll send us there? It's beautiful. Very green. Maybe you can ask—"

A loud crash of dishes followed by the bellow, "Shut *up*!"

A moment later Noel heard the sound of a sobbing woman, and Vega mumble, "Fuck."

The tape stopped.

Noel was furious. He was an outstanding judge of character, but he'd been wrong about Greg Vega. He loathed being wrong.

"I will take care of them," Noel said through clenched teeth. "Personally."

Sonia sat in a chair next to Riley's hospital bed while he slept. It was late, near the end of visiting hours, and she'd just kissed her parents good-bye. She was exhausted and wanted to go home and sleep for a week, but she couldn't leave without absolutely knowing her brother was going to be okay.

He looked so . . . helpless. "Helpless" and "Riley Knight" didn't belong in the same sentence. He'd truly been her knight in shining armor from the beginning.

After her rescue as a child, she'd lived with Wendell Knight for nine months. He taught her that she was a survivor. He showed her the first unconditional love she'd experienced. And then he died.

She was terrified to move to California and live with Wendell's brother and family, but it had worked out.

Sonia adored her adopted mother, but it was Riley she had bonded with. They'd gone through high school together—she was a year older than everyone in their grade and still struggled, but Riley helped her with homework every night. Without him, she'd never have graduated. Without him, she'd never have felt comfortable around boys. Around men. Without Riley, she would have been lonely and lost. He had always treated her like she was normal. And normal was good. That was what she needed, because she knew deep in her heart that she wasn't like all the other girls in her school. She wasn't *normal*. With Riley she could be anything, do anything, and grow into a *normal* adult.

He listened and didn't judge; he believed in her; he didn't tell her not to do something because of her background or because she was too emotionally invested. He called her to the carpet when necessary, but never had Sonia felt anything but brotherly love and respect.

"Damn you, Riley, you can't get hurt like this again. It'll just kill me."

"Hmmm."

She jerked her head up. "Are you awake?"

"Hmmm. Yeah." His voice was weak, but he was talking.

She took his hand and held it to her face. "You scared me to death."

"Nothing." He cleared his throat. "Nothing scares you, sis."

"Losing you scares me," she whispered. "You're my best friend." He was her only friend. At least the only friend she could truly talk to.

"I love you, sis."

"Love you, too, Riley. Now get some sleep."

"You too."

She leaned over and kissed him on the forehead. When healthy, Riley was the life of the party, cracking jokes and smiling. He shouldn't be in a hospital bed. He shouldn't have needed a blood transfusion.

Sonia would find out who was responsible for nearly killing her brother. She would make him pay.

Charlie's instincts were sizzling; something was going down. And none of it was good.

It was five to midnight and he was crouched among scraggly trees and shrubs along the bank of the Sacramento River. Jones wanted him to stay back, hidden, and observe. If anything weird happened, his orders were to shoot.

Jones didn't tell Charlie who he was meeting; when Charlie asked, Jones simply said, "My supplier." Charlie knew damn well that Jones had multiple suppliers, but he didn't push because Jones didn't know what Charlie knew.

You could have told Sonia about this meeting.

Stakeouts take time to set up.

Not for Sonia. She's sharp.

Charlie rubbed the bridge of his nose with his thumb. He had to stop thinking about Sonia. Focus on the goal: saving Ashley Fox. That's all that mattered. He'd almost broken the code in Jones's journal. As soon as he did, he'd have what he needed.

He'd rescue Ashley, then he'd send the books to Sonia. Not the FBI and that arrogant agent Dean Hooper, but Sonia Knight. He owed her . . .

You owe her nothing.

No, Charlie owed her his honor. He wasn't a bad person, no matter what she thought. He would prove it to her. He had to. Isn't that why he sent her intelligence every now and again when something crossed her jurisdiction?

You didn't tell her about Xavier Jones.

Obviously, he didn't need to. She already knew something was up with him. She must have found the missing kid. Jones was still looking for him, which was good news. The kid didn't know much, but when Charlie learned that he was to be killed, he couldn't in good conscience allow it to happen. Not to a ten-year-old boy. Charlie *would not* be party to the murder of a child.

Jones walked around the perimeter of the restaurant, as if checking out his property. Charlie wasn't quite sure whether it was an act of nonchalance or if he was truly inspecting the place. It was after midnight; Jones's meeting was late.

Headlights cut the darkness on the road above Charlie. Gun in hand, he crouched and waited for the vehicle to pass.

It didn't.

The car turned into the parking lot of the closed riverfront restaurant, cut its lights, and parked.

Two men got out.

They met at the rear of the car and spoke quietly.

Charlie could barely make out shadows let alone features. The car started rocking back and forth. The larger of the two men opened the rear door and a tall, beefy man emerged. He seemed agitated and his voice rose over the still, warm air.

"I don't like the water!" he exclaimed.

The others admonished him. Jones emerged from behind the restaurant.

Charlie braced himself, gun in hand.

Noel turned from Mr. Ling and Tobias and smiled at Xavier Jones. "Good to see you again." He extended his hand.

Jones took it. His palms were dry, but his grip wasn't as firm as Noel would have liked. Nervous? Perhaps. As well he should be.

"Did you bring the kid?"

Jones shook his head slightly, clearly somewhat disconcerted by Tobias's bizarre behavior. "The kid's still missing. But he hasn't been picked up by the police or social workers. He's in hiding. I'll find him. I have good men on the job."

Noel scowled. "I thought I made it clear that I wanted the kid tonight."

"Yes, you did. But I'm certain he's not anywhere he can do harm. He's very likely lost. Dead."

"Then why can't you find him?"

"I would know if he were in custody."

"I'm sure you would." Noel emphasized each word.

"I don't like your tone."

"I don't ask for a lot from our agreement, Mr. Jones. I expect solid negotiations, clean deals, and prompt payment. So far, you've provided such."

"That's my job."

"Exactly." Noel grinned. Jones cowered. Good. He should be scared. Noel had been told he looked more dangerous when he smiled.

"I'm confident that he will be found. I promise to deal with the problem swiftly. The shipment from China is secured. Everything is on schedule."

"And the FBI?"

"I explained that. They're fishing. They didn't get anything incriminating because there is nothing incriminating to find."

"And why do you think the FBI is looking at you at all?"

"Because they always look at the rich. I have money, therefore I must be dirty," Jones replied sarcastically.

"You are, Mr. Jones."

"I am extremely diligent. I've been in this business for a long time, Noel, without a single blemish. None of my people have been arrested; none of my people are a threat to me or you." Jones was working himself up, playing the indignant, righteous victim. "The FBI didn't even mention anything related to our business arrangement; it was all about money. I've been through three audits in the last ten years and twice the IRS ended up paying *me* money for *their* mistakes."

"All it takes is one slip-up and we're all in jeopardy."

"The FBI can't touch you."

"They can work with other agencies with a longer reach. I don't want to have to disappear. I happen to like my current situation very, very much. I've had to reinvent myself far too many times; I'm content."

"You're safe." Jones waved his hand dismissively.

The gesture fueled Noel's silent rage. "No one is safe."

Jones was not taking this situation seriously. Noel expected him to be contrite, repentant—he should be on his knees begging for one more chance. Instead, he was brushing aside the government investigation as if it were an annoying mosquito. People died from mosquito bites. The FBI was the malaria-carrying mosquito; Jones would be its victim. His cavalier attitude confirmed it.

Noel continued. "I know who ratted you out to the FBI."

"Not one of my people!" Jones's odd loyalty to his employees made no sense to Noel. "But it's a moot point: the FBI has nothing. They are going away. My attorney is already working on harassment charges."

"Greg Vega," Noel said.

Jones laughed nervously. "Greg is one of my most dedicated, disciplined employees. He has been with me for eight years. He is completely loyal."

"And his wife is pregnant and he's thinking about the future. And that future has nothing to do with you or your business."

"I want proof. If it's true, I will take care of it."

"My word is proof enough." Noel took his hand out of his pocket and said, as he pulled the trigger of the 9mm Beretta, "You have become a liability."

Jones fell to the asphalt, clutching his gut. He tried to reach inside his jacket. Tobias jumped up and down and clapped, looking ridiculous. "Can we do that again?" the idiot begged. "Please?"

Noel shot Jones three more times, then put a final bullet in Jones's head just because he was pissed off.

Noel commanded his brother, "Pick him up. We need to move him."

Tobias picked up the body with ease, without regard to the blood, and asked, "Where?"

"Behind the restaurant."

Noel followed as Tobias carried Xavier Jones down to the dock. He stopped in the middle and frowned. Noel said, "To the end. You have to drop him into the river."

Noel didn't care if Jones was found or not; he simply wanted to get Tobias to the edge.

"I don't want to fall in," Tobias whined.

"You won't."

Cautiously, Tobias approached the edge of the short pier. He dropped the body into the water without preamble. "He's sinking!" Tobias called.

He'd surface soon enough, Noel knew from experience. "Thank you, Tobias."

His brother turned and beamed at him with that sick, excited grin. How Tobias could have killed so many women was a shock in and of itself. Their father, who had watched Tobias in action once, remarked that Tobias didn't understand the difference between fantasy and reality. *"He's the type of boy who didn't understand that fish die from lack of food or water, or that puppies' skulls are easily crushed. He takes what he wants with the girls and enjoys himself, and sometimes they die."*

It wouldn't matter anymore.

"Mr. Ling. Please." Noel had some compassion for Tobias. It wasn't solely his brother's fault he was a stupid brute.

Mr. Ling raised his gun and fired three bullets into Tobias's chest. Tobias stared at Ling, stunned, raw emotions emblazoned across his face as he stepped backward. He turned his dark eyes toward Noel, his mouth opening and closing, no sound coming out. He fell back into the river with a splash.

"Mr. Ling?" Noel said.

Ling walked over to the edge and shined a bright light into the water.

"He's gone."

"Good riddance. Let's go."

CHAPTER
ELEVEN

As if her subconscious was on guard duty while she slept, Sonia was pulled violently awake, remnants of a disturbing dream slipping away while her heart raced. Her peripheral vision registered movement just as a hand fell over her mouth and a voice said, "Don't be afraid. It's me."

Too late, she thought, as her instincts told her body to fight even as her sleep-deprived, disoriented mind recognized the voice.

Charlie grunted when she kicked him in the balls. He let go of her mouth as he doubled over in pain, and she rolled quickly off her bed, landing on both feet in a pouncelike position. She reached for her gun, but it wasn't on the nightstand. She crouched in attack position, waiting for his next move.

"You *asshole*. How dare you break into my house. Into my *bedroom*!" She swallowed, her mouth dry, her heart pounding painfully in her chest. She'd had nightmares about just this thing. Being attacked in her bedroom, restrained, unable to fight back. She was thirteen again, being dragged from her hut, hearing her father's voice.

"She's a virgin. I expect to be paid well for her."

She had fought back and won, not once but twice.

First as an untrained, scared child; then as a fully trained cop, though just as scared as she'd been when she was sold the first time.

"Good defense, Sonia." Charlie grimaced as he adjusted his stance. "*You* wanted to see me."

"What?" Her head cleared. Dean Hooper. He sure acted fast. Sonia wondered what he'd said to push Charlie to contact her tonight. She glanced at her clock. 3:30. She'd slept a mere four and a half hours. There'd be no more sleeping this morning. "You were supposed to call me, not come to my house! How do you know where I live?"

Charlie waved off the question as if it were ridiculous that she'd even asked. He looked old and weary under the dim yellow streetlights streaking shadows across her room through the blinds. Not a surprise; he was nearly fifty, and while in shape, years of hard living, extensive physical activity, and hopelessness had eaten away at him. He cared about the victims of human trafficking, of that Sonia had never doubted, but their pain had eaten him alive, and he couldn't get out of the pit. He suffered and became a predator as much as those who preyed on the innocent. Sonia didn't want to be Charlie. She didn't want to become so emotionally involved that her humanity leaked through mortal wounds in her soul and she became a monster hunting monsters.

Without taking her eyes off Charlie, she leaned over and turned on her bedside lamp. Her bed separated them, but he was blocking the doorway. In his hand was her gun. He saw her looking at it.

"I'm not going to hurt you, Sonia. You are so predictable—keeping your gun on your nightstand. I'm disappointed that your instincts are so shoddy and I got close enough to take your only weapon."

"You don't know it's my only weapon." It wasn't, but her other gun wasn't in her bedroom.

"If you had another gun within reach, you'd have it in your hand right now."

Waves of conflicting emotions ran through her like hot lava followed by an icy avalanche. Charlie, her mentor and onetime friend, had taught her so much about duty, about compassion, about pride in herself and overcoming obstacles. He'd worked with her tirelessly to teach her everything he knew about the business of human trafficking, signs to watch for, questions to ask. He'd been infinitely patient with her as a new INS investigator, knocking the chip off her shoulder that had come from being on the other side of the line—a victim.

"They win if you act like a victim. Stand tall, Sonia, and be the warrior I know you are."

A warrior. Is that how Charlie saw himself? A warrior in a one-man army? Or Don Quixote, battling windmills?

Because he'd been such a huge part of her early career, when he left her to die she almost wanted to. She fought back and survived because she *knew* there had to be an explanation. Charlie wouldn't have set her up. He had her back and must have been injured or dead to leave her trapped with a rapist and killer.

She'd never believed, while she fought for her life, that he had intentionally left her, lying to her about backup, lying to her that their boss knew about the operation in the first place. She'd been terrified in that locked room, knowing she was bait, even while believing there was a team with eyes and ears on her even though she couldn't see or hear them. She didn't know there was no one watching, no one ready to jump in and save her before the man who Charlie had sold her to came to claim his property.

And when everything came out about the things Charlie had done, things she'd been blind to even while working side by side for nearly two years, Sonia had wanted to quit. If not for the support and faith that Riley lavished on her through tough love, and the unconditional love of her adoptive family, she would have left Immigration and . . . done something else. Been miserable. Feeling sorry for herself.

She had gotten over it, and seeing Charlie in her bedroom now hadn't turned her into a quivering mass of pathetic Jell-O. She'd been thrown off-stride, but she regrouped. He would give her the answers she needed, or she would take him into custody. She glanced again at her gun in his hand. It wasn't pointed at her. If she could get close enough without him suspecting her intention, she could disarm him.

"You are investigating a known trafficker in my jurisdiction," she said to Charlie, "and didn't have the courtesy of calling me?"

"You would have let me go in?"

"Hell no."

"There you go."

"You always start a job for the right reasons, but when did finding a missing, presumed dead teenager turn into working as the driver for Xavier Jones for God knows how long?"

"You've talked to Rogan." He frowned.

"Kane is your friend. Your only friend."

"Rogan is not my friend. Just because he didn't break my neck after the mishap in New Mexico—"

"Mishap?" She knew she shouldn't talk about the past with Charlie—it wasn't good for either of them—but *mishap*? "You sold me without telling me beforehand. Then you lied to me about having my back. I had to kill him to save my life."

"Good riddance. I knew you were strong enough to take care of yourself."

"I don't believe you!" She ran both hands through her thick, tangled hair. "He almost raped me!"

"But he didn't."

"Fuck you." She closed her eyes and took a deep breath. What Sheldon Rasmussen had done to her haunted her when she didn't have her guard up. She'd have the scars from his knife for the rest of her life. Because of Rasmussen, she'd never be able to have children.

Because of *Charlie* she was scarred and barren.

"I *am* sorry."

"No, you're not. Because you were a hero for a day. You saved all those girls while I was attacked by a vile monster thinking you were there to take him down."

Charlie spoke quietly. "It was a hard choice to make, Sonia, believe me. But they couldn't save themselves. They'd all be dead by now. But they're alive and free, and so are you."

"And if I had died, you would have justified it because you saved fourteen other girls that night."

He looked pained, and Sonia was glad. She hoped he couldn't sleep.

"I've paid for what happened. I take jobs where I can.

Rogan gives me the lost causes, but I know that Ashley Fox is alive."

Even though she was still angry, Sonia was curious how Charlie had ended up with Jones. She asked, "Did Jones have something to do with her disappearance?"

"Not directly. I found the gang who kidnapped her off the cruise ship. One of the stewards, a Mexican gang member, spilled everything when I tracked him down."

Bile rose into her throat. She didn't ask what Charlie had done to get the gangbanger to talk; she didn't want to know.

"She was shipped to Belize and forced to work at a sex club. They kept her drugged, got her hooked on coke and pills. Uppers and downers. I'm not surprised— when she found out she was trapped, she probably needed the mental escape."

A familiar strategy—breaking the victim's will to fight back using drugs, and physical and mental abuse. Sonia put the images out of her head; she had to focus on the facts.

"And then?"

"I'm unclear on why they moved her, but she came up through one of Jones's major suppliers into America. She may be in Canada now, but she came through here, Sacramento."

"How do you know?"

"You don't want to know."

Sonia slammed her palm against the wall. The picture over her bed slid on its wire and hung crooked. "I'm supposed to trust you?"

"I got the information. I don't care if you believe me."

Goose bumps ran down her flesh. She bit back her next scathing comment; she wouldn't be able to convince Charlie that he was no better than them. But this vigilante campaign had to end, one way or the other.

"Jones knows what happened to her. Where she went. I'm *this* close to figuring out his codes. I was going to come to you once I saved Ashley."

Sonia frowned in confusion. "Codes? What codes?"

"I'll give you everything when I get the answers I need."

"Tell me now! Are you honestly aiding and abetting a killer? You fucking bastard! Who made you judge and jury? You're not leaving here, so help me—"

"What are you going to do? I have your gun." Charlie laughed, then added wistfully, "Oh Sonia, I've missed you."

"Don't."

"We were a great team. I don't blame you for what happened."

"Blame me? What am *I* to blame for?" She asked too quickly, realizing that Charlie was deliberately side-tracking her. "No—"

Charlie cut her off. "For having me fired."

"I'm not going there again." She couldn't do it. She was losing her focus: her goal was to gather evidence on Xavier Jones so she could haul his ass into interrogation and get names. "You have information. You can testify. Names, places. What kind of codes? You mean he's writing everything down?"

"Yes. He has a journal. Every sale, every player, every exchange. How much money he made on the deal and what his expenses were and the threat level. He charges more for higher-risk endeavors. I made a copy of his current journal. But I can't figure out—yet—how he codes the people he sells. Without that, I don't know where Ashley is."

"Why don't you just torture the information out of him?" she snapped sarcastically.

"Jones wouldn't rattle under torture."

So he had actually considered it. Sadly, Sonia was no longer surprised by Charlie's decisions. "I know you're the one who contacted me about Andres Zamora's escape. Where's Maya?"

"I don't know."

"I don't believe you."

"I don't care. She wasn't with Andres."

"You should have called the police."

"Not without blowing my cover."

"You're no better than they are. You fit right in with Jones *and* my father."

Charlie's face hardened and he took a step toward her, his knees touching her bed. He shook the gun at her and she involuntarily shivered. Charlie was volatile. He could kill her, even if he didn't want to. "I'm just the driver."

"Bullshit. I want Jones's journal."

He ignored her demand. "I got Andres out. You found him, didn't you?"

She wasn't giving Charlie any information about Andres. "I want the journal and a signed statement detailing everything you know about Jones and his operation. Then maybe you won't be spending time behind bars."

He glared at her. "So you're working with the FBI?"

Sonia saw no reason to give Charlie any information, so she simply said, "Yes. And I need to debrief you. Let's go."

He shook his head. "I have—"

"There's a shipment of girls coming in any day and I need to nail Jones with them. We know that he uses Omega Shipping, and we searched their ships coming through Stockton last week, but found nothing." As Sonia said it she realized that she and Dean Hooper had been in the middle of that conversation when she heard about Riley's attack. She needed to compare her notes with Dean's.

She rubbed her temples, tense from this verbal and emotional battle with Charlie.

"I need the names and players. I want to stop Jones from selling people. Not just one—all of them. You're there. You have to help! We can arrest him red-handed. What do you know about it?" She didn't want to sound desperate, but her frustration level had reached the breaking point.

Charlie didn't say anything for a long minute. Sonia fidgeted but didn't take her eyes off him. "I know he keeps them somewhere in the foothills. I don't know where. The shipment is planned for midnight on Saturday. That's all I know. If I had found out what happened to Ashley, I would have tipped you off."

"If you didn't find her would you have tipped me off? What about those girls?"

Charlie was obviously torn. "I would have found a way to rescue them, too." He didn't sound as confident.

"You are but one man, Charlie Cammarata. You can't do it all. It's amazing you're still alive."

"Hell, Sonia, you didn't even know the day and time."

She glared at him. "You're in over your head. You're under arrest, Charlie."

"No, I'm not. Honey, I—"

"Don't call me honey."

"I've always cared for you. You know that. I never wanted you to get hurt."

"You care for no one but yourself."

"I love you."

"Don't, don't, don't!" Charlie had told her ten years ago, after she had testified against him, that he loved her. She didn't believe him then. Maybe in his own warped way he had affection for her, but he had no concept of how to love. She'd never thought of him as anything more than a respected mentor. She had loved him like she loved Wendell Knight, the Texas Ranger who had saved her twenty-one years ago. But Wendell had never lied to her, never betrayed her, never left her to die.

Charlie said flatly, "Jones is dead."

It couldn't be true. "Did you kill him?"

"Hell no!"

"What the hell is going on, Charlie?"

"I drove him to a meeting at his restaurant—the one under renovation in Clarksburg, on the river—and he told me to stay hidden and keep watch. If things turned, I was supposed to kill the man he was meeting. There were three of them. I couldn't hear what they were saying, and it was dark. I don't know who they were—two were well over six feet, one, the man in charge, was not more than five foot ten. Lean."

"You don't expect me to believe that you don't know who these men were."

"I don't."

She didn't believe him. He was lying to her yet again. When she was younger, she had believed everything Charlie said, now she saw his "tell"—he could look her in the eye and lie, but he was calm. Too calm. "And?"

"They spoke. The short man, the one in charge, and Jones. Jones was angry about something. Ten minutes into the conversation, without warning, the stranger shot Jones in the stomach. When he was down, he shot him four more times. One of the other men picked up the body and carried it to the end of the pier and dropped it in the river. Then he was also shot, point-blank range three times, and fell into the river."

Charlie was sincere. She saw it in his eyes and posture. This part, at least, was true.

"You're telling me that the UNSUB shot his own man?"

"It's true."

"And you couldn't see them? You don't know who they are?"

"I couldn't see them. Sonia, I don't care if you believe me, but I now have free access to all of Jones's material. He doesn't keep his documentation in his house. The FBI are a bunch of spineless idiots. Going after Jones for racketeering. Bullshit. They just alerted him to be even more careful. He has bank accounts the FBI doesn't even know about."

"And you do?"

"Some. And I have a copy of one of his journals. I've almost cracked the code."

"I want that journal, *now*."

"You're not getting it, Sonia, not until I know where Ashley Fox is. I promised her mother—"

"You're going to let an unknown number of girls die or disappear this weekend to *maybe* save one? Ashley disappeared a year ago. These girls who are being sold Saturday night? They have a real chance!"

"So does Ashley."

"Damn you! Give me the fucking journal!" She had been edging closer to him, and now she lunged, tackling him and slamming him against the wall.

He grunted and hit her with the butt of her gun. God, she thought as she fell to the floor, her eyes burning with unshed tears and hot anger, she had been a fool.

He grabbed her arm and pulled her up. Held her close to him, face-to-face while she shook her head to clear it. "I shouldn't have come here. I thought you could fish out the bodies in the river. Jones has his current journal on his person."

"Waterlogged."

"Maybe. But I'm sure your friends in the FBI can work with it. Maybe in time to figure out where the exchange is Saturday night."

"I can't let you walk out of here, Charlie."

"You have no choice."

He pushed her down hard enough so she couldn't quickly follow, and fled the bedroom. Her cheek hit the edge of her nightstand and she bit her tongue, blood filling her mouth. She swallowed with a grimace and pulled herself up, shaking off a dizzy moment. She grabbed her backup gun from the drawer in the hall as she ran after him.

"Stop!" she shouted as she followed Charlie.

He was already in her backyard. She ran after him, barefoot because she hadn't taken time to put on her shoes.

But by the time she hopped the fence and ran to her front yard, he was gone. He'd left her gun on the hood of her car.

CHAPTER
TWELVE

Noel Marchand had lost his patience with the turncoat.

"Greg," he said with a heavy sigh, "I'm unhappy with your answers. For the last twenty minutes I have been asking very simple questions. Who's your contact in the FBI? What did you tell them about Mr. Jones? What did you tell them about *me*? I cannot understand why you refuse to answer."

Jeremy Ignacio had met Noel and Ling at Vega's house to disable the alarm system, which had been the primary reason Noel had had to wait until after four that morning to break into the traitor's house. Fortunately, the Vegas had been sound asleep in bed, the wife easy to grab with her large belly sticking up.

Mrs. Vega was tied to a chair where Greg Vega could see her. Ling stood behind her, a gun at her head.

Vega was hard to shake. He had been a good employee for Jones until he went running to federal law enforcement; he would have made a good employee for Noel.

"Let my wife go." His voice had begun to quiver slightly, but he'd maintained for twenty minutes that he wasn't a traitor and had never spoken with the FBI.

"I was surprised it was you," Noel admitted. "I'd

planned on taking you on when Xavier became too great a liability. Losing that little kid was truly the final nail in his coffin, and since you've been with him longer than anyone, well, I thought you'd be his natural successor here in the West."

He nodded to Ignacio, who walked over to the adjoining kitchen.

Noel continued. "Jones and I disagreed on one key point. He picked men with families because he felt that the implied threat to your 'loved ones' would keep his men in line. I, on the other hand, prefer employees who are unattached. Individuals who enjoy the unique benefits of our business. And until now our different philosophies have never been a problem."

Ignacio retrieved the bug he'd planted earlier from under one of the kitchen chairs and held it up. Noel gestured at the bug and saw the fear in Vega's eyes. Fear was useful in getting information, but it wasn't a beneficial emotion. Especially since there wasn't anything Vega could say or do to save himself.

"Now we're done with the lies. Answer my questions or your wife will suffer."

Noel bent over Vega, who futilely fought his restraints. His nose had been broken from the brief scuffle in the bedroom, and dried blood covered his face. Noel had already cut off one earlobe, which continued to slowly drip blood onto the white T-shirt Vega wore. His legs were bare, only boxers covered his ass.

Noel took his knife and stabbed it into Vega's bare foot so hard that it went all the way through the carpet and padding and into the hardwood floor beneath.

Vega screamed and spouted profanities. No one heard

him, though; he lived in the country, a nice five-acre spread in Galt. Probably thought it was a good place to raise kids. Probably thought it was safe.

"Talk now or the next knife goes through wifey's stomach."

Kendra Vega screamed against the cloth in her mouth. Noel had told Ling to gag her when her sobs and pleas began to irritate him.

Vega's teeth clenched and sweat poured off his face. Noel impatiently tapped his own foot. He nodded to Ling, who hit the woman across the head so hard her chair fell over on its side.

"It wasn't the FBI!" Vega screamed. "Don't touch her again, you fucker! Don't touch her!"

"You're lying—" Noel considered Vega's words. "If you didn't talk to the FBI, who did you talk to?"

Vega's squeezed his eyes shut. "I'll tell you. Please don't hurt my wife. I'm begging. Kill me. Don't hurt her. Please."

Noel didn't respond. He waited.

Vega had been in this business long enough to know there would be no survivors. His choice was to die with pain, or without pain. Vega broke down when the silence extended into the third minute.

"Immigration."

Noel pulled a blackjack from his pocket, the leather-wrapped weight solid and comfortable in his grip. He hit Vega across the cheek. Blood and a tooth fell from his mouth and onto the floor. "You brought ICE down on my operation?" Noel's voice was a mere whisper.

Vega shook his head, spat blood onto the carpet. "Not you. Just Jones. I swear to God, just Jones."

"You never mentioned my name?"

"No! No one. I told them I didn't know any of the players. I just wanted out. I wanted to disappear. She only wanted Jones."

Of course ICE wanted Jones. Jones knew all the players, knew where all the money came from and where it went. Noel was certain Jones had records, somewhere, of his activities. Jones was a meticulous bastard, he'd have *something*. By the time the FBI found it, Noel would be out of the country, so he wasn't hugely worried about incarceration. What bothered him was rebuilding his business. It would cost him an extaordinary amount of money, not to mention rebuilding trust with his clients after something like this.

If Vega was lying, ICE—and probably the FBI at this point—knew him as Noel Marchand. That name was now in their ridiculous law enforcement database. But Jones didn't know the Devereaux identity he used in the States, and therefore Vega also couldn't know it.

But there were still other issues to contend with.

"Does ICE know about the pending shipment?"

"No details. Just that it's going to happen. I didn't have the time and location. Mr. Jones always tells me right before. I swear. God, please, let my wife go."

Noel asked, "Who's your contact?"

"Agent Sonia Knight. I swear, she's the only one I've talked to, and I haven't spoken to her in days. I'm supposed to call when I have the details about the next exchange, and that's it. I swear, I never mentioned you or anyone else, she's just after Jones. God, please, I swear."

Noel's blood ran cold. "Sonia Knight."

"Y-Yes."

He hadn't thought about Sonia Knight in some time. He'd known she'd been in the San Francisco office of Immigration and Customs Enforcement, but had not known about her transfer to Sacramento's regional office. Or was she here solely because of Jones? What did she know? This was a complication Noel couldn't afford.

"How did you pick Agent Knight?"

"I-I didn't. I contacted their hotline. Two months ago. She's the one who met with me. I've only met her face-to-face once, talked to her a couple times. I swear to God, please—"

"What does she know?"

"She has no proof. I think . . . I think she has theories but no proof."

"And you were willing to give her the proof?"

"Only on Jones! I swear, it was just him. I needed out. I needed out, and he doesn't let people walk."

"Of course not." Noel didn't like this development. The FBI played by strict rules. Homeland Security, and ICE, had arms that stretched much farther and crossed U.S. borders.

"What *exactly* did you tell her?"

"I told you!"

"She wouldn't get you out without something tangible."

Vega swallowed nervously, shaking, glancing at his wife. Noel stepped to the left and blocked his view. "You will answer me."

"I confirmed information that she already knew."

Noel pulled the knife from Vega's foot and the traitor

cried out, his muscles straining as he fought the pain and restraints. He put the knife to Vega's neck and said, "Specifics."

"The Omega Shipping Lines is controlled by Jones's people. That he uses the Sacramento Deep Shipping Channel but moves the merchandise before they reach the Port of Stockton. I confirmed the operatives she knew, but didn't give her any she didn't—she had about half of Jones's people."

"I want the list that she has."

"Okay."

"Now."

Vega recited names and Noel ordered Ignacio to take them down.

"What else?"

"J-Just that he uses multiple holding facilities. She'd discovered one two years ago and— You must know this, she took the girls."

Noel didn't know; Jones had hidden that raid from him. If he weren't already dead, Noel would kill him far more painfully than the easy way he had, the bastard.

But Noel wasn't going to tell this *cabrón* that he hadn't known. "I only confirmed it," Vega said. "And I gave her two more abandoned facilities—you know, for g-good faith, so she'd get my wife protection."

"She's certainly done a good job, hasn't she?" Noel stepped aside so Vega could see his wife, still tied to the chair, lying on the floor.

"God please God please, please, please," Vega begged.

"Does she know how we move the women when they get here?"

"No, she assumes trucks, and I didn't correct her. I

was holding back in case she tried to renege on our agreement."

Vega seemed motivated by Noel's calm demeanor to keep talking, as if his compliance now would save his life. "She knew about the Omega shipment from China, and they searched Omega ships headed for Stockton, but couldn't find them. She's frustrated, and—"

He was rambling and saying nothing important, so Noel cut him off. "Do you know where the Zamora kid is?"

The confusion on Vega's face made it clear he didn't know the kid's name. Noel elaborated. "Last week, Jones made a mistake and brought a boy to his house. He escaped. What do you know about it?"

"He was kept in the garage of the old house, over a mile away. I didn't even know he'd been brought there until I was told he'd escaped. I looked, couldn't find him, and Jones was worried about it, and— Oh!"

"Yes?"

"Someone told Agent Knight about the kid. Anonymous."

"Not you?"

He shook his head. "No, not me, I didn't tell her, someone else told her. I swear to God."

"Who knew?"

"A lot of people. Everyone on the inner security team. We all were looking. Donny, Juan, Chuck, Lars, his accountant I think, Chris—"

Ignacio interrupted. "There's no Chuck on this list."

"Who's Chuck?" Noel demanded.

"Ch-Chuck Angelo. Jones's driver."

"Why is he not on your list?"

"That list was the people Agent Knight knew about. She didn't ask about Chuck, so I didn't tell her. He's new, three or four months."

Driver. Noel had made a mistake. He'd assumed Jones drove himself to the restaurant. Jones often met with principals alone—or so Noel had thought. Where was the driver last night? Had Jones's driver witnessed his assassination? Or had Jones left him home?

"Where can I find Chuck Angelo?"

"He lives on the property. The old caretaker's house."

"Is that anywhere near where the kid escaped?"

"I-I-I guess. Walking distance."

"Is there anything you have neglected to tell me? Anything?

"No. I swear."

"If you lie to me, I will know. And your wife will suffer greatly. Perhaps you'd like to see your child carved out of her stomach?"

"Please, please, I told you everything Knight knows, everything I know. I don't even know where the shipment went after it arrived in Stockton. I don't know, I don't know where they are, I don't know where the meeting is, please, please let us go. I'll disappear, I'm so sorry."

Noel said to Ling, "I think we're done here."

Ling aimed his gun at Kendra Vega's head and shot her three times.

Vega screamed. "No! *NO! You bastard! You promised!*"

"I said she wouldn't suffer. I didn't say you wouldn't."

Noel took the knife he had in his hand and cut out Vega's tongue. Vega's screams of agony gave Noel neither pleasure nor remorse. Murder as punishment was simply a job that needed to be done; Noel didn't dwell on it. He stabbed the blade into Vega's stomach up to the hilt. He'd live ten minutes. Maybe a little more, or a little less. Though Noel was certain he wouldn't survive, he wasn't about to take chances.

"Ignacio, stay for a while. If he's not dead in twenty minutes, put a bullet in his head."

Noel left with Mr. Ling. The sky was just on the lighter side of night. "Will he be alive at sunrise?" he asked.

"What time is sunrise?"

"Four fifty-eight a.m."

"No," Ling said.

"Do you want to wager?"

"A hundred?"

"You're on," Noel said.

They got into the rental car and Noel said, "Find everything you can on this Chuck Angelo. He may be a mole. And I want renewed efforts put into tracking down the boy. If he's in federal custody, we have a problem." Two kids—the Zamora boy and the girl Tobias failed to kill and dispose of properly—were the greatest threats to his freedom. "I want that boy and the woman in the hospital dead."

"Yes, sir."

"I have to take care of Agent Sonia Knight."

"I agree."

"She's not going to be easy to take out." His anger had been simmering from the minute he heard Sonia's name. She had been a pain in the ass since the minute he laid eyes on her. He should have killed her years ago when he'd had the chance. "Mr. Ling, when we get back to the hotel, pull together whatever information we have on her. Address, adopted family, friends, habits—anything you can find."

"Sir, if I may?"

It's what Ling always said when he had an idea Noel wasn't going to like.

"Go ahead."

"A sniper's bullet is the best way."

Noel knew he was right. But it wasn't what Sonia Knight knew about this upcoming transfer, it was her activities in general that negatively impacted his business. He wasn't going to give up the entire western states because one bitch had made it her personal vendetta to stop people like him. In actuality, Noel offered poor girls a chance to get out of the farms where they were already virtually slaves by being born into the decrepit, poor villages. He removed them from the squalor they lived in and employed them. Sex was a viable commodity. They provided a good fucking—or whatever the client wanted—and Noel and those he sold to made sure they had a place to live, food to eat, and medical care. Hell, most of the girls he handled had never seen a doctor before Noel took them for brothels around the world.

Sonia Knight would never be able to stop this profitable business. It was getting stronger every day. But she could hurt *his* bottom line, and Noel took that very seriously.

Especially coming from her. He wanted to see her face when he killed her. He wanted her to know who he was before she went to her grave. He wanted to make her suffer for every dollar she'd cost him over the years.

Of course, he didn't want to be caught. He was in his

prime, his business thriving especially after he took over when his father died.

"Very well, Mr. Ling. We'll do it your way." He sighed. "Too bad I can't take her back to Mexico and make her work off all the money she's cost us—on her back."

CHAPTER
THIRTEEN

The sun had barely crept over the Sierra Nevada Mountains far east of the Sacramento River when the Sheriff's Department underwater rescue team dove to recover the first body.

Dean crossed the parking lot of the closed restaurant. One deputy muttered, "We have Sac P.D., Sac Sheriff's, Immigration, and now the FBI."

Not being based in Sacramento meant that Dean was not only an outsider because he was a fed, but also because he didn't know any of the local cops. He should have brought Callahan with him, but he'd left him in charge at Jones's house. Or, rather, the cabin that Cammarata had been staying in. Until there was confirmation as to whether Jones was in fact dead, Dean couldn't enter his house without permission. And he didn't see Jones's attorney giving it.

Dean walked to the back of the restaurant and spotted Sonia. Maybe it was just seeing a familiar face, or maybe it was because she was so beautiful and regal that Dean stopped for a moment just to watch her.

She stood straight, legs slightly apart, hands behind her back, in the middle of the pier in a short-sleeved black T-shirt with POLICE ICE in large white block letters. Her hair was up and looked more red than brown in the early-morning light. Her tan face glowed from the morning chill, colder here on the river.

Her call to him had been brief. He had a million questions for her but couldn't ask until he'd swept Cammarata's cabin.

"Charlie broke into my house this morning. He told me Jones is dead, killed by an unknown associate, and dumped in the river behind his restaurant. Can you check on Jones at his place? If there's anyone who's seen him since last night? Then check out Charlie's cabin. If he's there, arrest him. Breaking and entering, assault on a federal police officer, and anything else you can think of."

She'd sounded professional and calm on the phone—too calm. Dean would have preferred her fiery anger at Charlie's invasion into her home over her cool detachment. Something was troubling her over and above the events of last night; Dean aimed to find out what.

When Sonia turned her head toward him, as if sensing she was being watched, he saw a large Band-Aid on her cheek. That bastard had hit her. The sudden urge to protect Sonia surprised Dean, but more than the need to stand guard was his instinct to hunt down Cammarata. His hands clenched and unclenched, the only physical sign of his outrage.

Sonia raised her hand and beckoned him over, meeting him halfway. "They're bringing up a body now," she said. "It was caught in the roots of a tree about a hundred yards downriver." She gestured to the sheriff's rescue boat. Several divers were in and out of the water. "Ten minutes or so, they think."

She seemed distracted. Before Dean realized what he

was doing, he reached up and lightly touched the bandage on her cheek. "Are you okay?"

"I'm fine," she said, but averted her eyes.

"Why did he break into your house? Just to tell you about Jones's body?"

"I don't know. That was part of it. I guess you rattled him a bit last night when you told him I wanted to talk to him." She smiled, but Dean didn't see the humor.

"If I had known he would attack you in your own home, I'd have been there watching the place. I'm sorry."

"You have no reason to be sorry. You're not the problem. Charlie doesn't play by anyone else's rules." She turned from Dean and looked out at the river. "Did you find anything at Jones's house?"

Dean suspected there was far more about Charlie Cammarata that Sonia wasn't saying. She'd alluded to some of their history yesterday, but there was more, and it was eating her up. Still, now was not the time or place to ask. "Locked up tight. I have Richardson looking into getting a warrant whether or not we recover his body. Cammarata's cabin was clean. I suspect he cleared out either right before or after the alleged murder."

"You don't believe him?"

"Do you?"

"Yes. There was no reason for him to lie, and there's a fresh body down there."

"Confirmation that it's Jones?"

"Not yet, but if the time line holds, it's only been about six hours and the body won't be too damaged. We should know immediately after they bring it up." She glanced at him. "Charlie said Jones kept a coded journal documenting everything."

"Coded?"

"He has a copy, wouldn't give it to me, that asshole. I put an APB out on him, I have everyone looking. He's so damn fixated on this missing girl, Ashley Fox, he can't see the bigger picture."

"We'll find him."

"Don't be so sure. He's good at hiding. He said he didn't know where the girls are now, but he did know that at midnight Saturday the exchange would be made."

"Even with Jones dead?"

"I don't know. But if Jones isn't there, those girls will die. My informant didn't know when, but I'll bet he knows where."

"I don't follow."

"He's been involved with dozens of sales. There has to be a limited number of places Jones can keep twenty to thirty young women. He gave us two places Jones no longer used as a sign of good faith, but insisted that if he said anything else, Jones would know it was him talking. We raided the two places—one an abandoned farm not far from here, another a warehouse in Stockton near the river. There was evidence that a large group of people had been there—biological matter, garbage. Vega promised to contact me when he had an exact time and place, and I'd have about four hours to set up the raid. But now I have to push him."

"There's a pattern," Dean said. "Even when criminals attempt to randomize, people unknowingly create patterns."

"If Charlie would have just given me the fucking journal, this wouldn't be an issue! Between the FBI and ICE we could break the code in short order."

It bothered Dean just as much. "Why is he doing this?"

"He wants to save the girl I told you about yesterday, Ashley Fox. She's been missing for a year. A few days more isn't going to matter for her, but it could mean the difference between more young women suffering her same fate. Dammit!"

She turned her back on him so he couldn't see that this had gotten to her, but he hadn't missed the pain and frustration in her expressive eyes.

"Are you certain Charlie was telling the truth about the journals?"

"Absolutely."

"They're not anywhere at his house," Dean said. "We searched extensively, had Jones open his safe. But most criminal enterprises keep two sets of books—their public books and the real books."

"Have you been to his offices? The consulting firm and the security business?"

"Someone from our office has, but only to retrieve financial data per the warrant. Not to search the establishments for journals or anything else."

"If you can't get another warrant, I will. We need to push hard, whether Jones is dead or not. We don't have a lot of time. Two and a half days."

"If the books aren't at his businesses, then maybe one of his employees is working with him. Maintaining the second set of books."

Dean shook his head. "His businesses are what kept him legit. When laundering money, the more people who know how it works the more risk. But I can't figure out how Jones was doing it. His office expenses are a little high, but in line with the income he generates from his clients, which is substantial."

"Do you have a list of his clients?"

"Of course. We didn't have time to get to it yesterday."

"Maybe after we're done here and we talk to my informant, we should go back to your office and look again at his clients." The sheriff's boat started toward the pier. "Jones is getting money from buying and selling people, and I doubt he's hiding it under his mattress," Sonia said.

Dean and Sonia approached the vessel when it docked. The deputy coroner was on the boat bagging the victim. Floaters were put in clear plastic to preserve evidence and fluids, as the body decomposed much differently than it would on dry land. Then the victim was put into a body bag for transport.

Dean had a sudden realization. "I'm going at Jones all wrong," he admitted. "I was focusing on the money trail. Ninety-five percent of the time, going backward in financial records gets you exactly what you need. But with Jones, that hadn't been working. All *his* records check out. I need to spend more time looking at his clients."

"But you said not ten minutes ago that you looked into his clients."

"I did. They're all legitimate businesses with no red flags on their tax filings or bank accounts. But I need to dig deeper on them like I was doing with Jones."

Sonia frowned. "That sounds like it's going to take hundreds of hours of manpower. We don't have the time."

"That's why I need your help. You know this area. With you and Sam going through the names and addresses, I think we can narrow it down to a handful of possibilities."

"It still sounds like a long shot."

"Perhaps, but unless we find a safe with gold, cash, or black-market diamonds on Jones's property, a client is the only way he can clean his money."

Trace Anderson jumped off the rescue boat and approached them. He said, "It's not Jones."

"Charlie said there were two victims," Sonia said.

"Yeah, but who the hell is the second victim?"

Sonia watched as the deputy coroner and his team carried the body from the boat to the dock. A white sheet had been draped over the gurney. Charlie's story about the man Jones met with killing one of his own people was now far more terrifying with a body. There was a predator in town even more ruthless than Xavier Jones.

The head diver said to Trace, "We're headed back out to see about the second possible. You coming?"

Trace looked at Sonia, and she nodded her approval. "I'm coming," he called to the diver, then said to Sonia and Dean, "I'll let you know as soon as we find the other body."

"Thanks, Trace."

The boat left, and Sonia approached the deputy coroner and introduced herself and Dean. "I need to see the victim."

The wiry Asian man nodded and said, "I have him bagged already, but the outer bag isn't sealed yet." In a homicide, they locked the external body bag until the medical examiner's office was ready to perform the autopsy; then the lock was broken and all biological and trace evidence logged.

He removed the sheet and Sonia stared at the victim through the clear plastic.

He was middle-aged with a receding hairline, skinny but with a slightly pudgy middle. Tall—six foot two at least—with muscles still defined even though the water had saturated the skin, turning it a white and pasty color in the middle, with the limbs beginning to turn green from the buildup of gas and bacteria in the body. The bicolor stage of decomp helped establish time of death: generally, if a body was discovered within thirty-six hours, plus or minus, the M.E. could closely estimate time of death. Beyond that, the TOD became an educated guess.

The bullet holes in the chest were clean from the fresh water, the edges black suggesting that the killer was only feet away from the victim.

"He's pretty fresh," Sonia said. "Do you have an estimated TOD?"

"I have to factor in time, weather condition, water temperature—"

"I'm thinking four to eight hours," Sonia said. "I've seen enough dead bodies to know this one is new."

"You're probably right. Certainly less than eight hours, otherwise he'd be a lot darker. It's always darkest before the dawn." The coroner laughed at his morbid humor over the stages of water decomp, the two sheriff's deputies joining in. Sonia smiled, but she wasn't in a humorous mood. There was something bothering her about this victim, but she couldn't put her finger on it.

"What are you thinking?" Dean asked quietly.

"Look at his clothes."

The victim wore a white T-shirt under a dark blue, unzipped windbreaker, jeans, and bright-red running shoes.

"I haven't seen a floater," Dean admitted. "Is there something unusual? Should the current have stripped his shoes or something?"

"No, not necessarily. Maybe it's the red shoes. They look . . . different."

Dean said to the coroner, "When you get the body back, can I send an agent over to observe the autopsy and possibly help with evidence? My office has committed all resources necessary to assist the county in this investigation."

"Sure, whatever floats your boat. I'll let the supervising pathologist know to expect one of your people."

Dean said to Sonia as the coroner finished bagging the body, "I'll mention the shoes. Maybe they're rare, only available in a specific store."

"Yeah, but in the age of online shopping that doesn't matter much anymore," Sonia said, frowning. She asked the coroner, "Do you think you'll be able to get prints off the body?"

"Good chance. He wasn't in long enough to destroy them completely. We get his hands dried out, we can print him. You'll have to give us a couple hours."

"That's fine. Thanks for your help."

She and Dean walked back around to the front of the restaurant and into the parking lot where the crime-scene van was now parked, the techs combing the area for evidence. She motioned to the blood on the pavement near the restaurant entrance, then observed the riverbank to the southwest. "Charlie said he was hiding on the edge of the riverbank among the trees and had a clear line of sight on Jones. But the pier isn't visible from here."

"Depends on where he was hiding," Dean said.

"It couldn't have been too far, otherwise he wouldn't have seen the second victim shot, yet at an angle where he could observe the first shooting."

"And?"

"I think he knows damn well who killed Jones."

"I could have told you that. That guy is dangerous." Dean lowered his voice, brushed his hand again along her injured cheek. She resisted the urge to lean into his light caress. She wanted five minutes to just release the pent-up frustration and deep sadness that warred within her at what her mentor had become. She'd known—dammit, she had seen firsthand—Charlie's warped sense of justice, but she had hoped he'd realize he couldn't sacrifice honor and the law. Otherwise, he was just like the people they fought. A vigilante? Vigilantes didn't hurt innocent people. Vigilantes didn't let a truckload of Chinese women die because of a missing girl. He could save both if he would just be honest with her. She didn't understand what he was doing.

"We're getting close," he said, brushing loose strands of her hair aside. Dean's eyes were full of quiet compassion and potent focus. He didn't look much different than he did the other night at the raid, except that he wore only one gun under his jacket. That he was an accountant amazed Sonia. She never imagined being attracted to a numbers cruncher, but she'd never met one who looked so . . . hot. That he was also smart—she'd always been attracted to the smart, athletic guys—was an added benefit; that he was so commanding in his quiet intensity had her swallowing involuntarily and averting her eyes.

She wondered what would happen if all his attention was focused solely on her.

Sonia dismissed that thought, at least for now. Maybe after this case was over, she and Dean could indulge in wild, mindless sex before he went back to Washington. She was attracted to him, and the way he was looking at her right now she knew he felt the same. She didn't have a life designed for serious relationships, and suspected Dean didn't either.

His fingers brushed over her lips, whether on purpose or accident Sonia didn't know, but a hot shiver went down her spine. Suddenly she realized they were still in public. Two deputies were watching from afar. Sonia stepped back.

"I need to go," she said.

"Do you want to see Vega now?" Dean asked.

"Yes, but let's take a detour to the hospital. Ann is in surgery and I want to get that GPS chip and see if we can trace it. Detective Black is working on moving her to another hospital, but it's going to be delayed until she's stable. Even with the additional security, her attackers were ballsy enough to walk right by a uniformed officer and try to kill her. I'll send two agents to Vega's house to tell him we're putting him and his wife into protective custody. We can meet up with them later this morning."

They walked up to the road where they'd parked separately. "How's your brother?"

"My mom called from the hospital this morning. Riley had a good night and will be released tomorrow. He'll be off duty for two weeks, and on desk duty for at least two more. I'm sure he's not happy about that, but I thank God he's alive." Her voice hitched and she mentally berated herself. "Sorry," she mumbled as she squeezed back the tears. "Riley's fine, I don't know why I'm getting so emotional."

"Because you were scared for him and didn't have any time to think about it until now."

She stopped at her car. "Yeah. Maybe."

Dean wrapped his arm around her shoulders and pulled her to his chest. It was a warm hug, like Riley, yet very *unlike* her brother. She was acutely aware of Dean's clean scent, his subtle cologne, his crisp, lightly starched shirt, his hard biceps pressing firmly against her body. Sonia wrapped her arms around Dean's waist and hugged him back, her cheek on his shoulder, savoring the moment, in awe of how perfectly they fit together, of how comfortable she felt.

She hadn't been held like this in far too long. Her relationships were brief and largely uncommitted. She didn't have time for small romances. The hugs, the dinners, the movies. Her administrative assistant Grace joked bitingly about Sonia's "boyfriend of the month," and Sonia let the friendly criticism roll off her back, but in some ways she was saddened by the reality of her life. She didn't have the time or desire to get close to anyone. She had her family and her job and barely enough time to manage both well. Where did a boyfriend fit in? A husband? Besides, most of the good men wanted kids of their own, something Sonia couldn't provide.

A car passed them and Sonia jumped back, startled. Where had her mind wandered? Why was she even thinking about "FBI agent Dean Hooper" and "boyfriend" in the same thought?

"I'll meet you at the hospital," she mumbled and slid into her car before he could respond, before he could touch her again. That was it, he'd touched her. He was exactly her type: tall, lean, muscular, smart, with a *GQ* face and strong square jaw. One touch and she was getting sloppy.

She drove off, mumbling, "Just wait, Sonia. Go to bed with him, get him out of your system, and he'll be gone. He's safe. He lives three thousand miles away. No long-term commitment."

It seemed unwise to be waxing at length over the long-term potential of a one-night stand. The realization that Dean would be leaving as soon as this case was over left Sonia feeling even emptier than when she'd pulled back from his embrace.

CHAPTER
FOURTEEN

When his people reported that federal agents had been to Jones's house early that morning, Noel snapped the ballpoint pen he was holding in half.

"How do they already know Jones is dead?" he asked no one in particular. Ling and Ignacio were with him in his suite. "Mr. Ling, what do you think happened?"

"The dr—"

"The driver," Noel said before Ling finished. "Who the *fuck* is this *bastard* Chuck Angelo? Where did he come from? Where is he now? What does he drive and why don't I know him? Why is it that every *fucking* person I've spoken with in the last three hours has *never heard of Chuck Angelo!*"

He didn't like surprises, and because he took incredible precautions, he rarely had them. The few that had arisen over the years had been the direct result of a certain ICE agent messing up his plans. What particularly irked him was that Sonia Knight screwed up his life without intending to. She had no idea who she had pissed off.

She would find out.

"I think," he continued, "that no one knows this Chuck Angelo because he's a cop. An agent working with Sonia Knight. What I want to know is how this *fe-*

male agent managed to infiltrate Jones's operation with both an undercover cop *and* an informant? Jones was clearly an idiot. I'd love to kill him again."

"I have the report on Knight," Mr. Ling said quietly.

"And?"

"She's single. Her adopted parents live in Sacramento."

"I hope you have more than that."

"Her adopted brother was the cop Johan stabbed yesterday."

"He's not dead, is he?" Noel hoped. A dead "brother" would force her to take time off.

"He'll be released tomorrow, according to my source at the hospital."

"Find out where the parents live, where the brother lives, where Sonia lives. I want to know her best friend, her worst enemy, where she eats, the make and model of her car, and where she'll be every fucking minute of the day. I'm going to kill her, I swear, and when I find this Chuck Angelo I'm going to slowly pull out his intestines and strangle him with them!"

Noel was livid. When he looked at his face in one of the numerous hotel mirrors this ridiculous suite had, it was beet red.

"Mr. Ling, send a team to check on the merchandise and make sure it's being delivered from storage exactly when it's supposed to be. If they're five minutes late, kill them all. I'm not in a forgiving mood. I want our best people—except you—sitting on the whores. I want a patrol. I want no surprises. When the buyers arrive, I want a nice, clean transaction, and then we're out of this fucking country.

"We'll have our money, a permanent new distribution

channel, and ICE agent Sonia Knight will be dead. Then I'll put a headstone with her name in my backyard and bury another whore in it and dance on her *fucking* grave. If I had known that bitch would have been such a problem, I would have put a bullet in her head when I had the chance."

Ann was still in surgery, so Sonia slipped into Riley's room. He was awake, sitting up in his hospital bed, looking both in pain and antsy.

"Hey, sis. It's about time."

"I was here last night."

"They had me on so many painkillers I didn't know my own name. John Black said the guy who stabbed me isn't talking, but they I.D.'d him as Johan Krueger, a German national with a work visa for Omega Shipping."

"Omega?" The shipping company Jones contracted with to bring illegal immigrants into the country to sell to his "clients." Once again, their name surfaced. "Black didn't call me."

"I'm sure he plans to. He's been waiting for word on Ann's surgery."

"She's still in there. Dean's observing now."

"Dean?"

"Dean Hooper, the FBI agent I mentioned yesterday."

"Dean?"

"Excuse me?"

"Not Agent Hooper?"

It took Sonia a moment to realize that Riley was teasing her. "Oh, leave it alone, it means nothing."

"I'm just joshing you. Not much else I can do. Did Mom tell you I'm stuck on leave for two whole weeks?"

"Yeah. I'll make you cookies."

"Please don't. You'll burn down your house. Or worse."

"It's the thought that counts."

"Then think up some chocolate cupcakes from Free-port Bakery . . ."

Dean stepped into the room. "Sonia, I've just spoken with Detective Black. They have an I.D. on the man who tried to kill Ann. Johan Krueger. He's—"

"From Germany and works for Omega Shipping."

"You heard."

Sonia pointed at Riley and made quick introductions. Dean continued. "Omega is one of Jones's clients."

"Clients?"

"At his lobbying firm."

"Omega is also the shipping company that Greg Vega confirmed is responsible for transporting Jones's human cargo."

"This is our first solid connection," Dean said. "I don't want to pull you away, but . . ."

Riley waved them off with a frown. "Go catch the bad guys without me. I'll live vicariously through your stories for years to come."

Sonia kissed him on the forehead. "I love you, Riley. Take it easy, okay?"

"Be careful, Sonia. I don't have to tell you how ruth-less these people are."

"You don't," she said, "and I'm always careful."

Riley didn't look one hundred percent convinced.

Dean spoke up, "I'll keep an eye on her, especially after last night."

"What happened last night?" Riley said.

"Thanks, Dean," Sonia muttered.

"I assumed you told him. I'm sorry."

"I should have." She said to Riley, "Charlie paid me a visit last night—"

"He sought you out?" Riley was outraged and tried to sit up.

She gently pushed him back down on the bed. "Relax, you're not supposed to be up yet."

"Did he do that to you?" Riley pointed to the small bandage on her cheek. "I swear, Sonia, that guy is a ticking time bomb. He should have been locked away after what happened in Costa Rica."

"Riley," she said quietly, "it's okay. I had Dean get him a message that I needed to talk to him. We argued, he has a selective memory. But he shared some interesting information that we're pursuing."

"Are you sure he's not sending you on a wild goose chase so he can go about whatever it is he's planning without your interference?"

Sonia knew Riley was being overprotective, but she didn't like her judgment put into question, especially in front of an FBI agent, even one she was getting along with. "I'm not blind."

"You know I didn't mean it like that."

She continued. "We're closer than we've ever been— Dean has boatloads of intelligence and we're comparing notes. Charlie knows more, but he's working his own fool mission. However, he witnessed Xavier Jones's murder."

"*What?*"

"We haven't found the body yet, but there's evidence that Charlie is telling the truth. We're keeping it quiet for now."

"Who am I going to tell? So Jones is dead?"

"I think so."

"Well, *damn*. What does that mean? A new leader in town? Turf wars?"

"I have no idea," Sonia said, "but it's somehow connected to our investigation into the shipment of young Chinese women. Jones knew his killer, voluntarily met with him and didn't appear concerned until the moment he was shot. I'm thinking it's a rival taking over, but we really don't know."

Her cell phone rang and she excused herself and left the room.

Dean smiled at Sonia's brother. Riley Knight was a likeable guy. "I'm glad you're okay. Sonia was really worried yesterday."

"Thanks. Now what really happened with Charlie last night?"

"He broke into her house at three-thirty in the morning. Woke her up." Dean didn't want to worry Sonia's brother needlessly. "You can see she's no worse for wear."

Riley wasn't convinced. "He just walked in?"

"It won't happen again, I assure you. I'm putting a couple of agents on her house. I haven't told her yet, so . . ."

"I gotcha." Riley relaxed and smiled. "You seem to know my sister pretty well."

"Well enough to know she won't like the idea of two FBI agents babysitting her."

"Do you believe the story Cammarata fed Sonia? About a meeting that ended up with Jones dead?"

Dean had been skeptical, but so far Cammarata's story held up. "I don't know. So far the evidence confirms everything he said, but they're still searching for Jones's body. No one on his staff has seen or spoken to him since yesterday evening."

"Could be that Cammarata killed him, dumped the body, and ran to Sonia with the story of three suspects. He didn't give a name?"

"No. Claims he didn't recognize anyone at the meeting, but he was hiding."

"Bastard. I can just see him pulling this off. Fashions himself a vigilante, but he's nothing but a killer. Probably thinks he's doing Sonia a favor by killing Jones."

"Why?" Dean said. "He apparently wanted information from Jones."

"Maybe he got it. Killed him. Made up this story to divert Sonia's attention from him, so he can slip away."

Dean hadn't actually considered that Charlie Cammarata had killed Jones and the unknown victim, though his story of what he claimed happened certainly seemed incredible. The evidence should prove it one way or another.

Sonia walked back into the room. Her face was pale, her eyes in shock. "The Vegas are dead. They were tortured and murdered in their home early this morning."

I'm too old to rough it in the wilderness.

Charlie's bones creaked and his muscles protested as he trekked out of his makeshift camp near the Pardee Reservoir outside of Mokelumne Hill, a small town with a population of less than a thousand. He'd hidden his car near Highway 49 and Electra Road, camouflaged it, hiked in to further separate himself from his vehicle in case anyone came looking for him. He watched for clues that someone else was in these deep woods, using his tracking skills to avoid a predator instead of finding one. But when it appeared no one was following him, he had time to regroup and finish what he'd set out to do.

After leaving Sonia's house early that morning he didn't dare go back to his cabin on Jones's property. Either the bad guys would kill him, or the good guys would arrest him. Neither option appealed to Charlie. So he opted to go camping. He'd certainly endured far worse conditions than one summer night in the wilderness.

He felt shitty about scaring Sonia last night, but he hoped she'd realize that he'd risked everything to give her the information about Saturday. She was smart, she'd figure it out. She had most of the information she needed; it was a matter of trusting her instincts and taking those leaps of faith he'd tried to teach her. But those leaps often coincided with breaking the rules and the law, and Sonia wouldn't go that far.

And because she wouldn't, she'd never be able to stop predators like Xavier Jones. It was a war. She had to start treating it like one.

Charlie wasn't heartbroken over one predator taking out another. If he could find a way to get all of them to fight and kill each other off, ICE might finally be able to make some substantial inroads into the vast enterprise of human trafficking.

It pained him to think that Sonia thought so poorly of him. He wasn't willing to sacrifice the girls from China, but he had to find Ashley Fox first. There was no reason he couldn't do both. Rescuing Ashley was his job; he was focused on saving the one. He couldn't afford to think too hard about the many who died of AIDS and syphilis and beatings and suicide. He didn't have to think about the mistakes he'd made and how he'd hurt people he cared about because of this drive to do anything to help the weak and innocent.

On one level, he realized that he had crossed the invisible line between right and wrong, but really, wasn't that line arbitrary? Who decided which law to follow and which to abandon? They played fast and loose with the laws every day, it was just a matter of getting caught. This was war, and in war the rule of law could be suspended. People talked about the moral high ground, but the moral high ground meant a whole lot of nothing if you were dead.

Charlie stopped his brisk walk through the forest and leaned against a tree, a sharp pain in his chest making him want to cry out. It wasn't his heart, it was the pain of being unable to stop *it*. What he'd seen in his lifetime was enough to break anyone. The mass graves in Central America. The brothels of women and young girls all over the world. The "tourist sex trade"—predominantly men who traveled from developed countries into third-world countries where child sex laws were lenient or nonexistent. The money they spent to indulge in their perversion . . . Charlie harbored no guilt in stopping them, even if he'd broken not only the law but the Ten Commandments. No one else was willing to do it, and frankly, Charlie wasn't going to wait around for Satan to claim his own. He'd send the bastards down to the pit early, maybe saving one child in the process.

Head in hand, sitting in the dirt and pine needles, memories roared to life. The sight and stench of the dead, the dying, the desolation. There were so many, too many, and still he moved forward, doing what he could. If he did less, he couldn't live with himself. The law didn't matter to him. He'd paid lip service to it as a young, idealistic recruit in the former INS. He'd been in ROTC, did his time in the Marines, came into the job with the idea that he would help people and feel good about it. The only son of a man from Costa Rica with a green card and a woman from California who'd met after World War II while working in a factory. Good people who raised him to help others. He'd been an altar boy, a football player in high school, believed in the American Dream.

The American Dream that predators used to lure those who had nothing into their deadly web.

The sheer mountain of corruption and hate, of slavery and despair, and Charlie was a small nothing compared to all the evil in the world.

He wasn't sure exactly when he snapped, when he decided working within the law wasn't helping. There had been crime scenes he would never be able to forget, that came to him not only when he slept, but when he was awake. The prostitutes with syphilis who were shot and buried in a mass grave—unmarked and unremembered. The young teenage boys kidnapped and forced to fight in wars they had no hand in creating, in countries not their own. How many of these child soldiers had Charlie buried? But the one pivotal moment, when he knew they'd lost the war, was in New Mexico on a scorching August afternoon.

The big rig had been left by the side of the road when it broke down on Highway 10. It was a refrigerated rig that had air holes drilled into each corner because the truck wasn't being used to transport food. It held thirty-

six women, young and old, who had been left in the hot
sun while the driver fled because he'd brought them into
the country illegally to work in a sweatshop in Southern
California. Charlie knew that because he'd tracked
down the driver and extracted the information from
him.

When the truck broke down, so did the cooling system. The compartment became an oven. Eighteen hours
in a slow cooker. The coroner said they'd suffered for
eight to twelve hours before dying. While alive they endured heat stroke, their core body temperatures quickly
rose to over 110 degrees, at which point they suffered
brain damage and hallucinations, and severe—fatal—
dehydration.

The hot, moist environment sped up the rate of de-
composition and insect activity. Their bodies were fully
bloated with bacteria and gases, and the skin had begun
to slough off.

The cop who opened the back of the truck and first
witnessed the morbidity quit that day.

Charlie couldn't stop them, and when he thought
about the masses of people who were bought, sold, tortured, abused, and murdered each and every day, he
couldn't breathe. So many times he had wanted to kill
himself, moments when the burden of memory stripped
him of all sanity.

Then he'd think of Sonia.

She had escaped. One of the few, she had fought back
and won. She was a survivor, refused to be a victim. She
turned around and became part of the solution, using
her knowledge and skills to take down those who traded
in human lives.

If Charlie focused on saving individual victims, he

could make it through each day. Ashley Fox had become his salvation. If only he could find her, reunite her with her mother, he'd be a hero to two people. He could point to Ashley as someone he'd saved. He could put her pretty face in his mind when the dead and dying haunted him. Like he'd done with Sonia until he'd hurt her.

"I didn't mean for any of it to happen, Sonia," he whispered, his voice raw and dry. "I never wanted you to be hurt. Please believe me. Please understand why I had to do it."

He'd saved hundreds—thousands—of people over the years, but it all blended together. The bloodshed still outweighed the souls he'd salvaged. He was drowning in it.

Charlie slowly rose to his feet. He drank half a water bottle and ate a tasteless protein bar. Then he started the hike back to his car.

He was close to breaking the code in Jones's journal. He just needed some time at the library. The main library in downtown Sacramento was large enough to have the information he needed, and discreet enough that he didn't worry about anyone paying him any attention. He'd put on a long-sleeved shirt to hide his recognizable tattoo, and he looked average enough that no one should remember him. As soon as he had it all figured out, he'd give Sonia the rest of the information.

And if he didn't figure it out, he'd still tell her where the girls were being exchanged. He'd lied to her last night, but it hadn't been the first time.

He had indeed recognized one of the killers last night: Sun Ling, a Chinese American who Charlie knew to be a player. Ling was a vicious killer who could snap a man's neck in two without expending much effort or showing any remorse. Charlie had gone up against Ling in the past and the bastard had slipped away. But Ling was always the number two. An enforcer. Charlie hadn't recognized the man who had shot Jones, though he was confident *this* was the man in charge. Jones had said he was a major player who controlled more than half the trafficking out of southern Mexico, Central America, and South America. He operated from a little place south of Acapulco. But Charlie didn't know his name or nationality or anything else about the prick.

But the information was in Jones's journal, Charlie was certain of it. By the time this was over, he planned on killing both of them. First, he needed to find Ashley.

Focus on the goal.

A few hours at the library and he would have the answers he needed.

When he shared those answers with Sonia, maybe she'd forgive him.

CHAPTER
FIFTEEN

The Vegas' sprawling, secluded ranch-style house was located in the farming community of Galt, on the Sacramento–San Joaquin County border. The privacy probably made the Vegas feel secure, but it also gave their killers freedom to kill.

Torture and kill, Sonia thought as she stared at the bodies.

Kendra Vega had been tied to a straight-back chair that had been pushed onto its side. By the look of the blood spatter, she'd been on the ground when she was shot in the head.

Compared to her husband, her suffering had been mercifully short. Greg Vega had been grossly tortured and beaten. Blood had soaked his entire shirt so none of the original color showed. The deputy coroner—a tall, slender woman in her fifties—said that he'd likely bled to death from the stab wound in his abdomen.

"The autopsy can confirm, but it took him several minutes to die. The hilt of the knife kept some pressure on the wound to prevent rapid blood loss, but the internal body damage is severe."

"You can tell how long he was alive?" Sonia asked.

"We'll have a scientifically sound estimate, but it's still

a guess. He probably went into shock after a few minutes and then his body would begin to shut down. The whole process could take three minutes or an hour, depending on a variety of factors. He wouldn't have been conscious the entire time."

Sonia touched Dean's arm to whisper something. His muscles were taut, his entire body tense.

"What?" she asked.

"They shot his pregnant wife first. Made him watch her die, then stabbed him and left him to slowly die."

"They couldn't be certain he'd die from the wound," Sonia said.

The deputy coroner disagreed. "I think they probably could—there would be no surviving this without immediate medical attention. Immediate meaning within minutes. Even then, I doubt he'd make it to surgery."

"They probably waited for him to die," Dean said.

The deputy coroner was still examining the body. She frowned when she looked into his mouth.

"What's wrong?" Sonia asked.

"Someone cut out his tongue."

Sonia's stomach rolled and she became light-headed. Dean grabbed her arm. "Let's go outside."

It wasn't the crime scene itself that disturbed Sonia so much—she'd seen other death scenes that were more grotesque. But she'd been responsible for the Vegas.

"Oh God, Dean. This is my fault. I should have—"

"You are not to blame," Dean interrupted. He found a semi-private spot on the back patio.

"How did Jones find out—" she stopped. "But Jones is dead. The Vegas weren't killed before midnight."

"It's looking more and more like Cammarata was

right," Dean said. "There's no sign of Jones at home, his offices, or his known haunts. His Escalade is in the garage and his plane is in the hangar."

"Did the killers think Jones was going to turn state's evidence?" Sonia thought out loud.

"Or the murders had to do with a territory battle and not Vega's agreement with you."

"They cut out his tongue! They knew he'd talked to the authorities."

Dean didn't respond. He was looking beyond her into the house as if trying to recall something important.

"You know I'm right," she said.

He turned to her, his dark eyes more intense than she'd ever seen them. "You're in danger."

"What are you talking about?"

"He told them. Everything they wanted to know."

"He had no reason to—he had to know they'd kill him either way."

"Vega's pregnant wife was tied to a chair not ten feet from him. He watched her suffer, he saw her fear—you think he wasn't going to tell them everything?"

Sonia swallowed uneasily. "But there's no reason for them to go after me. If they thought I knew something that could lead to an arrest, they'd also be smart enough to know that my boss would know, there'd be reports and documentation."

She wasn't concerned for her own safety. She was a cop, and while she had no death wish, she understood and accepted the risks inherent with her position.

"I appreciate your concern, really, but what we need to figure out is their next step. We assume Vega told them everything he told me, but would that change their plans? They killed Vega because he was an informant, but why Jones? Jones was a big player in this business. Taking him out, and his chief lieutenant, will cause a huge void in the western United States. Are they seeking to fill it? With who? Jones's team? Their own people? Where are they coming from?"

Dean said, "All good questions, but do not minimize their vendetta. They may have thought Jones was part of Vega's deal. Or that Jones was losing control. Either way, they are ruthless, and just because you're a cop isn't going to stop them from going after you. They are old school." He waved his hand toward the Vega house. "Restraints. Torture. Executions. Cutting out his tongue. Hell, I'd think they were old-style gangsters. And we have no idea if Jones was killed by the same people or not."

"There's an easy way to find out," Sonia said. "Ballistics."

"You need a body first."

"We have one. The first victim they dragged out of the river."

Dean rubbed his temple. "Okay. I'll pull every string I have to expedite ballistics. The sheriff's department has been great in sharing jurisdiction."

"Because state and local government dollars are scarce. They're happy to share the credit and have the feds foot the bill. But it works in our favor most of the time," Sonia said. "I think we should pull in every known Jones associate for questioning in his disappearance and Greg Vega's murder."

"Arrest them? On what grounds?"

"Not at first. Just to ask questions. Last time they saw Jones, last time they saw Vega, what they know about

Omega Shipping and a shipment that was supposed to arrive this week."

Dean nodded, excited about the prospect. "You know, this might work. They don't know what evidence we have. We play them up, see where the questioning goes, follow anyone who isn't cooperating. I think we can pull it off. I'll call it in, get S.A.C. Richardson to free up some agents, talk to the sheriff's department about a few plainclothes."

Deputy Sheriff Azevedo approached them. "The killers did a mighty fine job of destroying the victim's office. Computers, papers, books—the damage is extensive, and probably permanent."

Dean asked, "Would you mind if the FBI's Evidence Response Team came by to process the office?"

"Not at all. We can use whatever help you can offer."

"I appreciate it. And as I just told Agent Knight, I can help expedite ballistics, at least on the national database end."

"Fantastic. I'll let the coroner's office know. Thought you might be interested in this." He held up a small plastic evidence bag. Inside was a tiny metal circle that looked like the battery for a garage door opener or other small device. But it wasn't.

"A bug?" Dean and Sonia said simultaneously.

"Where'd you find it?" Sonia asked. "I know Vega swept the place regularly."

"His wife's cell phone. There was another just laying on the table. I thought maybe it was the victim's, until we found this."

"Why were you looking for a bug?"

"I wouldn't have been, except for the one we found in plain sight. Then I thought maybe we should sweep the place. This was the only one we found so far, and we neutralized it."

"Now we know how they figured out Vega was an informant," Dean said. "I'll bet Kendra Vega talked to someone. It could have been as innocuous as asking about a school district in Georgia. Anything that implied leaving Sacramento would make Jones nervous."

"But Jones is dead. Who else was listening?"

"Like I said, someone making a move on the territory."

Sonia turned to Azevedo. "Agent Hooper and I are going to talk to the victim's colleagues. You should know that Greg Vega was a federal informant and Xavier Jones is under investigation for money laundering, racketeering, and human trafficking."

Azevedo was obviously surprised. "Xavier Jones the philanthropist? He just had some arts center downtown named after him."

"That's him. And we're investigating a witness statement that Jones is dead."

"I heard about the body they found in the river. That was Jones?"

"No. We think he's still under. But we need to talk to his employees, and they may or may not be involved with Jones's criminal enterprises."

Dean explained. "We may need the sheriff's department to help tail those we flag as suspect. See where they go, who they talk to."

"I get it. I'll talk to my boss. My men want whoever did this. The woman was pregnant, for chrissake. Yeah, we'll help, I'll just clear it. Give me a couple minutes."

"Thank you, Deputy," Sonia said as Azevedo walked away. She frowned. Maybe this wasn't a good idea.

"What's that frown for?" Dean asked.

"We might spook them," Sonia considered. "Should we wait until Saturday and follow key people?"

"Don't second-guess yourself." Dean put his hands on her shoulders and squeezed lightly. That familiar, hot tingle returned full force as soon as he touched her. "For all we know, Vega's killers are going to completely cut out Jones's people. The more information we have now the better, especially if anyone knows who did this, or who is capable of doing it. We need names. The killers are still in town. They'll be here Saturday night, otherwise these killings were for nothing. We have less than sixty hours to find out where those girls are being kept."

"We should go to the security office first," Sonia suggested. "That's the entity that paid Vega, and where most of Jones's goons were employed."

Dean disagreed. "The first person we need to talk to is Craig Gleason."

"The lobbyist? Isn't he a little white collar to be involved with such a brutal crime?"

"You'd be surprised at what white-collar criminals are capable of, especially when a substantial amount of money is involved. Remember, we track the money, we'll figure out Jones's entire operation."

"Even where the Chinese women are being kept?" she asked, skeptical.

"Oh, yeah. It's there, somewhere. We just have to figure out the pattern. If Gleason isn't involved, he may still know which of Jones's clients are suspect."

"And if he is involved?"

"Then he'll be crying lawyer before we say good afternoon."

"You sound confident."

"Nine times out of ten I'm right."

She gave him a half-smile, remembering their conversation the day before. "No ego?"

Dean raised an eyebrow. "Me?" He handed her the keys to his car. "Why don't you drive so I can pull out Jones's client list and we can talk about how to proceed with Gleason before we meet with him."

"Sounds like a plan to me."

CHAPTER
SIXTEEN

Like Jones's house, the decor of XCJ Consulting was minimalist and functional. Sterile, Dean thought as he and Sonia entered Jones's suite of offices in the Senator Hotel Office Building.

There was no receptionist in the small waiting area, but a secretary leaned through the doorway and asked, "May I help you?"

Dean showed his badge. "Craig Gleason, please."

If the secretary was flustered, she didn't show it. "Would you like to wait for him in the conference room? He's on a call."

"Thank you," Dean said.

They walked through the common area to the glass-walled conference room on the far side. There were two small offices with closed doors and a larger office in the opposite corner with open double doors. Jones's spread, no doubt. Odd, considering his schedule showed he was rarely in the office. Three other desks, including the secretary's, filled the common area.

"Coffee? Water?"

"No thanks," Sonia said impatiently.

When the secretary left, Dean leaned over and whispered in Sonia's ear, "Not many employees. A company with the revenue he has?"

"Is that suspicious?" she asked. "Some small businesses do very well with only a couple people on staff."

"Some." Dean didn't believe Jones's was one of those, especially since he was not an active principal in the business by all appearances.

Craig Gleason stepped into the conference room. He was in his mid to late thirties with sleek black hair and blue eyes. Dean figured women might find Gleason attractive—he was well dressed, polished, in shape—but Dean saw him as too slick, too perfect. Smart, and he knew it. Criminals who thought they were smarter than the cops were often the easiest to catch.

"We weren't properly introduced yesterday, Mr. Gleason," Dean said, shaking his proffered hand. Gleason was the late arrival to Jones's lunch.

Gleason's smile didn't waffle. "Mr. Jones mentioned the unfortunate situation."

Dean kept his face impassive, didn't say a word.

Gleason waved his hand in the air as if to dismiss the whole conversation he'd had with Jones. "Just that you were barking up the wrong tree, something like that. He's a very private person."

Gleason turned his white smile on Sonia. His eyes quickly scanned her entire body, as any warm-blooded man would do, but without the discretion most men employed. Dean didn't like it, but he was interested in how Sonia would react. She didn't seem the type to succumb to a pretty face and affected flirtation.

"Craig," he said, extending his hand to Sonia. "A pleasure to meet you."

Sonia shook his hand, squeezing harder than necessary. Gleason rubbed his hand after she let it go. Dean swallowed a laugh as he cleared his throat and coughed into his fist.

"Sonia Knight, supervisory special agent with Immigration and Customs Enforcement."

By her tone, she was playing the bad cop. Dean adjusted gears to be more conciliatory. They should have discussed it before they came up—Sam Callahan was the perennial "good cop" and Dean had naturally assumed the stern role. But he had a different partner now, one who obviously didn't like to mince words or play games. He liked it.

Gleason's smile faltered for a moment and Dean saw a flash of worry in his eyes. He expected Gleason's next words would be asking for a lawyer; Dean was surprised he was wrong.

Gleason said, "How can I help you?"

"We have some questions about your employer," Sonia said.

"Is it about the FBI raid yesterday morning? I really don't know anything about that. Perhaps you could enlighten me." He chuckled as the three of them sat around the large black lacquered executive table.

Dean let Sonia run with the questioning. He was more interested in observing Gleason's manner: his body language, the way he twirled slowly in the chair—left to right, right to left. How even when the questions were serious, half the time he glanced at Sonia's breasts before answering. Subtle, but Dean was looking for physical cues as to whether Gleason was being honest with them, or lying.

For starters, Gleason didn't seem surprised that they'd shown up, though he might have been expecting it after yesterday's raid. It was more his tacit agreement that he'd willingly answer their questions, no attorney present. Someone as sharp as Gleason—a major lobbyist in a major state—shouldn't be this easy for federal law enforcement to talk to. Even those with nothing to hide liked to have an attorney to cut off the conversation when it went off the narrow path of the investigation. Guilty or innocent, having an attorney present was a good idea to protect the rights of the witness or suspect. It also helped the prosecution because the presence of a defense attorney ultimately made the system run more smoothly. The biggest legal hurdles Dean went through in court were getting confessions admitted as evidence when defense counsel hadn't been present.

"When was the last time you saw Xavier Jones?" Sonia asked.

"Yesterday afternoon. We came here after lunch to talk about the office and our clients, bills that we are tracking. It's that time of year, June in Sacramento." His smile said *what can you do.*

"What time did he leave?"

"Three, three-thirty."

"Was he alone or was someone with him?"

"Alone. Though he had his driver pick him up."

Cammarata was his driver. Dean played dumb and asked, "His driver? Through a service?"

"His personal driver."

"Do you know his personal driver?"

"I've met him."

"Do you know his name?"

"Angelo."

"First or last?"

"I don't know."

Gleason didn't seem to be evading or showing any concern about Jones or his driver.

"Have you talked to Mr. Jones today?" Sonia asked.

"No, but he's supposed to be in later this afternoon for a meeting with clients."

"What time?"

"Five."

"And you know this how?"

"I set up the appointment yesterday. Why is this important?"

Sonia ignored the question and asked, "Do you know Mr. Jones's employee Gregory Vega?"

"Vega? I met him a couple times, but he works for Mr. Jones's security company in Stockton."

"He's dead."

Dean watched Gleason's face, and while his voice sounded surprised, his eyes were too calculating. Had he known Vega was dead? Suspected? That surprised Dean; he didn't think Gleason was a killer or accomplice to murder. Money laundering, racketeering, sure. But Gleason seemed the sort of man who didn't like to get his hands dirty.

"Greg Vega? Are you sure? What happened?"

"He and his wife were tortured and murdered early this morning in their home," Sonia said bluntly. She leaned forward. "We have evidence that your boss may have met a similar fate."

Gleason paled—a hard reaction to fake, Dean acknowledged.

"Wh-who would do that?" he sputtered.

Dean said, "We were hoping you might be able to help us figure that out."

"*Me?*"

"You're close to Xavier Jones, right? You've worked for him for six years." Dean looked at his notes, though he had the information memorized. "You graduated from USC with a degree in public administration and business economics. Worked for the governor for a year as an intern, then took a legislative consultant position with one of the Senate leaders. Two years later you went to work for the new governor—a different political party, showing you work well with everyone, right?" Dean gave him an impressed smile. "Four years later you became chief of staff to the Senate Pro Tem, and then after two years joined XCJ."

"Why is my background important? That's all on the XCJ Web page under my bio. What's that got to do with anything?" He seemed irritated. Agitated. Guilty or worried?

"I'm simply trying to understand your relationship with your boss. He needs you—you have the contacts in the legislature and the governor's office—Jones is a businessman who had a small lobbying firm with a handful of clients. Until you."

Something clicked and Dean went through his mental checklist on this case. It suddenly became crystal clear. Dean knew exactly how Jones was laundering his money. If he was right, it was brilliant—Dean could almost admire the man for his criminal intelligence. Proving his theory would be difficult. Unless someone talked—and Dean knew how to work the system and cut deals better than most.

He said to Gleason, "Is there anything you want to tell us?"

Gleason was now visibly rattled. "Xavier was a much sought-after lobbyist. He brought me on because he couldn't manage all the clients who wanted to hire him."

More likely Jones brought in Gleason to hide the volume of cash moving through his then-small company.

Dean wanted to wrap up the conversation and get back to FBI headquarters, but there was still more information he needed about Jones's clients. He didn't want to rush it, because if Gleason *did* know about the money laundering and was involved in any way in human trafficking, he was in a perfect position to continue Jones's operation, business as usual.

"But you do all the work," Dean continued. He forced himself to sound impressed. "You're the lobbyist of record for the overwhelming majority of clients. You have more clients than the two junior lobbyists—Eric Danielson and Rich Mercer—and Jones combined. You're the top gun."

"Mr. Jones is in charge," Gleason reiterated.

"You wouldn't know it looking at the lobbying reports," Dean said. "Your name is on virtually everything."

"I don't know what you're getting at."

Sonia spoke up. "Has Mr. Jones received any threats that you know about? Has he seemed preoccupied lately?"

"Threats? Of course not. He's always preoccupied. He's busy. I know the raid yesterday upset him greatly." Gleason fidgeted. "Maybe he killed himself. He was really upset about the situation. He was afraid word would get out and his associates would be concerned. Any hint of impropriety in our business is severely damaging to our reputation."

Sonia turned her BlackBerry around so Gleason could read the screen, then handed it to Dean. "Really hard to kill yourself with five bullets."

Dean read the message from Trace Anderson that had come in ten minutes ago, after they'd sat down at the table. He hadn't even seen Sonia checking her messages.

Divers found Jones on the bottom of the river. The current pushed him farther downstream than the unknown victim. Five entry wounds. Call me.

"Wait," Gleason said after Sonia showed him the text. "Wait a minute. Mr. Jones was murdered? Who's this other victim?"

"We don't know." Sonia pushed over a photo of the first bloated corpse pulled from the river. "Have you seen him before?"

Gleason was obviously disturbed by the photograph, and Sonia made no move to take it away. "No," he whispered.

"Are you absolutely sure?"

"I don't know him."

"Do you know who would want to kill Mr. Jones? Maybe a client who didn't get his bill through?"

Gleason was shaking his head before Sonia even finished her sentence. "This is America. People don't kill over legislation."

Dean said, "Did you know that XCJ Consulting has twice the revenue of any other lobbying firm in California, and more than any in Washington? That tipped my office off that there might be something else going on here."

"That something else," Sonia said, "is human trafficking."

"That's ridiculous."

Gleason said the right things, but his mannerisms told Dean that this wasn't news to him. Why was he talking?

Why hadn't he called an attorney? The guy couldn't be that arrogant, or that stupid.

Gleason continued. "What proof do you have?"

Dean pulled out the client list of XCJ Consulting. Driving over they'd decided to go through the list alphabetically. There were two or three they were specifically interested in, but they didn't want to tip their hand.

"Astor Manufacturing. Owner, Dale Trevek. Has Mr. Trevek spoken with Mr. Jones in the last two weeks? How satisfied is he with the work you've done for him?"

Dean and Sonia alternated between names, running through them as quickly as possible to get to the key companies Sonia felt were most likely involved with human trafficking, or were already on her radar like Omega Shipping.

Sonia asked, "Omega Shipping. One of Mr. Jones's personal clients. How long have they been a client?"

"Omega? Since before I started," Gleason replied. He was agitated and tired, and no longer stole looks at Sonia's chest. "Hasn't this gone on long enough? You still haven't told me why you want to know all this." He ended with a whine.

"As we said at the beginning," Sonia answered, "Jones was suspected of being involved in several illegal activities. We are completing the investigation, because the likelihood is that whoever killed him benefits from his death. So, please, let's talk about Omega. They've been a longtime client of Mr. Jones. Owned by George and Victoria Christopoulis. According to shipping records, they transport cattle, poultry, and other perishable goods from the United States—mostly California—to China, Japan, Russia, Brazil—all across the globe."

"And?"

"The single most common method of transportation in international human trafficking is by ship. Omega is in all the right places to bring illegal immigrants into this country."

Gleason laughed, wholly out of place considering the conversation, and said, "You don't need to bring them in by boat. There're tens of thousands willingly crossing the border every day."

Sonia slammed her fist on the table and Dean saw that the anger was not an act. "Do not make light of this situation, Mr. Gleason."

"Look, I don't know what's going on. You're the people who raided Jones's house. You didn't come up with anything, or you wouldn't be asking such stupid questions."

Dean pushed on through the list. There were two other entities that had been with Jones since the beginning of XCJ. "What about Rio Diablo Rancherita? According to Fair Political Practice reports, the tribe spent over $100 million on a statewide referendum related to a gaming agreement. A huge chunk of that money came here."

"It was a political campaign. They're expensive. Why are you interested in Rio Diablo?"

Not *that* expensive. "We've asked you about all of XCJ's clients," Dean said innocently.

"There's only two more on the list," Sonia said. "Weber and Sons Trucking and Zing Productions. Why would a local moving company need a lobbyist?"

"Joel Weber is a friend of Xavier's. It wasn't a major account. His son Jordan runs the day-to-day business."

"They paid over $100,000 to XCJ last year," Dean said.

Gleason shrugged. "Xavier charges a lot for his services. And maybe there was a special project. I don't know, it wasn't my account."

"And Zing," Sonia said, "I haven't found any films they've produced."

"Again, not my client."

Dean was surprised at how quickly Gleason went from shock over Jones's murder to spending nearly an hour running through XCJ's client list. He was someone to watch, closely.

"Thank you for your time," Dean said, standing. Sonia looked irritated, but there was nothing else they could learn from Gleason. If he knew more, he wasn't talking now. They'd have to bring him in to FBI headquarters or arrest him before they could pressure him to squeal. But Gleason definitely knew more than what he'd said. Dean would put two of his agents on Gleason, separate cars, to track him.

Dean's theory that had nudged him earlier took on substantial weight. He just hoped he could prove it.

CHAPTER
SEVENTEEN

Sonia was eager to head down to Stockton and talk to the key people in Jones's security offices, but Dean turned east on Business-80 instead of south on Highway 99.

"Wait, Stockton is the other way."

"Didn't Gleason rub you wrong? Aren't you suspicious?"

"Hell yes, but we still have several people who work for XCJ Security to interview."

"It's nearly four, and with traffic we won't make it to Stockton until after five."

Sonia was frustrated. She'd wanted to talk to the security staff today since Vega technically worked out of that office. But Dean was right—it would be a lot of driving for nothing. "Gleason didn't react how I expected when I showed him the text from Trace. He said all the right things, but . . ."

"I caught that, too."

"You know the one thing that really stood out? When I dropped the big bomb about human trafficking. Gleason didn't bat an eye. No shock or outrage or surprise."

"He knew all along."

"Or he's been a player all along." Sonia glanced over at Dean with a half-smile. "So we agree that Gleason is most likely part of Jones's illegal operation?"

"Yes."

"He didn't cry for his lawyer like you said."

"I know. It's been bugging me because he's dirty. I feel it. But he's also arrogant. Narcissists often balk at bringing in anyone to help them, even an attorney to protect their rights. I just assumed he was smarter than that."

"Maybe he was feeling us out," Sonia said, "trying to figure out what we know."

"Perhaps. The only organization he pushed back on was Rio Diablo. I definitely want to look into them."

"You started asking questions about Jones's personal clients. What are your thoughts there? I thought we'd planned on focusing on Omega and the trucking company."

"I think I figured out how Jones was laundering his money."

"How?"

"I want to look at a couple files first to make sure I have it straight in my head."

Sonia didn't say anything. What'd happened to the trust Dean had preached over the last two days? That they should work together and share information? She'd never liked working with the FBI in the past, but she'd thought that this time was different. Dean Hooper was smart and focused—two attributes she appreciated—and they'd developed a rapport. But now it was just another mistrustful relationship, like all the other Fibbies she'd worked with before; suddenly, she was on a need-to-know basis.

"Sonia?"

"You don't need me, do you?"

"Of course I do. Your knowledge about how human

traffickers operate and the specific players under Jones is essential to proving—"

"But you don't trust me with your theory?"

"It's not that. I don't have it all straight in my head yet."

"Okay."

They drove in silence. Commuter traffic was heavy and Sonia was trying not to be angry with Dean for his unwillingness to share his thoughts. But the slower the car moved, the higher her temper rose. Trust was a two-way street, wasn't it? Hadn't she been open with him about everything she knew? About Charlie breaking in? About what he said and how it might fit into their investigation. She was trying here, dammit, and she wished Dean would trust her—even if he ended up being wrong.

Maybe that was it. He didn't like being wrong. He wanted to go over his files to be satisfied that he was right, then he'd share. Maybe that's why his record was so strong, he didn't jump to conclusions, but worked methodically to be assured that his assumptions were correct. Sonia reacted to situations immediately, relying on instinct and experience. Sometimes it ended up saving lives because she was quick on her feet. Other times she found herself having to backtrack and refocus. She couldn't fault Dean for his diligence, just like he didn't fault her when she jumped down his throat after he interfered with her stakeout the other night.

Five minutes—and one mile—had passed when Dean said, "You're angry."

"Yes, but I'm getting over it." She glanced at him and saw a half-smile on his face. Her residual anger dissipated. Dean Hooper was too sexy to stay angry with for long, especially when he grinned.

Dean said, "Something Gleason said had me thinking. Before Gleason, XCJ Consulting was just Xavier Jones and a handful of clients, including Weber Trucking, Rio Diablo, and Omega Shipping. I know Jones's current finances well, but I didn't spend much time on his old finances because the statute of limitations for money laundering and racketeering is five years. I needed something current, so I only gave the older documents a cursory examination."

She sensed he was taking a leap of faith by sharing his theory with her. He didn't like brainstorming.

"When I saw the name Rio Diablo Rancherita on the list, and that they'd been clients of Jones since before Gleason, it set off some bells. Indian gaming is relatively new to California. There used to be a handful of casinos, now they're breeding like rabbits. Las Vegas and Atlantic City have always been under our watch because of the opportunities for money laundering. It's very easy to slide money into the casino and 'clean' it—the illegal money becomes profit for the casino owner, reportable and taxable, but still illegally obtained. They claim the cash came in through gambling losses, but in reality it came in through drugs or illegal prostitution or a host of other racketeering scams."

Sonia asked, "But how do the criminals themselves profit? Are all casinos criminal enterprises?" She didn't know much, if anything, about gambling.

"No, most are fairly clean, it's better now than in the past. But there are many ways for criminals to use casinos—frankly, any businesses that have large cash flows are at risk, even if the owners are clean. There are two primary ways that the criminal element profits from casino action. When the casino owners themselves are part of the illegal activities, they wash their own money and don't technically have to 'pay' anyone. They clean it, pay taxes on it as revenue, and they're free and clear. The other way is for a criminal to go into a casino, exchange cash for chips, usually under ten thousand, gamble a little, then cash in those chips. Now the money is 'clean.' He'll ask for a receipt for his 'winnings' and the casino has no way of tracking whether he won all the money or not. There are reporting thresholds that casinos are required by law to report, but just like running money through banks, the criminals know if they stay below the threshold they can run the scam indefinitely. And they will walk into multiple casinos with different players, washing tens of thousands of dollars all over town in a single night. We watch for the same people, have informants, and some owners are willing to work with us. Catching them is hard, but proving it is virtually impossible. That's why it takes on average two years of intensive, full-time investigating to collect enough evidence for an arrest warrant, and ultimately, a conviction. We have to show the pattern. Two or four or six times and a good defense attorney can get the guy off. Thirty lucky days a year? A jury isn't going to buy it. And of course we build our case with additional evidence, like known associates, lack of a stable job, living a lifestyle above reported income. It's a labor-intensive investigation, but it never fails to satisfy me when I can build a case and take down a criminal enterprise."

"I can see it now that you lay it out, but I never realized how easy it was."

"It's become harder over the years with security cameras and incentives for casino owners and staff to work with us to identify these people. But it's also harder for us with fewer resources, and criminals are finding new and innovative ways to launder their illegal money."

"And you think Jones found an innovative way?"

"Remember when I said that the revenue coming into his company was high for a lobbying firm?"

"Yes."

"He claimed the money, provided client lists, and has a real, legitimate business. There's no crime in charging high consulting fees, and while we looked hard at quid pro quo—where there was an agreement between a lawmaker and Jones to pass or not pass legislation in exchange for money—we couldn't find even a blemish related to Jones in the capital. So I put the idea aside, figuring Jones's clients felt he was providing a service and they were willing to pay his steep fees.

"However," Dean continued, obviously energized by his discovery, "when I saw Rio Diablo on the list, and Gleason asked specifically why we were interested in them, but not any of the other clients, I looked at my notes and saw the connection between the small operation Jones had before Gleason and the much larger operation he has now. I suspect Jones set up the consulting firm fifteen years ago specifically *to* launder money."

Sonia considered the idea. "If that's the case, it would be a huge conspiracy. A great number of people involved. Secrets are revealed proportionately to how many people know. I don't see how Jones could have kept something of that magnitude under wraps."

"That's the thing, he doesn't need a lot of people.

Only one in each business. And if the Indian tribe is one of those entities, there's no way in hell I would have figured it out. They investigate themselves, and trust me when I tell you they are not going to bend over backward to help us prove one of their own is laundering money through one of their casinos. That gets out to the public and public trust plummets. So do their casino profits."

"But Jones isn't a gambler," Sonia said. "I've been following him nearly as long as you have. He doesn't gamble."

"That's why I think this worked. If he was a gambler, I would have seen the gambling 'winnings' in his reportable income. That would have been a huge red flag. He's the one receiving the money from human trafficking. He likely keeps a large stash of money somewhere—probably in a safe-deposit box—and perhaps he pays his people some of their salary in cash. But his profits are going to far exceed his expenses. How can he ever use that money? He needs to deposit it in a bank eventually. While he can do a lot of business in straight cash, and that's how many criminals get away with their crimes, Jones has many expenses and property holdings that cost him capital outlay at some point. Deposits of over ten thousand dollars are reported to the IRS, as well as repeat deposits that are just under the ten-thousand-dollar threshold, at the discretion of the bank. Legitimate deposits would be payroll, consulting fees, and the like, so the IRS and FBI would be informed of a fifty-thousand-dollar wire transfer from one person or business to another, but if it's 'legitimate' on the face, it's not going to receive additional scrutiny."

"I don't see the connection here to Rio Diablo."

"Cash flow into traditional casinos is hard to track, but we have years of data and experience, and tough federal regulations to make it extremely hard to launder money through casinos. But those regulations don't apply to Indian gaming. They police their own, and their Indian council doesn't have the experience with money laundering and criminal enterprises to know what to look for."

"So Jones sent his employees to pretend to gamble and then collect winnings?" Sonia was confused.

"No. This is why it's so brilliant. I think he's *giving* his clients cash—and they are paying him for lobbying and political consulting—even if they don't need it. They probably keep a percentage off the top, and the rest goes back to Jones as income into his legitimate business.

"That's why I think he brought Gleason on six years ago. I suspect his illegal revenue had grown to the point he feared his small client list would become a red flag to the IRS. So he brought Gleason on with the charge of growing the business. Gleason and the other two lobbyists work ninety percent of the clients, but it's the few original clients who are still responsible for the bulk of the income. At least, that's what I think."

Dean turned into the FBI parking lot and showed his badge to the guard, who opened the electronic gate. "That's why," he concluded, "I need to analyze the older records before I can state with certainty that this is how he did it."

"But you are pretty certain."

"It's the only thing that makes sense. And it works every way I look at it."

As they got out of the car Sonia said, "I never thought

white-collar crime was so exciting. But you definitely have my interest piqued."

"You know human trafficking, Sonia. Together we can figure out exactly *how* they're helping him. Because they must have known about Jones's illegal activities from the start." Dean's gaze hardened. "I want to take every last one of them down."

It took Charlie all day researching, until he had a headache and could hardly see, but he had finally figured out Jones's code.

And it didn't help at all.

The code was so simple—a numeric code—that had he access to a government computer, it would have been broken in minutes. However, the numeric code revealed *another* code, this one seemingly random. The words were clear, but Charlie didn't know what they meant. And he feared their meaning would be clear to only one person: Jones.

There were columns of dates, which Charlie focused on, but this journal only went back six months, if Charlie had decoded it right. And Ashley Fox was kidnapped nearly a year ago.

He could hardly believe all of his work—the crimes he'd committed, the crimes he had to allow lest he reveal his identity—were for nothing. He needed the older journals, and he had no idea where Jones kept them.

Charlie was certain they weren't at Jones's house or in any of the outbuildings. Jones wouldn't have left them in either his consulting or security office because Jones trusted no one. He'd had a fear of being blackmailed, so Jones had held everything close to the vest.

But even if Charlie found the older journal, he still wouldn't know what the damn words meant! Odd words and phrases like *lipid* and *fresh news* and *rose* and *coffee time*. The words meant something—the transportation method, how many people were brought in, expenses, and income. Lacking access to a high-end computer-decoding program, it would take him much longer than decoding the numbers.

All this work and he was no closer to finding Ashley.

Her mother's voice rang in his ear.

"All I want, Mr. Cammarata, is to know. I want her back home, but if she's dead I want to know that, too. This not knowing what happened to her—the not knowing is killing me. I'm in limbo. One morning I'm sure she's gone, the next morning I'm positive she's still out there, crying for me. Help me find her, dead or alive. I have to know."

Charlie didn't yet have an answer for Ashley's mother. It was killing him. How could he go back and tell her he didn't know what happened to her daughter?

There was nowhere he could turn. Ten years ago he had burned every bridge and betrayed the one person he'd never wanted to hurt. But Charlie couldn't let this one go. He had to find Ashley. But looking at this code—it made no sense. Jones had put together a fail-safe against law enforcement and his illegal business associates.

Damn you to hell, you bastard.

Charlie should have found a way to torture the information out of Jones. Now he was dead and the bizarre code dead with him.

Even with a code-breaking program and a top-notch analyst, the chance information about Ashley Fox would be in the journal that began in January of this year, while Ashley was abducted a year ago last April, was slim.

But for certain the key information about the China dolls being sold in the foothills to the unknown buyer was here. Charlie would give Sonia the journal—on the condition that she promise to find Ashley Fox.

The key players involved with the Xavier Jones investigation assembled in the conference room crowded with all Dean's computers and files. In addition to Dean and Sonia, ICE agent Trace Anderson and analyst Maria Sanchez were there; FBI agent Sam Callahan and two analysts who'd been assigned to Dean full-time; and sheriff's deputy Brian Azevedo brought detective Melanie Montgomery, who'd been assigned the Vega double homicide and, because of the connection between Jones and Vega, the riverfront double homicide as well. Quantico's top profiler, Dr. Hans Vigo, was on speakerphone. Dean introduced everyone who didn't already know one another, gave a brief rundown on Dr. Vigo's credentials, and started the task force debriefing.

It was after hours, and while the atmosphere was charged with energy and hopes that they were making progress on the case—or cases, as it were—the men loosened their ties, drank coffee, water, or soda and munched on snacks Sam had brought in.

"Thank you all for coming on such short notice," Dean said. "As you now know, ICE and the FBI formed this Xavier Jones task force two days ago when we learned that we were running parallel investigations. However, in light of the primary suspect's murder last night, our purpose has changed. It's important that we lay out everything we know and reexamine it together. There's an urgency we didn't have until now. An unknown number of Chinese women, likely minors, are being brought in illegally from Hong Kong and are being sold Saturday night into illegal prostitution or slave labor. We have an unconfirmed day and time, but no location. They may already be here in the Sacramento area, or still en route. Agent Knight will summarize what we know so far."

Dean nodded at Sonia, who'd been sitting casually on the corner of the table by the door. She was drinking coffee but not eating, and Dean vowed to get some food into her before she left for the night. Though she was holding up well, Sonia still blamed herself for the Vegas' murders.

Sonia stood and walked over to one of the whiteboards where earlier she had written a general time line. "Omega Shipping, affiliated with Xavier Jones, has long been suspected of transporting illegal immigrants, not only to the U.S., but to Canada and other countries in the Western hemisphere. No country is free of trafficking. Women, girls, and boys are enticed or kidnapped for illegal prostitution, child soldiers, and slave labor. Over eight hundred thousand individuals a year are trafficked across international borders, and that doesn't include those captive in their own countries, such as the child soldiers in Africa.

"My office has been looking at Xavier Jones for a couple years, but we never had enough evidence for a warrant. We had some suspicious travel, his name had come up in other, unconnected investigations, and his affiliation with Omega Shipping, who we had been investigating on another trafficking matter, had us on the edge. It took an informant to give us the in we needed to finally make strides in building a case against him." Sonia drained her coffee, and Dean handed her a water bottle. She nodded her thanks, sipped, and continued.

"Our informant was one of Jones's top lieutenants, and as everyone here knows, when you have a criminal like Jones in a major racketeering case, it's usually the inside man who gives us what we need to build a case for the U.S. attorney. My informant confirmed what we already knew, and provided us with some additional but outdated intel regarding facilities used for temporary storage of their prisoners. Unfortunately it was his word alone: he had no hard evidence to give us Jones. He wanted immunity and witness protection. We agreed, provided he obtained the physical evidence we needed to prosecute."

Sonia sighed almost inaudibly; if Dean hadn't been standing right beside her, he wouldn't have noticed the defeated heave in her chest. She said, "Greg Vega, my informant, and his pregnant wife were murdered early this morning. Any evidence he may have collected for us is gone, though I doubt he had anything significant. He wanted out, and would have given me the moon if he could have. We were both counting on the shipment of the China dolls—what we sometimes call Chinese women sold or lured into forced prostitution—to give us what we wanted. I wanted Jones; Greg Vega wanted freedom."

Deputy Azevedo spoke up. "Vega was tortured and left to die with a knife in his gut. The coroner estimated it took him twelve to fifteen minutes to bleed out; he was probably conscious for half that time. Conscious and looking at his dead wife who had been shot execution style while tied to a kitchen chair."

Grimness set in among the assembled group. Dean spoke. "Xavier Jones was murdered prior to the Vegas. Though we're waiting for the crime scene and ballistics reports, it's clear the four homicides are connected. Theories as to why are welcome, but Agent Knight and I believe that there's some jockeying for power within the Jones organization, or that one of his competitors saw a weakness and exploited it." Dean paused. He had been uncomfortable with his realization all day, and hadn't spoken of it. He would probably never know if his actions were the catalyst that led to this chain of violence. "Our raid early Wednesday morning may have been the signal that now was the time to make a move on Jones's territory."

Sonia said, "The problem remains that, if our intelligence is accurate, we have young women in jeopardy. We don't know where they are at this precise time, but we know they'll be in the greater Sacramento area late Saturday night." She pointed to her time line. "Twenty days ago, a small tanker owned by Omega left Hong Kong. ICE agents on site informed us that the ship was likely to have a minimum of thirty females between the ages of fourteen and seventeen who had been kidnapped from an illegal convent. These girls had been orphaned or abandoned as infants and raised to maturity by an underground church. They were being transported to a safe haven when the girls were abducted. We believe they are to be integrated into the illegal sex trade here in the United States, or that they'll be traded to other Western countries."

"Why Sacramento?" Sam Callahan asked. "We're inland. Wouldn't it be easier to do this in a major port, or offshore, or in Mexico?"

"Yes and no. First, we have a vigorous watch in all ports in California, and because Omega is flagged, we search more of their ships. Second, Mexico is not the safest place to engage in trades if the destination country is elsewhere. There's border patrol, for one." Sonia paused. "However, we have unconfirmed intelligence that once the victims hit American soil, they are transported by air. Small aircraft, including helicopters, which have virtual autonomy to travel within our borders."

"But Sacramento isn't a major port," Sam added.

"No, but Stockton is. We don't think the women are being unloaded in Stockton. Based on another witness, we believe the victims are transferred at night from the main ship to smaller boats, which then traverse the delta to private docks where the women are moved to trucks or small aircraft." Sonia pointed to the whiteboard. "Six days ago we had word that the ship with the girls would be stopping in Honolulu. They never came. We don't know why, we don't know if they sank, we don't know if they went another route. Or they could have moved them in the middle of the ocean to another ship. But based on the business-as-usual tone of Jones's people and another informant, the girls are still expected in Sacramento on Saturday." She paused. "They may already be here. We don't know."

"That's a lot you don't know," Detective Melanie

Montgomery said. "Why isn't the Chinese government doing anything to find their citizens?"

Sonia glared at the detective. "As I said, the girls were kidnapped from an illegal church. They can't go to the authorities, there's no record of the girls being born."

"So they're illegal in China?" Montgomery asked skeptically.

"The one-child-per-family policy has created a sub-class of girls—unwanted by their families because they are not boys. Especially in the farming communities, where a son can help keep their plots working. Those babies born female are often killed or abandoned. Illegal churches and other human rights organizations will take them in. They can't go to the authorities or risk their lives and freedom. But that's neither here nor there, it is what it is."

Montgomery frowned. "I have four bodies and no suspects," the detective said. "Do you have suspects you're not sharing with local law enforcement?"

Dean saw Sonia bristle. He was about to respond to smooth tensions, but Sonia said, "I've told you everything I know about the murders. If I had any idea who killed Xavier Jones, believe me, I'd tell you. Jones was a ruthless bastard, but whoever killed him is colder, more calculating, and completely without remorse. Jones was a businessman; he was in it for the money. He never thought about the fate of the women he'd sold; to him it was simply a business transaction. Whoever killed him is in it for power."

Dean glanced at Sonia. He hadn't realized she'd been profiling the killers, but what she said made sense to him. He leaned toward the speakerphone. "Dr. Vigo? Did you hear that?"

Hans Vigo sounded like he was in the room when his voice came through the speaker. "Yes, Dean. And I think Agent Knight is dead-on. I read your report on the homicides and came to the same conclusion."

"So who are these people?" Detective Montgomery said. "I feel like we're in the middle of a war. I haven't seen so many dead bodies outside of gang turf wars."

Vigo said, "That's actually a good comparison, Detective. Xavier Jones is a top lieutenant of a 'gang'—or, in our case, a human trafficking ring, who'd been given autonomy to operate within a defined territory. In fact, he's been working the territory for so long he thought of this criminal enterprise as *his* organization. He got into a bit of trouble with the law. The leader of the ring doesn't tolerate this kind of attention, so he kills Jones. Takes out his top lieutenant as well."

Sonia interrupted. "I agree, Dr. Vigo, except your last point. The killer *knew* that Greg Vega was a government informant. Vega's tongue was cut out. Jones wasn't tortured; Vega was."

"It could be that Jones was killed because his man was an informant, but the informant was made to suffer because he'd committed the more egregious sin."

Montgomery said, "So who is this top gun?"

"Someone who has little fear that he'll be caught," said Vigo over the speakerphone.

"Most criminals don't think they'll be caught," Sam said.

"But this killer is extremely confident. He's stealthy. He's not someone you've talked to or interviewed. I don't even think he's from the area. If he were, there'd be more dead bodies."

"Four isn't enough?" Montgomery sneered.

"This killer leaves a trail of dead wherever he goes. He punishes people fatally. He does not tolerate dissent; he does not tolerate imperfection. He rewards those who do what he says when he says it—he prizes loyalty. At the same time, he surrounds himself with smart people. He loathes not only incompetence, but stupidity."

Sonia looked stunned. "You can tell all that by a written report on the murders?"

Vigo chuckled. "Not exactly. I have copies of the preliminary autopsy reports, as well as Agent Hooper's psychological assessment of Mr. Jones after their meeting the other night. I'm also drawing upon my knowledge of known individuals involved in human trafficking, and my own experience.

"For example," he continued, "the killer considered Jones incompetent; he was shot and killed. Simple and effective. He considered Vega a traitor. Traitors anger him far more than incompetence, therefore the torture. Cutting out his tongue while he was alive shows that he wanted to make it clear to not only Vega but to everyone in his organization that if they talked, they'd meet a similar fate."

"This sounds like mob activity," Sam said.

"Similar," Vigo concurred, "but different in one key area."

"What's that?"

"Your killer has every reason to think he's untouchable. He's not an American citizen."

After the verbal shock and comments subsided, Dean asked, "How can you be so sure about that, Hans?"

"Because he is unconcerned about evidence."

"No prints were found on the knife or anywhere in the Vega house," Montgomery interjected.

"He wore gloves, but he left the knife. He didn't weight the bodies he dumped in the river because he didn't care if they'd be discovered sooner rather than later. He left the Vegas in their house without disturbing the scene—no arson fire, no body removal, he didn't care if or when they were found. The dead are in the past, unimportant, problems that have been dealt with. This is, ultimately, what's going to trip him up."

"What?" Sonia asked. "That he didn't destroy the bodies?"

"That he considers them the past. Dealt with. He's not concerned about evidence because even if we got his prints, they wouldn't be in our database. He doesn't believe he's been photographed by American law enforcement; he is most likely in this country under an assumed name. This is why I've made initial contacts with Interpol and our attachés in Central and South America—they may have information on him or his M.O."

Sonia said, "My boss, Toni Warner, can help with those contacts as well as finding out what, if anything, Homeland Security has on a similar M.O. Though without a name, description, or even a home country, it'll be impossible to narrow suspects down. There will be far too many possibles."

"You're right," Vigo concurred, "but we can assume he's here right now, and that he's likely to be present Saturday night."

"Would a man in his position normally come in for what appears to be a routine exchange?" Dean asked. "That would increase his risk and the chance that someone could I.D. him."

"I honestly can't say why this man chose to come here now."

"Maybe it's not the leader," Sam said. "Maybe he hired someone to kill Jones and Vega."

Vigo said, "I suppose it's possible, but if that's the case, would a man who is operating for power relinquish control to an underling? One of this case's fundamental problems is that we don't know exactly why *this* shipment is so important. Not to diminish the humanity of the victims, but Chinese girls are trafficked in the tens of thousands every year. Why are these three or so dozen girls so important? Agent Knight? Do you have an insight here?"

"I hadn't thought of the situation in that light," Sonia admitted. "But you're right—there is no lack of Asian girls."

"What about smuggling?" Trace spoke up for the first time.

"Like what?" Dean asked. "Drugs?"

"Not from China," Trace said. "It wouldn't be typical, at any rate. But there are other commodities. Pirated software, fake brand-name pharmaceuticals, weapons. I could go on."

"Trace is right," Sonia said. "China has a huge black market export business. The women trafficked within their borders are predominantly used as slave labor. What the media likes to call 'sweatshops.' But why would they mingle the two illegal trades?"

No one had an answer. Vigo said, "If it was a hired hit, I don't think that the Vega murders would have been that brutal. That *personal*. But I may be wrong. It is interesting, however, that Jones was killed twenty-four hours after the FBI raid. That's enough time for the leader to travel from virtually anywhere in the world. Maybe he wasn't planning to come until Jones was seen as a risk. He felt he needed to be onsite to ensure everything went smoothly."

There was silence for a good minute as they considered the various theories.

Vigo continued. "Our target is unassuming, of average build and appearance, well-groomed. He does not draw undue attention. He could walk right past any of you, and you wouldn't look twice. He's not on the FBI's Ten Most Wanted; he's not even on our radar. *If* he's wanted by anyone, it's as a name that means nothing, because as soon as the name goes on a list, he changes it. And I guarantee you that this is no young turk jockeying for territory; it's someone with decades in the business, with extreme confidence and a strong organizational structure. No one within his inner circle is going to turn on him because they have seen the results of disloyalty many, many times.

"But make no mistake: there is one leader. He is indisputably in charge of his territory, which is far larger than northern California, which Jones commanded. He is feared by his equals because he seems to have no weak points. He's not married, he has no children, he is likely an only child or oldest child. He also lives well, enjoys the good things in life. But not physical collections. He won't be collecting art or other treasures that some cultured criminals judge their worth by; he lives simply, with fine meals, expensive wine, premium liquor, expensive suits. Disposable or consumable wealth. He is well-educated, but easily angered. If a waiter gives him poor service, he might wait all night to snap his neck in the dark."

"Sounds like a peach of a guy," Montgomery mumbled.

"Thanks, Hans. That's terrific insight we need." Dean turned the meeting back to their current situation. He appreciated Vigo's assessment—it had proven invaluable when he'd planned the raid on Jones in the first place—but right now they had a tight time frame.

"The sheriff's department has provided assistance with stakeouts on several key Jones people that Agent Knight has identified as part of Jones's inner circle," Dean said. "By that I mean individuals involved in Jones's criminal enterprises. They may be in danger from whoever killed Jones, or are already part of the UNSUB's group. We don't know who is working for this guy locally, or if everyone he brought in are foreign nationals."

Sonia added, "One thing you need to understand about human trafficking is that it's solely about the money. Twenty minor girls here for this brothel, forty teenage boys for this war. They also deal with special orders, so if a wealthy 'client' wants a virgin, the sellers will find one to desired specifications." Sonia drained her water and looked uneasy. Dean wished that for just a minute, he could get Sonia alone and . . . just let her know that he was there to listen. Her past as a victim of these crimes was no secret. She had testified in court against those who had held her captive, and had provided key information that had helped law enforcement in figuring out some of the tricks and lures criminals employed. At this moment, however, she seemed so forlorn and lost, though by the looks on the faces of the other cops in the room, Dean was the only one who had noticed.

"We're pulling out all the stops for the next forty-eight hours. In addition to monitoring Jones's security, we are closely tracking his head lobbyist."

"Lobbyist?" Azevedo questioned.

"Craig Gleason is under suspicion as an accessory, but we're keeping that under wraps. Agent Knight and I interviewed him earlier about Jones's clientele and both of us got bad vibes from the guy. It could be that he knows about the money laundering, but not the human trafficking. He's hiding something. Agent Callahan is digging into Gleason's background and monitoring his whereabouts. So far, after our meeting this afternoon, he let the XCJ staff go home early, but he's still in the office."

"Maybe he's dead," Montgomery quipped. "There seem to be a lot of bodies popping up today."

"We actually considered that," Sonia said, "and put an undercover agent in the building. So far, Gleason is still alive."

Dean added, "He has clients and the legislature is in session tonight. It's entirely possible that Gleason is working. With Jones dead, he's also probably getting a lot of calls."

"When was that released?" Trace asked. "We only confirmed it late this afternoon."

"We released the information about Jones's death in time for the five o'clock news," Dean said. "After consulting with Dr. Vigo, Richardson and Warner agreed that holding the information would empower the killer. Giving it to the media puts more pressure on him, which increases the chance he'll make a major mistake."

Dr. Vigo's voice came from the speakerphone. "That's important," he said. "This isn't a guy you can easily rattle. Any move we make, he's already thought about and has planned a half dozen possible responses. But the more pressure on him, the fewer options he has. Only when he feels trapped will he do something reckless, which increases our chances of catching him. Every time we take away a choice, we ratchet up his stress level. There is, however, a problem with this approach."

"What?" Sonia asked.

"He'll kill without thought if it gets him out of immediate danger or perceived danger. The more stress he's under, the more paranoid he'll get. This means he may go after more of Jones's people or anyone blocking his end goal. While the benefit to us is that he's more apt to make a major mistake, we should not underestimate him."

"Great. Don't underestimate someone we don't know," Sonia said.

"Exactly. I didn't say it would be easy."

After Dr. Vigo hung up, the rest of the team laid out their plans for the next day. Sonia finally looked at her phone—someone had been trying to call her for the last ten minutes, but it was an unfamiliar number. She dialed her voice mail.

"Dammit, Sonia, I need to talk to you right now. Call me back. It's Simone Charles."

Sonia's stomach did a little flip as she thought that something had happened to Riley or their unconscious "Ann." She excused herself and called Simone.

"It's about friggin' time," Simone snapped.

"I've been busy."

"Me, too. You'll never believe it."

"What?"

"I was going to make you guess, but that was fifteen minutes ago so I'll just lay it out. I'm at the Sacramento County Coroner's Office and am looking at two bullets that match perfectly. Okay, I'm not a ballistics expert but I can see the similarities under the microscope."

"What bullets?"

"The unknown vic pulled from the river and Kendra Vega. And—"

"Anticlimactic, Simone," Sonia cut her off, wanting to get back to the meeting. "We already suspected that the two double homicides were connected."

"You interrupted the best part."

"Sorry," she mumbled and rubbed her head. She sat down at the nearest cubicle. She needed to find some Tylenol or something. She glanced at the desktop. The tidy employee had classic cartoon strips pinned precisely on the thick, rough fabric walls, humorous quips and scenes from "The Far Side," "Blondie," and "Peanuts," some yellowed with age. A corkboard held a collage of pictures, most of them three happy blond girls of varying ages. Laughing. At the zoo. Eating ice cream. Being hugged. Being loved.

Sonia's chest heaved and she bit back the self-pity that threatened her calm professionalism. It wasn't these kids' fault that she hadn't had a normal childhood. It wasn't their fault they had a loving mother and father who wanted to spend time with them. She was blessed with an adoptive family who loved her, and she was grateful for them, but sometimes when she thought of all the children who never had that support, never had the hugs, the unconditional love . . . She thought of Ann lying in the hospital after being raped and strangled and left for dead. She might be all of sixteen. Who were her parents? Had they sold her or had she been kidnapped like Charlie's Ashley Fox? Where was she from? Was she going to make it? Could she have a normal life? Would she find a family like the Knights or be sent back to where she came from?

"Hey, I can't believe you're that speechless."

"I'm sorry."

"So?"

"So what?"

"Damn, you didn't even hear the news. I can't believe it!"

"I'm distracted. I'm sorry, Simone, it's been a tough day."

"Okay, I'll cut you some slack. The head forensic pathologist performed the autopsy after hours on Jones instead of waiting until the morning, knowing that this case is red-hot. So get this: his bullets don't match. Not one of the five match the unknown vic or Mrs. Vega."

Sonia straightened. "You're positive?"

"Of course I'm positive. They're not even the same caliber. Jones was shot with nine-millimeter slugs; the other two vics with forty-five caliber hollow-points. And based on the angle of the entry wounds and knowing that Jones was shot in the parking lot, I assumed that both men were standing face-to-face. I did some preliminary calculations using the county lab, and I'm pretty confident that the killer is between five foot nine and five foot eleven."

"You're incredible."

"So I've been told. I have more."

"Give it to me." Sonia grabbed a notepad from a neat

stack in the corner and opened the top drawer for a pen as she listened to Simone.

But as the criminalist spoke, Sonia froze. She was speechless.

"Did you hear me?" Simone asked.

"Are you one hundred percent positive the knives match?"

"Well, technically, ninety-nine point three percent positive. But I'm looking at both of them now."

"I'll call you back. Thank you."

Two minutes later, Sonia stepped back into the war room as Dean was finishing up his explanation of how he suspected Jones was laundering money. He glanced at her as he said, "We need to tread carefully with regards to Rio Diablo. We have no jurisdiction on their land and will have to work with the multitribe council to gain even minimal access."

Trace Anderson looked at Sonia and said, "Something happened."

"I just spoke to Simone Charles from Sac P.D. She confirmed that Mrs. Vega and the first victim found in the river were killed with the same gun; however, Jones was killed with a different gun. Time of death is the same. The blood evidence collected at the scene indicates that Jones was killed in the parking lot and carried to the edge of the dock where he was dropped into the river. The second victim was shot on the dock and fell into the water. There wasn't much blood, so he must have been near the edge."

"Like walking the plank," Trace said.

"Simone also said, based on the angle of the wounds, whoever killed Jones was between five foot nine and five foot eleven. They shot him three times point-blank in the chest. When Jones fell, he was shot two more times, once in the chest—it went through at a completely different angle—and once in the head.

"The second victim was killed with a different gun *and* likely a different killer," Sonia continued. "The second victim was six foot two inches and his killer was about the same size. He wasn't dead when he hit the water. He drowned, though the two gunshot wounds would have been fatal."

Dean said, "So our top guy has a henchman? That makes sense."

"There's more. The knife used to kill Greg Vega is unique. In fact, though the company has several factories around the world and in the United States, this particular knife is only manufactured in Argentina."

Sam Callahan said, "Please tell me there were custom initials or engraving that leads directly to the owner."

Sonia glanced at him. "We're lucky, but not *that* lucky."

"How are we lucky? Are we going to be able to get the database of buyers from the company? In the U.S., sure, but in another country?"

"I sent an email to my boss to work on it," Sonia said. "But here's the big news: the knife used in the hospital attack on Officer Riley Knight, my brother, is almost identical to the knife recovered from Vega. The same company, and only made in Argentina. Which means that Ann, the Jane Doe at the hospital, is connected to *this* case."

Suddenly, Sonia yelped and everyone stared at her. Dean crossed over to her, but even his commanding presence couldn't stop the fear from invading every cell in her body. "Andres. Andres is connected to Jones, and he's from Argentina. What if the killers are looking for him? He's at my parents' house. Oh, God—" she ran from the war room, punching numbers on her cell phone as she went.

CHAPTER
NINETEEN

Sonia had never been so relieved to see anyone than when she ran into her parents' house and saw them sitting at the kitchen table with Andres, their German shepherd curled at their feet. They were playing cards, but both Owen and Marianne looked strained after Sonia's phone call. Owen wore his holster and gun, which he hadn't put on since he'd retired five years ago.

She hugged all three of them in turn. "Okay. Okay." She took a deep breath.

Dean stepped into the kitchen. "The grounds are clear."

"Did you meet FBI Agent Dean Hooper at the hospital yesterday?" Sonia asked her parents.

"Briefly," Owen said. He extended his hand. "Owen Knight. My wife, Marianne. And Andres."

"Pleased to meet you. I wish it were under better circumstances."

Owen asked, "Are you sure you're not overreacting, Sonia? From what you said you're making some huge leaps to arrive at the conclusion that we're in danger."

"I don't care if the risk is less than one percent, that's still too great with people like this." Sonia scratched the German shepherd's ears. Sarge sensed she was tense and stood beside her like a sentry. Petting him calmed her, and in response the former K-9 relaxed as well. She wished she had a dog, but with her erratic hours she'd feel guilty leaving a pet home alone.

"I called in a bodyguard," Sonia said. When her dad was about to protest, she put her hand up. "Please, Dad. This is serious. The next forty-eight hours are going to heat up. With Riley out of commission and Max in Afghanistan, there's no one else here to keep an eye out. His name is Duke Rogan. He's the brother of a friend of mine."

"Rogan," Owen said flatly. "You mean Kane Rogan."

Sonia's father had never liked Kane, nor did he approve of his daughter's longtime friendship with him. Kane was a man who, like Charlie Cammarata, had forged his own path in the world and played by no one's rules. The difference, a crucial difference, was that Kane Rogan never put anyone but himself at risk.

Owen Knight believed absolutely in the rule of law. He didn't like that Kane had influence over Sonia.

Sonia trusted few people, but Kane was on her list. When she'd called Duke Rogan as Dean sped through the streets from FBI headquarters to her parents' house, Duke had said, "Kane told me you might call, and that if you did I was to drop everything. I'm at your service, fair lady."

A knock on the door interrupted the tension. Dean offered to answer it and left the kitchen.

"Dad," Sonia said quietly, "Kane is one of the good guys. I wouldn't trust him if he weren't, you know that."

Marianne spoke up. "Your dad is just concerned about the long-distance relationship. When you love someone who won't give up his career to be with you—"

"What?" Sonia exclaimed. "You think—" and she

laughed. God, it felt good to laugh. Maybe she laughed a little too hard, a little too long, but it was either laugh or be worn down by the intensity of facing the potential threat to her family by a ruthless killer who had already killed four people, including her informant.

Dean walked in with two men.

One looked like a younger version of Kane Rogan—in fact, much like the Kane Sonia had met ten years ago. But it was the older, taller Rogan, with hair so deeply red it could have been mistaken for dark brown, who had to be Duke Rogan. His bright blue eyes were framed by laugh lines that became more pronounced when he smiled at Sonia's laughter, revealing the same solitary Rogan dimple that the darker, brooding Kane also had.

"Duke?" Sonia said, extending her hand.

Duke took her hand, but pulled her into a hug. "Kane speaks highly of you," he said. "And as you know, he doesn't praise widely."

"I can attest to that," the other man said.

Sonia turned to the black-haired Rogan. He must be the youngest Rogan brother "Sean?"

"At your service." He smiled, with two dimples, and gave a slight bow.

Duke said, "I thought under the circumstances two bodyguards were better than one."

"I really appreciate your help."

Duke shook Owen's hand, then Marianne's and finally Andres's. Andres was overwhelmed and trembling. Sonia spoke to him softly in Spanish. "It's going to be okay. These are my friends. They'll make sure you're safe."

"How is this going to work?" Owen asked, still standing, trying, Sonia realized, to keep authority and control over his house. She felt awful that she'd never fully explained her relationship with Kane to her parents, but she'd never thought to. That her dad had believed she was pining for an unattainable mercenary made her realize how little about her personal life she shared with him, not that there was much to tell.

Sonia appreciated that Duke had assessed the situation quickly and correctly, and said, "Sir, I think you should walk me through the house, pointing out the strengths and weaknesses of your home security. I'd like Sean to stay upstairs with your wife and the boy, and you and I can monitor the perimeter."

Owen nodded. "Our alarm system is a good one," he said.

"Terrific. Security systems are my specialty. I'm not a full-time bodyguard, only when asked by friends of the family." He winked at Sonia. While he could act serious, Sonia realized that Duke was far more fun-loving than his older brother. "In fact, my primary responsibility with our company—Rogan-Caruso Protective Services—is providing electronic security to local businesses. I designed the systems for the university as well as the new biotech research lab in Auburn. I might have a few tricks to beef up your alarm system for the duration."

"I heard about that lab." Owen sounded both impressed and interested.

Sonia breathed easier. "You have my contact information. I'm headed home because we have an early day tomorrow."

"It's already after eight. You haven't stopped working in days," Marianne said. "I kept some stew on the stove. Please let me warm it up for you and Agent Hooper."

"Mom, you don't—" she saw the determined look on her mother's face. "Okay." She glanced at Dean. He was looking at her . . . oddly. As if he could see under her professional shield. She cleared her throat, feeling scrutinized and suddenly nervous. "My mom is a terrific cook."

"I'm famished," Dean said and sat down. He picked up the deck of cards. "What are you playing?"

"We were teaching Andres crazy eights."

Dean smiled. "How about five-card draw?" He turned to Andres and said to him in Spanish, "Would you like to learn how to play poker?"

Andres's eyes lit up. "I know how to play poker."

"Well, let's get a game on."

Owen Knight left the room for a moment and came back with a box of poker chips. "A penny a chip."

"You've gotten cheap, Dad," Sonia said.

"We have federal law enforcement in the kitchen, I don't want to be under indictment for illegal gambling."

"I'll grant you immunity tonight," Dean said.

Dean watched Sonia interact with her family. She was still a bit on edge, but the events of the day, starting with Charlie Cammarata breaking into her house at three-thirty that morning, had to have worn her down. The adrenaline from the fear for her family had been replaced by relief, and now she was simply exhausted. But content. She seemed to draw both strength and comfort from the Knights. He'd seen how close she was to her brother, Riley, and now he realized that Sonia was all business, all the time, except when she was with her family.

She wasn't playing cards with them, but stood at the counter and ate stew, chatting with Sean Rogan who

was young—maybe twenty-two, twenty-three. Duke
Rogan sat with Owen, Dean, and the ten-year-old Andres as they played a couple rounds of five-card draw.

Dean had a good childhood, but he wasn't particularly close with his family. His dad died years ago; his
brother, now married, lived in San Diego, three thousand miles from Dean's home in D.C. He and Will had
been pals growing up, but time and distance and demanding careers had separated them. Then their mother
relocated to Florida and spent half the year traveling
with her seniors' group. They connected in person once
or twice a year, and Dean had thought that was good
enough.

Seeing Sonia with her family made him realize that it
wasn't. He should have made more of an effort to stay
in contact with Will. The last time Dean had seen his
brother was over a year ago, at his wedding. Dean had
taken a week's vacation, but cut it short by two days because of a break in one of his cases. That was two days
he could have spent with his brother.

He envied the closeness Sonia had with her family.
And he certainly now saw her in a different light. This
smiling, relaxed Sonia was the Sonia hidden inside the
fiery, passionate ICE agent. When she let her hair down,
she was happy. Because she had her family to support
and love her come hell or high water.

Dean caught Sonia watching him playing poker. He
couldn't read her mind, but she didn't avert her eyes. He
was drawn to her in ways he shouldn't be thinking
about, physically attracted but also with feelings that
went deeper than lust. Feelings he shouldn't be experi-
encing. She was a colleague, not a potential girlfriend.
Still, he couldn't help that he was seriously attracted.

Sonia Knight was beautiful, but she was also far more than a pretty face and hot body. She was smart and dedicated and driven. She didn't let up on the job, she didn't pretend to be anything but what she was. She had confidence, but in that confidence she was able to listen to others and allow others to help. Yet there was a vulnerability inside that showed itself only when she was worried. About Ann in the hospital, or the Vegas, or her family.

Her mouth parted slightly, full lips begging to be kissed. She glanced away with a hint of a blush tinting her tan, regal cheeks. What was she thinking? The same private thoughts that Dean had? That he wanted to be alone with her? That he wanted to touch her? He wanted to do more than touch her.

Her profile was elegant, aristocratic. Her nose long and slender, her neck even longer. Her large breasts were barely restrained beneath her standard black T-shirt. She'd taken off her light jacket; it was draped over a kitchen stool. Her stomach was flat, her waist narrow, and her long, long legs encased in well-worn, fitted jeans.

Ignoring the cards in his hand, Dean soaked all of her in. He noted that though Sonia was relaxed, she hadn't stopped moving, a bundle of nervous energy. She helped her mother rinse out the bowls and put the remainder of the stew away, then wiped down the counters, though to Dean they looked clean enough to eat on. And when that was done, she grabbed a broom from the cabinet and swept the hardwood floor.

He wondered if she ever stopped moving, even when she slept. He wondered if he'd get a chance to find out.

She caught him staring again.

"I think you just lost to a ten-year-old," she said with a smirk.

Dean returned his focus to the game. Andres was grinning, as were Duke and Owen. "Full house, right?" said the young card shark.

"Sure is." Dean pushed his chips over to Andres. "Well, I'm out. We have a long day tomorrow. The stew was delicious, Mrs. Knight."

"Thank you, Agent Hooper. You're welcome anytime."

Duke walked outside with Sonia and Dean. "Don't worry about your family," Duke told Sonia. "I'll keep them safe."

"Thank you," she answered, though Dean knew she'd continue to worry until this case was over.

"No thanks necessary." Duke took her hands in his and said with intensity, "You be careful, too. Kane said these people are vicious."

"I'm always careful," Sonia said.

"And I have her back," Dean added, not quite sure what the relationship was between Sonia and the Rogans—specifically, the elusive Kane Rogan—and fearing that maybe she wasn't a free woman.

He aimed to find out. Tonight.

CHAPTER TWENTY

Dean walked Sonia into her small, tidy bungalow. There was a small light on in every room and Sonia felt the need to explain, though she sounded a bit sheepish. "I don't like walking into a dark house. I have night-lights on a timer."

Though Dean knew what Sonia meant, he let her save face and said, "I don't blame you. Smart, from a security perspective." Her bungalow wasn't homey and well lived in like the Knight family house two blocks away. Dean suspected Sonia didn't do much but sleep here, but it had a certain charm in the details: a collection of stuffed teddy bears dominated the love seat in the corner of the living room, lacy curtains covered generic venetian blinds, and perhaps the most revealing, an entire wall in the dining room was decorated with photographs of Sonia with her family.

But he was surprised that she didn't have a security system.

"Why don't you have an alarm?"

"I never felt the need for one," she admitted. "Until now. But I'm okay."

"You won't mind if I stay here tonight, will you? There are two agents outside, but—"

"Wait." She stared at him pointedly. "You have two agents watching my house?"

"I was going to tell you," Dean fibbed. "It's been a busy day." Sonia was obviously irritated but too tired to argue. "Get some sleep," he told her. "I'll kick back on the couch."

"I have a guest room," she said.

"I'd rather be out here."

"I'll keep you company for a while." She went into the kitchen and called, "Thirsty?"

"I'm fine." He looked at the pictures on the wall. Sonia seemed to have been born a teenager. There were no childhood photos of her.

She came back with a half-glass of white wine and sipped, standing next to him. "That's Max," she said, pointing to a tall dark-haired young Marine in full dress. "He's in Afghanistan right now. Career military."

"Good for him, and for our country. I was in the Marines for three years."

"*Semper Fi,*" Sonia said with pride. She gestured to another picture. "That's Riley and me at graduation. I'm a year older, but because—you know, my past—I had to play catch-up."

"You're close to your brother."

"He calls me his twin."

She sounded so forlorn.

"Your family is in good hands," he told her, clearing his throat.

"I know Duke and his brother will keep them safe."

"The Knights are good people. I can see why you're close to them."

"Owen and Marianne have unlimited love and compassion. I couldn't have picked better parents."

She didn't say anything for a long minute as she stared at her photographs. "You know I'm adopted, right? You know about my history."

"Some," Dean said. "You don't have to talk about it if it makes you uncomfortable."

"Good."

She didn't sound like it was good.

"Sonia?" he asked quietly. "You okay?"

"What exactly do you know?" she whispered.

She sounded scared and defensive. Dean refused to be anything but honest with Sonia. "When you were thirteen you escaped from traffickers who planned to sell you into prostitution. You bravely testified against them, foreshadowing the strong, smart, determined woman you are today."

Her voice cracked when she said, "You make it sound heroic."

"It was heroic," he said. He took the wineglass from her hand and put it on the table, staring at her in silence until she looked him in the eye. "I have never met a woman I've admired half as much as you."

She opened her mouth to say something, then closed it, sheepish. The tip of her tongue ran across her lips. The physical response hit Dean all at once.

Sonia turned and walked into the adjoining living room, her back to him. He followed.

He wanted to hold her, run his tongue over those soft, red lips, taste the wine on her tongue, taste Sonia. Dean wasn't impulsive in anything he did, especially with relationships. Each one had been carefully planned. All the women picked for their calm reasoning, their self-sufficiency, their intelligence. Dean's love life was always separate from his job, and his job always came first. He did nothing spontaneously, he'd never wanted to. Until now.

It was all he could do to control the unfamiliar primal urge to grab Sonia and kiss her. Sonia was anything but calm and cool. She was smart and self-sufficient, but hotheaded, impulsive, and passionate. He couldn't get her out from under his skin. She'd infected him with a desire he could barely keep under wraps. He was pretty damn sure he didn't want to fight it anymore.

"Sonia—" he began and stopped.

She turned to face him, their eyes locking. Tears had dampened her lashes and a powerful urge to hold and protect her almost brought Dean to his knees.

"Sonia?" he said quietly, reaching for her, touching her cheek, moving his fingers to her neck, her shoulder. "What's wrong?"

Her voice cracked. "I feel like my past is coming back to hurt the only people I truly care about."

He picked her up and carried her to the couch, sitting with her in his lap, their closeness intoxicating. This wasn't planned or logical, it probably wasn't even the right thing to do. But Dean couldn't imagine this was wrong, not the way he felt or how Sonia felt in his arms.

Her arms went around his neck and she leaned in with a sigh that sent a jolt of carnal heat through his body. She was pressed so closely against him she had to know that he wanted her. She felt so good, so right; the aroma of flowers and sweat, femininity and strength. He brushed her thick, wavy hair away from her face, an intimate gesture, then cupped his hand under her chin. He ran his thumb the length of a faint scar across her cheek.

Over her lips. Her mouth parted, her breath warm as
she drew his index finger in with her tongue. She
watched his face, and Dean absently wondered what she
saw. Did she see that he found her amazing, wondrous,
and beautiful? She sucked on his finger, then released it.
A quiet groan rumbled in his chest.

He couldn't imagine being anywhere in the world but
right here, right now.

Sonia held Dean's gaze, her face inches from his. She
was practically shaking from restraining herself. She'd
wanted him since the moment he'd walked into her
house. At first, she thought it was her need to unwind,
release the tension of the day, but when he looked at
her—when he reached out and touched her—something
had shifted inside. She didn't want this to end. She
wanted to know Dean. Intimately. Not only tonight, but
tomorrow. As long as it took to rid her mind and body
of this wanton desire for this man. Outside of her family, she'd never felt like she knew anyone well enough to
make them part of her life. But in just a few short days,
Sonia could anticipate Dean's thoughts and ideas, she
craved his deep voice in her ear; she admired his logical
approach to his job; the way he listened to everyone but
always stood by his decision. He was a man of deep
thought and decisive action, and there was nothing sex-
ier than a man who knew what he wanted and went
after it.

The way Dean was looking at her right now told her
he wanted her as much as she wanted him.

Their lips touched.

Her breath hitched as soon as his mouth met hers.
This was no sweet kiss; her hands were in his hair, hold-

ing his head to hers, her mouth opening to draw in his tongue. Urgent. Needful. The kiss wasn't enough, she wanted more, she needed all of him now. And by the way his lap danced beneath her, only her jeans and his slacks kept the heat between them from combusting. That he wanted all of her just as much spurred her forward.

Her hands couldn't touch anything but his head from this position, which was no good at all. Not when this incredible man had a long, lean, rock-hard body that begged to be caressed. She sat up, not taking her mouth from his, her hands never stopping. Touching his hair, his ears, his face rough with a day's growth of beard.

Sonia straddled him and impatiently unbuttoned his tailored shirt. Dean dressed his ripped body well, and she loved the smooth, rich feel of the Egyptian cotton. But she wanted what was underneath far more than she wanted to play with the fine material. She pulled the shirttails from his slacks, then shoved the sleeves down his arms. He was trapped beneath her and she savored the playful restraint. His scent was intoxicating, and she buried her face in his neck and breathed deeply.

She kissed his throat, ran her tongue up his neck until she reached his lips. He claimed her lips. His arms fought with the sleeves of his shirt, but she held him down, returning the kiss with as much intensity as he gave her, then pulled away, licking his strong, square jawline, all the way to his ear. She drew in his lobe and Dean couldn't restrain the guttural groan she felt deep in his chest, felt it in his lap as he pressed hard against her. He fought again to pull his arms from his sleeves, the friction of his struggle sending shivers up and down her spine. There was no turning back now; nor did she want to. From the moment she had set eyes on him, she'd felt this deep and startling connection; maybe at that moment her subconscious knew this was their fate.

His right hand pulled free and he wrapped it around her waist, holding her tightly against him as his mouth did the same thing to her as she'd done to him. His breath was warm against her flushed neck, but he didn't stop there. He pulled his left arm free and with one fluid movement had her T-shirt off, tossing it somewhere behind her. She pulled his face to her breasts and he licked everywhere her flesh was exposed. Licking and suckling and kissing until her mouth was dry and her body wet. With one hand he unhooked her bra and she shook herself free. She pushed her hands beneath his undershirt and massaged his deltoids, relishing his hard, fit body. Damn, but she loved a man who took care of himself, who kept his muscles finely tuned.

"Oh, God, Sonia." Dean's fingers skimmed over her breasts, his thumbs circling her nipples until her chest heaved and perspiration clung to every inch of her flesh. Then his mouth claimed one breast and suddenly she couldn't move, she couldn't think, as Dean focused all his attention on that one part of her body. An involuntary gasp escaped her throat, and the sound urged him on. He switched his mouth to the other breast, while his hands grabbed her ass and squeezed. The dual attention had Sonia on the edge, ready to go over. She fought with his buckle. There was a time to go slow and savor every new sensation, but she didn't want slow and easy; she wanted fast and hard. And she wanted it now.

Dean could have spent an hour on Sonia's incredible, responsive breasts, but as soon as her hands unzipped his pants and reached inside, grasping him firmly, he groaned and pulled back, willing himself to stay in control and not let loose like a frat boy. Staying in control with a woman like Sonia in his lap was not easy. Hell, it was damned impossible.

She pulled his wallet from the back of his pants and handed it to him. "Tell me you're prepared."

He would have laughed if she didn't look so damn serious, her skin flushed, her rapid breathing making her chest heave erotically. "I was a Boy Scout." His voice was rougher, deeper than usual. "Go ahead."

She opened his billfold and frowned as she checked the few slots. Then she smiled like a siren when behind his driver's license she found one foil package.

She stood up and he thought she wanted to go to the bedroom, but when he tried to stand she pushed him back down. "Stay right where you are."

She pulled his pants off him, her hands never stopping. Her body practically vibrated with electricity. She stepped out of her jeans and lacy panties and sheathed him herself, her fingers playing while at work. He grunted, then pulled her mouth to his and kissed her long and hard. Over and over, bringing in her tongue, and giving her his. She responded in kind, straddled him, and with one deep thrust pushed herself onto his cock with a high-pitched gasp from her lips as she sat on him.

Dean watched Sonia's flushed face, her hair damp, one side tucked behind an ear, the rest loose and wild, making her look both sexy and wholesome at the same time.

In this position, he couldn't control their lovemaking; he wanted to show her how much he cared, how much he craved spending hours getting to know every inch of her. But Sonia wanted him now, impatient and passionate, and after only a moment of stillness that seemed foreign for her, she started moving her hips up and down, her breasts rubbing against his bare chest, and Dean lost all conscious thought as he grabbed her hips and held on.

Sonia was a passionate woman in everything she did, but Dean took her beyond passion into deep lust, a need so great that she didn't want to let him go. She moved fast and deep, feeling him inside and outside of her, his hands firmly holding her hips, pushing her down on him, as they developed a rhythm that promised a quick, powerful release. The heat inside her boiled over, and she clenched her muscles to prolong it, in contrast to her hips, which moved faster, pushed harder.

"Sonia," Dean whispered roughly.

She opened her eyes and he kissed her hard, then held her on his lap and thrust his hips upward, his body pressed hard against her most sensitive spot as he adjusted their position just slightly. His whole body stiffened beneath her; her back arched as she lost control, her orgasm developing a mind of its own and shocking her with its intensity. She cried out, and Dean pulled her to him as they rode out the waves until they completely subsided.

She collapsed, panting, parched, and completely satiated. Dean kissed her neck, her hair, her face, her lips. He entwined her hands in his and squeezed them.

"God, Sonia," he murmured. "I wanted you since I first saw you."

She saw he spoke the truth, in his unwavering gaze, heard the truth in his firm voice. Warmth spread through her body and soul, a sense of peace, of belonging. Could she have found her soul mate when she wasn't even looking? In her entire adult life, she'd had half a dozen relationships lasting months, but had never felt this close, this intimate, this loved.

She touched Dean's face, kissed him lightly on the lips, put her forehead to his and sighed.

Dean sensed a change inside Sonia, and he was at a loss for words. He was embarking on something new, something incredible, and didn't want to blow it. Not with Sonia. This wasn't a woman to be put aside for all but the few hours of the month he was willing to put his job on the back burner. She would be part of everything he did, work and play. He didn't realize until then that he'd wanted someone he could share everything with. He'd always been reserved and demanded his privacy, but with Sonia he could bare everything.

A moment later, Sonia eased herself off his lap and held out her hand with a sly grin. "You're not sleeping on the couch, Agent Hooper."

He grabbed her hand. "I'm not?"

She yanked him up off the couch. He wasn't expecting it, but Sonia was stronger than she looked. He stood easily, enjoying how her hard, defined muscles bulged just enough to give her the strength to lift him. She looked absolutely glorious standing in front of him completely naked.

"I have a very comfortable bed." She glanced at her watch. "Not even midnight. My alarm goes off at six-thirty, I think maybe we can sacrifice thirty or forty minutes of shut-eye. You're already pretty hot-looking, you don't need much beauty sleep."

Dean enjoyed this rare playful side of Sonia Knight.

He kissed her, then picked her up like a bride. "Direct me to your chambers."

Her eyes brightened, and a curve of a smile had him wanting to take her away from everything and into a private world where he could discover her deepest thoughts and dreams, and fulfill her most intimate fantasies.

She pointed down the short hall, her finger waving lazily to the right, then lifted her head to kiss him.

He followed her direction and pushed open the door on the right, carrying her across the threshold. Her bedside lamp was on low, casting long shadows across her lacy white bedspread. The lazy movement of her ceiling fan overhead cut swatches in the dim light, but something was interfering with the perfectly symmetrical blades.

They both looked up at the same time. Sonia stifled a scream and Dean put her down as he reached for his gun that wasn't there.

But a gun wouldn't have done any good.

Hanging by a thin string from the edge of a fan blade was Greg Vega's missing tongue.

CHAPTER
TWENTY-ONE

Sonia watched the FBI Evidence Response Team process her house as she sat stiffly in the passenger seat of Dean's car. Dean had insisted on his people taking jurisdiction, and she didn't blame him—the FBI would give priority to her case, not just because it was related to an ongoing federal investigation, but because she was a federal agent targeted by a killer.

Her house. Her case.

She hated feeling like a victim again, and worked on battling the fear that came with the invasion of her sanctuary.

Her cell phone rang. She answered immediately when she saw Duke Rogan's caller I.D. "You're on your way?" she asked.

"Left the hospital five minutes ago. Had no trouble getting Riley released. Sean is tailing us, making sure no one is following, and one of your brother's friends is playing tag team with Sean. I'll get them to the safe house in Lake Tahoe without trouble, I promise."

A huge weight lifted off her shoulders. As long as her family was safe, Sonia could focus on finding Greg Vega's killer. Already her fight was returning.

"Thanks, Duke."

"What about you?'

She knew what he meant. "It's my job."

"It's not your job to get killed."

"I have no intention of getting killed. I will find and arrest this prick. He picked the wrong person to fuck with."

Dean slid into the driver's seat, keeping his door open. Tension filled the car, his body so tight she could feel his anger. She wrapped up the conversation with Duke and told Dean, "Duke Rogan has my family and is heading for Tahoe."

He said, "The agents I had sitting on the house swear no one entered. But they didn't arrive until six-fifteen this evening."

"You think the killer broke in before then?"

"Hell if I know. There's evidence of a picked lock at the kitchen door. It's partly hidden from the street. But ERT hasn't been able to pick up any footprints in the backyard to suggest the killer hopped a fence out of sight. The only activity in the house was when your lights went on at eight p.m."

"They're on a timer."

"ERT is finishing up here. They'll confirm the tongue belongs to Vega—"

"Like there's a doubt."

"We still need confirmation. They've printed the place, searched extensively for any other surprises, but so far nothing. The UNSUB wore gloves, left nothing obvious behind. They're pulling trace evidence and fibers to see what they can find." He caught her eye. "I told Brian Stone, the team leader, everything."

Sonia blushed and averted her eyes. She was embarrassed. Not because she and Dean had had sex in her living room, but because it was no longer a private, intimate moment. "I'm sorry."

Dean grabbed her hand and squeezed it tightly, so tightly she had to face him. He said, "Don't apologize. I'm not sorry. I really hope you aren't, either."

She shook her head. "No," she whispered.

He relaxed. "I had to tell him the truth so they don't pursue a false lead. Stone is discreet. He's a former Marine, our head firearms instructor, and he directs our SWAT team."

"Why is he here with ERT?"

"Half our agents are ERT certified. We pull them for their expertise, and Stone understands psychological warfare."

"The killer hung the tongue to scare me. It doesn't take a rocket scientist to figure that out."

"But they broke into your house to do it. Your bedroom. Where you should feel the safest. They want to wear you down, break you, so you make a mistake."

"Then they're going to be waiting a long time. I'm not broken over this. Pissed off, a little upset, feeling damn guilty I didn't see the danger Vega was in. But not broken."

He reached up and caressed her cheek. She closed her eyes and willed her body to relax.

"When can I check into the hotel? I'm beat and"—she looked through the windshield as three agents emerged from her house—"I really hate watching my house being invaded by your people. Or anyone."

"Ten minutes, okay? And you're not going to any hotel. You're coming home with me."

He jumped out of the car and shut the door. If he thought she was going to argue about it, he was wrong.

*   *   *

Dean watched Sonia sleep.

It was barely dawn, but Dean could only sleep a few hours before his internal clock woke him at five-thirty Friday morning.

He'd brought Sonia back to his sublet apartment. The FBI agent he was renting from was due back after the Fourth of July, four weeks from now, and Dean had expected to have his case against Xavier Jones wrapped up long before then.

Things had changed. Not only was Jones dead and the entire case spinning out of control, but he didn't want to leave. Specifically, he didn't want to leave Sonia.

Sonia had fallen asleep on the way to Dean's apartment. She'd barely woken up as Dean led her up the four flights of stairs and into bed. She'd brought an overnight bag and barely managed to brush her teeth and pull on a tank top before collapsing into bed. Dean laid next to her and went out as soon as he heard her evenly breathing.

She was still asleep, but she'd kicked off the covers and lay sprawled on her stomach, taking up over half the bed. She had just as much energy while sleeping as she did awake, but once she'd settled in this position an hour ago, she hadn't moved.

Light crept through the half-closed blinds and cast long, bright orange shadows across her near-naked body. Dean stirred below his waist as his gaze moved up Sonia's lean body. He wasn't going to wake her for sex, but he hoped she woke up on her own before they had to rush to leave.

Dean noticed a tattoo on Sonia's upper arm. It wasn't cute or feminine, but crude and rough. He leaned forward, his chest tightening when he realized the mark wasn't a tattoo. Three stars had been burned into her skin. He gently touched them, wishing he could take away the pain she'd suffered. Then he saw a faded scar on her shoulder blade, partly concealed by her tank top. He pushed the material aside, revealing a dark puckered double circle.

Sonia stiffened, and he realized he'd woken her.

"I'm sorry," he said.

"I know they're ugly, but there's not much I can do about it."

"That's not what I was thinking."

He rolled her over to her back and brushed her hair away from her face. "Who did that to you?"

"Which marks? The circles when I was thirteen, or the stars when I was twenty-four?" She pushed him aside, sat on the edge of the bed, and pulled off her tank top. The circles appeared more like a rounded infinity symbol, four inches long and two inches wide. Long, faint scars crisscrossed her back. Dean could scarcely breathe, rage swelling in proportions he'd never felt before.

She stood, crossed to the bathroom, and shut the door.

Dean swore under his breath. He'd never considered that Sonia had been abused as a child beyond what her father had done . . .

"*. . . or the stars when I was twenty-four?*"

Charlie Cammarata *branded* her? And he hadn't been thrown into jail? Dean hoped he'd never meet the bastard again, because he didn't know if he could stop his fist from connecting with Cammarata's jaw.

He should have realized she'd be sensitive about the scars, but at the same time she'd been so matter-of-fact about her past, he didn't think. He wouldn't hurt Sonia for anything. He hoped she knew that.

When the shower turned on, Dean rose and considered joining Sonia. He'd show her that the marks didn't affect how he felt about her. But thinking about what she had suffered, that her former partner had been involved in her trauma, further enraged him. He didn't want Sonia to think his anger was at all directed toward her, nor did he want her to think that he felt sorry for her. Sonia would not tolerate pity, and he didn't want to give her any excuse to walk out.

Instead, Dean walked down the hall to the kitchen to make coffee. A fluffy white cat improbably named Mouse rubbed his lean body against Dean's legs and meowed loudly. He reached down to scratch Agent Elliott's cat, who instantly began to purr. The deep rumble was surprisingly soothing and Dean began to relax.

"Maybe I should get a cat," he mumbled.

Sonia heard Dean walk away from the bathroom door. She almost wished she'd invited him in, but the embarrassment of her overreacting to Dean touching her scars had her hesitating. She owed him an explanation. First, she'd shower.

Sonia stepped into the icy water to wake up, then turned on the hot water. As the shower warmed, she washed. She shouldn't have been so snippy with Dean about the brand. But even though she thought she'd put what happened behind her, it still hurt to talk about it.

She turned off the water, wrapped a towel around her body, and brushed her hair back into a wet ponytail. When she stepped from the bathroom, she smelled rich coffee in the air, and the white cat meowed a good morning at her. She absently scratched him behind the ears, then pulled fresh jeans and a black ICE T-shirt from her overnight bag. She didn't have much variety in her work attire, but she was always comfortable.

She stepped from the bedroom into the main living area. Dean sat at the small table drinking black coffee and reading the newspaper. He wore nothing but boxers and looked like a Greek god, muscles clearly defined even at rest.

He glanced up when she walked in and smiled sheepishly. "I'm usually a better cook, but I haven't had time to stock up." He gestured to a box of cereal and milk on the table. He was eating an apple. "I have more of these, plus bananas, oranges, strawberries, melon."

"Sounds like heaven to me." She sat down after pouring herself a cup of coffee, added a generous amount of milk to the cup, and sipped. A man who cooks, even if it was just putting out cereal and fruit, was a keeper in her book. She had apples at home. They were squishy and in the bottom of the refrigerator drawer, which looked none too clean.

"I'm sorry," they said simultaneously.

Dean said, "You don't have to talk about it. I shouldn't have said anything."

"No, it's just . . . I put it behind me. I probably didn't deal with it well, didn't want to think about it after the internal affairs investigation and everything that happened ten years ago. I never talk about it. I told Riley after it happened, and he's the only one who knows. Other than Kane, of course."

"Kane," Dean said flatly.

Did he sound jealous?

"Kane saved my life. He's like a brother to me."

She paused, wondering what to say and how to say it.

"Sonia." Dean took her hand. She looked at him, saw the respect in his eyes. No pity, not anger. Just raw affection and honesty. Dean was rock solid. "You don't owe me an explanation. But I want you to know that nothing you say to me will affect how I think of you."

Her chin quivered, and she swallowed and forced herself to toughen up.

"I should start from the beginning, but it's a long story."

"I'm not going anywhere."

Sonia would never forget the night the men came to the village.

"My father was a missionary who traveled from village to village throughout Central and South America teaching the people how to grow crops, how to preserve food. I didn't see him much until my mother died and he returned to Argentina. I was four. He took me with him on his missions, and for nine years we lived in more villages than I can remember. We stayed four to six weeks before moving on. I didn't remember anything from my early childhood, this was the only life I knew. And I liked helping people. I became good at figuring out different languages and dialects. I learned about farming and basic medicine.

"My father was cold. From my earliest memories, he never hugged me or talked to me."

Dean said, "He didn't talk to you?"

She explained. "He didn't have a conversation with me. You know, *How was your day? Did you meet anyone today?* It was all work. *Translate for me. Get out to the field and show them how to pull the vegetables without destroying them.* I did everything he asked, hoping to find favor—hoping he'd love me. He left for weeks at a time. Left me wherever we were. He told me he had business back in Argentina and he would come back for me. Once he left me in a village for ten months. I thought he was dead. I worked three times as hard as anyone because they didn't like me. I was too white, too urban, too . . . I don't know."

"How old were you?"

"Ten. That time. I began to wish he'd never come back, then I'd feel so guilty that I didn't like my own father. I thought he was a good man—someone who helped others—but he hated me. I didn't acknowledge it then, maybe I didn't even understand. I thought he blamed me for my mother's death. He leaves for a mission and six months later returns and she's dead."

"What happened to your mother?"

"She died suddenly. She'd always been sad, and my father told me she had cancer. I didn't understand it then. But one day she was there, the next she wasn't."

Sonia rose from her seat ostensibly to refill her coffee, but she needed to move. She paced the length of the great room, from the kitchen to the living area and back to the kitchen.

"I was thirteen when he sold me. It was the middle of the night. I knew what was happening, but I didn't believe it. Complete denial until he looked at me with contempt and said I had become a liability. That I was too curious."

There's an American saying, Sonia. Curiosity killed the cat. You're damn lucky you're not a cat right now.

"It took nearly two weeks to get to Texas. There were a lot of us, picked up from small towns as we moved north. Some girls came willingly, excited that they were going to America. That was how I found out about my destination. Some of the older girls said they were mail-order brides being delivered to their grooms. Others were going for work. Others didn't talk, they were like me. Sold. Or kidnapped. I knew the eager ones were being lied to, but they didn't believe me or I wasn't convincing. I tried to figure out why my father gave me away—*sold me*—and I didn't know. I thought I'd done something unforgivable, and this was punishment. I blamed myself for something I didn't know I'd done. But deep down I knew he'd never loved me, never wanted me except to do things for him." She laughed bitterly. "I had been a slave and didn't even know it."

"Sonia—"

She didn't look at Dean, couldn't look at him right now. Damn, why was this so hard? Had she convinced herself that she had gotten over the past, only to be lying to herself yet again? Just like she had while growing up with a father who didn't love her?

"One time I tried to escape. We'd passed a church and I knew it was my only chance to find help.

"That's when they whipped me." She thought she was dead. And for a time, she wished they had killed her. But her will to survive was too great. She had to be smarter. Patient. "Then the bastard in charge burned me. I didn't know then that he was branding me on purpose—I thought it was another punishment."

She sipped her coffee, her hands steady even though her stomach quivered.

"Izzy and I were separated from the group and taken to a house in Texas, though I didn't know where we were at the time."

"Who's Izzy?" Dean asked.

"I met her on the truck. I don't know why we were separated from the other girls. Anyway, Izzy and I were locked in a basement. We barely understood each other but we were all we had. I wanted to escape but Izzy had accepted her fate."

Sonia stared out the partly open blinds into the bright sunrise. "Then one of them came down into the basement. He—" she closed her eyes, but when she saw Izzy's dead eyes staring at her, she opened her own. Heart racing, she swallowed uneasily and said in a monotone, "He raped Izzy."

"God, Sonia—"

"Not me. He just wanted me to watch. Told me since I was a virgin I'd make them a lot more money, but this would be my life. He was a brute, so large, so violent and he was hurting her—he killed Izzy. I saw it happening and tried to stop it, but she was already dead."

She turned to Dean. "I killed him. Shot him with his own gun that had slipped from his pants while he raped and murdered my only friend."

"You had no choice."

"I know. I know." She took a deep breath. "Wendell Knight was the Texas Ranger who found me. My adopted dad's brother. Wendell took me in because he didn't want me to face the alternatives—juvenile hall or foster care. Obviously I couldn't be sent home since authorities were looking for my father.

"When he sold me, I thought I'd done something wrong. Thought I deserved it. In fact, for a while, I thought he'd buy me back, that he'd needed the money for something important, but he'd buy me back when he could. That delusion didn't last long.

"After the ring was arrested, Immigration tried to find him and couldn't. I don't know how hard they tried, I don't even know if they believed everything I said. Some of the people I talked to looked at me like it was my fault. Some wanted me to disappear, go back to where I came from. Others wanted to help. I testified in court. It was a small town and everyone knew what had happened."

"I loved Wendell," Sonia said, her voice cracking. She cleared her throat. "He was the father I should have had. Then one day he was gone. Killed in the line of duty."

Dean put his hands on her shoulders. She hadn't noticed that he'd even gotten up from the table. "I'm so sorry," he whispered, rubbing her shoulders, sharing his strength with her. She leaned into him, just for a moment. But she had more to tell.

"Owen and Marianne came for the funeral and asked if I wanted to live in California with them and their two sons. I would have done anything to get away from the rumors and mean kids and the numbing loss I felt. Without Wendell, there was nothing for me in Texas but bad memories."

"They're good people, and they obviously love you." He rubbed his hands up and down her arms.

Sonia smiled warmly. "I'm really lucky. I even went to college. Amazing really, because I never thought I'd have the opportunity. Working for INS was my only goal. I wanted a degree. I wanted to get into the program, and I was going to stop human trafficking. Single-handedly." She stared at the ceiling. "I was young, idealistic, and stupid."

Dean said, "There're a lot of people in our business who start out idealistic. I'm glad."

"But not you." She couldn't picture Dean charging windmills. He was too intense and focused. She turned to face him, saw that he hadn't changed the way he looked at her even after her story. Her body began to relax as if it had a mind of its own. Or maybe it was because Dean took her hands and held them firmly.

"My dad was a beat cop in Chicago. It's all he was," Dead said. "Unlike Owen Knight, who obviously loves his family and spent time with you. My dad was a good cop, but he didn't know how to be a father or a husband. I came into the FBI a little jaded, I suppose. It wasn't my first career choice."

"What was?"

"After getting out of the Marines, I went to college to be a CPA. I was recruited into the FBI. Fifteen years ago, they wanted accountants. And I have a knack for numbers and financial connections." Dean led her back to the table and poured cereal in a bowl for her.

"Fifteen years and you're already assistant director?" She took a bite to make him happy, though she was too wound up to eat.

He waved the achievement away. "It's not just tenure, it's politics. I was successful on a few high-profile investigations early on, rose through the ranks quickly. In a way I wish I hadn't. I prefer the grunt work over being in charge."

"You're a natural leader," Sonia said. "It's obvious."

"So are you."

She shook her head. "I'm learning, but . . ." she stopped. Did she really want to go into this?

Dean took her hand and kissed it. The rising sun cast a filtered array of orange and yellows through the blinds. She'd never felt safer.

Sonia took a breath and said, "When I finished my training, I was assigned to El Paso. Charlie Cammarata was my training agent. We worked together for eighteen months. The first year was my training year; the second year was as his partner.

"I worshipped him, I admit it. He was smart, brave, compassionate. He knew about my past, and said it made me a better person and a better agent. The Knights loved me, but honestly? We never talked about what my father did. For the first time, I felt I *could* talk about it, and Charlie listened. He made me feel powerful. Like I could make a difference. I trusted him.

"Eighteen months after I became an agent, Charlie told me we were going undercover in Costa Rica. The INS wanted two agents to go in to gather intelligence on a human trafficking ring. Both Charlie and I spoke Spanish fluently, and I knew dozens of dialects. All those years living in remote villages, I learned to pick up languages easily. I was excited. This was my first real chance to do something bigger and more important than border patrol.

"What I didn't know was that Charlie had no sanction from the INS. He told them he was taking a vacation. I learned later that he told people that he and I were involved and wanted to take a vacation together." She shook her head. It still angered her how manipulative Charlie had been, and how readily she'd believed him.

"So we were in this bar and I thought we had backup. I was a waitress, and I took great notes. Every night I wrote down names, numbers, towns, destinations, everything I overheard.

"Ten days later, the bar was closing and I was waiting for Charlie to walk me back to the room we'd rented. He didn't show, and my boss in the bar was an asshole. He kicked me out, though it was late and the neighborhood was dicey. Still, I was young and stupid. I had no gun, no identification because Charlie told me that would be a giveaway. He gave me a can of mace and with that in hand, I started walking.

"I was grabbed by a meaty thug not twenty feet from the bar entrance. I maced the guy, then someone else grabbed me from behind, and the next thing I know, I'm in a truck, and we're moving. And there are dozens of girls with me."

"Where was Charlie?"

Sonia closed her eyes. "I didn't know it then, but he'd hidden in the alley and watched the whole thing. I overheard the men saying my brother had sold me to them, that I was a virgin and worth a lot of money. I didn't believe them. Charlie wouldn't do that.

"No one came to rescue me. We were heading south, toward Panama. I thought Charlie was following. He was, but not to save me. He was mapping the route because two months before, a dozen girls from a Costa Rican orphanage had been kidnapped and he didn't know where they were taken, but he knew which ring sold them. He'd sold me into that ring, hoping they'd lead him to the orphans."

"He sold you and didn't tell you his plan?"

She shook her head. "I was stupid."

"No. You were following orders. You were young and you believed your senior agent."

"Maybe, but in hindsight I should have seen it. Don't tell anyone, it's classified, *yada yada*."

"Sonia, don't blame yourself for the crimes of Charlie Cammarata," Dean said firmly.

"I don't. But I do blame myself for being blinded

by someone I trusted and considered a mentor and a friend."

"I think you're being too harsh on yourself."

Maybe Dean was right, but she'd never forget how stupid and terrified she felt when she realized she was once again a prisoner. She continued. "Two nights later, they took us to a farm outside Ustupo. That's when they branded us. All of us. Two, three, or four stars depending on our destination. I learned later that three stars was for a brothel on an island off the coast of Venezuela. Two stars was for a slave-labor camp in Brazil, and four stars was for domestic servants—indentured servants— for some wealthy families in Chile. They like to split the groups up because there's less chance of us bonding and trying to escape if we don't know who we'll be with.

"But because I was a virgin, I had a detour. I was separated from the girls after we were branded and sent to a small town outside Panama City, where I was put up in a crumbling motel and told to wait for the man who would, and I quote, 'fuck me good.'

"And you know what? I was scared shitless, but even though I was terrified, I still thought okay, this is what Charlie is waiting for, to arrest this guy. I'm the bait. I wish he'd told me, but it's okay because I knew where all those girls were going, and as soon as Charlie came in and took out this guy, we'd rescue the girls. A little scar on my arm was a small price to pay. I already had so many, one more wouldn't matter."

Sonia didn't realize she was crying until the tears dripped off her chin. She looked down and squeezed her eyes shut. "The guy came in. He looked at me and said that I was too old to be a virgin. He was enraged, thought he'd been cheated. I found out later he'd paid two thousand American dollars for a virgin. He would have paid five thousand if I was under sixteen. Bastard."

"Sonia—"

She put up her hand to stop Dean from talking. She wouldn't be able to get it out if he tried to soothe her or tell her it wasn't her fault. "He thought I was nineteen, though I was twenty-four. It happened so fast . . . He tore the dress I'd been ordered to wear. And that's when I knew I was on my own."

"He didn't—"

"No. He didn't rape me. He tried." Tried was an understatement. She had run around the room, had screamed her head off, but no one came. She'd tried for the door, but he'd stopped her. She hit him, kicked him, and he used her as a punching bag. He told her to lie down and spread for him. It was humiliating and disgusting and she would have rather died than let him touch her, let alone rape her.

She said softly, "I killed him."

Dean clutched both of her hands in his. "How?"

"I had five minutes alone in the room before he came in. There wasn't a private bathroom, just a sink with a small mirror on the wall above it. I removed it, hoped no one would notice, and cracked it in several pieces. I hid the shards in strategic places." Her voice hitched. This was harder than she'd thought. "I never told Riley this. I told him the big-picture stuff, but never . . . never how close he came.

"He had me on the bed and I pretended to accept my fate."

She'd never forget his hands on her, his foul, fishy breath, his crudity. He'd promised to teach her how to be a good whore, after he made her one.

"And when he didn't expect it, I took one of those hidden shards and stabbed him in the neck."

There'd been so much blood. It spurted—she'd hit a major artery. He was dead in minutes.

"I didn't know what to do. I ran, tried to find help, but I was so sick. I didn't know what was wrong with me. I collapsed and was taken to the hospital. I needed surgery because he'd beaten me pretty badly and there was internal bleeding. It was a small hospital, and they removed my uterus. I don't know, if I'd been in the U.S., if it could have been saved or not. I'll never know."

She looked at Dean for the first time since she envisioned herself back in that awful room. He had moved closer to her, his hands entwined tightly with hers. He brought them to his lips and held them there, his eyes red with suppressed emotion.

"As soon as I was out of surgery and conscious, they arrested me for murder. Forget the phone calls, I'd apparently killed someone of importance. I found out later he was a popular local politician and the father of nineteen kids."

"What did they say when you told them you were a U.S. Immigration cop?"

"At first, they didn't believe me. This town had their own law. Conditions in their jail weren't—stellar." She'd killed Sheldon Rasmussen, a man with a wife and kids. She paid the price. "They didn't believe that I'd been kidnapped. One of the cops convinced others that I was an assassin. Rasmussen was a criminal, but he provided for the town. His own mini kingdom. Then, I think they did finally believe me, but were scared of possible repercussions. It would have been easier to make me disappear than to face the U.S.'s wrath. The fact that no one

came around asking about me made my 'story' less be-
lievable."

"I can't believe he left you." Dean's voice was rough
with anger. He kissed her hands again, holding them so
tightly her fingers almost went numb.

"Do you know who saved me from being hanged?"

"Don't tell me Charlie."

"Indirectly."

"Do I want to hear this?"

"You asked about Kane Rogan. This is where he
comes in. I was in prison, I wasn't getting a trial, and I
thought I was going to die. I didn't get a phone call, I
didn't get to talk to anyone. Charlie hadn't followed me
from the farm. He didn't know where I'd been taken. He
was tracking the other girls. He called Kane—they'd
been in the Marines together—and told him what happened. Some of what happened. Kane specializes in
hostage rescues. He tracked me down, broke me out of
prison, and brought me back to El Paso. I asked him
where Charlie was and he thought I already knew. He
said, 'Charlie said you'd gotten yourself in trouble. Tell
me what happened.' I told him everything."

Dean massaged her palms. He didn't say anything,
but she felt his support through his touch.

"I thought Kane was going to kill him. Really. He
ended up testifying on my behalf during the OPR hearings."

"On your behalf?"

When Sonia had first heard Charlie's lies, she'd been
devastated. Now it just made her angry. "Charlie had
fabricated a story. A lot of stories. Suffice it to say, he
was a hero. He saved all those girls who'd been branded
with me, and he found the dozen girls kidnapped from

the orphanage. No one wanted to believe that he set me up as bait so he could gather intelligence. But Kane believed me, and his word went a long way with OPR. If you ever meet him, you'll understand why."

"Sonia," Dean said, "I'm glad you told me."

She breathed easier, gave him a half-smile. "Me, too."

He leaned over and kissed her softly, holding her face with his hands. "You are amazing, sweetheart."

Dean's respect and affection empowered Sonia, as if sharing the entire sordid story had purged the last of her anger and resentment and self-pity. She'd been holding back for so long, keeping the details of that unspeakable time locked deep inside, not realizing how it still haunted her. Now, her heart felt lighter, she was stronger. Because Dean drew the truth out like no one else had been able to.

She said, "I kinda like you."

"I kinda like you, too." He kissed her again. No urgency, just a deep affection like nothing Sonia had known before.

He reluctantly pulled back. "It's getting late. I brought over the files on Rio Diablo and some of the older documentation I have on Jones, if you want to take a look while I take a quick shower."

"I'll do that."

Dean pulled her from the chair and brought her lips to his. Lightly, a breath of a touch, but Sonia's body tingled in response. He wrapped his arms around her and held her tightly, her head nestled between his neck and shoulder. Just held her without moving for a long, peaceful moment.

"Okay. I'm going to get in the shower." He made no move to leave her. He kissed her head, her cheek, her neck, back to her lips. "Now," he said, his voice husky. Then he cleared his throat and stepped back. "The files are on the coffee table."

"Thanks."

She watched him walk down the hall. She was tempted to follow, but there was a time to play and a time to work.

She crossed to the living room. Mouse, the cat, followed her and jumped into her lap the minute she sat on the couch in front of the file box. She absently rubbed his fur as she took the lid off.

Most of the files were numbers. Rows and rows of numbers—they looked like printouts from tax returns or corporate filings. This wasn't her forte. She flipped through those quickly, looking at only the names.

She put those files aside and pulled another one. And another. The shower went off and she didn't see herself making any inroads.

She put the files back, moved the box, and looked at the files that were beneath it. They were marked THOMAS DANIELS. Smitty. The guy who had unwittingly clued Dean in to Jones's shady dealings.

She opened the thin file and stared at a black-and-white photograph of nine men and a woman who looked familiar, but Sonia couldn't put a name to her face. She recognized Xavier Jones and Smitty in the picture. She also noted Pieter Huffmann, a German who was wanted by Interpol and ICE for trafficking.

And she recognized one other man.

Sonia's mouth went dry, and her hands began to shake. She flipped the photograph over; there was nothing written on the back. No date or time stamp. Nothing to tell her when or where it was taken.

She turned it again and stared at the familiar face again, bile rising from her stomach. The picture had been taken outside. Most of the men held big-game fish of all sizes; a huge blue marlin dominated the picture, half-obscuring the bastard in the center. Her hands and face became clammy, and she bent over to stem the nausea that continued to rise. Mouse jumped off her lap with an annoyed *meow* and reminded her that she was safe, safe in this apartment with Dean in the next room.

Only in her mind, only in her memories and nightmares could he hurt her.

"What's wrong, Sonia? Are you feeling okay?" She hadn't heard Dean return over the ringing in her ears.

He put a hand on her back. "You're shaking. Sonia, talk to me."

"This picture." She still clutched it in her hands.

"Yes, I told you about it. It's what—"

She interrupted. "Do you know who this is?" She straightened and tapped the man in the middle, the man with the blue marlin.

"No, we don't have an I.D. on three of those men, him included."

"When was this picture taken?"

"Sonia, what's going on?"

"When!"

"We believe seven to ten years ago."

"I know who this is. This is my father. My real father—Sergio Martin— who sold me twenty years ago."

CHAPTER
TWENTY-TWO

Dean was halfway to FBI headquarters when Sonia got the call from Detective John Black that "Ann" was awake and coherent. Her prognosis had been upgraded from critical to serious and the doctors were optimistic.

He turned off the freeway, then looped around and headed back downtown to the hospital. Sonia was optimistic that Ann could help them. The man who tried to kill her had used the same type of knife that had been used to kill Greg Vega; there was a connection but they needed more information. Information that Sonia was certain Ann could give them. Or maybe it was just wishful thinking on her part. But right now Sonia needed every last detail she could get to find the Chinese girls before they disappeared.

If it wasn't too late already.

Ann had been moved into the psychiatric ward, which had the best security in the hospital, for her protection. Used only for assessments, Ann was the only patient in this wing.

"I need to warn you," John Black said when he greeted them, "she can't talk, and Dr. Miller doesn't think she'll regain her voice. But there doesn't seem to be any brain damage. The problem is she doesn't read or understand English or Spanish."

"She doesn't need to read anything," Sonia said. "I'll ask yes-and-no questions."

"But if she doesn't understand—"

"She knows *a* language. We just have to figure out which one."

"How many languages do you know?"

"Enough to get by. I'll figure it out. Unless it's Russian. If that's the case we'll find a translator."

A Sac P.D. cop was stationed at both the nurse's station and Ann's door. Dean and Sonia showed their identification, and entered Ann's room. Black followed.

The patient's bed was tilted up and she was watching cartoons on television. The white bandages on her face stood out against the dark bruising on her cheek and nose. Her neck was grotesque, a dark, swollen purple. Her white-blond hair had been washed and brushed. She looked younger now, though based on her teeth and bone growth Dr. Miller had said Ann was over fifteen but not yet eighteen.

The nurse in the room rechecked their identification, which pleased Sonia. The staff was taking this matter seriously. The nurse said, "Dr. Miller doesn't want her to try to talk. There's a dry erase board on the table next to her bed. I don't know if she understands anything we say. She does enjoy cartoons, though."

"How is she emotionally?" Sonia asked. "Nightmares?"

"She woke up last night in a panic. I wasn't on duty, but the night shift told me she pulled out the IV and jumped out of bed, then collapsed. They sedated her, monitored her, and played classical music. When she showed signs of waking again they spoke softly, assuring her she was safe. She was better this morning. She kept pointing to the television until I turned it on, and she's been hooked for two hours."

Ann had been watching them from the moment they came in. Sonia smiled at her. Ann didn't smile back, but continued to watch with distrustful blue eyes.

Sonia sat down on the edge of the bed. She started in English. "I'm Sonia Knight, and my partner is Dean Hooper. We're here to find the man who hurt you."

No recognition.

Sonia pointed to herself and said, "Sonia." She pointed to Dean and said, "Dean."

She handed Ann the whiteboard. Pointed to her chest and then put her hands out and motioned to the board.

She got it on the first try. She wrote in sloppy letters with her right hand.

KIRSTEN

"Kirsten," Sonia said.

The girl nodded and pointed to herself.

Kirsten was a common name in Scandinavian countries. If she didn't speak English, she might speak French. Sonia said in French, "Do you understand French?"

The girl perked up a bit, nodded tentatively. She understood well enough to know what Sonia had asked.

"Where were you born?" she asked in French.

"SURINAME," Kristen wrote.

"Suriname? Wouldn't they speak Spanish?" Dean asked.

"They have several dialects, but Dutch is the official language."

"Dutch?"

"Suriname was colonized by the Dutch. It's had an interesting history, but there are few Boers left. They were the descendants of the Dutch settlers. They teach English in the schools, as well as Dutch. There are many languages spoken. Most of the population is trilingual."

Black asked, "Does that mean she didn't go to school? Because she doesn't understand English?"

"Maybe she's been gone for a long time," Sonia said, her voice tinged with sadness.

"Kirsten, how old are you?"

Kirsten wrote on the board: SEIZE.

"Sixteen." Sonia smiled at Kirsten. "Good."

Sonia then asked a harder question. "Do you know when you left Suriname?"

Kirsten wrote, "Six or seven years. Don't remember." She frowned and averted her eyes.

Her heart went out to this poor girl. "Kirsten, you're safe now. If you want, we can find your family." She waited for the response—if her family had put her in this situation, Kirsten wouldn't want to go back.

But her eyes looked into Sonia's with hope. Her mouth opened but no sound came out.

The nurse said, "Tell her not to try to talk."

Sonia did what the nurse asked and Kirsten nodded, her expression pained. She erased her last message and wrote in another language—Dutch, Sonia suspected. She said, "I don't read Dutch, Kirsten. I'm sorry."

Kirsten erased it and wrote in French, with enough misspellings that Sonia had to guess what it meant.

"Sonia?" Dean prompted.

"I think she's telling us how to find her family." She nodded to Kirsten. "I'll find them," she said.

Now for the hard part. Sonia would give her right hand to spare the girl the pain of this conversation, but it couldn't be avoided. She touched her wrist, covering the tattoos with her hand. "When did you get these marks?"

Kirsten started shaking. Sonia tilted her head and made Kirsten look at her. "It's okay. Kirsten, I know you're hurting. I know how you feel. I want to find him. I want to put him in jail. But I need your help. I need to know who did this. I want you to look at some photographs for me, okay? You tell me if you recognize any of them. They can*not* hurt you. I promise you are safe here. Understand me? You are *safe*."

Kirsten nodded almost imperceptibly, but she understood.

Dean handed Sonia the stack of photographs and sketches they'd compiled of everyone involved in the Xavier Jones investigation.

Sonia first showed the picture of Xavier Jones. Kirsten didn't respond.

The nurse said, "She has a hard time moving her neck, and the doctor wants her to minimize movement while she heals. He tried a neck brace, but it terrified her when she woke up."

Sonia wasn't surprised after Kirsten had nearly been choked to death.

She said, "Sonia, if you recognize the man, touch the picture. Okay?"

She gave a weak nod.

Sonia asked about Jones again. No response. Then she put a picture of Craig Gleason up. Nothing. She had the picture of Charlie Cammarata that she'd showed Andres. Nothing. Greg Vega. No. Kendra Vega. No. She ran through the other photos of Jones's key people and no one popped. She finally showed the picture of the nine men.

She pointed to one of the men and frowned.

"That's Thomas Daniels," Dean said. "He's dead."

"Kirsten, this man died four years ago."

The girl motioned for the whiteboard. She wrote in a combination of Dutch and French:

He took me from Mama.

"Smitty kidnapped her." She asked Kirsten, "He took you from your mama in Suriname?"

She wrote, *Yes.*

Sonia asked Kirsten. "Do you know where he took you?"

She either didn't understand the question or didn't know.

"Did someone force you to do things you didn't want to do?"

Kirsten frowned. She grabbed the marker and wrote, *I am whore.*

Sonia wanted to cry, but let the fury rage instead.

"No, you're not," she told Kirsten. "You never have to do that again. You understand? *Never.* You're safe. *You're safe.*"

Dean put a hand on her shoulder and squeezed. His support meant everything to Sonia, but right now all she wanted was to destroy the people who subjected inno-cent girls like Kirsten to sexual abuse.

Dr. Miller entered the room. "You're not tiring her out, are you?"

"No. She speaks French and Dutch," Sonia said. "She's from Suriname, a small country in northern South America originally a Dutch settlement."

"You did good, Ann." He smiled.

"Her name is Kirsten."

"Kirsten," he said. He added in French, "Beautiful."

The girl lit up. Though Sonia had found Dr. Miller cold, he'd warmed up around Kirsten.

"I have some more questions," Sonia said. "This really will help us find out who did this."

"All right, but don't distress her. I want to kill the creep who did this to her." His voice was calm, but his words were clear. "The man was a brute. Huge."

"How can you tell?"

"Other than the internal damage? The marks on her neck. He had fingers like sausages."

Sonia showed her the last picture she had. Johan Krueger, the man who had tried to kill her while she lay unconscious. "Do you recognize him?"

She pointed and her eyes watered.

"Did he do this?" Sonia gestured to Kirsten's neck.

Kirsten grabbed the whiteboard and wrote frantically. Sonia wasn't sure she translated it right, but said to Dean, "He didn't try to kill her, but he did something else." To Kirsten, "What did he do?"

Kirsten was frustrated, erased her words and thought, then drew a crude picture of a bird.

"A bird?"

"Helicopter," Dean said. "Ask her if she came to Sacramento in a helicopter or plane."

"Did this man fly you? Take you in a plane?" When Kirsten looked at her quizzically, Sonia said, "Did you fly in the air? Was this man a pilot? Or did he come with you?"

She wrote in French: *He drove plane in air. He did sex to me.*

"Did he hurt your neck?"

No. Crazy man want to kill me.

Dean said, "Sonia, the river victim."

"I can't show her that picture."

"You have to. He's connected to Jones as well. He's big with large hands."

Sonia didn't want to show Kirsten the dead man's photo, but the girl was strong and wanted to help. Sonia said to Kirsten, "The next picture might upset you. The man is dead. He doesn't look right, okay? I want to show it to you, but be strong."

Dean handed her the crime-scene photo.

The recognition was instant. Her eyes widened and she nodded and pointed.

"Kirsten, calm down," Dr. Miller took her hand and petted it. "Shh, you don't want to hurt yourself."

Sonia reiterated what Miller said, then added, "He hurt you?"

She wrote: *He wanted to kill me while we do sex. I didn't want to die. I hurt him, too.*

Sonia asked Dean, "Did the autopsy report any scratches or injuries to the victim?"

"I haven't seen the report. I'll call."

He stepped from the room, and Dr. Miller said, "Your crime-scene gal, Ms. Charles, took a rape kit that included scrapings from under Kirsten's fingernails."

"I'll talk to her," Sonia said. "We might have something to compare it with."

"He's dead?"

"Yes. He was found in the river yesterday."

"Apropos. I hope he suffered."

He didn't suffer enough, but at least he can't hurt anyone else.

*   *   *

Noel Marchand was not pleased with being interrupted while he meditated. He didn't ask for much from his staff: competence, loyalty, and peace. He rarely got what he wanted.

"What is it now?"

Mr. Ling said, "Raul is on the phone. He is at the hospital and hasn't seen Agent Knight. Wasn't able to find the brother, either. I called and Riley Knight was released at one a.m."

Noel tensed. "Are you certain?"

"Yes. Raul then checked the residences, and all are empty—no one home. He's watching, but he'd like direction."

"The kid is first. He's always been first. He needs to be dead. Where is the fucking kid?" Raul was his best sniper, had served him well over the years, and he'd called him in last night specifically to kill Sonia Knight. But the kid could identify him, and that would not do. Until Noel was safely back in Tres Palos, or the kid was dead, he couldn't be certain the kid wasn't a risk.

Anyone who escaped was a potential danger to his organization. Look at that bitch Sonia Knight.

"The kid is the priority. But he needs to be prepared to take care of Agent Knight on my command."

"Are you sure—"

Noel looked at Mr. Ling. He didn't have to say a word, but Ling understood.

"Yes, Mr. Marchand. I'll let Raul know."

CHAPTER TWENTY-THREE

Dean wasn't one hundred percent confident that letting Sonia interview Johan Krueger was the best use of their time. Krueger hadn't talked to anyone but his attorney since he was arrested, not even a word to his cell mate. But Sonia was adamant that she must see him.

"I can get him to talk," she vowed. "He used a knife from Argentina, just like Vega's killer. He brought Kirsten to Sacramento to be killed for the sick pleasure of that bastard in the morgue. I just wish he'd suffered a hell of a lot more."

Sonia was highly stressed. Dean suspected it had more to do with the photograph of her biological father and Kirsten's comment about being a whore. Sonia was taking it personally. Sometimes, cops who put themselves in the victim's shoes ended up turning the case for the good. Other times, it ate them alive.

Dean didn't want Sonia hurt anymore. While there was no doubt in his mind that she could handle anything life threw at her, he wanted to keep her safe. She was well-trained and sharp. Smart. But this case had gotten too personal for her to be wholly objective.

Krueger was brought into the interview room of the county jail.

He sat down and stared blankly at the wall behind Sonia.

She introduced herself and said, "Mr. Krueger, the charges against you are serious, and I have additional charges that my office will be bringing."

No reaction.

"The girl you tried to kill Wednesday night at Sutter Hospital? She's awake. She's talking. And she pointed a finger at *you*. You flew her to Sacramento. You raped her. And you handed her over to—" she slid a photo of the river victim in front of him, "this man who tried to kill her. Now, he's dead."

Krueger couldn't resist glancing down at the picture of Kirsten's attacker. Surprise crossed his expression before he became stony again. Dean was surprised that after hours of interrogation and nothing, five minutes with Sonia had sparked a reaction.

"I have your DNA. I have an eyewitness identification. I have *you* and I have your knife, and surprise surprise, your knife matches another knife used in another murder."

Nothing.

"Who do you work for?"

Nothing.

"Where did the girl come from?"

Nothing.

"Who paid you to kill her? To bring her here?"

Nothing, nothing. The man was a statue. Clearly frustrated, Sonia slammed her fist on the table.

"I work for *Immigration*. You are a *German national*. You are going to pay for this, no matter what, no matter who you know, who you pay, who wants you alive . . ." she paused. "That's it. You talk, you die."

A blink.

"Oh. I get it. Great. You don't want to talk to me? Fine. Don't. You don't have to say a fucking word."

She turned to Dean and he knew exactly what she had in mind.

"Agent Hooper," she said, "can you put a press conference together?"

"Absolutely. When? Who do you want there?"

"As soon as possible. In time for the noon newscast. Radio and television, might as well get print in as well. We have a witness." She glanced at Krueger, then turned to Dean. "Do you think we can get witness protection?"

"If he gives us information."

"Can you work on that? I want to prepare for the press conference announcing that we have a witness who is in protective custody. I don't want to give away his identity . . ."

"Why not simply say it's the pilot of the helicopter who was the last to see the minor rape victim before she was attacked?"

"Oh, that's good! Thanks."

Krueger spoke with a growl, "You won't say a word."

Sonia whirled on him. "Watch me."

She left the room.

"Bitch," Krueger said.

Dean looked at him. "If you don't think she'll hold that press conference, just wait."

"She doesn't scare me."

"Who does?"

"Someone who should scare you, Agent Hooper."

Dean left and heard Sonia telling the chief corrections officer to monitor the prisoner's phone calls.

"We aren't allowed to eavesdrop without a warrant, and not if he's talking to his attorney."

"But you can find out what phone number he dials, right?"

"You're certain he's going to call someone?"

"Oh, yes."

"I can get the number."

"Who's his attorney?"

The guard looked it up. "Bernard Cline."

"Cline? Is he a big defense lawyer or a public defender?"

"Private. Never heard of him before, never seen him in the pen."

"Thanks." She gave the guard her contact information. "Just let me know what number he calls and when."

They walked out into the bright mid-morning sun. Dean said, "You rattled him."

"Good. Sometimes you just have to shake a lot of trees before you spook a rat."

"I don't think I've heard that expression before."

"I just made it up."

Dean stopped walking, took Sonia's arm, and pulled her to him. She was surprised, but then got a shy smile on her face and her incredible eyes stared at him seductively.

"I'm really beginning to like you, Agent Knight."

She licked her lips. "I'm right there with you, Agent Hooper."

He kissed her. He couldn't resist those lips. "Let's solve this case fast so we can do something fun."

"Are FBI agents allowed to have fun?"

"Twice a year. It's in the manual."

"You're on. What do you do for fun?"

"Is this a trick question?"

"You brought it up. I don't think I know what 'fun' is. The last time I remember having fun was at Disneyland with my family when I was sixteen."

"That does sound like fun. So, how about Disneyland again?"

Sonia laughed. Dean loved the sound coming from her. Sonia was passionate in everything—in her job, how she laughed, with her family, in his bed. Though technically they hadn't made love in a bed. Yet.

"Agent Hooper, you just solved the most complex case in human trafficking. Where do you want to go? Disneyland!" She giggled and kissed him. "You're on."

Her phone rang and she grabbed it. "I knew he'd call someone."

She frowned when she answered the phone. "I want to talk to you . . . Dammit, Charlie, this is . . . No! Don't—" She slammed the phone shut. *"Fuck!"*

"What happened?"

"Charlie! He said he could only decipher part of Jones's journal and left it in the main public library."

"That's a big library. Where?"

"Behind a book on serial killers by Harold Schechter. Let's go—the library's right down the street."

CHAPTER
TWENTY-FOUR

Sonia:

I decoded Jones's journal and discovered that he created a secondary code. I'm sorry, I should have given this to you earlier. I know you'll figure it out, or know someone who can.

I lied to you the other night. I recognized one of the men who killed Jones. Sun Ling. He's an American citizen born in Chinatown, San Francisco. He's ruthless and has been involved in trafficking for as long as I've been in the business of stopping it. I don't know who he works for now, I've been out of the game too long. But he's not in charge. He's never in charge.

Please forgive me for everything. I'll make it up to you. I have a favor to ask. Find Ashley Fox. I know she's in this book somewhere. Find her and return her to her mother. Please. I've worked too long and hard on this to have it mean nothing. She needs to be rescued. I know you'll save her.

I've always loved you, Sonia.

C.C.

Sonia sat alone in the FBI's task force room, surrounded by humming computers and mountains of paperwork. But all she saw was Charlie's letter.

She read and reread the letter he'd left with the journal in the main Sacramento Public Library. She was so frustrated she wanted to throttle him. Damn straight he should have given her the journal the other night. The thirty-six hours they'd lost because Charlie wanted to play the hero could mean the difference between life and death for those young Chinese women.

Dean had taken the journal to the FBI cybercrimes unit, which was also responsible for code breaking. If they didn't think they could handle it, they'd scan the code and send it to Quantico.

Time was running out. Jones's killer could have moved the women, killed them, or traded them—and they'd never know. It pained Sonia to think that they'd been so close.

"Damn you, Charlie!" How dare he write *I've always loved you.* He was delusional. Or trying to manipulate her yet one more time.

Dean returned and said, "They're working on the journal. But I should tell you that it's sophisticated in its simplicity."

"I don't understand."

"Jones used random words—so it seems—that mean something to him, and there's a pattern of sorts, but until we figure out what one of the components means, we can't figure out any."

"I get it."

Dean pulled the letter from her hand. "You've read this enough. Don't let him tug at your heartstrings."

"Where is he? Why did he give this to us now? What's he up to?"

"I would love to know the answer to those questions, but right now, Cammarata is the least of my concerns."

He sat down at the table, comfortably poring through property records of Jones's old clients, focusing on spreads in the Sierra Nevada foothills.

Sonia was hugely frustrated that the clock was ticking and they didn't know where the girls were. She hated sitting in an office looking at papers and maps when she wanted to be in the field.

Dean said, "Hey, did you know that two of the three good-faith locations that Vega gave you were adjacent to Rio Diablo land?"

"No," Sonia said. "You think that means something?"

"Hmm." Dean rose and, sleeves rolled up, marked his main wall map. She watched as he quickly added boundaries in different colors.

"What is it?" She just saw lines. They meant nothing to her.

"It's coming together. Almost there." He went over to another box and pulled more maps out, then traced more boundaries on his map. "What do you think?"

She stared. "I don't—" she tilted her head. There did appear to be some pattern, but she didn't know the relevance. "What do the different colors mean?"

He had pins and color-coded sticky notes and highlighter marks.

Dean said, "The red lines mark the Rio Diablo boundary. The blue lines are Jones's property. Green are Omega and purple are Weber Trucking."

She stared. "They almost connect."

"Not exactly, more like a connect-the-dots moving from one safe zone to another."

"I see." And she was beginning to. "How does this help?"

"They practically give a perfect path from the Port of Stockton to the foothills with plenty of private roads to avoid major highways." Dean pointed to the holes. "All this is owned by the Port of Stockton. And here . . . and here . . . and here I'm having ownership researched. But it's mostly unused land. No route goes through a major town. I'm thinking that they stick to areas where they're comfortable moving freely, where there would be minimal chance to encounter people or police."

Sonia tilted her head back and forth. "Jones's restaurant connects the land to the river. We already know they don't transport their victims all the way to the Port of Stockton. The restaurant could be a temporary storage facility."

Dean asked, "Why don't they simply transport them directly to their final destination? Wouldn't that minimize problems?"

"Sometimes, but when you're dealing with a large number of victims, you want to disperse them quickly. The longer they're in your possession, the greater the chance of being caught. If Charlie is right and they're using small planes and helicopters to move them out of the area—"

"Damn, I didn't factor that in!"

Dean went back to the maps and flipped open books, made marks on the primary map, traced things that Sonia couldn't see. She had never seen him so animated. It was like he was seeing a completely different map, a different world, than she saw.

"Okay." Dean stood back and surveyed his work. His tie was loose and he'd lost the jacket long ago. But he still looked like a beefy stockbroker, sleeves rolled up after the exchange closed. "I marked off all areas where private aircraft can't land—in these areas because of the proximity to military or commercial air facilities. This area because of power lines—no way a helicopter can get in there. And terrain. You don't need a large flat space for helicopters, but you can't land on a slope."

Sonia leaned forward. "Amazing. You've cut the search area in half." She pointed to a stretch parallel to Highway 99. "What's this? What does purple mean again?"

"Weber Trucking. Their business is here"—he pointed to a dot just outside of Stockton—"but the company or the owners own all this land just outside Lodi. Is that important? It doesn't look like there's much there."

"I've driven past that area hundreds of times and never thought much about it, but I think there's a small industrial area right off the freeway here."

"You think they'd keep the women that close to a major highway?"

"Well, look at this. Right here, this is a deep-water channel. Omega would come down this way. There are at least a half dozen places where they could off-load the women and take them by small boat upriver—here, here, here—damn, all over the place. It wouldn't be difficult, and at night? Unless we were there twenty-four/seven monitoring, we wouldn't see it. Of course, it's seasonal. These tributaries are fed by one of the reservoirs to the east, I think. I'd need to double-check, but I'm sure parts of these waterways are too shallow for boats of any kind, or dry by the end of summer. But now? End of spring? With all the snowmelt in the Sierra Nevadas, they'd still be usable. They could stop in the deep-water channel and in less than fifteen minutes have the women transferred to a small boat and headed virtually anyplace along the river . . ." She traced a route with one finger like a maze. She backtracked once and found she could get from the Sacramento Deep Water channel to the small industrial area completely on water.

"That's it!" she exclaimed. She was giddy with excitement.

"You're brilliant." He kissed her.

"So are you."

"I'll get a warrant," Dean said. "Give me a few minutes. I'm going to have to do some fast talking." He gave her another quick kiss and left the task force room.

Sonia watched the door close behind him. She'd never met a man like Dean Hooper. She had a forceful personality and tended to be the dominant partner in her relationships. She always said when to jump, when to go out, when to have sex.

Dean Hooper would have none of that. He was in charge, and if she wanted to be in charge, fine, as long as he was her equal. Sonia didn't realize how much of a turn-on that was, to have a man spontaneously kiss her. Maybe it was her fault, she tended to scare off prospects because of her job and her hot head. Riley once told her she played the tough girl just to see who was still standing at the end. "Most guys run away, but the one still standing? You'll fall for him."

Dean hadn't run, and in fact, he had maneuvered himself so easily into her life that she felt sick to her stomach thinking about him going back to Washington.

He'll leave. He has to. It's his job.

She couldn't fault him for that. Just like he wouldn't be able to fault her for staying in Sacramento. How could she leave her family?

How could she let Dean walk away?

She turned her gaze from the map and looked at the

copy of Charlie's letter where Dean had dropped it on a stack of files. She read it again.

Sun Ling. She knew the name, everyone in the business did, but she'd never come up against him, and no one in ICE knew where he was. That certainly said something about their state of intelligence, didn't it? She knew their focus was on terrorism, but right now she felt a far bigger threat from human traffickers than she did from a small-minded extremist bent on killing Americans for the sake of killing Americans. It was a valid focus, but why couldn't they do both? Why couldn't they fight terrorism *and* stop criminals from buying and selling people?

She took a deep breath. This was getting her nowhere. She had no time for self-pity.

She called Kane. He didn't answer, of course. She left a message.

"Sun Ling. Chinese American, born in San Francisco. Trafficking. I need everything you know. I owe you big-time, Kane. Duke and Sean are godsends. Thank you."

Sonia snapped her phone shut and it immediately vibrated in her hand. But it wasn't Kane returning her call, it was her boss, Toni Warner.

She almost didn't want to know what Toni had learned about her biological father, but she'd never hid from the truth before, and she wasn't going to hide now. "Hi, Toni," she answered. "What have you found?"

"I don't have good news."

"I wasn't expecting any. Just answers."

"Then you'll still be disappointed. There are no records of Sergio Martin."

"None? There have to be records."

"Nothing, except for your deposition. The agents assigned to find him twenty years ago never did."

"I knew that, but—"

"They concluded that he may not have existed."

"That's bullshit."

"I know that, you know that, but this is in the records. They couldn't find a birth certificate they could prove was his. I don't have to tell you Martin is a common name in Argentina."

"So they never continued looking for him?" When Sonia became an agent with Immigration, she'd received permission to read her file, which included minimal information about her father. Now she realized that she knew everything they knew, which was almost nothing. She had always been certain that there was a file somewhere, maybe classified, but that one existed, so she could rest assured that someone was trying to find him and punish him. The statute of limitations on her case was long up—and the United States didn't have the laws then to prosecute him—but traffickers were like drug addicts. They didn't stop. The money and power were addictive. Many considered it simply a job, and the cries and pleas of the victims nothing more than the bleating of lambs being led to the slaughter.

"No one knew what he looked like," Toni said.

"I do!"

"Sonia—"

"I sent you the picture this morning."

"I know, but it's not a lot to go on and the image is fuzzy. Are you certain?"

"One hundred percent certain. It's him. Sergio Martin. I promise, I'm not hallucinating or making it up or guessing. It's him."

"I believe you, but—"

"No one else does?"

"It's not that. It's just that we don't have a name, one that has any meaning or record. We have an old, unclear photograph. And we have the twenty-year-old deposition from a minor. It may not be related to this case—"

"Toni, my father was from Argentina. That's where I was born. The knife used to attack Riley and kill Greg Vega were available exclusively at an Argentinean knife factory. He's in the same picture as known human traffickers, including Xavier Jones, taken less than ten years ago."

"On the surface it sounds good, but—"

"It sounds good because the intel *is* good! I know it's vague, but honestly, we've gone after cases with less. We need to send someone to talk to the manufacturer of the knives."

"I put in your request for a legal attaché to do so, and it's been approved. They're on their way."

"And you said there wasn't good news? That's great. It's a huge lead."

"It's Friday afternoon. There could have been hundreds, thousands of those knives sold. We don't know how old, we don't know when they were sold—"

"They could be limited editions. We have to follow every lead."

"Sonia, you're not thinking your father is involved in this in some way?"

Not on the surface, but deep down, as soon as Sonia saw the photograph, she had suspected just that.

"Toni, let me lay it out. Yes, I think my father is still involved in trafficking, but I don't know how. Finding him is my priority after this case. But one of those other

men in the picture could very well be our killer. Making
his move, taking out Jones and staking out this territory.
There are already two people in that photo who are connected to this case. If we can identify the other men, and
the female, we may find the killer. I need to find Charlie.
He saw him."

"You told me he didn't see him."

"He said he didn't recognize him. I want to show him
this picture."

"He hasn't contacted the office."

"If I find him, can I offer him limited immunity?"

"Sonia, you can't offer him anything, but if you find
him, I'm not going to send you up the river if you let him
walk. Once."

"Understood." Sonia had to locate Charlie. Dammit,
where would he be hiding out?

Toni said, "You're working closely with the FBI,
Richardson tells me."

"Yes."

"Stick close. This is messy and multijurisdictional, but
it's also dangerous. Traffickers are rarely this bold
within our borders. I fear this is a new operation, someone who has the money and power to control it from a
distance, which makes him that much more difficult to
capture."

"I'm not going to let Greg Vega's killer leave this
country. I will find him, Toni." Sonia wished she was as
confident as she sounded.

"I hope so. I don't like how he's made this personal."

"It's not personal—"

"It is. These people broke into your house!"

"Toni, I'm being careful."

"Are you too close to this? Maybe you should join your family—"

"No. I can't believe that after ten years you'd think I would run away and hide and let someone else stand in my place. I know this is dangerous, we're dealing with dangerous people. But I'm not too close to it, and I'm not leaving. In fact, my connection with Charlie and Jones and everyone else in the case gives me inside knowledge. I'm doing everything I can to minimize the threat, but I'm not walking away when dozens of women are in jeopardy. My entire career has prepared me for this."

Toni said, "I didn't think you'd step down. Keep me informed as often as possible. If you need anything, call."

"I will."

She hung up and made several calls trying to find Charlie.

Dean walked in a few minutes later and said, "We have the warrant."

"That was fast."

"Two double homicides in one day has everyone wanting results. Bob Richardson has been fielding calls from the media and politicians ever since our office's involvement came out."

"Let's get rolling." Sonia headed for the door.

Dean followed and said, "I contacted the San Joaquin County Sheriff's Department. They'll meet us at the warehouse to help serve the warrant."

"Where's Sam and Trace?" Sonia asked when she didn't see them around the white-collar crimes area.

"While I was getting the warrant, Sam thought he'd check out Omega and feel the staff out. See if any of them will talk. Sometimes, all you have to do is ask the right questions. I should have had them talk to you before okaying it."

"No, that's fine." She frowned. Something didn't quite add up, but she wasn't sure what was bugging her.

"Any sign of Cammarata?" Dean asked as he slid into his car. Sonia sat in the passenger seat.

"He hasn't called. If he does, I'm going to meet with him. I need to show him the picture of the men with Jones. He might be able to identify one or more of the UNSUBs."

"Then we arrest him."

Sonia didn't say anything.

"Sonia, dammit, we will arrest him. He withheld evidence, for one. He broke into your house. He *assaulted* you."

"I'm giving him a onetime pass. I need his information, and there's no way in hell he'll meet with me unless I promise not to take him into custody."

"Fine, I will."

"Dean—" Sonia rubbed her eyes and stared out the window as Dean drove south toward Lodi. "I need the information."

"This is about your biological father, isn't it?" Dean asked.

"No." She paused. Dean deserved honesty. "Partly. Charlie may recognize him. He knows most of the major players. It's obvious he's no longer using the name Sergio Martin. He may not—" she stopped.

"Sonia?"

"My whole life is a farce. What if I had never been Martin? What if *that* name was an alias? I feel like I don't even know who I am anymore."

"You're Sonia Knight," Dean said firmly. "Cop, sister, daughter . . . lover."

She glanced at Dean and something shifted inside her. A calmness blanketed her, a wholly unfamiliar sensation. He reached for her hand. Held it. She wondered if he felt what she did.

She wanted to ask, but she feared voicing her feelings would somehow threaten this new beginning. And the last thing she wanted to think about was Dean returning to Washington. But maybe . . . maybe now would be the time to clarify their relationship. Their careers and family and residences on opposite coasts.

When Sonia gathered the courage to finally speak, Dean said first, "This is the exit. Ready?"

She nodded. "Let's do it."

CHAPTER TWENTY-FIVE

By all appearances, the small industrial warehouse north of Lodi was abandoned. Weeds pushed through cracks in concrete, and garbage from nearby Highway 99 had blown against the buildings, making the row of fifties-era cinder-block and metal buildings look like a ghost town.

Except for the brand-new padlocks on the doors.

Four San Joaquin County sheriff's deputies were already on-site. Brian Stone and three trained FBI-SWAT agents pulled up behind Dean and Sonia in a black Suburban.

"I hope this isn't a wild-goose chase," Sonia said. "We don't have the time to screw up."

"Don't second-guess yourself. Ready?"

"Absolutely."

She got out of the car and stepped into the dry valley heat. The noonday sun glistened off the river—Sonia thought it was the Mokelumne River, but she wasn't certain. Traffic from the highway was audible, but not visible. At night the area would be pitch-black except for sparse street lighting and security lights above each door.

If the traffickers were using this waterway to maneuver inland from the deep-water channel, they could walk the women into any of these buildings at night without fear of discovery.

Stone and his team inspected the perimeter, then Dean directed them to break down the door of the main warehouse—the others branched off this one.

Guns drawn and their badges clearly displayed, the six federal cops and four sheriff's deputies prepared for a possible attack even though there was no sign of anyone.

"On three." Stone used his fingers to count down.

A SWAT team member broke the padlock with one swift hit with the heavy handheld battering ram. As soon as the doors swung open, a foul stench of vomit and human excrement hit them.

Sonia's stomach turned, not from the stench but from what it meant. No sounds—no shouts or cries—came with the smell; there was no one inside.

The SWAT team rolled into the warehouse, Dean and Sonia on their heels. Calls of *clear*! rang out as they inspected the interior.

The filthy windows let in only a minimum of sunlight, and the only noise was their own movement, their own voices. It was clear that the huge storage room was empty.

A door on the far side was open, leading to a darker room.

"Sonia," Dean said in a low voice. "Do you smell it?"

He wasn't talking about the urine. Only blood smelled so sweetly metallic.

She nodded. Her training and extensive experience kept her calm and alert. Adrendaline sharpened her instincts.

They had their guns poised over their flashlights as they cautiously entered the dark room.

"Lights?" Sonia whispered.

"None here either," Stone said.

She felt along the wall. "I found them," Sonia said. "Be ready on three—they could be bright. Three. Two. One." She flipped them on, narrowing her eyes.

Old-style fluorescent lights flickered on. This room was empty of cargo, but they found the source of the blood.

Three partially clothed Chinese women lay in a heap against the wall, their throats slit. Arterial spray on the wall closest to Sonia said they'd been killed right there, one after the other. Their hands were bound but not their feet.

"Dear Lord," one of the deputies muttered.

From the pile of feces in one corner of the room it was apparent that at one point far more than three women had been held captive in this room.

Sonia slipped on gloves and touched the bodies. "Full rigor. Twelve to twenty-four hours, my guess, but we should get the coroner in here ASAP."

"They moved them at night," Dean said.

"Yes. Last night." Sonia looked at the women. *Girls.* They were sixteen or seventeen. Long black hair and too-thin bodies. These were the girls she had wanted to save.

Where had they taken the others? Had they been killed too?

She wanted to cover the bodies, but knew better than to disturb them.

"Hooper!" Stone called from the far side of the room.

Sonia turned at the same time Dean did. At first she didn't see anything.

"Shit," Dean said, taking a step toward Sonia.

Then she saw. In block letters, written in blood on the gray cinder-block interior wall, was a message.

YOU ARE TOO LATE.

*   *   *

Sam Callahan had been emboldened by Assistant Director Dean Hooper's confidence in handling the Jones investigation, starting from the minute he came to town, through the execution of the warrant on Jones, and the subsequent confrontation in the restaurant downtown. He'd convinced Hooper to give him this shot at Omega—they might get lucky and find someone who knew something, and was willing to talk.

Trace Anderson had clued him in on more details of Omega's suspected involvement in trafficking. He finished by saying, "We have no hard evidence. It's one thing to know in your gut that someone is guilty, it's quite another to prove it."

"You're telling me."

Omega Shipping, on the books, was a huge enterprise; their headquarters on Washington Street were small. One car was parked in the front of the industrial building. Activity on the opposite end was heavier, but they weren't Omega facilities.

"Is this it?" Sam asked Trace.

"Yep. Sonia and I came out here last year, not to talk to them, just to check it out. It was the same."

"Looks like a front."

"Looks like."

"Let's go."

The interior was bigger than the outside suggested. The warehouse had been converted into large offices, all of which were dark. The reception area was cheerful with bright, fake flowers and a tidy reception desk. The young woman who sat behind it was typing triplicate forms on an electric typewriter. When they stepped through the door, a bell rang overhead and she turned to them, smiling brightly. She was blond and petite, and seemed thrilled to have potential customers.

"Can I help you?"

Sam smiled back, showed her his badge. "I'm Sam Callahan. And you are?"

She was a bit flustered, but responded. "Daisy Sajeck."

"We're following up on a murder investigation—"

"Someone was killed?"

He nodded solemnly. "Xavier Jones. Did you know him?"

"Mr. Jones! That's awful?"

Sam wanted to ask if she watched the news, but refrained. "I know he did business with Mr. Christopoulis, and I hoped I could have a word with him. We're trying to find out who might have had a grievance with Mr. Jones."

"George and Mr. Jones were very good friends. He's going to be shocked when he hears."

"He's not here?"

She shook her head. "He's on the *Crius II*. They're taking medical supplies to Argentina."

Argentina. Again. Sam mentally filed the information and asked, "Is Mrs. Christopoulis available?"

"*Ms.*" Daisy corrected. "She's divorced."

"And they still work together?" Trace asked.

She blinked. "Well, George was upset about the divorce—I think he likes his dad a lot more than his mother—but they get along okay."

Sam glanced at Trace. They'd assumed that Victoria Christopoulis was George's wife.

Trace said, "The senior Christopoulises are still Greek citizens, correct?"

"Oh, yes. Ms. Christopoulis would never want to live here."

"Is she in Greece now?"

"No, she's in town. She stays with George, which is why I think he took this extra assignment." She leaned forward conspiratorially. "I wouldn't want to live under the same roof with her. And I thought my mom was bad." She rolled her eyes like a teenager. Sam realized she wasn't much older than one.

"How long have you worked here?" he asked.

"Ten months. Longest job I've held. My daddy says if I can keep the same job for one year, he'll buy me a convertible. I'm almost there."

"Good for you. We were hoping Mr. Christopoulis could help with our investigation. Was he in town Wednesday night?"

"Wednesday? I don't think so. He docked late Tuesday, after I was gone for the day. I had a manifest and billing on my desk Wednesday morning. He came in late in the afternoon to work, then told me about the *Cruis II* shipments."

"It wasn't scheduled?"

"It was an emergency. Another shipper canceled at the last minute, and Mr. Christopoulis took the job. He works so hard." She sounded like she was infatuated.

"Does Ms. Christopoulis come in to work here?"

"She hates coming down here. She works from the house. But I can call her for you, you can set up an appointment—"

"No, that's okay. It's not important right now." It was hugely important, but Sam didn't want Daisy talking to Victoria Christopoulis about him before he could track her down. "When is George coming back to town?"

"Two weeks," she said.

"Great. We'll call then."

"I can tell him you came by—he calls every night."

Sam raised an eyebrow. It sounded like something might be going on between George and Daisy. By the light flush in her cheeks, he suspected he was right.

"That's okay, Daisy. Two weeks is fine."

Sam and Trace left Omega. "That was interesting," Trace said. "Want to go chat with Mommy Christopoulis?"

"Absolutely. Christopoulis's house is only a couple miles from here, on Country Club Drive. Let's see what she has to say."

CHAPTER
TWENTY-SIX

Noel stood on the pathetic excuse for a balcony on the tenth floor of the Hyatt Hotel and spoke to his buyer.

"Everything is running smoothly," he assured the man on the other end of the phone. He went by the name Richter. Noel knew that wasn't his name; Noel knew far more about "Richter" than the buyer, and the organization he represented, suspected, but information was crucial at this stage of the process. He'd reveal his intelligence only when and if it became necessary.

"We're getting nervous with the increased federal activity," Richter said.

"They are chasing their tails. They don't know what to think or where to turn. The merchandise is secure. I confirmed it personally."

Noel knew what Richter's plan was, and Noel wasn't going to let the bastard undercut him. He had far too much invested in this deal to allow Richter's organization to cut the price. Reduce the cost once and no one would ever pay full market value again.

"Because of the increased risks and security measures, we feel that a reduction in price is warranted."

Noel would have smiled at being right had he not been so irritated that they wanted to stiff him.

"Price is not negotiable."

"We have additional costs, and it's not our people who brought the feds swooping down."

"If you're concerned, feel free to back out. I have another buyer lined up," Noel bluffed. He could get a new buyer with time, but that would mean staying in America beyond Saturday night. That was not a true option. Noel would rather destroy the merchandise and relinquish this particular market than stay in the United States longer than he had planned. This corridor had always been profitable, but his freedom was more important. He could open another route easily enough. Annoying, but not deadly.

Richter attempted to bluff as well. "That's your decision. We feel that fifteen thousand a head is too high."

"Fifteen thousand is the group price. Individually, they go for twenty to twenty-five thousand each, and you know that with good management you'll make back your money in a year. You're getting thirty ripe vessels. You can sell a few yourself to recoup some of your costs, but I don't need to tell you how to run your business."

"We're offering ten thousand."

"I am not open to negotiation in this matter."

"I'm afraid we're firm. We can cancel the exchange."

Noel's hand clenched the metal rail so tightly the edges left impressions in his palm. The stifling air, not even a breeze, had him burning inside and out. Yet his voice was calm when he said, "Very well, the deal is canceled. You understand that I don't take these setbacks lightly, Roger."

There was silence on the phone line. Noel fumed, unable to enjoy this judicious release of information. *Yes, Roger Applegate, I know who you are. I will expose you and destroy you if you fuck me.*

He hoped there would be an opportunity to break this idiot's neck during the exchange. It would please Noel to see him dead.

"I need to discuss this with the organization," Richter said, his voice cracking just a fraction.

"You have twenty minutes."

Noel hung up the phone. Ling said, "Well done, sir."

"Trying to renege on me. He'll pay, maybe not tomorrow night, but one day."

"They say revenge is a dish best served cold."

"Whoever came up with that is an idiot as well. Revenge is best when you can see its results, hot or cold."

Ignacio walked in without knocking. Noel glared at him.

"Excuse me, it's urgent," Ignacio said.

Noel continued to stare.

Ignacio left the room and closed the door behind him. A moment later, he knocked.

"Ling," Noel nodded toward the door.

Mr. Ling opened the door and Ignacio walked in. "Sir."

"Yes?"

"The feds found the warehouse."

Noel smiled. Government cops were so predictable. *People* were predictable. No one surprised him anymore. Sonia Knight had once, but she wouldn't again. Dread and panic would keep them occupied and following the wrong leads. It bought him time.

He hoped she liked the message he'd left for her.

"Find out where they're headed and keep me informed."

*   *   *

Driving back from Lodi after the ERT arrived to process the crime scene, Dean was worried about Sonia's silence.

"Are you okay?"

"Hmm? Oh, yes, I'm fine." She was absently drumming her fingers on her door handle.

"What are you thinking?"

"I don't know—I'm just wondering about the time line."

"Talk it out."

"Jones was killed around midnight Wednesday, twenty-four hours after the raid of his house. But those three women weren't killed until last night, twenty-four hours after Jones."

"Right." He didn't see the connection.

"If the killer thought Jones or Vega had talked, he would have moved the girls before last night."

"We don't know that he didn't," Dean said.

"But it doesn't make sense to move the girls the night Jones was killed, then bring three of them back to kill."

"It was a message. He knows we're close. He's trying to throw us off."

"It's going to take a hell of a lot more to scare me off this case." Sonia shifted in the passenger seat to face him. "I'm going to find these people and bring them all to justice. I don't think they were moved until last night. It's not easy arranging transportation of that many illegal aliens who are being held against their will, even if they're too terrified to attempt escape. He had to have had inside information, information that *he* knew could lead to the girls even if we didn't know."

"Like that we were looking into Weber Trucking."

"Exactly! That's it. I've been after Omega since the

beginning, but Weber is new. It was only a matter of time until we pulled Weber property records and started looking at places the women could be safely kept. So he moved them—"

Dean interrupted. "I don't know. That means he has a mole in ICE or the FBI. I don't think so. Not many of us were privy to our investigation into Weber. That only came up yesterday when I went further back into Xavier Jones's client records—"

"—after realizing the importance," Sonia said, practically jumping up in the seat. "When we talked to Craig Gleason."

Dean sped up. "You think he's involved."

"It's the only way. He's the only other person who knew we were even asking about Jones's clients. If he knew who was involved, he could tip them off."

"I think you're right. I hope he's in the office right now, otherwise I'm putting out an APB and he can talk to us from jail."

"Where do you think the woman is?" Trace asked Sam as they sat in their car down the street from George Christopoulis's stately home in Stockton. They were parked under a tree and had the windows rolled down, but still the heat was nearly unbearable.

When they first arrived an hour ago, Sam had gone up to the front door alone and knocked. There was no answer, and a small dog barked incessantly from the interior. Sam checked the garage through a window; there was no vehicle. The house had a silent, empty feel. He returned to the car and called the office to research Victoria Christopoulis's immigration status—she was in the

United States on a vacation—and he had her passport flagged.

"Maybe we should call Sonia," Trace said, "and get her take on this."

Sam liked Trace, but he was young and overeager to please his boss and seek her approval. "We're okay for now. We don't have anything to report, not of substance. Let's see what happens."

Ten minutes later a Mercedes pulled into the driveway. Sam peered through binoculars at the figure in the driver's seat.

An attractive, middle-aged woman with dark red hair and excessive makeup drove. The garage door went up and she pulled in, and Sam lost sight of her.

"Shall we talk to her?" Trace had his hand on the door handle.

The woman was familiar, but Sam didn't know why. "Hold on." Where had he seen her? Dammit, it was just outside his memory.

"Sam?"

It wouldn't come if he forced it. "Let's talk to her. Casual. Inform her of Jones's murder, ask the last time she saw him, see what she says. Nothing about trafficking."

"Got it."

Sam turned the ignition and drove the car down the street, parking in front of the Christopoulis house. "Let's go."

"Don't bullshit me!" Sonia slammed her fist on the conference room table. Gleason blinked rapidly. He should be scared. Sonia was in no mood to play nice with criminals. And he was sitting here lying to her about Weber Trucking.

"You're the only person who knew we were asking about Weber Trucking," she said. "You alerted them."

Gleason shook his head. "No. I didn't. Check my phone records. Check my emails."

"I'll do that, with your permission," Sonia said, waiting for him to balk.

He didn't.

Dean sat casually on the edge of the table while Sonia stood, palms down on the surface, glaring at Gleason.

Dean was cordial, but firm. "You can see where we are having a problem believing you didn't alert someone to our investigation."

"I see what you're saying, really, but I didn't talk to anyone. I answered your questions, worked here until eight, nine at night, went home, and came back at eight this morning. This is a busy time of year for us."

He was telling the truth about his whereabouts, Sonia knew, because they had had an agent sitting on him all night. But she didn't believe for a second that he hadn't told someone.

"Three women are dead," Dean said calmly. "In a warehouse owned by Weber Trucking."

"That's awful."

"They were illegal Chinese immigrants," Sonia snapped. "Kidnapped and brought to this country by Omega Shipping—another of your dead boss's clients. Where does that leave you? Either dead, or an accessory. So tell us exactly who you talked to and what you said."

"You're barking up the wrong tree."

He was lying. His skin was pale except for his bright-red cheeks. He tapped his fingers on the table and kept looking from Dean to Sonia and back to Dean with a wide-eyed innocent stare. Sonia wasn't buying it. But nothing she said could make him talk. It infuriated her. She was usually much better at getting suspects to tell her everything they knew.

Maybe Toni was right; she was too close to the case. Yesterday, Gleason had hit on her. She should have played off that; instead, she'd let her anger and dislike of the man impede her judgment. Why hadn't she seen it before?

Her phone vibrated. She glanced down at the number. It was restricted.

"Get your cell phone and call your phone company to give us permission to access your phone records here and at home, or we'll get a warrant." Gleason shifted uncomfortably. "Now," she commanded.

Gleason jumped out of his chair and scurried from the room.

"Sonia—"

"I have a call. He doesn't need to listen in." She answered. "Hello."

"I gave you everything I have."

Charlie.

"I need to meet with you."

"You can't believe I'd fall for the oldest trick in the book."

"Charlie, I'm not going to arrest you. I give you my word. I need ten minutes, that's it. I have a picture taken in Mexico. I think you can help me identify these people."

"How can I trust you?"

Sonia wanted to scream. Instead she said, "Think back, Charlie. Have I ever lied to you? *Ever?* No! You lied to me right, left, and upside down, but I have always been honest, to my detriment. Dammit, you owe me! Five minutes of your fucking time and you walk away. This one time, I won't follow. But I swear to God, if you burn me I'll hunt you down and you'll be in prison or you'll be dead. I need you just this once to listen and tell me the truth."

She took a deep breath. Dean was staring at her, an odd look on his face, and it made her feel uncomfortable. As if he had just now seen the real Sonia Knight and didn't like what he saw. She turned her back to him. She didn't want to blow it with Dean, there was something about him she couldn't shake, but she couldn't change who she was. She didn't think she'd ever find anyone who could look at her and accept her, warts and all. Did she think Dean might be the exception just because he knew so much about her and hadn't already walked away?

Right now, she would do or say nearly anything to get Charlie to look at the photo of her father and the others and identify the man, or woman, who'd killed Jones and the Vegas. That person was starting up a far more ruthless human trafficking ring than even the vile Xavier Jones had created. Her experience and the little evidence they had told Sonia her instincts were right. And trusting her instincts had saved her life, and her career, many times over. Her instincts were all she had left to trust.

"Where are you?" Charlie asked.

"Downtown."

"Twenty minutes, Raley Field. River Cat dugout. Don't be late, there's a game tonight. I'll be gone in thirty, and I'm not coming back."

"Charlie, please—"

He hung up.

Sonia swore. "He'll meet."

"Are you sure you want to do this?"

"Of course! We need that information."

"Where?"

Sonia didn't want to ask, but she had to. She'd promised Charlie that she would give him a pass this time. She had to believe that Dean would support her decision. "You're not going to try anything?"

Dean's lips tightened. "I told you I wouldn't."

"I'm sorry, I just—"

"You don't trust anyone."

"That's not true." But he was right. She had a hard time with trust.

"Then it's just me you don't trust?" She felt the hurt and anger behind his softly spoken words.

"Of course I trust you." She wanted to. God, she wanted to. "More than anyone," she added honestly.

"Then you need to trust my word."

Was trusting Dean that hard for her? Hadn't he proven himself? Why was she fighting it? Not everyone was Charlie. Not everyone was her father.

"Raley Field. Twenty minutes." She saw that her brief hesitation hurt Dean. She wouldn't have hurt him for the world—and now, she didn't know if she could take it back. God, she wanted to. She didn't want him angry with her. "Dean—"

He interrupted. "We'd better get over there. Is it close by?"

"A couple minutes." She took his hand, squeezed, and dropped it as Gleason walked back into the room with two cell phones and said, "I gave Pac Bell permission to talk to you and faxed them the signed authorization. I swear, I didn't talk to anyone with Weber Trucking yesterday. You'll see."

"Thank you," Sonia said. "We'll be in touch." She walked out, and Dean followed.

In the elevator, he said, "I have your back, Sonia."

She tensed. Charlie had said the exact same thing to her before he had sold her.

"I'm not going to let anything happen to you, you know that," Dean said.

"I know," she said softly.

"What is it then?"

"Nothing."

"Don't lie to me. Don't clam up. Tell me what you're thinking."

Sonia didn't like being yelled at or ordered around. She stood toe to toe with Dean Hooper and said in a low growl, "Charlie told me he had my back, too, and look what happened there."

His face darkened. "I can't believe you're comparing me to that bastard."

Sonia stepped back. She couldn't believe she had said that either, especially on the heels of their recent conversation upstairs. She hadn't meant it. God, she didn't mean it. "I'm sorry," she mumbled lamely.

The elevator doors opened and they walked out in silence. Sonia didn't know what to say or do to fix it, but she feared she'd lost something important.

CHAPTER TWENTY-SEVEN

The River Cats minor league baseball team was playing at six that evening at Raley Field, and at three in the afternoon there were already employees and vendors showing up. Along the main entrance were places to eat and drink; inside everything was clean and well maintained. It was one of the nicest stadiums Dean had been in, though he'd admit that he hadn't been in many over the years.

Dean didn't know whether the team was already onsite. He wasn't expecting trouble, but any time he went into an unknown situation he was cautious. It had saved his life, and the lives of his fellow soldiers, during his years in the Marines, and it had helped avoid danger when he was in the field for the FBI.

Dean showed his badge and told the security guard they wouldn't be long. "When do ticket holders usually start to arrive?" Dean asked.

"We don't open up the gates to the public until ninety minutes before game time. But there's a high school singing the national anthem, and they're already here getting ready. The players start arriving two hours before. Is something wrong? Should I notify management?"

"Just routine." Dean was getting concerned. He didn't

like this arrangement, but being in the open stadium minimized the risk of being surprised. Still, there were civilians around, and that always increased the chances that something could go wrong.

They walked to the wide mezzanine level that curved around the back of the stadium, offering shade from the heat and a view of the field, plus access to all seating levels, restrooms, and food. A groundskeeper was walking the field and someone else was working near the scoreboard. But aside from employees in the corridor, the interior of the stadium was empty. Dean couldn't see if there was anyone in the shadows of the home team dugout. He hated sending Sonia in there alone.

"He'll know you brought someone," Dean said. "You're not so reckless as to walk into this alone. I'll stand back, let you do the talking."

"You would be a threat to him," Sonia said. "He won't come. I need him to look at this picture."

"Do you think he knows that's your father?"

"It's not something I like to discuss, even though everyone and their brother in this business seems to know."

That bothered her, Dean realized. The lack of privacy. Most people could dismiss a bad childhood, or simply not discuss it with their peers, but colleagues usually knew only what you told them. For Sonia, her childhood case had been high profile and well known among law enforcement. She didn't shy away from her past, but she didn't wear it on her sleeve, either.

"You didn't answer my question," Dean said.

Sonia closed her eyes and took a deep breath. When she opened them they were troubled. "Charlie might know what name he's using, but if he knows this man I doubt he knows its my father. Since no one could find him twenty years ago, it makes sense that he would be using a different identity. But Xavier Jones knew him, and Thomas Daniels—both men who worked out of northern California. I'm going to do this right. One step at a time. First, the case in hand. Then my father."

Dean lightly rubbed Sonia's arm. He greatly admired her inner strength. "I'll help you any way I can."

She gave him a half-smile. "That means a lot to me, Dean."

He reiterated, "Whatever happens here, whatever you learn, wherever you find your investigation headed, I'll be with you every step."

Her eyes glistened, then she blinked the emotions away. She opened her mouth to say something, then looked away, unsure.

He put his fingers on her cheek and turned her to face him. "You have my word." He kissed her softly, but felt surprising power between them in the light touch. It was a jolt of knowledge, something far more than he expected. "Be careful."

She whispered, "I know you have my back."

Dean felt the sincerity and weight of the trust she'd just placed in him. He skimmed his hand over her cheek, realizing this hadn't been easy for her.

"I'll watch you go down, then I'll find a place to keep an eye on the dugout. Text me if you get in trouble."

She cocked her head. "If I'm in trouble, I'm not going to take time to text you."

He pulled her phone out of her belt and typed his phone number into a blank message, then locked the phone. "Just press unlock and send. You can probably do it in your sleep."

"Thanks." She put the phone back in its pouch, then jogged down the stairs and leaped over the small fence that led to the field.

Dean wished he hadn't reacted so poorly when Sonia raised her hackles earlier. She'd simply reacted from her gut. She tried to backtrack, but Dean's ego had been bruised. He'd thought after last night she would know he was not only on her side, but capable of assisting her on all levels of this investigation. He should have cut her some slack from the beginning, knowing trust didn't come easy to her. But when she had compared him to that bastard Charlie Cammarata, Dean saw red. He didn't lose his temper often, but for a moment he was blinded when he should have understood it wasn't personal and, in fact, she'd been sharing something important with him. That she'd been betrayed and disappointed and was looking to him to prove that she could believe in him, trust him, love him.

She wanted to believe, but life had taught her differently. She wanted to trust, but people had proven they couldn't be trusted.

Dean would die before he disappointed her again. He never wanted to see the doubt in her eyes, the disbelief.

Their relationship may be just beginning, but they shared something valuable. Dean felt it deep down where he rarely allowed himself to look because it had always been empty. With Sonia around, he no longer felt the emptiness.

When Sonia slipped into the dugout, Dean maneuvered around the stadium and reached the stairs that led to a private observation deck on the first-base line. While it afforded a good view of the dugout, it was a little farther than he would have liked.

Movement to his right had him leaning against the back wall of the stadium. A group of teens dressed in identical attire descended noisily from the observation deck toward the field. He pulled the teacher aside and identified himself. "Can I ask that you hold off a moment?"

"Is there something wrong?" the young woman, who didn't look much older than her students, said.

"No, but my partner is checking into something. That young man over there"—he gestured toward one of the larger students—"can I borrow his T-shirt?" The shirt had the name of their school in white on blue.

"Um, would it help if I just gave you one of the extras?"

"It would help a lot. Thank you."

"When can we go down?"

"I'll let you know. Not more than thirty minutes."

He took the shirt from the teacher and stretched it out. It was an extra large, but still clung tightly across his shoulders. Fortunately, it was square cut and concealed his sidearm nicely.

"If you're going to use a disguise, I don't know if that will help much." She handed him her clipboard, then the River Cats cap from her head. "You can borrow these."

"Thanks, ma'am."

As soon as Sonia reached the dugout, she heard noise at the top of the bleachers where there was a semi-enclosed booth high up from the first-base line. A large group of teenagers dressed in blue-and-white T-shirts congregated, but they stayed in the bleachers. Good, she didn't want to have any more civilians to worry about.

She looked over the dugout—fairly secure. No doors or access point except through the front. The area was quite large—she'd never been in a dugout before. There was a ramp and stairs that led to it, and it was set back a bit from the field. Private. Surprisingly quiet. The dugout was in the shade, the sun behind the stadium. Even now, in the heat of a Sacramento June, the temperature was comfortable.

There was no reason for Charlie to hurt her, but she liked knowing her escape options. She could run out anywhere along the dugout as long as she leaped over the railing, or slid under it. Good. And it would be fairly easy to get to the bleachers or across the field. Not that she needed to escape. As she walked the dugout, her senses sharpened and she twitched. A million needles pricked her skin and she began to sweat. She took a deep breath, not letting her anxiety—she refused to call her fear of dark, enclosed places a phobia—take control. The needles went away, but her eyesight and hearing still felt heightened and she was jittery, as if she'd had too much caffeine.

She blamed her father for this fear. After he had sold her she'd been stuck in the back of a dark truck for nearly two weeks, allowed out only under cover of night and then watched by heavily armed guards. And in the basement, where Izzy was murdered. She hated being underground. The dark, the bugs, the foul, moldy smell—she felt as if she were thirteen again. Trapped. The dugout had been dug into the ground and the fresh earth reminded her of a new grave. That was what was getting to her. Damn Charlie. But she couldn't blame him completely; he didn't know. She didn't talk about it, she had never talked about it, hoping that by ignoring her reaction it would go away.

Another deep breath, and she grew calmer. She willed herself calm. She paced, unable to stay still, constantly checking each possible approach.

Twenty-two minutes had passed since Charlie called her. Where was he?

Movement on the field caught her sight, and she watched as a man in a blue shirt and cap crossed the field writing on a clipboard. It took her a couple seconds, but then she realized the man was Dean. She squinted and saw there were words in white printed on the back of the shirt. Resourceful. She had to admit to herself it relaxed her to have Dean in close proximity.

She sensed movement and turned, facing the far side of the long, narrow space. Charlie leaned against the wall, on the outside of the dugout, partly hidden in the shadows. When she saw him, he stepped inside and walked toward her.

"It's good to see you," he said.

Complex emotions battled. She did not like Charlie, but she couldn't forget that her training under him had been stellar. He was a lying, gloryhound bastard, but he also knew what he was doing and had freely shared his skills with her. It was ironic that the self-defense moves he'd taught her had saved her life when he put it in danger.

"You should have given me that journal two days ago. Three of those women are dead."

His expression hardened. Whether out of guilt or her refusal to pretend they were still friends and colleagues, she didn't know. "You wanted me to look at a picture."

She handed him the photo without comment.

He looked at it and she knew he saw something. "Where did you get this?"

"Through my investigation. It's seven to ten years old. You recognize Xavier Jones, of course. And Thomas Daniels—he was killed four years ago during a police investigation."

"The FBI. I remember hearing about it. It wasn't related to trafficking."

"Not directly, but he was a competitor of Jones," she said. "As I'm sure you knew."

"This looks like Mexico or Central America."

"Analysts believe it was taken outside of Acapulco."

He said, "Ashley was last seen near Acapulco."

"And you said there was a link between her and Jones. I need to know who the other men are. We don't have I.D.s on these three." She pointed to her father, the man next to him, and a man in the back on the far right. "Or the woman."

"I want this picture."

"No."

He stared at her.

"Why?" she prompted.

He didn't answer.

"Damn you, Charlie!"

"I can I.D. two of those men for you. If you want their names, and additional information, then you'll give me that picture."

Though it wasn't Dean's original photo, only a copy,

Sonia didn't want to give it to Charlie. She didn't want to help him in any of his vendettas. But he was stubborn. He wouldn't talk without getting something in return.

She handed it to him. "Name them."

"I don't know the man on the far right. But these two in the middle—Jaime Huerrera on the left. He's a drug dealer. Trafficking is a sideline, only when it furthers his goals. More money in drugs. But he provides routes. He was nobody ten years ago, a mid-level hack whose only claim to fame was he kept under the radar of law enforcement. He's also a great master of disguise. You probably have photos of him and don't know it. He's from Colombia and never crosses into the United States. I suspect that your friend from the FBI, the one watching us while pretending to be a choir boy, might be able to prove Jones was laundering drug money for Huerrera, once you decipher the journal."

"And the other man?" Sonia's heart raced and she was dizzy, whether from the confines of the dugout or what she expected to hear.

"I don't know his name. But I have seen him."

"Where? With who?"

"He's the man who killed Xavier Jones."

Charlie pocketed the photo. "I hope you catch him."

"Do you know who the woman is?" Sonia asked, her voice surprisingly calm. "She looks vaguely familiar, but I can't place her."

"You know who she is," Charlie said.

"No, I don't—" Dammit, she did. She'd only met Victoria Christopoulis once, over a year ago. And she looked much different now—older, with darker red hair. "Christopoulis."

"Bingo."

"I thought it was her son, not her—"

"He's involved, but she's in charge." Charlie took a step toward her. "Sonia, this is too big, too deadly. That's why you need people like me. I can go in and take care of—"

She put up her hand. Her voice was firm, though her insides burned. "Don't say it. I don't want to know what you've been up to, I don't want to know who you've killed. I'm not a vigilante, Charlie. I'm a cop. And I can't condone what you've done. This was your freebie. Now go. Before I arrest you."

Dean walked along the base of the bleachers in the red clay gravel that separated the stands from the playing field. He'd seen Cammarata slip into the dugout, so Dean moved in closer. He heard voices but couldn't make out the exact words. Then he heard Sonia distinctly say, "Go."

He tensed, every instinct on alert. His phone didn't vibrate, she wasn't in trouble. Still . . . he didn't like her tone. Practically hugging the wall, he ran to the edge of the dugout, then stood flush against the low wall.

Cammarata stepped from the dugout.

"Sonia—"

A flash of light in his periphery sent Dean back twenty years to his days in the Marines.

"Before I arrest you," Sonia said.

Dean didn't think; he acted solely on adrenaline and instinct.

"Down!" He rushed Cammarata who was in the line of fire and tackled him, pushing him down the short flight of stairs into the dugout.

Sonia hit the ground before they did, reacting on Dean's command to get down while he was still moving.

The sniper's bullet hit the wall where Sonia had been standing. It had been aimed at her chest, a perfect military sniper aim from more than three hundred yards. Which meant that the sniper was on the fence surrounding the stadium—the only buildings tall enough were across the river or not at the right angle to see into the dugout.

Dean crawled over to Sonia. "Are you hit?"

"No."

"Stay down, in this corner. He can't see you here. Flush against the wall. Do not move."

"What the fuck?" Cammarata exclaimed.

Dean crawled over to him and grabbed him by the collar as they lay on the hard-packed dirt floor. "Did you set Sonia up?"

"I didn't do anything."

"No one knew we were meeting you here. Someone followed you or you led them here."

"No one followed me."

"I don't believe you."

Charlie pulled away from Dean and Dean barely resisted the urge to hit him. What that bastard had done to Sonia, he didn't deserve to be walking free. But the movement would get them shot.

"Stay *down*!" Dean shouted, pushing himself up against the short wall and hoping the sniper wasn't at a high enough angle to see fully into the dugout.

The ground in front of them suddenly jumped as bullets hit on the edge of the ground.

They were sitting ducks.

"I called nine-one-one," Sonia said, "and emailed Richardson and Trace."

"Quick thinking."

The bullets stopped and they heard shouts and screams from the bleachers. The choir.

Charlie started to sit up.

"Down!" Dean pulled him down, though he deserved to get his head blown off.

"Don't touch me!" Charlie scooted away. "I wasn't being stupid."

"There's a first." Dean glared.

"What's your fucking problem, Fibbie?"

"You."

There were sirens in the distance.

"Are we clear?" Sonia asked, her voice quivering.

"No," Dean said. The sniper had aimed right at Sonia. Sonia was the primary target. Not Cammarata, not him, Sonia. What did she know that was dangerous to the traffickers? Who wanted her dead? Dean was ninety-nine percent certain no one had followed them, and had they, there'd been at least a dozen easier shots to take—getting in and out of the car, for example—than a sniper's rifle from more than three hundred yards.

Charlie Cammarata had to have led the shooter here.

Dean pulled himself over to Sonia. She was shaking and her hands were ice cold. "Are you hit?" he asked again.

"N-no."

"Stay low."

Suddenly, rapid fire hit the wall behind them. Sonia's fingers dug into his biceps.

Then it stopped. The sirens were closer. Dean waited. Waited. Minutes passed. Sonia was still shaking.

Someone called into the dugout. "Police! Is anyone there?"

Dean crawled to the dugout stairs and peered over. Police were all over the field, a large number by the fence halfway between center and right outfield.

"Special Agent Dean Hooper, FBI," he shouted.

"You're clear."

Dean rose and offered his hand to Charlie Cammarata, who ignored it and stood on his own. Two West Sacramento police officers came over to them. Dean showed his I.D. and badge.

"Take this man into custody, please," Dean said.

Cammarata fumed. "Fucking prick, that wasn't the arrangement—" he pulled his arm back to hit Dean. Before the cops could run interference, Dean decked Cammarata square in the face with the palm of his hand. Blood spurted from his nose, and the two cops took him into custody. They read him his rights.

A third cop, this one a black man with rank, approached. "Chief of Police Rob Morrison."

"Dean Hooper, FBI. Did you get him?"

"No. Had a driver waiting for him. We're searching, but word is when they hit Cap City Freeway heading east, they lost the vehicle. We have a partial plate and description of the SUV, plus a possible witness. We're on it."

"Sounds like it. Though you have the lead, please work with my office on this. It's part of an active investigation."

Morrison jerked his head toward Cammarata. "Is this guy a suspect?"

"In the shooting?" Dean glared at Cammarata. "I don't know."

"Fuck you, Hooper."

"What charges?"

"We'll start with obstruction of justice." Dean's blood was still pumping.

"Sonia!" Cammarata shouted. "Dammit, Sonia! Tell him to let me go." He fought against the cuffs and one of the cops tightened them.

Sonia.

Dean ran back into the dugout.

Sonia was sitting up, her back against the wall, her arms wrapped around her knees. She was shaking, ghostly pale, and he heard her mumbling something to herself.

She was whispering, "Get up, Sonia. Don't be a wimp. On your feet."

"Sonia?" He squatted in front of her, touched her face.

She looked at him and he saw she was scared, as if suddenly the reality of the attack had hit her. "It's over. He's gone."

She shook her head. "I—I." She swallowed. "Dammit." She took a deep breath. "I'm claustrophobic. Just give me. A minute. One minute." Sonia sounded angry with herself, over and above the fear.

He picked her up and carried her from the dugout. As soon as the sun hit her face, he felt her sigh deeply.

Cammarata called out, "Sonia, are you hurt?"

Dean glared at him and said, "Take him to jail. I don't want to look at him. I'll be in contact with you later."

"Bastard," Cammarata said.

He didn't respond, but walked Sonia to the middle of the field and sat her on the pitcher's mound. The color returned to her face and she let out a deep breath.

"I'm sorry," she said.

"No apologies."

"Time hasn't changed anything. Twenty-one years hasn't fixed me."

"You're so wrong." He turned her face to his, made her look into his eyes, and said, "You didn't panic when you had to act. You did what had to be done first and foremost. That's what's important."

She closed her eyes and leaned her forehead against his for a moment, then said, "I'm okay now."

"We can sit here as long as you want."

"It's my father."

"Excuse me? The photo— You knew that."

She looked so sad and lost, but she was getting her fire back. He saw it with each breath she took. Dean was relieved; he didn't like seeing her weak. It reminded him that she wasn't invincible, that people wanted her dead. He couldn't let it happen. He *wouldn't* let it happen. They'd have to kill him first, and Dean was hard to hit. His former Marine buddies nicknamed him Sylvester because he had nine lives. He'd seen a lot of combat, but had never gotten so much as a scratch.

"Charlie didn't know his name, but positively identified my father as the man who killed Xavier Jones."

"You think he was telling the truth?"

"Yes. He didn't know it was my father, and I didn't tell him. The man standing next to him, one of the others you didn't have an I.D. for, is Jaime Huerrera, a drug smuggler from Colombia and Charlie thinks Jones might have been laundering money for him, and proof will be in the journal."

"I'll pass the name and photo on to the DEA."

"I gave Charlie the picture. That was his requirement."

"Why?"

"Probably for his own vendetta. I don't know, but I needed the information. I'm sorry. You can get it back now. Did you really arrest him?"

"Yes."

"I promised—"

"That was before he led a sniper to you."

"There's no reason—"

"Maybe not on purpose, but there's no other explanation. No one knew we were coming here, except my boss and your boss. And I didn't tell Bob we were going to be in the dugout. I told him the stadium."

"I didn't tell Toni anything other than I was meeting him."

"I don't think I'm the best person to interrogate him. I can't be impartial." Dean ran his hand up and down Sonia's arm. "Not after what he did to you. But I thought Callahan and your partner, Trace Anderson, could take it on. Cammarata has information about tomorrow night, I feel it in my gut."

"I agree."

Dean was relieved they were on the same page.

"There is one other possible explanation."

"What's that?"

"Craig Gleason. I got the call from Charlie when we were in his office. What if he eavesdropped on us?"

"Gleason was never in the military. He has no firearms training in his background and, frankly, I don't see him having the balls to kill."

"He could have called someone."

Dean agreed. "I can see him giving out information. The time line is so close, though. To put all this together in less than thirty minutes—from the time you got the call to execution? They had to know exactly where you would be. Cammarata called you, he decided on the venue, right down to the dugout. It has to be him."

"There's no reason he would want me dead."

"Maybe he planned on saving your life and getting into your good graces again."

She didn't say anything for a long moment. "That's stretching it."

"But it's in his personality. To play the hero, the great savior." He couldn't see Charlie Cammarata caring about anyone but himself.

"It's not Charlie," Sonia said, but in her tone Dean heard doubt. "I'm putting my money on Gleason."

"Then let's get over there and push hard," Dean said. He stood and held out his hand to Sonia.

She took it.

"You're filthy," he said.

"So are you," she said as he pulled her to her feet. "Nothing that sun and the clear blue sky can't fix."

CHAPTER TWENTY-EIGHT

When Dean and Sonia arrived downtown to visit Glea-son at XCJ Consulting in the Senator Hotel, less than two miles from Raley Field, they couldn't get anywhere near the entrance.

Sonia glanced at Dean. He looked disheveled, his nor-mally neat hair hanging loose across his forehead, and they were both covered in dirt and grass stains. Her el-bows were scraped from where she'd cowered in the corner against the cement in the dugout. The panic was so far behind her now that she almost didn't believe it had happened, except for residual embarrassment.

Dean walked to the tape and flashed his badge, then went under. He was stopped.

"Sir, can I see that identification again?" the female cop asked.

"We don't look like federal cops," Sonia told Dean. She recognized the cop from Sac P.D. "Sheila, right? I'm Sonia Knight, Riley's sister. With ICE."

"Sonia. Right. You look like you've been through the wringer."

"We both have," Sonia said. "This is Agent Hooper with the FBI. What happened?"

"Guy killed on the fourth floor."

"When?"

"About an hour ago. Call came in at two fifty-three p.m."

She looked at Dean. "That's right after we left," she said. "Not ten minutes."

"Excuse me?" Sheila said.

"Who's the victim?"

"I don't have a name, I'm just holding the masses back."

"We need to get in. We were interviewing a potential suspect in a multijurisdictional murder investigation on the fourth floor this afternoon."

"Go right ahead. But tell the detective in charge you're here."

"Who is it?"

"Detective John Black. And I heard Riley is out of the hospital. That's great news."

"It is," Sonia agreed, and she and Dean went to the fourth floor.

Black was standing in the hall talking to two uniformed officers. When he saw them, he said, "I thought I'd be seeing one or both of you as soon as I found out the murder was at XCJ Consulting."

"Gleason?" Dean asked.

"Bingo."

"Murder?"

"Right again. Want to go for a grand slam?"

Dean frowned.

"Never mind. It's been a long week. Come in and see for yourself. They haven't moved the body. The crime scene techs are still working the scene."

"Simone?"

"No, but they're still good."

Gleason had been shot in his office at his desk. His

brains and half his scalp were plastered on the window behind him.

"The bullet went out the window?" Dean asked.

"Almost," Black said, "but it's actually in the window. It looks like a forty-five slug."

"One shot?"

"It did the job."

Sonia looked at the angle of the body and the blood spatter on the wall and window. "He was standing when he was shot. The impact pushed him back into his chair."

"Good call. That's what I was thinking, too. I think the killer was looking for something."

"After shooting Gleason? How do you know?"

"Our shooter was interrupted by one of the other lobbyists coming into the office. I was about to interview him, he had an interesting story to tell the responding officer."

"Where was the killer searching?"

"The conference room."

"Did he find anything?" Dean asked.

"We don't know. The lobbyist doesn't think so. I have a team going over it carefully, but we don't know what we're looking for. There's really nothing in the conference room."

"Let's talk to the lobbyist," Sonia said.

Black led them out of XCJ offices and down the hall. "I have him settled into another office. I didn't want to let him go; he might be the only one who can identify the killer."

Rich Mercer was a tall, slender thirty-something with a hairline just beginning to recede and silver wire-rimmed glasses. He sat on the leather couch of the office—a political consulting office, according to the door plaque—and jumped when they walked in.

"Mr. Mercer," Black said, "Dean Hooper with the FBI and Sonia Knight with Immigration and Customs Enforcement. We'd like to follow up with your statement to the responding officer, while it's still fresh in your mind."

"Absolutely, Detective," Mercer said in a voice stronger than his appearance. "Anything to help."

"Why don't you start from the beginning? Mr. Gleason let the staff go early?"

"Yes. We came in this morning and he told us to go home, that he was closing the office due to Mr. Jones's murder. Is this connected?" he asked.

"We don't know yet," Black responded. "Go on."

"He was insistent, even when I told him I had meetings lined up and dozens of phone calls to return. He told me to work from home.

"I took my files and went home. I had a one o'clock lunch meeting at the Esquire, and after that walked back to the Capitol with the senator, we parted at the entrance, and I was going to return to my car, but I was worried about Craig. He hadn't taken Mr. Jones's murder well. I honestly didn't think they were that close— that doesn't sound good. I mean, everyone is upset about Mr. Jones, but no one really knew him. He came in once a week and that was it. He had his own clients, didn't care anything about the rest. That was Craig's domain. He managed ninety-five percent of the workload."

"Can you give specific examples of why you think Mr. Gleason wasn't handling the murder well?" Dean asked.

"I don't know. He looked like he hadn't slept last night. He had on one blue sock and one black sock. Craig is meticulous in his appearance. He wouldn't make that mistake."

Sonia concurred. "So you came back here. What time?"

"Just before three. Ten to three, five to three. I don't know for sure, but when I walked past the bank on L Street the digital clock said two-fifty. I remember because I had two hours on the parking meter and that gave me ten minutes to get back to my car."

"You don't have a parking garage?"

"Sure, but the lot is on the opposite end of town from the Esquire, and I was running late. My wife—" he stopped and blushed. "Well, I'm not usually home during the day and the baby was napping."

Sonia didn't need to hear more. "So you noticed the time—"

"And considered not even going up. Parking tickets are like thirty bucks now, ridiculous, and I swear those traffic cops have a sensor that tells them when a meter is about to expire, because I always get nailed. But I thought about Craig, thinking maybe we'd go for drinks or something. Let him talk it out. Maybe he was worried about the clients, but except for Jones's own clients, I don't think anyone would have left. They all liked Craig.

"So I went up the stairs—the elevator is incredibly slow—and while I was in the stairwell I heard a gunshot. I ran up to the fourth floor and—"

"Excuse me for interrupting," Black said, "but you ran *toward* a gunshot."

"I thought Craig had . . . killed himself. I didn't know why but he had all the signs of being depressed. I didn't think murder until I walked in and saw the guy in the conference room."

"How many minutes lapsed from the sound of the gunshot and when you saw the man?"

"One? No more than ninety seconds."

"What was he doing in the conference room?"

"I have no idea. He saw me and pointed the gun at me and I ran out, came in here."

"It was open?"

"Margie was here. She's the secretary. She had called the police when she heard the gunshot and was still on the phone with them when I came in. I locked the door and put a chair up and told her to tell you guys to hurry. I thought he'd follow me, but he didn't."

"Can you describe him?"

"Chinese. Tall. Had a pockmarked face, like from teenage acne, though this guy was in his forties or older. Wore a dark gray suit. Looked expensive."

"Had you ever seen him before?"

"Not recently, but last year he was here and had a meeting with Mr. Jones at Chops."

"Just him and Jones?"

"No. Two of Jones's clients were there as well, from Rio Diablo."

"And you remembered him after a year?" Sonia asked.

"Sure. You don't forget a face like that."

Dean retrieved the photo he'd taken back from Charlie. "Do you recognize any men in this photograph?"

Mercer looked closely at the picture. "There's Mr.

Jones, of course." He started to shake his head. "No . . . oh, yeah, I know him."

His finger tapped on the face of Sonia's father. She tensed.

"You know this man? From where?"

"It's been a long time." He closed his eyes and didn't say anything for a minute.

Sonia was getting antsy, wanted to push him, but Dean put a hand on her knee and held a finger to his lips.

"Devereaux!" Mercer exclaimed.

"Devereaux?" Sonia repeated.

"Four years ago he was here."

"In XCJ offices?"

"No, it was at the Hyatt. Dawson's, the restaurant downstairs. My top client wanted a dinner meeting with Mr. Jones. Jones didn't want to, but finally agreed so we went to Dawson's. On our way out, Mr. Devereaux was coming in. He didn't seem very friendly when Mr. Jones said hello, but he congratulated him."

"On what?"

"I have no idea."

"How'd you know his name?"

"The hostess came up and said, 'Mr. Devereaux, we located the Scotch you requested. Your table is ready.'"

"He was alone?"

"I think so."

"And you remember that? A brief meeting years ago?" Sonia asked in disbelief.

"I have a good memory for names and faces, it's part of my job, especially with the turnover we have in that building now after term limits." He jerked his thumb behind him in the general direction of the Capitol building. "But I probably wouldn't have remembered at all except that after Mr. Devereaux was seated in the far back of the restaurant, Mr. Jones asked the hostess what the Scotch was that he had ordered. Laphroaig. You just don't forget Scotch whisky like Laphroaig. The man has good taste."

The Hyatt Hotel was across the street from the Senator and John Black pulled together all the cops he could spare to cover every exit, then he, Dean, and Sonia went to the general manager and confirmed that a guest named Pierre Devereaux was currently registered and staying on the tenth floor.

"How many people are staying in the room?" Dean asked.

"Three."

"Names?"

The manager looked on the screen. "Mr. Devereaux, his brother Tobias Devereaux, and Lee Chin. There's a king bed in each of the adjoining bedrooms, plus a Murphy bed in the meeting room."

"When did they check in?"

"Late check-in Tuesday night."

"When are they scheduled to leave?"

"Sunday."

"Please pull all security disks since Tuesday night," Dean said, "and find out which housekeeping staff has cleaned the rooms. I want them all brought to a secure area, but I don't want them talking to each other. And call each guest on that floor and tell them to stay inside their room until you call again. Understand?"

"Yes, Agent Hooper."

Black spread the information around to his men. Dean pulled Sonia aside. "You can't come upstairs. It could—" he didn't finish.

"I know," she said reluctantly. "We have to protect the integrity of the case. We're close, Dean. Be careful."

"I don't want you down here alone," Dean said. "If he somehow slips through and sees you." He motioned for one of the uniforms.

"Officer—" he looked at his badge.

"Jerry," Sonia said. "How are you?"

"Good. Glad to hear Riley's better."

"Me, too. Agent Hooper thinks I need a babysitter. Care for the job?"

He straightened. "Is this about the Devereaux guy?"

"Yes. It's complicated."

"Jerry?" Dean said. "No one gets near her. Find an office and stay there until I call."

"Yes, sir."

Dean turned to Sonia. "Okay?"

"I understand. He wants me dead." She steeled herself. "I'm good. But you be careful, too."

They took the elevator to the ninth floor, then Dean and Black got off and took the stairs up one floor while three uniformed cops took the elevator up. Black had a master room key.

The Park Capitol Suite had three separate doors. With two cops on each door, they counted and entered simultaneously.

Three. Two. One.

Black inserted the passkey and pushed down the handle while pushing the door in. He went in high while Dean went in low.

"Freeze, Police!" Black shouted while Dean did the same thing with, "FBI!"

The room was empty. The beds were made, but disheveled. They quickly searched the room and confirmed that no one was hiding.

Devereaux and his cohorts had left quickly. There were toiletries in the bathrooms. A personal robe behind one door. But no suitcases, no clothing or computers.

"The killer knew he'd been seen. They ran," Dean said.

With gloves, they went through the drawers and closets more meticulously, looking for anything that would give them a hint as to where Devereaux and the other two men had gone. No airline tickets, no notes or receipts.

Dean opened the wet bar and carefully pulled out a half-full bottle of Laphroaig. He said, "Let's get this printed and tested ASAP. Detective, if you don't mind, I've taken the liberty of calling in my team. I need this place gone over with a fine-tooth comb." He swore under his breath. "We were so close."

Black said, "He's on the run. I'll talk to hotel security and get a better shot of him if they have one."

"Great," Dean said.

"We should release it to the media," Black said.

"I don't know." Dean frowned. He remembered what Hans Vigo said during the conference call. The killer would make mistakes when pushed, but if trapped he could be more dangerous. He already knew where Sonia lived, where she worked, and even had an assassin track her to the baseball stadium.

But he knew what Sonia would say if she were here. There were too many lives at stake *not* to push him.

"If not the media, all law enforcement," Black said. "Airports, train stations, ports."

"Absolutely," Dean said. "And I'll talk to Bob Richardson and Sonia about releasing the image to the media. But only a current photo, so if the Hyatt doesn't have anything recent—"

"Understood," Black said. His cell phone rang. "Excuse me." He stepped into the hall.

Dean stood in the center of the room and looked one last time at the expensive suite Sonia's biological father had been living in for the past three days. Trying to get into his head, to think how he thought.

Why had he gone after Sonia at the stadium? Attempting to kill a federal police officer would make law enforcement more resolute in tracking him down.

He also didn't need to kill the three Chinese girls in the warehouse. He's left a message—*you are too late*—as a taunt. He knew Sonia was involved in the investigation because of Greg Vega. And he had to have known Sonia was his daughter he'd sold.

The assassination was personal on the one hand—he wanted Sonia dead. Not because she knew something important per se, but because she irritated him. She was pushing, and he probably couldn't stand the fact that his own daughter—a woman—could get so close to taking him down.

But it was also functional. The attempt would divide their resources just as the murders of the Chinese girls did. As Hans said, the killer didn't care if they knew who was responsible because he believed he was untouchable.

And if Sergio Martin, aka Pierre Devereaux, left the country, he very well could get away with everything.

Dean would not let that happen.

Black came back inside. "I know what the killer was looking for in the conference room."

"What?"

"A listening device. The room was bugged."

Victoria Christopoulis had been gracious when she allowed Sam and Trace to come into her home, but she gave them no answers. She played ignorant. Yet Sam suspected the woman was shrewd. He saw it in her eyes.

So he drove away, circled the neighborhood, and came back, parking far down the street. Just barely able to see her driveway. If she left, he'd know.

Thirty minutes later, the Mercedes skidded out of the garage.

"Good instincts," Trace said as Sam pursued the car. He picked up his phone and called Dean.

As soon as Dean stepped into the office where Sonia paced while Officer Jerry Strong stood at the door, she knew her father had slipped away.

"I'm sorry," Dean said.

"Dammit," she said. "It's not anyone's fault. He's like two steps ahead of us! We need a break."

"We have one. The conference room was bugged. That's how the killer knew where to find you."

"How long were they listening?"

"I don't know—"

"Yesterday? When we asked Gleason all those questions about Jones's clients? That's why they killed those women."

"Don't—you have no idea why they killed the women. We've done everything by the book, we've responded immediately when we learned information, and we have been proactive. Excuse me." He picked up his BlackBerry.

Sonia tried to figure out her father's next move. He killed—or had ordered killed—three of the women. Why? To torment her. To send them on a wild chase. To keep them away from finding the truth. He wanted to jerk them around so they didn't know which lead to pursue—so he could sell the remaining women and leave the country before they could find him, or the victims.

It made sense. Throw a half-dozen murders out there and all of them were running around trying to make the connection. But it wasn't the murders that were important—at least, not right now. The only thing they should focus on was where the girls were taken when moved from the Weber warehouse.

San Joaquin County sheriffs were looking for Joel Weber and his son, Jordan, but hadn't found them yet. They could even be dead—Sonia wouldn't put it past her father. The Webers might be the only living people who could put a face on the man who now called himself Pierre Devereaux. Or maybe they felt the heat of the investigation and ran.

She and Dean had found the warehouse by tracking the property records of Jones's clients; would Devereaux use an existing location? Would he be able to find anything else? Based on the evidence at the warehouse, there had to be at least thirty women who'd been smuggled in. They wouldn't be easy to hide for long.

Dean said, "That was Sam. He's tracking Victoria Christopoulis."

"Oh shit, the woman in the picture—"

"Is Victoria," Dean finished.

"How'd you know?"

"Sam said she looked familiar and he went through the photos I'd sent him related to the case."

"Charlie told me but it slipped my mind, I'm sorry."

"After being shot at?"

She rubbed the bridge of her nose with her knuckle. "Maybe I am too close to this."

"We'll find him, Sonia." Dean's voice was full of anger and confidence. "He's not getting away this time." Dean glanced at his phone again. "It's headquarters." He answered, listened, then hung up and said, "Sonia, they broke part of the code in Jones's journal. They have a couple ideas where the women are being held. We have to get to FBI headquarters immediately." He paused, glanced at his dirty clothes, and back at Sonia. "I think there's time to change."

Noel threw a glass against the wall.

"Does no one have pride in their work? A military sniper can't take out one little woman? You couldn't kill one fucking *witness* and we have to leave my hotel?"

He hated the pressure of not being able to come and go as he pleased. He hated thinking that people were watching him, waiting for him to fuck up.

He wasn't going to. Noel had a backup plan, didn't he?

They were in a house on the Indian reservation. The Indians owed them—hadn't Noel made them rich? It had been Xavier's idea, and it had been brilliant, but it was mostly Noel's money. So he had no problem coming to collect.

Once the casino was built, they'd have far more freedom. He didn't need Gleason after all, Ling had developed a rapport with the Rio Diablo tribe.

He threw another glass against the wall. It felt good to destroy something. He turned to Ling. "Call in every pilot, everyone you can trust. Have them on call to meet at the exchange site tonight."

"Tonight?"

"We're moving everything up twenty-four hours. If the buyers don't agree to my terms, we'll kill the women and get out. I'm not staying in this fucking country to see another sunrise."

"And Sonia Knight?"

"She'll be dead before we leave." Noel rubbed his face. Damn, he wanted to kill her himself. He wanted to slit her throat and watch her die. He hated her, hated her with more passion than he'd felt for anything in a very long time. Some of his colleagues said they appreciated a worthy adversary. Not Noel. He preferred idiots he could fool, bribe, or kill.

"You put yourself at risk if you pursue her alone," Ling warned.

"Ten thousand to whoever kills her," Noel said reluctantly. "And I'll double it if they bring her to me, alive, before sunrise. But after that, I'll be on my way home. I'm never setting foot on American soil again." He spat on the floor to show his disdain.

"I'll make the arrangements."

CHAPTER
TWENTY-NINE

Dean drove a circuitous route to his temporary apartment so he and Sonia could shower and change after the sniper incident and subsequent raid of Devereaux's hotel suite. On Dean's orders two agents followed to keep close watch on Sonia, though Dean wasn't about to let her out of his sight.

While she showered, Dean called Sam Callahan to make sure he got the message about the task force meeting at headquarters. As far as Dean was concerned, they were on duty until Devereaux and the women were found.

"Callahan."

"Did you get my message about the meeting?"

"Yes, but I'm still following Victoria Christopoulis. She just left Bank of America. She was inside for sixty-nine minutes. I stayed behind, while Trace followed her in my car. I talked to the manager, found out that she withdrew two hundred thousand in cash. Also learned that she had a safe-deposit box jointly with her son. He didn't know what was in it, but she went in and cleaned it out—left the box on the table, open and empty."

"Go on."

"Trace called and said he thought she's heading for the San Francisco Airport. He contacted the DOT at the airport and learned that she bought a ticket—from the time stamp, while she was still at home—to Vancouver, British Columbia, with a connection tomorrow morning to Montreal, and a connection from there to Greece."

"She's fleeing."

"You bet. And getting out of the country as fast as possible. There's a faster way going through New York City, but she's headed across the border into Canada."

"Who won't extradite on a death penalty case."

"I need an arrest warrant, before she gets on the plane. Definitely before it takes off."

"I need a reason."

"Suspicious behavior?"

"You're funny."

"Seriously, we show up and she clears out Omega's business account, their joint safe-deposit box, and gets an international flight? She's associating with known criminals? The photo?"

"How long has she been in America?"

"Ten days, but she comes often for both business and vacation. She's in the country at least three months out of the year. We've been looking into Omega and no one has run before. There must be something more."

"Maybe she thinks we're closer."

"Or she found out something we don't know."

"Detain her. Attempt to flee to avoid questioning in a capital offense. We'll have her for seventy-two hours at least. I'll call the U.S. attorney right now, give them a heads-up."

"When Trace picks her up, where do you want him to take her? Immigration might have jurisdiction."

"Bring her back to FBI headquarters. This is a joint task force, we'll deal with jurisdictional issues later. Hell, maybe we'll both take a stab at her. She sounds like a peach. But have him take backup." He hung up and called the U.S. attorney he'd been working with.

The U.S. attorney wasn't pleased, but understood that they couldn't allow Christopoulis to get on the plane. If she left U.S. borders it would be far more costly to get her back. They'd likely have international diplomacy issues, but since ICE was involved, the Department of Homeland Security could take the heat.

Sonia came out of the bedroom, still flushed from her shower. She was putting her wet hair up. "Your turn."

Dean said, "Victoria Christopoulis is fleeing."

She paled. "Because I didn't tell you about the photo fast enough?"

"No. Sam and Trace have been following her all afternoon. She withdrew over two hundred thousand U.S. dollars, plus whatever was in a safe-deposit box, and made flight arrangements to Canada. I told them to detain her and bring her in for questioning."

"I want to be there for that one," she said.

"I'll be ten minutes, then we'll go."

Sonia called Simone Charles to find out if she'd learned anything from the three women who'd been killed and left in the warehouse.

"Actually, yes," Simone said.

"And?"

"They were all pregnant."

"Pregnant?"

"Anywhere from two to four weeks."

Sonia did the math. "Four weeks was about the time they were kidnapped."

"There were signs of repeated rapes. Bruising, tearing. I have the embryos for DNA testing against possible suspects. You find them, I'll nail them. Gladly."

"How'd they know the girls were pregnant?" Sonia thought out loud.

"What? You think they knew?"

"They had to. It makes sense." Her stomach churned and she swallowed uneasily. "You don't just kill your meal ticket for no reason. They must have given them pregnancy tests when they arrived."

"Oh shit, I think you're right."

"What evidence could you have?"

"The test sticks. You know—you pee on them and they turn blue if you're pregnant. When we were processing the scene we found dozens of them tossed into a corner with trash."

"Do you know exactly how many?"

"Just a sec—" Sonia heard the shuffling of paper. "Thirty-seven."

"And three were blue?"

"Possibly, I don't have that here, and the biological evidence would be contaminated at this point. But why kill the pregnant women?"

"Because abortions are more expensive than murder." Sonia's voice cracked. "And they wanted to intimidate me."

"That's sick."

"You don't know the half of it. Let me know if you find anything else." She hung up and squeezed her eyes shut. Took a deep breath, then another, then another. But the damn tears came out; she couldn't stop them. They were so close, but they needed more information. Better information. Jones's journal was their only hope, but the analysts had only theories, no facts.

But Charlie could help. He knew more than he was saying. He might not know exactly where, but he'd been with Jones for months. He could narrow it down, make an educated guess.

Dean walked in, dressed in a white T-shirt and Dockers. She hadn't seen him looking so casual. His hair was still wet and he was holstering his Glock. "Ready?" He looked at her and frowned. "What's wrong? What happened?"

She wiped away the remnant of her tears. "The women who were killed in the warehouse? They were pregnant. I think that's why they were killed."

Dean hugged her tightly. There really was nothing to say.

Sonia relished the comfort, breathed in Dean's fresh-scrubbed scent. She wished she had more time. She took a deep breath and said, "I want you to let Charlie help."

Dean's entire body stiffened and he stepped back, his face unreadable. But she felt his anger, and disbelief, vibrating off his rigid body.

Sonia continued, nervous but gaining confidence in her idea. She began to pace, a bad habit but the constant movement helped her focus her thoughts. "I promised him I wouldn't arrest him if he met with me. He gave us good information. He lived up to his end of the deal. And we now know he didn't lead the sniper to us, that was Gleason and the bug in the conference room."

"You don't know that he wasn't party to that," Dean said in a low voice.

"For what reason?" She threw her hands up in the air and stared out the window. Downtown traffic had decreased on the tail end of rush hour. Time was slipping away.

"You had him fired, for one."

"That was ten years ago." She turned around, faced Dean. She didn't like that she couldn't read him, that he stared at her so dispassionately. Bile rose up her throat as she thought about what might have been. She had thought he understood her, but maybe she had been wrong. Maybe she wasn't worthy of love or any of the security she'd longed for.

She said, "Charlie could have killed me the other night in my house. Dean, please listen. Please understand. He doesn't want to kill me, and he's not working with the bad guys."

"I cannot believe you are defending him."

Sonia took a deep breath. Her uncertainty and confusion turned to anger. "I'm not! I've never defended him or what he did to me. Dammit, Dean, you didn't live through it! You weren't there. I've lived with what happened for ten years. Not just what happened to me, but going through the hearings, telling what happened to a panel full of bureaucrats—most of whom had never been in the field, who had no idea what we faced every day. I was cross-examined, I was questioned, I was made to feel guilty even though I had nothing to be guilty about—except naïveté and trusting my partner. This righteous anger of yours—don't take it on for me. There're more important things at stake. Charlie can help. He was in Jones's operation for months. He may know something to help us find those women before it's too late!"

Dean stepped toward her and grabbed her by the arms, pulled her to him so their faces were inches apart. She thought he had been still as a rock, but she felt his muscles vibrating. "I hate him for what he did to you. That man is selfish, he doesn't consider anyone but himself, never thinks of the consequences or who might be hurt. I can't forget, it's eating me up inside. I can't forget because it happened to *you*. You, Sonia Knight, I can't get you out of my mind. You complete me. You make me want more than this job. I want *you*. I think about what he did and see red. I feel your pain here." He pounded his chest. "I look at you with such pride, knowing that most people would never have recovered from such an evil betrayal. Evil—that's what Charlie Cammarata did. He may not have thought it through, he made excuses to himself to justify it, but he should have been in prison."

Dean was shaking. Tears rolled down Sonia's cheeks and she reached for his face. His mouth turned and kissed her hand, then his arms were around her, holding her tight, his lips on her lips, pulling her as close as he could, close to his body, his heart, his soul. Sonia felt every ounce of anger and passion and love pouring out of Dean. It humbled her and empowered her.

She kissed him, her hands around his neck, his hands fisted in her back. He kissed her neck, her ear, got down on his knees and held her, his face pressed against her stomach. His body shook and she dropped to her knees, took his face into her hands.

"Dean—" she whispered.

He stared at her, his eyes red with unshed tears. "I can't lose you, Sonia."

Her breath caught in her throat. "You won't."

CHAPTER THIRTY

Dean sent two agents to bring Charlie Cammarata from the West Sacramento jail to FBI headquarters. Sonia was working with Sam Callahan in the war room putting together a map and search grid. She was certain that the women were being held on property owned by Jones or one of his three primary clients, and Dean concurred. Unfortunately, though the analysts were making great headway with Jones's journal, they'd been premature in their declaration of knowing where the girls were being held. They did confirm, however, that Jones had paid two thousand U.S. dollars for their abduction.

Sam and Sonia were more than capable of coming up with a game plan. Dean needed to meet one-on-one with the man who had become a wild card—not only in this investigation, but in Dean's relationship with Sonia. Whether Sonia realized it or not, Cammarata stood between them and the future.

The agents brought the former immigration agent into an interview room. Cammarata took one look at Dean and scowled.

Dean motioned for him to sit.

"How about taking off these handcuffs?"

"Not until we have an agreement," Dean said. He

waited for the agents to leave, then sat down across from Cammarata.

"You can't hold me. You have nothing on me. No case. I haven't done anything."

"Possession of fake identification and social security number, which is a federal crime."

"Misdemeanor."

"Possession of a concealed weapon without a CCW."

"Misdemeanor."

"Aiding and abetting a known trafficker. Obstruction of justice. Concealing information from a federal law enforcement officer. Resisting arrest. Breaking and entering. I think we're getting into some pretty good felonies now."

Cammarata scowled. "What the fuck do you want, Hooper?"

"I'd like you in prison. But I'm giving you an offer."

"I'll take my attorney."

Dean slammed his palm on the table. "That's not an option."

"I'm sorry, when was the Constitution repealed?"

"I don't like you."

"The feeling is mutual."

"The only reason you're here is because Sonia thinks you will help."

At the mention of Sonia's name, Cammarata's eyes shifted. He swallowed uneasily, asked gruffly, "She okay, after today?"

Dean didn't answer the question. "This is the deal. You help us locate the Chinese women Omega transported into the area, and I let you go."

"If I knew where they were, I would have told Sonia."

"Just like you gave her the journal? A day late and a dollar short?"

Cammarata leaned forward. "You don't know anything about me or Sonia."

Dean wasn't going to rise to the bait, but his gut churned. "I know you pretend to care about her, but she'll be the first you'll sacrifice if it gets you what you want."

"What do you know about what I want? My record was stellar."

"Your record was built on the backs of other agents you used or sacrificed so you could take the credit and glory. You're right, I don't understand you. I don't understand how you could sell your own partner and not even send in backup."

"We saved dozens of innocent civilians."

"And you were willing to let Sonia die." Dean stood. "Sonia has more compassion in her little finger than you have in that huge ego you carry. She seems to have forgiven you. I haven't. I never will. You have two choices. Agree to help, share all information you know, adhere to all my conditions, and I'll grant you immunity for your part in this fiasco. Or you can go back to jail and I will have you prosecuted for every last charge the U.S. attorney and I can come up with. But you will *never* get out of prison. Those are your choices. You have five minutes."

Dean walked out and shut the door. He leaned against the wall and closed his eyes, took a deep breath. He didn't want to do this. He didn't want to work with that bastard. But they had little to no choice at this point. Time was running out, and Sonia's idea was that somewhere in that man's memory was information that would lead them to the women. If that was the case, Dean had to use him. Lives were at stake. Sonia's life was at stake until they stopped this ring of traffickers.

He didn't have to like it.

Bob Richardson came around the corner. "Did he agree?"

"He's thinking."

"I sent out the press release and photos of Ling and Devereaux and am giving a statement as soon as the media gets here. This is a risk."

"I know. But we have to do it. Devereaux is in hiding and as long as he's free, Agent Knight is in danger. Not to mention the captive women. I feel like we're damned if we do, damned if we don't."

"I hear you. But you're right, it's our only option at this point. You take anyone you need."

"Thank you, sir."

Richardson walked away and Dean glanced at his watch. He walked back into the interview room.

Without looking at him, Cammarata said, "I'll do it. I want it in writing."

"My word is going to have to be good enough for you." He uncuffed him, but didn't let down his guard.

Cammarata looked like he wanted to punch him, but didn't.

"Show me what you have."

Sonia tensed when she saw Charlie walk into the conference room. Neither he nor Dean looked happy with the arrangement, and she wasn't one hundred percent sure they were doing the right thing. But they were stuck. Devereaux, or someone else on his orders, had already brutally murdered three of the women and Sonia had no doubt they would kill others if it would further the criminals' goals.

Sonia made a quick introduction of Charlie Cammarata as a civilian consultant in this investigation and caught Dean's eye. She couldn't read him again, but she'd never forget his brief, powerful emotions in his apartment. Dean Hooper was the personification of the saying "still waters run deep" and Sonia would never doubt his compassion or honor.

"Mr. Cammarata has some knowledge of Xavier Jones's movements during the weeks prior to his murder and can hopefully help us narrow the search."

Sam said, "I'm concerned that if we start an open search we'll spook them and they'll run."

"They'll kill the women first," Sonia said, glancing at Charlie for confirmation. He nodded. She continued, "Based on information Mr. Cammarata had from Jones, the women are likely being held in a secure facility in the foothills. It needs to be accessible to small planes or helicopters, as well as vehicle traffic. But it also needs to be remote and a place where a civilian wouldn't stumble onto it by accident."

Dean crossed the room and stood next to her. "It's privately owned and most likely on Rio Diablo tribal lands."

"Rio Diablo?" Sam said. "We can't go there."

"That's exactly why it's there," Dean said. He gestured toward a whiteboard where he had columns of numbers under the headings of RIO DIABLO, WEBER, OMEGA, XCJ SECURITY, XCJ CONSULTING. "After we went further back into XCJ Consulting records, we came up with these large transactions. The statute of limitations has expired on this, but it shows a pattern

that we were then able to overlay to current payments."
He quickly went through the list. "You can see that payments increased over a twelve-year period, from the
time Jones opened his consulting firm. Secondarily, the
three clients paid Jones's security company for personnel
and other security measures that are incredibly difficult
to track or confirm. The lobbying activities are suspect
as well, as the money paid to XCJ is far more than what
similar companies would make from the same sort of
clients."

Charlie asked, "So what's your point? They were paying Jones, probably paying him for protection or as a
bribe. Big fucking deal. There is far more at stake here."

Sonia cringed, realizing that she had thought something similar when she first learned of the racketeering
and money laundering investigation. She said, "Charlie,
the point is, Agent Hooper has figured out how Jones
laundered his trafficking money."

"He's dead, so there's no point. You can't put him in
prison, Eliot Ness," Charlie said smugly.

Dean ignored Charlie and said, "We now believe that
Jones was giving the three entities the money to pay his
fees. There was two hundred fifty thousand the first
year, three hundred the second year, and it's gone up ex-
ponentially since—last year it topped fifteen million."

Sam shook his head. "So he receives the money as legitimate income, pays taxes, and it's clean."

"Exactly."

"I don't believe this," Charlie rolled his eyes.

Sonia snapped. "I don't care what you believe, Charlie.
You're missing the big picture. Rio Diablo is a recognized
Native American tribe. We have no jurisdiction. We can't

go search their land or issue search warrants. We have to go through their tribal council—"

"Which will take time and cost us in leaks," Dean finished for her.

"That's it," Sonia said. "They're there, on that land." She turned to the big map, took a red Sharpie, and traced the boundaries of Rio Diablo land. "That's about a thousand acres."

"I'll go check it out," Charlie said.

"No," Sonia and Dean said simultaneously.

"We go in smart," Dean said. "No mavericks in this. If we're going to get a conviction we need to do it right."

"What about the girls?" Charlie said. "You fucking Fibbies only care about your clearance rate. Do you even care about the fate of those China dolls?"

"Charlie!" Sonia said and crossed the room. "Don't even go there. If we don't catch the people responsible, they'll keep doing it, and they'll be smarter next time. The only reason we're this close to nailing them is because ICE and the FBI are working together and sharing information. Something I know *you* have a hard time with. Either you help us or you can go back to jail."

"So you drank the Kool-Aid," Charlie mumbled.

"I don't know you," Sonia whispered, deep sadness spreading through her chest.

Charlie looked stunned. "Sonia, I am trying to help, which is why I need to go in alone. I know that area. I've been on Rio Diablo land. Jones went up there every week. He's tight with the three leaders of the tribe. There're only a dozen people in the tribe, I didn't think much of it, but what a scam. They're building a casino, great location, too."

"Even if I trusted you, you're not going up there

alone. But if you really want to help, go over to that map"—she pointed—"and identify where those girls are being held."

He wanted to say something; she saw it in his face, in the way his mouth opened slightly, then snapped shut. He walked past her and she breathed a sigh of relief and rubbed her forehead.

When she looked up, Dean was watching her. He gave her a half-smile and nod, and her headache faded to the background. He held her gaze for a moment, then followed Charlie to the map.

"This is all pretty heavily forested," Charlie said.

Sam stood next to him. "I know this area fairly well. Not Rio Diablo land, but the Sierra Nevadas. This was all mining country, from Nevada County up north, down to past Calaveras. Gold, silver, copper. There're roads all over . . . here, here, here." He highlighted them. "All those can handle a good-sized truck."

"Where's the casino going?" Charlie asked.

Dean pointed to a green pin. "It's almost complete. Supposed to open next spring."

"I don't see planes coming in and out of here," Charlie said. They don't need much room, but it's hard to see if there's a flat enough area to build a runway."

"Can they land on a road?" Sam asked. "Here's a straight stretch on Salamander Gulch Road, and the road ends here."

"Definitely possible, especially if the road is in good shape," Charlie said. "Though they'll land just about anywhere as long as they have the clearance."

"International private plane travel is heavily restricted and regulated," Sonia said.

Charlie dismissed her comment with a wave. "They

cross the border any number of places—no way we can cover every mile of border twenty-four/seven. They're damn geniuses when money is involved, and they take physical risks on land, air, and sea. Low-flying planes, commercial vehicles, boats of all sizes. Jones flew into Mexico last week and it was a snap. No questions."

"How?" Dean asked sharply.

Charlie didn't want to tell him, more out of spite than to keep a secret, but he relented. "He has two planes. They flew into a small private airstrip near the border in the middle of the desert, drove through showing fake I.D. and passports, and picked up a plane in Alicia."

"What was he doing in Mexico?" Dean asked.

"That has nothing to do with this."

"Let me be the judge of that."

Charlie turned to the map and ignored Dean. Sonia put a hand on Dean's arm, his muscles hard and tight. She squeezed.

Charlie said, "They need to be close. They won't require much space, but they'll need a place to wash."

"Why?" Sam asked.

"Would you buy a woman who'd been sleeping in her clothes for a week and walking around in her own waste?"

"Charlie," Sonia said sharply. "We're on the same team right now, aren't we?"

He glared at her, but lost his venom. Sonia was growing weary of the game.

"So water source," Sonia said, "and shelter. Secure, so they don't have any runners. Where no matter how loud the women were, no one would hear. Though they would be quiet, out of fear."

Trace Anderson came into the room. "I got her in your interview room." He stared at Charlie, stunned.

Sonia said simply, "He's helping us."

"I'll be right there," Dean said. To Sonia he said, "Do you want to interview Christopoulis with me?"

"Who?" Charlie interrupted.

"I don't believe this is your business," Dean said coolly.

"He said 'her.' There's only one female Christopoulis. The queen bitch, Victoria."

"You know her?" Sonia said.

"In my other identity as Chuck Angelo. Let me do this."

"Hell no," Dean said.

"I can bluff her. I know some of her dirty secrets— Jones shared them after I met her." Charlie's eyes widened in excitement and for a split second, Sonia saw the old Charlie, the younger, idealistic Charlie who had once been a good agent and a valuable mentor. "I'll tell her Jones was turning state's evidence. It'll freak her out. She'll turn. I promise, if you let me do it, she'll turn."

Sonia nodded to Dean and motioned to leave the room. She walked out with him and closed the door.

"I think he's right. If she knows where they are, this will save us a lot of time. Let him go with you."

"It'll open us up in court—"

"Dean, you don't even have to say who he is. It's a bluff. She'll think what we want her to think without either of you saying a word. He can lie. Hell, he can tell her we faked Jones's death and he's in witness protection as we speak. The only problem with that is if she was part of it."

"I see your point." Dean ran his thumbs down her

face, across her lips, dropped his hand. "How are you holding up?"

"I'm good."

"I don't like him."

"You don't have to."

Dean didn't want to do this, but he understood the strategy and he could see it working. He rubbed the back of Sonia's neck as they returned to the conference room. Cammarata was watching. "Sam, find out where the assistant U.S. attorney is—she's someplace around here—and ask her to observe. Cammarata, you're with me."

Dean knew the interview would be a success from the minute they walked into the room. Victoria Christopoulis's rigid back was to them and Dean walked around the table and introduced himself. "Ms. Christopoulis, I'm Assistant Director Dean Hooper with the FBI, and I think you've already met Charlie Cammarata—though you knew him as Chuck Angelo."

Cammarata walked around and sat down across from the regal Greek matriarch of the Christopoulis clan. He leaned back and grinned, looking younger and confident while he pretended to be laid back. "Vicky! Good to see you again. I had a feeling I'd be seeing you in prison one of these days."

The shock on the woman's face was priceless. The shock was followed by disbelief. "I-I don't understand. I don't know why I'm here." She gained confidence as she spoke. "I've been harassed by your government all day."

"I'll apologize for my partner, Agent Callahan," Dean said. "He can be a bit tenacious."

Victoria's eyes kept going back to Cammarata. "I don't understand what you're doing here."

"You don't? You're smarter than that, Vicky."

"Victoria," she snapped.

"Right. Tori. Got it. Well, I didn't exactly advertise it, but I was working undercover. Xavier was a very naughty businessman. You heard about the FBI raid the other day."

She stared at him with disbelief bordering on hatred. "You? You bastard."

"So I've heard." He glanced at Dean. Dean had never seen such calculation and cold strategy in anyone before.

"Well, see, after that Xavier realized he was dead meat. My man Dean, here—same guy who took down two mob families in Chicago and our own local home-grown boy Thomas Daniels—killed him, too, didn't you, Dean?—well, Dean had Xavier hook, line, and sinker. Xavier knew it and was willing to deal."

"I don't believe you."

"He sat right where you are. I know. I drove him here."

Victoria was doing her best to keep a stiff upper lip, but Dean saw her composure waver. Cammarata said, "I helped negotiate terms for his testimony against your son, the principals of Rio Diablo, Weber Trucking, and—"

He pulled out the photograph and pointed to the picture of Devereaux in the middle. "And him."

Victoria paled. "Noel—"

Dean didn't physically react to the new name. Cammarata hadn't clued him in on this part of his strategy. He was a loose cannon.

"Noel baby is going down."

"He'll kill you."

"Me? No, I don't think so. Thing is, Tori," Cammarata said, "Jones got himself popped. So did Greg, very sad." Cammarata sounded like he was dancing on their graves. Dean shifted in his seat. "So, babe, let me lay it out to you. My man Jones squealed. Gave us some good faith info for us to verify, but wouldn't take our protection. We thought he might run, so we confiscated his plane, froze his accounts, the whole nine yards. Hoop here was tracking him, lost him near the river, and bang. He's dead."

Dean interjected before Cammarata went too far. "We have Jones's statement, and it will hold up in court at least to the extent that I can get a warrant to verify everything he said, such as Omega's latest shipment from Hong Kong."

Victoria stared at him and didn't say anything. She played with her diamond and platinum watch with shaking hands.

Cammarata leaned forward. "Xavier told us about your penchant for young boys. Fourteen, fifteen? Georgie ran all the way to America to get away from you, but you followed him. Of course, he's too old for you to be screwing anymore, but there was that special order of yours."

Victoria looked down, lip quivering, and Cammarata slammed his hand on the table. "Look at me, bitch!"

She jumped, stared at him, eyes wide. "You think I don't know?" he said. "He was thirteen and your son brought him up from Chile, along with a shipment of slave labor into Mexico. Then he asked Xavier to fly down and retrieve him for you. You had him for two weeks, locked in a warehouse. When you had enough, you flew home. Only, you didn't tell anybody to fetch him, did you? *Did you, you fucking bitch!*"

Dean straightened. "That's enough," he said firmly.

Victoria said in a small voice, "I want immunity."

"No," Cammarata said. "You need to pay for the lives you destroyed and the people you killed."

"I've never killed anyone!" She sobbed, tears leaking, making her excessive makeup run in rivulets down her face.

"Leaving a minor to die of dehydration? That's murder in my book, babe."

"Immunity and protection. You don't know Noel Marchand."

"Tell us," Dean said.

"I want a deal on the table. I want my attorney and a deal and then I'll tell you everything you want to know."

Fuck, she'd asked for her attorney.

"Let's go, Cammarata."

"No."

"Now."

"There will be no deal. We have you dead to rights . . . unless you give us something we can verify. Something that might help. Where are the girls?"

"I don't know what you're talking about." She turned her head. She was visibly shaking, but held her chin high.

Cammarata made a move to backhand her and Dean grabbed his wrist and twisted his arm behind him. He pushed him out the door and slammed it shut.

"I don't care who she is or what she did, you will not hit a suspect in my interview."

Cammarata was red-faced. "That kid's not the half of it."

"Callahan," Dean said without taking his eyes off Cammarata. "Watch him."

The assistant U.S. attorney was frowning. "She asked for her lawyer, Hooper."

"I know."

He went back in.

Victoria was crying, her body shaking violently. "He'll kill me. He killed Xavier, he killed Gregory. He'll kill me. You have to protect me." She implored him. "Please. I'm not scared of dying. But you don't know what he does to people."

"I want to make a deal," Dean said. "But I have two questions and I need you to answer them truthfully, okay?"

She nodded.

"Where are the young women your son brought from Hong Kong earlier this week?"

"I don't know. I swear, I don't know!"

"Do you have a good guess?"

She nodded, eyes wide and her nose leaking as much as her eyes.

"Please, Victoria. If we find them in time, I will personally go to the judge on your behalf."

She sniffed, wiped her face with the back of her hand. Her spotty hands showed her age. "I don't know exactly where, but George told Jordan Weber to take them to the mine."

"The mine?"

"That's it. That's exactly what he said. I don't know where it is. I don't know, I swear, I don't know. If I knew, I would tell you."

Sam had said there were mines all over the Sierra Nevadas. Could there be one on Rio Diablo land?

"I believe you."

"You do?" She smiled. "Thank you. I'm telling you the truth."

"One more question."

Dean took out the photograph of the traffickers. "You said this man was Noel Marchand."

She nodded. "Yes. I've known him for years. But that fishing trip was the first time we met."

"Where was this taken? Our analysts believe Acapulco."

"Near Acapulco. It's a small town, Tres Palos. Noel lives in a fortress there."

"What was this fishing trip about?"

"I-I think," Victoria said, her chin held up, "I'll wait for my attorney before I answer any more questions."

Dean left the room feeling ill. He didn't want to tell Sonia the news, but he had to. Better to come from him than anyone else.

Cammarata said, "You did pretty good."

"You sound surprised," Dean said.

He shrugged. "Sonia doesn't like idiots."

CHAPTER THIRTY-ONE

Sonia knew something was wrong the minute Dean stepped into the conference room with Sam and Charlie right behind him. "Sam, you and Cammarata find out if there's a mine on or near Rio Diablo land. Sonia, can you step out here for a moment?"

Dean led her down a long hall past closed doors and wide openings with eight to ten cubicles set back in a work group arrangement. He opened a back door and led her outside to where the garage was bustling with activity around a burned-out SUV.

Dean took her hand and walked her around the side of the garage to where they had a modicum of privacy. It was dark; the sun had completely set. Sonia hadn't realized it was nearly ten at night. External lamps lit the entire area.

"Victoria Christopoulis is going to cooperate in exchange for immunity."

"Thank God. It's about time we had a big break. Does she know where the women are? What did you say about a mine?"

"She doesn't know the specifics, but she said they were taken to a mine. If we are right in our analysis and they are on Rio Diablo land, we'll have some major issues, but—"

"Homeland Security has jurisdiction in matters of national security. I'll take the heat. I'll take anything if we get to them in time."

"No need to do that. I think we have cause, and at this point, I'd rather ask for forgiveness than permission. I'm going to play with the time line a bit, contact the tribal council as we approach Rio Diablo boundaries, tell them what's happened and hope the council doesn't have huge loyalties to this little tribe."

"Charlie came through?"

"I hate to admit it, but yeah, he scared her half to death. It put her in the right mind-set to cooperate."

Sonia took Dean's other hand and squeezed. "We're close, so close, why the long face? She didn't tell you they were already gone?" She tensed. "Or worse?"

He shook his head. "No, no, no. Not that. I have every reason to believe they're still alive. It's about your father."

Sonia stifled a cry. "My dad? What's wrong? Is he okay? Is it his heart—"

"No, not Owen. Sergio Martin."

"Oh." She glanced down, breathed deeply. She was going to have to get used to this. Once it all got out— She'd just have to develop a thicker skin, a stronger spine than she already had. She looked Dean in the eye. "Just spill it. I need to know."

"He's Noel Marchand."

Sonia stared at Dean blankly at first, then the information—the name *Noel Marchand*—sank in.

She slowly shook her head. "I don't believe you. Marchand is the most notorious human trafficker in the hemisphere. Some people in ICE don't think he exists, at least as one individual. Some think the name represents a gang, not a person. It's not—not—not possible," she stumbled over her words.

"Victoria Christopoulis confirmed it. She met him that day in the photograph. She's scared to death of him, believes he'll kill her. Believed he was capable of killing Jones and Greg Vega. I'm sorry, Sonia, but I wanted you to hear it from me."

She turned and dry heaved, covering her mouth to hold in a sob. *No. No!*

Her father had sold her. Why was she surprised that he was infamous? But the knowledge that his blood ran through her veins chilled her, humiliated her, made her feel tainted and dirty. How could she face his victims? How could she look at herself in the mirror?

She braced herself with both hands on the cinder-block wall of the garage and took deep breaths as silent sobs of anger and sorrow wracked her body. She wanted to forget, she wanted to disappear. Self-pity invaded her mind. *Why me?*

"Sonia, you didn't know. You couldn't have known. But I had to tell you, even if you hate the messenger."

She shook her head wildly back and forth, her chest tight. "Why would I hate you? I hate myself. Hate that I didn't know!"

Dean took her by the shoulders and spun her around. "I never want to hear that again. You're not God. You're not all-knowing. You are Sonia Knight, a top-notch investigator, a compassionate cop, a beautiful woman. You are Owen Knight's daughter, and that man is a damn good dad. Don't forget it."

She wrapped her arms around Dean and held on tight. She sobbed, releasing the pain and anguish. Dean absorbed it, shared it. She loved him for it. He had reminded her of what was truly important. Her family wasn't the man whose genes ran through her cells, but a mother and father who wanted her, who'd taken her into their home and loved her unconditionally, treated her as much as their own as they did their two sons. Owen and Marianne were her true family.

She whispered into his chest, "Thank you . . . for reminding me."

"I love you, Sonia."

She breathed in sharply, holding his declaration inside, felt his love and devotion. He'd already shown her how much he cared. She'd shared her secrets, her fears, her frustrations, and he not only understood but made her stronger by telling him. As if he'd made her past his own. She never realized how much she needed to have someone in her life to trust explicitly, to love beyond family. That she could be this lucky amazed her, but she wasn't a fool. She wasn't going to turn Dean away.

They heard voices in the courtyard around the corner. "Has anyone seen Hooper?"

Dean called, "Over here, Sam!"

Sonia let him go.

Sam ran around the corner. "We found it. I'm certain it's where they are, if Christopoulis can be believed. It's an abandoned mine right on the edge of the Rio Diablo property. And get this: it's not tribal land. They bought it along with several other adjoining parcels over the last few years, probably with Jones's illegal money."

"Good work, Sam. Let's go."

Mr. Ling approached Noel as he finished loading his favorite gun.

They were both dressed in black. Once they were out in the night they could blend into the surroundings.

"They agreed," Noel said. "We have one hour."

"Mr. Marchand, the news." Ling turned up the volume of the television with a remote.

". . . Bob Richardson earlier this evening," the newscaster was saying.

The shot cut to film of FBI headquarters, evident from the seal on the podium and the American and California State flags behind him. The ticker moving along the bottom of the screen repeated:

FBI SAC Bob Richardson is releasing a new Sacramento Most Wanted list with a public plea for help in finding a dangerous fugitive.

Richardson said, "Tonight the FBI has learned that notorious human trafficker Noel Marchand is in the greater Sacramento area. We have a witness who puts him at the scene around the time philanthropist and lobbyist Xavier Jones was shot and killed near his restaurant in Clarksburg."

An old picture of Noel was put on-screen and Richardson's voice-over said, "We're releasing the first known photograph of Noel Marchand, taken seven to ten years ago in Mexico."

Noel turned red. Where had the FBI obtained that photo? He never allowed himself to be photographed, but it appeared posed. Then he remembered. He'd been fishing with friends in Tres Palos. On his own property. Tobias had a new camera. A present from their father as the old man died, half out of his mind with syphilis. Noel had let Tobias take pictures, but he'd destroyed the film every night. The hobby lasted less than a month, when Tobias broke the camera. Who had kept the film?

Jones. It had to be. The FBI was at his house, they'd found it. Not for the first time, he wished he'd made Jones suffer.

A computer-generated enhancement came on-screen with the voice, "An FBI forensic artist has aged the picture to what Marchand may look like now. Marchand is between five foot nine and five foot eleven inches tall and approximately one hundred seventy pounds. He has light brown or graying brown hair and blue eyes. He's approximately fifty-five to sixty years of age. He may be traveling with a Chinese American using the name Sun Ling." An old, shaded photograph of Ling popped onto the screen. "If you see either of these men, do not approach. They are armed and dangerous. Call the FBI or your local police department. A special tip hotline has been set up and will be answered by a trained agent."

Richardson came back on the television and the hotline number ran on the ticker.

"Marchand is the leading suspect in multiple felonies in the United States, Mexico, and Central and South America. He uses multiple aliases, including Sergio Martin and Pierre Devereaux."

Noel fired his .45 into the television. In rapid French, he swore. "That bitch! How dare she give them that name! I will tear her apart limb from limb. I will cut off her fingers and stuff them down her throat and leave her dying for the coyotes to eat for dinner. I hate that girl. I should have drowned her after I slit her mother's throat!"

He pressed the trigger again and again, until his ammunition was gone. He threw the gun across the room, picked up a knife, and cut deep gouges into the handmade leather couch that graced the small cabin. When he was done, the only sound was his rapid breathing.

"We should leave now," Ling said quietly.

"Right. The buyers." He shook his head to clear it.

"I mean, we should leave the country."

"No."

"Sir, it's too dangerous—"

"I said *no*! I'm not walking away from my money. I had to pay out of pocket to change the day and time. I'm not leaving half a million dollars behind."

"The first half million is already in your bank. I think—"

"No. Let's go to the mine."

"I would not do well in prison."

"You won't be going to prison."

"I will get your plane ready."

"You will be coming with me!" Ling looked at him with defiance. Noel fumed. How dare he disobey. Contradict him. Noel was in charge!

"I believe you've lost sight of the goal," Ling said.

Noel forced himself to breathe slowly. Lower his heart rate. Take it easy.

"Perhaps."

Ling relaxed. "Very well. Let's go to the airstrip." He turned his back to Noel.

That was his second mistake.

Noel threw the knife. It hit Ling right where he aimed, between the shoulder blades. It went in deep, deep enough that Ling couldn't scream or make any sound.

His first mistake was telling Noel what to do.

Noel never ran away, especially from a woman.

He retrieved his gun, calmly reloaded it. He felt much better now that he had a game plan. Headlights cut a swath of light across the room, then stopped. One long, three quick beeps of the horn and Noel was assured Ignacio had arrived.

He'd lost half his U.S. team during this operation. Someone had to pay for his losses. Hell, a lot of people were going to pay.

Noel stepped over Ling's body without giving him a second thought, for the years of service, for the people he killed on command, or for the friendship.

If he felt a twinge of regret it was only because he would miss Ling's perfectly steeped morning tea.

CHAPTER THIRTY-TWO

At Dean's command, FBI SWAT team leader Brian Stone pulled together a team of tactically trained agents within fifteen minutes. Dean had Sam Callahan dragging the curator of the Calaveras County Museum out of bed to meet them at the sheriff's department. Warren Sheffield had the only known map of the closed mine. Dean wanted to consult the man because Callahan's quick research told them the mine was severely unstable.

It was an hour before midnight when they gathered at the Calaveras Sheriff's Department in San Andreas, twelve miles from the abandoned mine off Salamander Gulch Road. Unfortunately, the twisting road was narrow and treacherous in places, and the sheriff said it would take thirty minutes.

"Do you have a helicopter?" Dean asked.

"Yes, Agent Hooper, two. We use them primarily for search and rescue."

"I need them."

"One of our pilots lives quite a ways—"

Brian Stone said, "I can fly a chopper."

The sheriff cleared it and called in the on-call deputy pilot. While they readied the equipment, Dean spoke to the curator.

Sheffield was skeptical. "The Grouch is dangerous. No one goes there."

"Grouch? Don't you mean the Gulch Mine?"

"Technically, it's called the Second Quartz Mine. The primary mine is about five miles from there, and is open in the summer for tourists. The caverns are amazing, and you can—"

"I'm interested in this one," Dean interrupted impatiently.

"The Grouch. The miners nicknamed it because it has a temper."

"A mine with a temper," Cammarata interjected, shaking his head.

Dean cringed. He hadn't wanted to bring Charlie Cammarata with them, but Callahan said the man would be valuable since he was the only one who had recently seen Marchand. Dean relented. They needed every advantage they could get.

Sheffield nodded. "Fourteen miners lost their lives in the twenty-six months the Grouch was operational. It took nearly five years to build it, and it was open less than half that. Shafts collapsed spontaneously. It's boarded up."

"Are these blueprints accurate?" Dean asked.

"As accurate as they were since the last inspection, which was five years ago. During the inspection one of the geologists fell thirty feet and broke both legs. It took them six hours to get him out of the hole he'd fallen into because they had to shore up the sides, otherwise he would have been buried alive."

"Sounds lovely," Sonia said. "We need to get up there, Dean. If Marchand saw that broadcast—"

Dean and Sonia had tried to stop Richardson from

broadcasting Marchand's identity, but it was too late. It had been the smart thing to do . . . until they learned the location of the women. Now they feared they'd forced Noel Marchand to act rashly.

"I'll go with you and explain the blueprints." Sheffield said, pushing his glasses up on his nose for the tenth time in as many minutes.

"It's dangerous."

"So is the Grouch! I understand the risk, but you don't."

Dean didn't want any civilians with him, especially this old nearsighted curator, but he didn't see another way. They needed Sheffield to interpret the arcane blueprints, but they couldn't sit around the sheriff's station.

"You're with me," Dean said, "Sonia, Brian, Cammarata and three of the SWAT team. Brian, we're going to have to send half your team on the road. Callahan will go with the other pilot and three SWAT. Trace, if you can lead the ground contingent and stay alert for any sentries. If Marchand is anywhere nearby, the longer he's in the dark about us, the better."

Brian pulled his team aside for orders.

Dean took out a highlighter and marked the map. "Sheriff, I need your men to put up roadblocks here . . . here . . . and here. That should effectively cut off all escape routes if someone is already up there, and prevent anyone else from showing up."

"We can't go there, that's Rio Diablo land. They're not the friendliest Indians around."

"Get as close as you can."

"That I can do."

Dean glanced at his watch. "Brian, two minutes."

"Roger that."

Dean made a call to the Western Regional tribal counsel leader. He'd obtained his home phone from a local congressman who was friends with the chief.

"Chief Raintree?"

"Speaking."

"My name is Dean Hooper, assistant director of the FBI. I'm calling as a courtesy to tell you that we're engaging in an operation adjacent to tribal lands that may cross over into your property."

"Which property?"

"Rio Diablo Rancherita."

"Ah."

"Sir?"

"We have our own investigation into Rio Diablo, Director Hooper. I'm not at liberty to share our ongoing investigation, but I appreciate the call, and you won't have any trouble from the Council if there's a need to cross into our sacred lands."

"Thank you, Chief. I appreciate your cooperation."

Dean hung up. That was easier than he'd expected. He hoped the rest of the operation would run as smoothly.

Sonia listened to the curator explain that the Grouch Mine had produced over seven million dollars in gold— a large haul for a small mine—but the preponderance of accidents had left the owner bankrupt. When the bank seized his property, he fought the police who came to remove him, then fell hundreds of feet to his death in a condemned shaft.

"The geologists who sited the mine made a critical error in judgment related to groundwater. There are hot springs a few miles from here, and we now know that they run deep underground, and because of a unique combination of rock and soil on just this small acreage, they caused underground floods and the shifting earth collapsed shafts. Had the owner simply built the mine one mile down the road, still on his property, he would have tapped into the same vein of gold without the tragic problems."

While Sonia appreciated the history lesson, she was more interested in what the marks on the yellowed blue-prints meant. "What's this?" she asked of a red X.

"Collapsed tunnel. Here . . . this is elevation. The entrance itself is stable, but you'll want to watch your footing. Right . . . here"—he pointed to a double red line—"the ground gave way between five and twenty feet. There are markings and warnings all over the mine, but you'll want to watch for neon orange marks. If you see them, stop. That's the sign for danger, and any step you take other than retracing your exact steps could land you in deep trouble."

Sonia pointed to what appeared to be a room. "What's this? It looks like an office."

"It used to be. The foreman worked from there, the men would break there. It's three stories belowground, and probably the only safe place in the whole structure."

"That's where they are," Sonia said. "It's secure, they can't get out, it's dark."

"What about air?" Dean asked.

"There's plenty of ventilation on the upper levels, but after a hundred feet I wouldn't guarantee it. I haven't been to the Grouch in years, it could have changed dramatically since the last inspection."

The night was clear and the mine seemed to come out

of nowhere as they approached from above. The towering metal roof had rusted with time, a narrow and for-
bidding remnant of the past. The three-quarter waning
moon backlit the peaks, casting a ghostly bluish light
over the land.

Brian asked Dean over the headset, "How close do
you want me to get?"

"As close as you can," Dean said. "The noise will
alert anyone near the mine, but we don't have a choice.
It's nearly midnight. We can't be running through the
woods in unfamiliar territory searching for the mine."

Sheffield said, "The road is right there. See? There's a
good-sized turnout just past the mine to the northeast."

Brian inspected the map and instruments. "I can do
that."

He radioed the other pilot with the information, then
said to Dean, "We can land, but there's only room for
one. The other chopper will land point-four miles west."

"Roger."

Sonia stared at the blueprints, searing them into her
brain as best she could. "How do we get to that room?"
she asked Sheffield.

"There's only one way. The old elevator shaft. It's a
manual elevator."

"Manual elevator."

"Crank, pulleys, ropes, chains. You get in and turn
the crank by hand to go up and down."

"Ropes," Sonia said. "They couldn't possibly be in
any condition to hold any weight."

"If they were worn the inspectors would have marked
them with a big orange X, and I don't see anything
here."

Sonia swallowed heavily. The closer they got, the more

nervous she became. She would not allow her claustro-phobia to stop her.

Dean looked at her. He knew. She hated that she was so obvious about it. She closed her eyes as the helicopter descended.

It was cold up here on the mountain. They jumped out of the choppers. Brian ordered one of his team members to stand guard, leaving only seven of them to approach the mine.

"Hooper," Brian said, "we should wait for the rest of the team before we go in."

"How long?"

"Twenty minutes."

Both Dean and Sonia shook their heads. "We don't know where Marchand is," Dean said. "Time is the one thing we don't have."

Guided only by flashlights and the waning moon, they walked briskly and cautiously down the road and around to the fenced entrance to the property. The lock looked new, and Sonia wondered if it had been put in place by Marchand's people. The *whirl-whirl* of the second helicopter faded into the night. Sonia tried to breathe easier, but the pounding in her chest vibrated so loudly she couldn't hear anything but the blood rushing through her veins.

She had to save those girls. But the mere thought of going down a manual elevator shaft to a room more than a hundred feet below the surface of the earth had her hands coated with sweat.

Brian cut the lock off the fence and they reached the mine minutes later, staying among the trees. Dean motioned for everyone to turn off their lights and be silent.

Sonia heard nothing but her fear.

Dean whispered, "Okay, two of us need to stay here on lookout. Under no circumstances is anyone to go off alone. You all heard Dr. Sheffield's instructions? You see neon orange, turn around. Cammarata, Knight, stay up top with Sheffield. The rest of you, with me."

"You need me down there," Sonia said. "You don't speak Chinese. I speak enough to at least calm them when you find them."

Dean shook his head. "I need you up top," he said. "You're the ranking agent. When the others arrive, you need to be here to give direction."

He was letting her save face.

"I'll go," Charlie said.

"No. I don't trust you, Cammarata. This isn't a game."

"I didn't think it was, Hooper. I speak mandarin and some Xiang. I can work my way through some of the others. This isn't the first time I've done this. But I'll bet it's the first time you have."

Sonia cringed. Why did Charlie have to be such an arrogant jerk? But he was right, he knew what he was doing; yet Dean had every reason in the book to mistrust him.

"You follow my orders, Cammarata, or I'll have you taken out of here on a stretcher."

Brian said, "Agent Lawson, you're with me. Agent Clinch, you're with Knight and Sheffield."

As they turned to leave, Sonia touched Dean's arm. "Be careful," she mouthed.

He gave her a wink and a nod, then disappeared into the mine.

* * *

They'd parked in a clearing on the backside of the mine and Ignacio turned off the engine. They'd taken the dirt road, forced to tread slowly over rocks and potholes even in the four-wheel-drive SUV. If they hadn't been forced into that awful cabin, they wouldn't have had to cross the virtually inaccessible Rio Diablo land.

Noel listened a beat, then swore. Helicopters!

"They're fucking early. I should have known. If they try to steal my merchandise, they'll be sorry."

He checked his guns, his knife— "Where's my knife?"

"I don't know, boss," Ignacio said.

"Right. I know." He'd had to kill Sun Ling and forgot to pull it out of his back. He'd get it on his way out of the country. He liked that knife, it was his favorite.

"Let's go. If they spring the mousetrap, at least I have half their money in the bank. But I want the rest. We're going to have to lay low for a while." He looked around. "Where are Don and Simon? You did tell them about the change." He reached for his gun.

"Yes, boss. I told them. They'll be here at midnight."

"It's nearly midnight. They'd better be on time."

Trace Anderson drove up the mountain with lights flashing and no siren, half a dozen deputies following. He urged the driver to go as fast as possible. They slowed a fraction to round a ninety-degree turn and saw taillights in the distance. He didn't like the look of the black truck in front of them.

"Catch up with them," he told the driver.

As they approached, the truck lurched forward as the driver pushed on the gas.

"It's a suicide run to go up this mountain at that speed," the deputy told Trace.

"Just keep up as best you can without driving off the edge."

"O-kay." The deputy pressed down on the accelerator again, then radioed in the license on the fleeing vehicle.

Trace sent Sonia a text message.

Suspicious black full-size truck plates 5EET608 refuses to pull over. In pursuit. Stand by.

Dean shined his light around the mine. Sheffield had provided them with hardhats and lights and Dean turned his on. The others followed suit. Cammarata approached the elevator cautiously.

"You know how to work that thing?" Dean asked.

"Yeah, but I want to check it out. Something feels . . . off."

"What?"

"No guards for one. You don't leave your prized possessions in the open."

Lawson said, "I hardly call this the open."

Dean agreed, but this was still an area he wasn't an expert in. He'd worked the field enough, but in white-collar crimes it was pretty cut-and-dried. Some resisted arrest and Dean dealt with each situation as it arose. This mine reminded him of his military tour, and that was a long time ago.

He didn't want to rely on Charlie Cammarata, but right now he didn't have much choice.

While Cammarata inspected the elevator, Dean shined his light around the entrance. There were several dark holes cut into the mountainside. One had a bright neon X painted on the side. Underneath was written: 200+ ft drop.

The other tunnels didn't have marks on them, but

Dean wasn't about to test them. He just wanted to go down, get the women—if they were, in fact, here—and leave. They'd stake out the place for a couple days, hoping Marchand would show up.

"God-fucking-dammit!" Cammarata exclaimed.

"What?"

"It's rigged."

"Meaning?"

"The bastard has another way in. This is a false bottom. If we step in it and start moving, the bottom would give way and wham! We smack down a hundred feet below. The actual elevator must be down in the room."

"How do we get it up?"

"Find the other way down."

"Sheffield didn't say anything about another way."

"There's always another way."

"We need to ask him."

"We have the blueprints. We're wasting time!"

"We're being smart," Dean said. "No rash moves. I'm not jeopardizing my team until I'm confident it's as safe as possible."

Cammarata glared at him. "I've worked in mines before. Undercover. There's another way down." He held out his hand and motioned toward the blueprints that Dean had folded and put inside his flak jacket.

If he was going to trust Cammarata about the elevator trap, then he would have to trust that he knew what he was doing in the mine. Dean handed him the blueprints.

Cammarata spread it out between them. He put his finger on the elevator, turned the map to face the same direction they were facing, and traced a line to one of the tunnels. He looked up.

Dean followed his gaze.

It was the tunnel with the two-hundred-foot drop.

"That's a red herring," Cammarata said.

"You're not going down there."

"Yes I am."

"No."

"It's the only way. Look, the inspectors haven't been out in years. These blueprints don't have that marking. I'll bet Christopoulis or Marchand himself painted it."

"No," Dean said. "I can't risk my men on a hunch."

"I'm not your man."

Cammarata started for the tunnel.

Dean grabbed him and pushed him hard against the rock wall. Dirt crumbled onto their heads. "This is why you lost your job. You put people in jeopardy."

Cammarata attempted to punch Dean. Dean countered, grabbed his fist, and spun him around, holding his arm high behind his back in a deadlock. He growled, "Don't try it."

"You're in love with her," Cammarata spat.

"Don't talk about her. Don't even think about her."

"The elevator is in the room. The only way to get it up here is from the room. The crank up here is booby-trapped. Therefore, the staircase is safe. I'm willing to risk my life. I'm not asking you to risk yours. I go down, verify the women are there, and bring the elevator up, thereby disabling the trap."

"Why not bring the women up the staircase?" One of the SWAT guys said.

"We may be able to, but we don't know what condition they're in until we get down there," Dean said.

Cammarata nodded. "They've been through hell, Hooper. Let me do this."

Dean let go of his arm. "I'll go with you."

"It's not necessary—"

Dean interrupted. "The rule is, no one goes alone. Including a bastard like you."

Dean told the others, "Be alert." He turned to Cammarata. "Lead the way."

Without hesitating, he turned and started down the marked path.

Dean followed.

CHAPTER
THIRTY-THREE

"Did you hear that?" Sonia whispered to Agent Clinch.

It had been only ten minutes since Dean and the others had descended the mine, but each minute felt like an hour, and Sonia caught herself beginning to pace a half dozen times.

"You mean your feet crunching the dry pine needles?"

She froze. Listened. Nothing.

Sheffield stood right next to her among the trees near the entrance of the mine. "What did you hear?" he whispered in her ear.

"A car door shut."

"It was from the mine. The elevator."

Maybe, but Sonia was poised. Every hair on her skin rose, and she sensed someone else in the woods.

"Shh." She closed her eyes and listened.

First, her own breathing. She internalized the sound, put it aside. Then Clinch's slow, steady, calm breaths. Dr. Sheffield's faster intakes, sounding a bit winded. Or scared.

Then the far distant sound of helicopter blades slowing down.

A *hoot* of an owl. An answer in return.

The scurrying of a rodent in the leaves.

She internalized all the sounds and focused her mind and senses on one: listening.

"Two people are approaching from the east," she whispered.

Clinch put his ear to the ground. "It's from the west. Callahan and the others."

She shook her head, removed her gun from its holster, and flicked off the safety. She put her fingers to her lips. "They're coming from the east, and it's not Callahan. Trust me."

Clinch was skeptical, but unholstered his gun as well.

"Slow down, Cammarata."

"It's Charlie."

Dean had no intention of being friends with Cammarata. They continued slowly another twenty or so feet down the mine in complete silence. The staircase had been cut out of the earth, with wood planks laid loosely, so old they cracked and splintered under their weight. As they descended, the air cooled and the hard-packed earthen walls seemed damp to the touch. The sound of distant running water echoed through the shaft, which was disconcerting considering they were at least fifty feet below the surface.

"You're taking care of her, right?" Cammarata asked.

He wasn't going to talk about Sonia with this man.

"I was never good enough for her," Cammarata continued.

"Where are you going with this?"

"Just making small talk."

"Bullshit." Dean refused to be sucked into whatever game he was playing.

"I've always loved her, you know."

Dean's jaw clenched. "You're treading on thin ice."

"I want her to be happy." The light bobbing from atop their hard hats cast shadows all around, showing darker tunnels leading off this main staircase. They turned again, spiraling down, and one tunnel to the left was marked with an orange neon X. Inside, Dean saw a large mound of earth sealing part of the opening.

Dean remembered a mission to rescue a trapped caravan in Kuwait. They'd occupied an abandoned bunker while fending off the enemy. When he and his unit went in, all they found were the dead.

"Hooper?"

"Shut up, Charlie." He was getting on Dean's last nerve. If he thought "I'm sorry" would fix everything, he was an idiot.

"Tell her I was wrong."

"She knows that."

"She doesn't know *I* know it."

"Sonia's moved on. Leave her alone."

"I want her forgiveness." Charlie's words were barely audible.

Dean paused in his step, wiped the sweat from his forehead.

"She asked me to drop the charges against you. Said your word meant something. She also insisted that even though you fuck up often, your instincts are good and we needed your help. But how can you expect her to forgive what you did to her?"

They descended ten more steps. Slowly, methodically, testing each landing.

Dean said, "I think you're in this because you care about the victims. I think you'll do anything to save the helpless. Including sacrificing your partner, your friends, the people who trust you. You justify it because they're trained, they know what to do or who to call. So you feel comfortable leaving them to fend for themselves because if they fail, it's not your fault. Except you lied to Sonia."

"I never lied to her."

"What the fuck do you call it, Cammarata? She didn't agree to be sold to a pervert. She didn't agree to be on her own in that room. She thought you were there."

"I never told her that."

It was all Dean could do not to push him down the rest of the stairs.

"Lies by omission are still lies. She had every reason to believe you were her backup."

Silence.

"I know."

Dean barely heard him.

Cammarata continued. "I haven't slept through the night since I found out Sonia nearly died."

"You lied to your superiors."

"Only after I knew she was okay."

"You wanted her to look like an idiot, a failure, and you to look like a hero. Screw that. You're a prick, you'll always be a prick. I don't like you. I don't want to get to know you or listen to your apologies or excuses. Sonia is who she is *in spite* of your influence. When this is over, never contact her again. If you do, I'll arrest you."

"For what?" he chortled.

"I'm sure you've committed plenty of crimes that have no statute of limitations."

Dean paused. *Scrape*. "Did you hear that?"

"Rats?"

"Listen."

Scrape, scrape.

A female voice. Dean didn't understand the faint plea. An overwhelming sense of relief washed over him. They'd found the girls.

Charlie said, "It's Chinese. Xiang. I think she said, 'Ming is dying. Help Ming.'"

"Let's go."

Sonia saw the men emerge from the east, at first two shadows in the filtered moonlight.

They grew distinct. One tall and dark. The other shorter, five ten, lighter hair. Pale.

Sergio Martin. Pierre Devereaux. Noel Marchand. She wondered if any were his real name.

She swallowed thickly, put her finger up for Sheffield and Clinch to remain quiet. She motioned for Clinch to silently alert Callahan and his team to hurry. She sank down behind a tree and watched.

The two killers paused on the edge of the woods, the trees obscuring them. Were they listening? Watching?

Sonia never thought she'd see her father again. She'd never wanted to. She hated everything about him, about her childhood and the lies. But he'd still raised her. She'd followed him from village to village. Why did he play the role of a missionary? Of someone who helps others? Was that all a lie, too? A front?

A gasp caught in her throat as she realized they'd never returned to a village. Why? Because he'd committed atrocities? How many girls had he sold without her knowing?

The men in the shadows moved through the trees. Toward the mine.

Dean was in there. She had to warn him. But how? How without being heard?

Dean was a Marine. Though the military no longer used Morse code, they'd used it when Dean was enlisted.

She tapped her walkie-talkie.

Danger. Two men approaching. Danger. Two men approaching.

She heard nothing in response. No Morse code, no voices, nothing.

"They'll be ambushed," she whispered to Clinch, itching to go into the mine and warn them.

Clinch put his hand on her shoulder. "Stay," he whispered.

The men stepped out of the trees and scurried into the mine. They had guns in hand.

Dean.

Sonia rose to her feet, rock in hand. She threw it as hard as she could toward the mine. It hit the wall with a *thump*. Fell to the ground. So did Sonia. Waiting. Waiting.

One of the men emerged.

Her father.

He looked in her direction. God, did he see her?

Then he turned back toward the mine. She heard his voice, "It's nothing. Animals."

No!

She jumped up and fired her gun, aiming into the high branches of the pine trees. *Snap*. A branch split.

"Shit!" she heard from the mine.

The two men emerged and hunkered down behind a stack of old lumber outside the mineshaft entrance.

They were at a standstill. Sonia whispered to Clinch, "Get Callahan and the others."

"I'm not leaving you."

"Dammit, we need them now!"

"Believe me, they heard your gun. They're on their way."

Dean stopped walking. "Did you hear something?"

"No." Cammarata stopped and shined his light on the door. "This is it. It's padlocked." He knocked on the door and spoke in Chinese. The women inside started shouting and crying.

"Can you tell them we're here to help? They need to quiet down," Dean said.

"They're scared."

"They're going to be dead if Marchand is here. I need to listen."

His walkie-talkie was making noise, but with the noise in the room he couldn't hear it.

Danger.

Someone was alerting him to danger. Was someone approaching the mine? Or was it the mine itself that was the danger?

"Charlie, someone's coming."

Charlie spoke firmly in Xiang through the door. The cries didn't stop, but they quieted a bit.

"We have to get them out. Several are sick. They need water. Shoot the lock."

"Wait. There's danger. Someone upside is trying to reach me using Morse code."

A faint echo hung in the air.

"That was a gunshot," Dean said.

"We have to get them out. Now."

Dean didn't have a choice. He shot the lock.

They were at a standstill, the two killers behind the trees. Sonia inched closer, staying under cover.

The darker man made a run for the entrance only five feet away, then fired his gun in Sonia's general direction while Marchand followed.

"They're going back in!" Sonia exclaimed. "Dammit, Dean is in there."

"And he gave us explicit orders—"

"To watch the entrance. Not to let that bastard breach it! How far away is Callahan?"

Sonia couldn't wait for the answer.

She slid out of hiding. "Marchand!" she shouted. "Dammit, you motherfucking bastard, show yourself!"

Silence.

Then her father stepped out from the mine. She wanted to shoot him right then. Be done with him and the misery he caused.

"Sonia. I somehow knew you were here."

"Sergio Martin, aka Noel Marchand, aka Pierre Devereaux and any other damn identity you use—you're under arrest."

He laughed. Her finger itched to pull the trigger. But she couldn't kill him in cold blood.

"Put your hands up!" she shouted. He laughed and dove behind a tree. But at least he was away from the mine. Away from Dean and the others.

She stood, obscured by brush, listening to the moving laughter. Where was the second man?

"Clinch, number two, where did he go?"

A volley of gunfire came from the mine.

Boom!

The ground shook, but Sonia stayed on her feet. "Shit, Clinch, that was an explosion."

Before Clinch could respond, the entrance crumbled, the sound of the collapse tearing at Sonia's heart. Dean. No, no, this couldn't end in death. She couldn't lose the victims. She couldn't lose the man she loved.

In the woods behind her, the laughter continued. "Are you going to try to save them? Please do. I'll find you, Sonia. Next week. Next year. I will kill you after I kill everyone you care about. And I will enjoy every minute watching you suffer."

Sonia inched toward the voice, which was too close. "Don't." Clinch put his hand on her arm. But he didn't understand. No one did.

The ceiling began to cave in around Dean, and the women inside the room screamed. Cammarata pushed open the old door and spoke rapidly in Chinese. He pushed past them, and a chunk of granite slid loose and blocked part of the doorway behind him. The smell of rotting food and feces clogged his nose and lungs.

"You'd better be able to get that elevator running, because I don't think we should go back up the stairs."

"Why?"

Dean pointed his flashlight at the staircase.

The last ten feet were gone.

CHAPTER
THIRTY-FOUR

Marchand was on the run.

Sonia glanced back toward the mine entrance. She had no tools to dig them out. Callahan was nearly here, with equipment and reinforcements. She could wait here, but her father would get away. Disappear into another country, waiting for her to let her guard down so he could kill her family.

If they didn't catch her father now, he would escape and go back to exporting people. She wouldn't be able to live with herself if he went back to his old ways. She wouldn't be able to sleep, waiting for him to make his move.

She ran after him, ignoring Clinch's command to cease.

Sheffield called after her, "The mine!" but she must have heard him wrong. She wasn't going into the mine, she was going into the forest. She had Marchand in her sights. If he resisted, would she be able to shoot her own father?

He's not your father. Owen Knight is your father.

She aimed.

A second, bigger explosion knocked her to the ground.

* * *

"Holy shit," Cammarata said as he pushed the door closed against the tumbling rock. "What the fuck was that?"

"I don't know," Dean said through clenched teeth. He couldn't think about Sonia now; he had these young women to think about.

The flashlights revealed that there were approximately thirty Chinese girls. These weren't women. None of them was over sixteen. They all wore simple, handmade dresses that were filthy. Empty water bottles lined the walls. Was water all they'd had for the last four days?

Cammarata was doing a good job calming them down. When the mine stopped shaking, Dean realized that this room was built like a bunker in the granite. He didn't know where the air was coming from; it tasted stale, but that might be from the perspiration of the women. But the explosions could have cut off their ventilation, which gave them little time.

"Get the elevator operational," Dean commanded. "Now."

For once, Cammarata didn't argue but went right to the elevator and started working.

Dean tried his walkie-talkie, but no one responded. Was he out of range? Could the signal not cut through this rock? Dean wanted to know that his men—and Sonia—were okay. He needed to know what the hell was happening up above.

All he heard was static.

Sonia lost sight of Marchand when he cut through the trees. She slowed, listening, but her heart was pounding.

Hearing laughter, she dove for cover behind a thick pine tree.

"You are a stupid girl," Marchand said.

"You're not going to get away. We know who you are, we know what you look like. I'll hunt you down until the end of time."

"No, you won't. You'll be dead."

She wasn't going to fall for his mind games. She looked around her, trying to gauge where she was and how she could lure him out of the woods. There was rustling, and movement—where was he going?

She closed her eyes and listened closely.

Crunch crunch crunch crunch.

She dove in the nick of time. A bullet whizzed past her head. And then she was falling.

She hit the ground with a thud, stunned.

Sonia looked up. He stood there, against the moon. She saw the silhouette of the gun in his hand pointed into the hole she'd fallen into. She quickly turned off her flashlight and prayed he couldn't see her. But the hole wasn't big. He could probably hit her with his eyes closed.

"Marchand!" she called. "You can kill me. Go ahead. My people will hunt you down like the fucking animal you are."

She felt around the wet, muddy slush for her gun. Damn, where was it?

A bullet hit the muck inches from her leg. No light reached this far down, which was the only reason he missed. Unless the bastard enjoyed this game of cat and mouse. She prayed Clinch or someone heard the gunshot and was close by. If she could stall Marchand just a few minutes, her team would be here to arrest him and toss her a rope.

She focused on staying calm, but the pitch-black of the hole, the small space, it all conspired against her. She was trapped. The panic started, escalating, and her hand shook as she continued to search for her gun. A sob escaped her chest, a barking pain. *No, Sonia! Don't give in to the fear!*

She heard Dean's voice in her head. *You're the bravest woman I know.*

Her father laughed from above and fired his weapon again. This bullet hit a good foot above her head.

"I'm not your papa, Sonia. I'm sure you've figured that out by now, haven't you?"

She didn't respond. He was goading her. He wanted to hurt her, or maybe he was low on bullets and wanted her to talk, give away her location in the pit.

"Your mother was a whore," he continued. "She worked for me and my father. She took four, five men a day. No one knew who your father was. We'll call him John." He laughed again, a low, creepy laugh that sounded almost crazy. "My father had a soft spot for Gabrielle. She was just a manipulative whore, like you. You could be my sister, since my father fucked her often.

"Sergio Martin worked for me. He was supposed to take Gabrielle to town for an abortion. Believe me, no one was more surprised than I was when the doctor called and said she'd never arrived."

Sonia didn't want to listen, certain Marchand was lying. Wasn't he? Why would he make up a story so insane?

"They hid for years. I never stopped looking. *No one* defies me. Not Sergio, not Gabrielle, not her daughter. I should have slit your throat like I slit that whore's throat. Painless, compared to poor Sergio's fate."

Marchand fired into the pit again. The bullet clipped one leg on the side of her thigh. She bit back a cry and rolled to the side. It hurt, but it wasn't serious.

She felt her gun under her back. It was wet and slick with the mud, and she tried to clean it as best she could with her damp shirt.

Sonia closed her heart and mind to what Marchand said. He wanted to scare her, to divert her attention from the danger she was in. And it was working. Her panic, her anger, everything. She was losing.

She barely remembered her mother. Only the sadness that spread like a sickness through their small cottage. But Gabrielle had risked her life, had died to save Sonia. Sonia would not allow Marchand to win after everything her mother had sacrificed.

"Why didn't you kill me then?" she screamed up the shaft. "Why play daddy to a four-year-old?"

His voice was cold. "Because everyone trusts a widower missionary traveling with a child."

Sonia's claustrophobia disappeared, dwarfed by the anguish and anger she felt at being used. She aimed her gun at the silhouette of the bastard up top and fired. The gun worked, and she pressed the trigger again. Again.

Marchand's body jerked against the sky, as each bullet hit its mark. He fell into the pit with her.

Sonia quickly rolled to get out of the way, then scrambled to gain hold of something as she started to slip. But everything was slick and wet and she rolled down, through loose, wet soil. Down, down, down faster and faster until she screamed, and her mouth filled with mud.

* * *

Dean came up with the last of the Chinese girls. It took only ten minutes to get them all out once Charlie got the elevator working. When he reached the landing, he saw Lawson sitting up against the wall with a bullet in his leg. He'd been given a field dressing. Another man he didn't recognize lay dead. The entrance had disappeared.

Brian Stone was on the radio, looking frustrated.

"What happened?" Dean asked

"Two men came in and then one turned and ran back out when he saw Lawson. The dead guy panicked when he saw us, started firing. There was a small explosion of some sort—I think he hit an old lamp, but I don't know what caused it. Then the ceiling came down. We fired back. It was a righteous kill, Agent Hooper."

"Did you search him?"

The SWAT leader tossed him a wallet. "Jerry Ignacio, lives in Sacramento. There's a passport on him, too, and about three thousand dollars. Couple guns, a knife."

"Have you tried to get out?"

"We've been in contact with Callahan, they're right on the other side. There's a small crawl-through. We've been sending the women out one at a time."

Dean spoke into his walkie-talkie. "Agent Knight? Callahan?" Nothing. "Clinch? Anderson? Anyone?"

"Hooper, it's Trace Anderson."

"Where's Sonia?"

"She and Clinch pursued the other suspect."

"The curator?"

"The guy with glasses? He's fine, sitting in my car. We came across a truck on the road. They fled when they saw us and went over the cliff right at the bend not half a mile down the road. You might have heard the explosion."

"It caved in part of the mine."

"You okay?"

"Yes. The women?"

"We have a sheriff's med unit and van here, and an ambulance on its way."

"Good. Now find Sonia and Clinch."

Cammarata heard the conversation. "She went after Marchand, did she?"

"I don't know." But Dean feared she had.

"Shit."

Dean was itching to get out and find her himself. His skin crawled, thinking about what might happen in a confrontation between Sonia and her father.

Clinch shined his light down the hole. "He's dead."

"Where's Sonia?" Sam Callahan looked around. "Sonia! Sonia Knight!" He asked Clinch, "Are you sure there were only two of them?"

"Yes," Clinch said. "Dammit, where is she?"

Sam took out a heavy-duty light and shined it into the hole. "Do you hear that?"

Clinch listened. "It sounds like running water."

Sam called Brian Stone on the radio. "We have a situation. We need rope and lights. Tell Hooper that Agent Knight may be in trouble."

Dean followed Trace and Brian to the edge of the hidden shaft that Sonia had fallen down. "Where is she?"

"Dr. Sheffield thinks she fell into an underwater river," Trace said.

Dean couldn't have heard that correctly. "I don't understand." His skin prickled and his chest tightened. "Where is she?"

Sheffield shined a heavy-duty light on the blueprints. "This river is flowing toward the mine. It was a huge problem for the original miners before they—"

"Stop," Dean said. "I just need to know where she is."

Sheffield continued. "It flows east to west, of course. It's heading toward the mine, but it's more a pool of water this time of year. If she didn't drown—"

Dean closed his eyes. "I'll go in. Get the rope, Brian. Lower me down."

Sheffield shook his head. "Not a good idea. All this movement and activity has disturbed the sediment. But I know where she'll end up."

"That's ridiculous!" Cammarata exclaimed. "She could be hurt, she could be—"

"Lower me down," Dean repeated. But it was too late. Cammarata jumped into the shaft and disappeared.

"Shit!" Dean turned to Sheffield. "Take me to where she'll be. Right now."

"It's dangerous—"

"I don't give a shit how dangerous it is. I need her back."

I need her alive.

Sonia coughed up muddy water. It was pitch-black. She couldn't see anything, not even her hands in front of her. She shivered, soaked through.

Where on earth was she?

Running water echoed all around her, deafening. She'd lost her gun when she fell—she felt around for it and her hand fell into deep water. She scrambled back up to where she'd landed. She'd lost consciousness at one point. She must have. She remembered falling and then . . . now.

More cautiously, she felt the surrounding area, crawling away from the water. Her knees and hands sank deep into mud. She sat and wrapped her arms around her legs, rocking herself.

It was so dark.

The familiar panic rose in her chest, her body breaking out into a sweat. But it was cold, so cold, and she shivered uncontrollably.

Her voice echoed eerily in the dark. "Don't move, Sonia. Sit tight. Someone will find you. Don't move. Don't move. Don't move.

But they would never find her. How long had she been here? How far had she fallen?

She had to find a way out herself. Or she would die here.

Come on Sonia! You're not a victim anymore.

She crawled again. Slowly. Carefully. The mud sloshing through her fingers. The ground became firmer the higher she went. Okay. This was okay. She wished she had a light . . .

Idiot! Brian Stone had given them all emergency lights. Shake and break, he'd said. The long stick was still in her pocket. She pulled it out with trembling fingers, holding it as if it were a life jacket. Shake. Break. A faint glow emanated from the stick. She held it up.

A skull glowed inches from her face.

She screamed.

Dean stopped walking. "Did you hear that?" he asked.

He, Brian Stone, and Sheffield were back in the original mine, going down a long shaft following metal rails that had been laid more than one hundred fifty years ago.

"I hear water," Brian said.

"Good sign," Sheffield replied, spry for his age. He led the way. "The cavern opens up down here. Unless the river has changed flow dramatically over the last hundred years."

Dean didn't want to hear it. He couldn't. He would find Sonia. He wasn't going to let her die, not like this.

They continued walking down the shaft.

"Help me!"

"Did you hear that?" Brian said. "She's not far."

She's alive.

Sonia cried out again. How were they going to find her in here? She held the light up, but the cavern was so huge she couldn't see the walls around her.

She heard a grunt and splash. "Help me! Help!" She cried out. "It's Sonia."

"Sonia! Thank God."

"Charlie? Where are you?"

"I see your light."

He grunted like he was in pain. She held up the light and saw a dark red shirt in the water as Charlie struggled to get up the slope she'd landed on. She slid down the mud and held out her hand.

He took it. Slowly, she pulled him out of the water.

His shirt hadn't been red when she last saw him.

"Oh, God, Charlie, what happened?"

"They said you fell. I didn't know if you had been shot or what. I came after you."

"Why?" She hugged him tightly. "Charlie, you're bleeding."

"There are rocks. I—" He coughed. "I hit them."

She held up her light and pulled up his shirt. His chest was bloodied; she saw a rib protruding.

"Charlie, lie still." She pulled off her flak jacket, then her T-shirt. She wrapped it as best she could around Charlie. Tears streamed down her face. Charlie was in bad shape.

"We have to get you out." He closed his eyes and coughed up water, mud, and blood.

"Why did you follow me? You didn't know. I could have been dead. I don't want you to die."

"That's a first," he said faintly.

"I hate what you did, Charlie, but I don't hate you."

"You should."

He didn't say anything for a long minute. Sonia heard something over and above the water. Faintly, "Sonia!"

She called out as loud as she could, "Over here! Help!"

"Sonia! We're coming."

She saw a bright light bouncing against the walls of the cavern.

"Help's coming, Charlie. Hold still."

He shook uncontrollably, going into shock.

"Charlie, hold on. It's just a little time."

"I want to die, Sonia. I need to die."

"No. No, dammit! You taught me so much. I'm stronger because of you."

"You're strong." He coughed and this time blood poured from his mouth. "Because of you."

"Sonia!" Dean called.

"Here!" She waved her glow-stick. "Charlie's hurt!"

"I'm coming!"

Sonia said to Charlie, "Dean's coming. Help's here. Hold on."

"Forgive me, sweetheart."

"I forgive you. I forgive you, Charlie, dammit!"

"Find. What happened to Ashley. Please."

"You'll find her. Dammit, Charlie, fight!"

The bright lights showed the cavern to be monstrous in size, and Sonia sat on a small cutout. She couldn't believe how much water was in here. She couldn't believe she'd survived.

"Don't die, Charlie."

There was a ramp and railing that went around the top of the cavern. Dean walked across the precarious edge to get to her. She willed him to be safe. She couldn't lose him. The five minutes it took to reach her seemed like an eternity.

He didn't say a word, just held her. He was trembling.

Sonia said, "Charlie's hurt."

Reluctantly, Dean let her go. He inspected Charlie's injuries and checked his pulse.

"Honey, he's gone."

"No. No." She let Dean gather her into his lap and hold her while she cried until Brian Stone came down with a rope to bring them all up, the living and the dead.

CHAPTER
THIRTY-FIVE

Four Weeks Later

Sonia had never seen so many people in her parents' house.

She put on her best smile and walked through the crowd, greeting everyone.

It had been a perfect day up until an hour ago, when Dean left their wedding reception after giving her a quick kiss and telling her he'd be right back.

To Sonia, right back meant five or ten minutes. Not—she glanced at her watch—sixty-seven.

She made her way to the kitchen, which was surprisingly devoid of people. She crossed to the window and looked into the backyard.

Her parents were there with Riley, Max, and their cousins. She had been tickled when Max showed up with a three-day leave for the Fourth of July weekend. "I couldn't miss my sister's wedding," he'd told her when he surprised her at the rehearsal dinner the night before.

The day had been perfect, but it would have been even more so if Wendell could have lived long enough to see her married to a man like Dean Hooper. He would have liked him.

Sonia didn't know if she'd ever put to rest the trail of blood left by Noel Marchand, but knowing he wasn't her biological father helped. It was hard to think of him as anything but—she'd lived nine years with him, traveling from village to village in Central and South America. And although she now knew he was using her to lure his prey, she remembered teaching the children English and French and basic math; she'd taken pride in the farms she helped establish. As Dean told her one night when she couldn't sleep, focus on the positive and the good, and put the bad on a shelf.

"I know you'll remember it's there, but if it's far enough from sight you'll forget for a time. And when you do remember, I'll be here. Always."

Sonia turned and jumped when a man walked in.

"Sorry," Dean's brother, Will, said. The Hooper brothers didn't look alike, but they had the same chocolate-brown eyes and square jaw. "You have a big family."

Sonia almost corrected him—her family was actually small—but then she realized her friends, her colleagues, Dean's colleagues, they were like family. She smiled. "I'm lucky."

"Dean's the lucky one. I never thought he'd get married to anything but his job. And giving up that post in Washington, oh, sorry. Is that a sore point?"

"Not at all." Dean had given up his prestigious position in Washington to relocate to Sacramento and take the job as assistant special agent in charge. Some might think it was a demotion, but Dean told her he wanted the change of pace, the challenge and her. "*Sacramento is your home. This is where your family is. They're going to be my family. I'm not leaving them. I love them, almost as much as I love you."*

Will said, "I thought I'd sneak away for a few minutes. My wife wanted to take a walk through that park down the street."

"It's a nice place. Riley and I played baseball and soccer and basketball there all the time. There's a little zoo if you walk all the way to the other side, right next to the church."

"You don't mind, do you? Thirty minutes?"

"Take all the time you want."

"Where's Dean?"

"I don't know. He had an errand."

Will's redheaded wife came running in. "Ready?" she said and they went off on their walk, hand in hand.

Sonia turned back to the window. The Rogans, two of them anyway, were there. Sean Rogan was showing Andres something—a card game, Sonia thought. Great, just what she needed—Andres beating them at yet another game. The kid was a whiz. She didn't know what was going to happen to him, but she was pulling every string, and she had a lot she could pull, to keep him here. Owen and Marianne loved him and wanted him. He had no one else.

Kane couldn't make it, but Sonia wasn't surprised. He rarely came to the States anymore. But he'd called her that morning and they talked about Charlie and the past, as well as the future. "You forgave him, he knows that," Kane had said. "And he died a hero. That's all he wanted."

"I'm looking for Ashley Fox," she'd told him. "We found Jones's old journals and are piecing together information. But—"

"You think she's dead."

"Yes, But I'll confirm it if it's the last thing I do. Her mother deserves to know what happened." And for Charlie.

She'd never forget the night in the mine. She'd never forget the cloying fear. It didn't matter that she'd come out on the other side and hadn't let her claustrophobia beat her, she still woke up shaking, feeling the weight of the world on top of her . . .

"Sonia."

She smiled, recognizing her husband's voice. She turned and was surprised to see a young pretty woman with him.

"Maya."

The girl nodded, looked at Dean with wide eyes. "Andres?" she asked.

"He's out back," Sonia said.

Dean walked Maya outside and Sonia watched from the window again. When Andres saw his sister, love and relief crossed his face. He ran to her and hugged her tightly. Tears streamed down their faces, and Sonia's own tears flowed as well.

She heard Dean return to the kitchen and turned and embraced him. "You found her."

"I didn't want to get your hopes up again," he said. Ever since they'd cracked Jones's code a week after the mine incident, they'd thought they'd found Maya twice. Each time they'd been mistaken, though they'd rescued several underage prostitutes in the process.

"How is she?"

"She's okay." He wiped away her tears. "She's strong, like you. She'll need help, but she'll make it. Because of

family." They looked out the window as Andres introduced his sister to Owen and Marianne. "I told your
parents yesterday morning. They want Maya, too."

"I'm going to cry all over again." She took a deep
breath. "That was a wonderful surprise. You are incredible."

"Just call me Mr. Incredible."

She laughed and kissed him, savoring his taste. "I can
hardly wait until tonight, and you'd better be Mr. Incredible."

He raised his eyebrows. "Tonight? What's tonight?"
He smiled and kissed her. "I have one more surprise."

"I don't think I can handle any more excitement."

"Just this one."

"All right. One more." She grinned as she followed
him out the side door. They walked down the street. It
was the most beautiful Fourth of July—hot, blue, and
free. She was free, and she would never forget anything—
the good and the bad—that had brought her to this
place, these people, this peace.

"Where are we going?" she asked when they turned
the corner.

He didn't answer her, but pulled her along. He was
grinning and practically bouncing on the balls of his
feet—very unlike the serious Dean Hooper she knew.

"Dean, what's going on?"

"Be patient."

"I'm not a patient person."

"Fifty feet."

"What?"

He stopped in front of a two-story Mission-style
house with a wide porch and flowers everywhere. It

fronted the quiet side of South Land Park, two blocks from her parents' house.

There was a real estate sign in the front yard. Underneath it was a sign that said SOLD.

Her heart thudded. "What's this?"

"Our home."

Read on for an excerpt from

Cutting Edge

the final book in the
unputdownable FBI trilogy,
by

Allison Brennan

coming soon from Piatkus

The arson had been hot, fast, and lethal.

The cloying, acrid scent of the extinguished fire had FBI agent Nora English breathing through her mouth as she walked carefully through the extinguished remains of the research wing of Butcher-Payne Biotech, her boots sloshing through the water left behind by the firefighters. Tens of thousands of gallons of water had flowed into this wing to put out the blaze, and the crew was surveying the building, axing the remaining interior walls that had been charred to ensure there were no hot spots.

They'd been damn lucky. The summer had been particularly dry, and the trees surrounding BPB in a canyon off the two-lane highway could easily have caught fire, spreading through the crisp timber and underbrush faster than they could respond. Fortunately, there'd been no wind to push the fire, and the first firefighters to respond had done a magnificent job saturating the roof and surrounding grounds. In addition, the solid exterior and internal firewalls of the five-year-old building had contained the fire wholly within the research wing.

"And the fire sprinklers didn't go on as they were supposed to," the Placer County fire chief, Ansel Nobel, said as he escorted Nora to where the body had been found. He sat on the standing Multi-Jurisdictional Do-

mestic Terrorism Joint Task Force—DOMFOR—that
the FBI had implemented shortly after 9/11. "The most
recent inspection was three months ago. They were
functioning properly. I don't understand."

"Have you checked the water pump station? Is this
area on a city pump or well water?"

"There's a water storage tank uphill for—damn,
that's it."

"Excuse me?"

"The water storage tank is for the hydrants. The
sprinklers are on another system maintained by the
county. When we hooked up to the hydrants without
any problems, I assumed it was faulty sprinklers."

"I'll ask my partner to check it out." She called Harry
Antonovich, a senior long-time agent with the FBI who
led Sacramento FBI's Domestic Terrorism Squad and pi-
oneered many of the Evidence Response Team protocols
related to domestic terrorism. Harry had trained her
when she was a new agent right out of Quantico, and
Nora didn't want to think about his retirement at the
end of the year.

"Harry, it's Nora. Chief Nobel said the sprinklers
didn't go on. The pump may have been sabotaged—can
you talk to the sheriff's department and get a team over
there to check it out?"

"Absolutely. What's it like inside?"

"Wet."

His voice had a modicum of restrained humor. "I
meant damages."

"Same apparent burn pattern. Started in the lab and
was contained ninety percent in the lab and adjoining
offices. The lobby walls have some damage. Hot enough

to melt some of the equipment, but that's beyond my expertise."

"When's Quin going to get here?"

Nora hesitated a moment. Her sister had a reputation, and she hated to fuel it. But this *was* Harry. "She had a date."

"It's five in the morning."

"In San Francisco. She promised she'd leave immediately. She wasn't on call tonight," Nora defended.

"I'm not being critical, but we need her. I don't need to tell you they're escalating."

The arson gang they'd been investigating for eighteen months had never killed before. The three previous arsons had targeted the same industry—biotechnology—but the first two were in warehouses, and the third fire was in a small genetic research building at the zoo. BPB was a multimillion-dollar company that employed more than fifty people.

Other than the dead body, the MO was the same. Why BPB? Why now? Why kill? Accident or premeditated murder?

"Something else is going on. This just doesn't feel right to me." Nora caught herself twisting her short hair between her thumb and forefinger. She tucked the curls behind her ear and dropped her hand.

"Have you seen the vic?"

"I'm heading that way now."

"I did a field test on the graffiti. The paint matches the other arson fires."

"Dammit, Harry, they haven't killed anyone before."

"It was just a matter of time, kid. You know that. I'll go check the pumps and get back to you." He hung up.

Chief Nobel said, "It's happened before."

"Excuse me?"

"Arsonists. Set the fire not knowing someone is inside."

"It still makes them murderers, whether they intended to kill him or not."

Nobel stood in front of the opening into Jonah Payne's office. "Brace yourself, it's not pretty."

"I've seen worse."

Nora buried her emotions deep. It didn't matter how many times she saw a dead body, or in what condition, the anger and deep sadness at a life taken too soon could overwhelm her if she didn't close off her feelings. She couldn't afford to impair her critical judgment. Cops learned to compartmentalize to do the job or they ended up dead or drunk. There was a reason cops had nearly twice the suicide rate as the population at large.

Her ability to fully detach herself had earned her the reputation as level-headed by those who liked her, and a cold bitch by those who didn't.

Chief Nobel stepped aside. Bright crime-scene tape crisscrossed the charred opening leading into Dr. Jonah Payne's office off the main research laboratory. The office itself wasn't large, approximately fourteen feet square. Paper fueled the flames in here, soggy remnants of pulp everywhere, higher piles of ash and partially burned paper on the credenza behind the large desk. No windows, no natural light—Nora couldn't fathom how anyone could work in such conditions.

The victim, presumed to be Jonah Payne, was flat on his back on the floor in front of his desk, which instantly seemed odd to Nora. She'd only investigated one domestic terrorism case that had resulted in fire deaths: in that case, the fourteen victims had been trapped in a burning building and all had died of smoke inhalation. The bodies had either been in fetal positions or prone.

Payne had third-degree burns over all exposed areas of his body. His hair had disintegrated—which would help the M.E. determine how long he was exposed to flames—and the metal from his glasses had melted into his charred skin. His shirt was completely gone but he'd been wearing jeans, she noted, and while they were black with soot they appeared intact. Denim could withstand fire longer than some other materials. All details they'd need to figure out exactly what happened.

Fire fatalities were some of the most difficult crimes to investigate. Much of the damage came from necessary fire-suppression activities, but when the firefighters discovered a body, they did everything they could to preserve evidence while putting out the flames.

"Chief," the man inspecting the body said with a brief glance up.

"Kevin, this is Special Agent Nora English with the FBI's domestic terrorism unit."

"Don't come in," he said.

"We're not. Nora, have you met our M.E., Kevin Coffey?"

"No," she said. "Dr. Coffey, does it seem odd to you that the victim is on his back?"

He stopped his inspection and looked up at her. "Yes, it is odd. But I don't want to jump to conclusions before the fire inspector gets here."

"She's on her way," Nora said. "She was out of town and—"

A raspy voice behind her bellowed, "She? Last I checked, I'm still a man, sugar."

Nora bristled and turned. The smoker's voice belonged to a man who looked old enough to be her father—or grandfather. He wore black pants and a red plaid shirt on which was clipped a fire marshall's badge.

The man grinned at her and winked. "Yep, still a man."

"Ulysses, this is Special Agent Nora English with the FBI. I told you about the task force—"

Ulysses waved his hand in the air. "Task force," he said with derision. "All talk, no action."

"We should discuss this, Mr—" Nora began.

"Ulysses."

"I've brought in a consultant from the state fire marshall's office who's been on the task force since the first fire eighteen months ago—"

"This is my jurisdiction, or are you going to flex your federal muscles and screw everything up?"

Nora didn't want friction with the locals, but she would flex her federal muscles if she had to. Domestic terrorism fell squarely on the FBI's shoulders. She was about to say that when her sister Quin bounced into the room, the polar opposite of the craggy old fire marshall.

"Ulysses!" Quin exclaimed, a petite blonde ball of energy bounding over to the graying man. She gave him a hug that was longer than it needed to be and Nora watched, bemused, as Ulysses turned to putty.

"If I'd known you were coming, sweetheart, I'd have put out the red carpet."

Quin laughed. "Nora is my sister. Cut her cute federal ass some slack, okay?"

"Anything for you, sugar."

Quin caught Nora's eye with a happy smugness that had Nora twisting her mouth to avoid smirking back. At least the victim was in good hands. Quin didn't take anything but her job seriously, which had been a bone of contention between the sisters, but there was no one Nora trusted more than Quin with this case. And Quin would catch Ulysses up on the previous arsons, freeing Nora to focus on interviewing Payne's partner and staff. While there was little doubt that this arson was connected to the others, she needed all documentation of threats either in person or written, any trespassers over the last few weeks, and information on what BPB was working on.

Ulysses turned to Nora. "To answer your question, Agent English, I've never seen a case where the victim was on his back except if he'd been dead or unconscious when the fire started."

Quin crossed over to where Nora stood by the entry and said under her breath, "Sheriff Sanger is here, and he's on a rampage about the Professor. That slimy reporter Buttface is here—"

"Belham—"

"Right, Buttface. He's hanging around Sanger, who's giving this hot, dark, and sexy hunk an earful. Don't know if he's Payne's partner, but—" she gave Nora the *I think he's stirring up shit* sideways glance.

"Thanks for the heads-up."

"I'll take care of Ulysses. He's ornery, but he's one of the smartest in the business."

Nora excused herself with one final look at Jonah Payne's remains.

Unconscious or dead before the fire. That would mean his death wasn't an accident—he'd been intentionally murdered. Had he caught the arsonists red-handed? Why not hit the panic button? What happened to the alarm system? Why not call the police? Had he confronted them and been killed? Had he known them? Was it an inside job? Was his murder premeditated, and the arson a way to cover up the crime and destroy evidence? That would make this crime far more personal.

Quin took command of the crime scene like she commanded everything in her life—quickly and completely, with a sugar coating so no one knew what hit them. Jonah Payne was in good hands.

Now Nora had to control whatever damage Sheriff Sanger had done by talking publicly about Professor Leif Cole. This investigation was already sliding down the slippery slope of legal posturing and games, the press circling like vultures because biotech was controversial, and high-ranking politicians were calling Washington wanting to know what was being done in Sacramento and why they didn't have an arrest—and shit runs downhill fast.

Sanger was going to jeopardize the entire case if he didn't keep his big mouth shut.

SUDDEN DEATH

When by-the-book FBI agent Megan Elliott realises
that the murder victim she's investigating carries
military ID, what seemed to be a simple murder
enquiry turns a lot more serious. An unusual
mutilation on the body causes Meg to suspect the
murder is target specific, especially when she
discovers other recently murdered soldiers
with the same disfigurement.

Then military police take possession of the
body and Meg is forced to partner up with
burn-the-book mercenary Jack Kincaid. All too
soon she realises that the killer's primary target is
closer to home, and that Jack really is more
trouble – dangerous trouble – than either of
them had bargained for . . .

978-0-7499-0955-0

KILLING FEAR

Six years ago, lawyer Theodore Glenn was
convicted of brutally murdering four strippers in
San Diego. But as he was dragged from the
courtroom, he made a vehement promise to kill all
those who testified against him . . .

Robin McKenna, a former stripper, had shared a
stage with all four of the victims. Over the last six
years Robin's worked hard to turn her life around,
transforming the strip joint where she once worked
with her friends into an upscale bar. Self-defence
courses, a good security team – and the fact that
Glenn is rotting on death row in San Quentin have
helped her to feel safe again. But not a day goes by
when Robin doesn't think of her friends. Or – if
she's honest – of homicide detective Will Hooper,
the man who put Glenn behind bars. Their fledging
relationship has not survived beyond Glenn's trial.
But when a freak earthquake hits California,
Theodore Glenn escapes San Quentin. Convicted of
four murders, he knows he's guilty of only three
and is determined to find out who framed him for
the fourth, whilst systematically eradicating all
those who put him in prison . . .

978-0-7499-3919-9